A NEST FOR LALITA

A NEST
FOR LALITA

A NOVEL

KEN LANGER

Dryad Press ◗ Washington, D.C.

This book is typeset in Bembo on 11 over 17
Book and cover design by Megan Katsanevakis

Library of Congress Cataloging-in-Publication Data

Names: Langer, Ken, 1949- author.
Title: A nest for Lalita : a novel / Ken Langer.
Description: Washington, D.C. : Dryad Press, 2020.
Identifiers: LCCN 2020018969 | ISBN 9781928755555 (paperback) | ISBN
    9781928755579 (ebook)
Subjects: LCSH: India--Fiction. | GSAFD: Mystery fiction.
Classification: LCC PS3612.A5534 N47 2020 | DDC 813/.6--dc23
LC record available at https://lccn.loc.gov/2020018969

DRYAD PRESS
15 Sherman Avenue
Takoma Park, Maryland 20912

To JLS, NL, and AL

PROLOGUE

Babai, May 1970

The commute from Bombay's financial center to Babai was living hell. Lalita's feet ached as stinking workers crushed in on her from all sides, some on purpose, and eyes like hot coals raking over her body. As the rickety bus approached her village and slowed, she mustered all her courage and jumped off. Her mood lightened on the walk home. Finally, no jerks brushing against her breasts or pinching her buttocks.

She thought about Mr. Behera, so kind and gentle. Who would have imagined the big boss's son—heir to the Behera Group—would take an interest in a barefoot Dalit, an invisible sweeper girl? He noticed her burn marks and offered to take her to a real doctor. She pictured the gold necklace he gave her, saying she could sell it if she ever needed money to escape her husband. But how could she? For someone who grew up in Bombay's sprawling shantytown, it was like owning a piece of the sun.

Lalita valued the necklace more than her life.

Most of all, she treasured the man, who treated her like a goddess. The young heir to the Behera Group was always respectful, gentle, never trying to take advantage of her. Unlike every man she'd ever known, starting with her useless father. A pair of ruddy shelducks soared above. She shook her head—if only humans were so loyal to one another!

Lalita passed the neighborhood shrine to Shiva, where a yogi sat cross-legged meditating under a majestic banyan tree. A garland of *rudraksha* seeds hung over protruding ribs. Long coils of matted hair looked like aerial roots, as if he had merged with the tree. What a blessed life, sitting day after day in a trance. No job, no chores, no money problems, and best of all, no useless husband. She had been married only two years, but that was one and a half too many. The trouble started when Ram lost his position guarding a sprawling bungalow on Malabar Hill. Soon he was drinking away her meager earnings and stubbing out cigarettes on her arms.

She finally arrived at her hut at the edge of a wide field of bright yellow sunflowers. She made herself a cup of dark-brown tea—*ek sau mil chai*, the kind that could sustain a trucker for one hundred miles. She drank from the saucer and waited for the caffeine to kick in. After checking the rice and dal for small stones, she threw a cow dung cake into the mud stove and sprinkled it with kerosene. She was about to light the fire when Ram burst through the door.

"What's for dinner?" he yelled, slurring his words.

"What do you think," Lalita snapped, "beefsteak?"

"How about some meat, you slut? I'm craving goat curry!"

"Then stop banging every girl in the village and get a goddamn job!" Lalita could smell fresh coconut oil wafting from Ram's direction. Who's he screwing now?

"Fuck you, whore! You're the one who's sucking every dick at that fancy office of yours!"

On most days, the conversation would have ended there; Ram would make his way to the string cot in front of the hut, fall asleep, and snore like a bulldog until dinner. After filling his belly, he would slobber her face with kisses or rip off her sari. But not tonight. He stumbled around and kicked the earthen jug. Water gushed onto the dirt floor.

"Bastard, I got up at 5 a.m. to fetch that water!"

Ram pulled a small bottle of whiskey from his pocket, took a swig, and swaggered over to the shrine where Lalita did her daily *puja*. He grabbed the stone goddess and threw it across the room. Lalita scrambled to pick up the deity. It had landed at the foot of a small trunk, which she had recently inherited from her mother. Ram staggered over to the trunk and kicked it.

"What's in there, anyway?"

"I've told you a hundred times, my wedding dress and some old clothes. Now get out of my way so I can cook."

Ram flipped open the top and pushed the trunk over. The contents flew onto the floor. Lalita quickly charged her husband, hoping to distract him.

"What the hell is this?" he growled, picking up a folded silk sari from the wet dirt. The necklace tumbled out. Ram's face turned red. He looked like a *rakshasa*, a wrathful deity full of bloodlust. "You tramp! Where'd you get this?"

"I bought it with money I've saved up."

"Stupid liar." He seized her by the hair and pushed her against the wall. Then he started rummaging through the items. "And what's *this*?" he roared, holding a pen and ink drawing of Lalita dressed in a shiny green sari. The gold necklace hung from her neck. He slammed the drawing into her face, crushing her nose.

"It's a drawing, what do you think?"

"It's you, isn't it? Wearing a silk sari and that motherfucking gold necklace! Who did this?"

"Shree Behera, the big boss's son. He likes to draw. He draws all his employees. I don't know why."

"Even scum sweepers like you? He gave you the necklace, didn't he?"

"No! I told you, I—"

"He's fucking you in the ass, isn't he, you wench?" Ram grabbed the tin of kerosene near the mud stove. He caught hold of Lalita's arm and dragged her behind the hut. She squirmed and struggled, finally freeing herself. She ran like the devil, but he tackled her in the neighbor's field. He doused her with kerosene, from head to toe.

"No! No!" she screamed, her lithe body flailing like a caught fish.

Ram jammed his knees onto her legs and chest, pinning her to the ground. With his arms free, he lit a match and tossed it onto her. Then he jumped back. In seconds, Lalita turned into a living torch. She screamed, running this way and that until she collapsed in a patch of yellow flowers. A woman rushed out of a nearby shed with a bucket of water. But it was too late.

PART I

APRIL–MAY 2005

CHAPTER I

Sompur, India

Meena dreaded the evening commute. Sompur's streets were a dusty, tangled mess—nothing like New Delhi, with its wide boulevards and stately bungalows. The roads were far too narrow for the crush of cars, trucks, and scooter rickshaws, let alone bullock carts and bony cows. They were clogged, like an old man's arteries. *And why do people think there's one lane when there are three?*

But the commute was a small price for her dream job. No one else in her master's program at Delhi University was already heading up a nongovernmental organization. Stopping for a group of men who had stumbled into the street, she worried about her husband. Kesh had not been himself since they moved to Sompur five years ago. He was too far from his office in New Delhi and missed the hustle and bustle of his architectural firm.

As Meena maneuvered through the city, she recalled a conversation with Madhav Behera soon after they had moved to Sompur. The industrialist behind Behera House could not understand why she would refuse a car and driver. Even at thirty, Meena was not confident behind the wheel and surely would have benefited. But no self-respecting activist would dare to be seen in a chauffeured Mercedes. Behera finally gave in, but not without some stern advice.

"Meena, Sompur is not New Delhi. If you insist on driving, please remember to leave your manners at the door. To get anywhere, you must act as if you own the road. And don't forget the streets have their own caste system. Oversized lorries and sacred cows are the Brahmins. Don't mess with them. Then come Mercedes and other luxury automobiles—the Kshatriya warriors. After that you have Marutis and all the other mid- and low-priced cars—they're like the Vaishya farmers. Finally, the Shudras, the bottom feeders, common scooters and rickshaws. Everything on two wheels or legs is untouchable."

She remembered shuddering at the word *untouchable*, which nobody used any more. But, as a new hire, she was too shy to speak up.

"You must first know your place in the pecking order," Behera had said. "Yield to those above you, negotiate with your equals, and sit on your horn to blow everyone else out of the water."

Even the roads had their bloody caste system! Meena knew she could never change the country's ancient social structure, but she was determined to make a difference. After all, domestic violence was a cancer eating away at the country. And after five years, Behera House had helped hundreds of women.

Meena drove around a cow standing perfectly still in the center of the road. She imagined what the new campus might look like. Their current address, Behera's ancestral home, was charming, but they had outgrown it. The new site was an abandoned cement factory located twenty miles outside the city. How nice to be settled into a quiet rural area, perched on a hill overlooking the ocean. She could hardly believe Madhav was willing to donate the land and fund the design and construction of buildings that would accommodate 250 women—four times the current number. Women of different castes, maybe even some Muslims and Christians. Would they change their name? After all, a campus could no longer be called *Behera House*, could it?

She swerved to avoid a herd of goats. When the coast was clear, she found herself thinking of her phone call with Madhav that morning. Her jaw tightened. He wanted to bring in a Western architect to design the community center—the flagship building proposed for the new campus. And he insisted *she* call her husband to deliver the news. Madhav should have made the call himself.

What an awful morning, with Kesh ranting about those "bloody Western *starchitects*." He had every right to be angry. Hadn't *Time Magazine* recently named him India's premier sustainable architect? The first to design a building awarded LEED certification by the US Green Building Council—a full three years before India established its own association. And didn't *Architectural + Design Magazine* call him a "game changer, crusading to break India's addiction to fossil fuel?" She pictured one of his latest projects, a prize-winning concert hall in Mumbai. But what could she do? Still, Madhav didn't have to go on forever about how Kesh couldn't be trusted. How her husband was *too goddamn green*.

Meena turned a corner and almost hit a bicyclist. Her nerves were frayed; she leaned forward, almost pressing her nose onto the windshield. But she couldn't stop thinking about Kesh. It wasn't just that new buildings had to be green, but they had to produce one hundred percent of their energy from wind and solar. *Net-zero-carbon buildings*, his mantra. Maybe Madhav was right. And so what if her boss wanted to show off his company's latest air-conditioning system? Why shouldn't those women enjoy a little creature comfort after all they've been through? Especially this time of year, when the sun's rays pierced your skin like red-hot spikes.

Suddenly, a deafening horn jolted her back to the present. She looked in the rearview mirror and saw a Tata truck barreling toward her. The road vibrated under its weight. She veered to the side until the eight-wheeler whipped by, belching clouds of smoke. As it sped into the distance, the motley crew of vehicles and creatures sprung back into action, and the scene returned to its normal state of mayhem.

Then, a thunderous crash, as if the monsoon had come three months early. But the sky was deep blue without a single cloud. Except for a few scooters and bicycles, everything ground to a halt. That dreadful lorry must have driven off the road and hit something! She turned off the engine and poked her head out the window, but all she could see was a line of cars and, in the distance, a wall of people. Soon sweat was trickling down her armpits and her sari clung to the vinyl seat. Spotting a brawny young man clomping toward her from the direction of the accident, she got out of the car and asked what happened.

"A lorry swerved to avoid a bicyclist and went paunch up," the man replied in the local language. "It fucking crushed a young boy standing on the side of the road." The man flipped the bottom of his shirt up and exposed his navel, an outie. He moved toward her as he muttered something about her sea-green eyes.

"Step back, young man, and don't raise your shirt like that at me!" Meena pulled her sari tight around her lithe body. She was used to men undressing her with their sleazy eyes whenever she walked through the bazaar, but this youth had crossed the line.

"All right," he snapped, "but you don't have to get all puffy." He backed off and let his shirt fall over his belly. He pointed in the direction of Chanakya Market and said the dead boy worked for the sari emporium, bringing customers chai from the nearby tea stall. Tall plastic glasses were scattered around the overturned vehicle.

Meena felt like her limbs had been painted with varnish. Wasn't that A. J. Kalbarta & Sons? The rotund proprietor served his patrons chai, brought in by a wisp of a boy no more than ten or eleven. He had an angelic face and smiled whenever Meena entered with a new resident. She squeezed the end of her sari and blinked her eyes, burning from car exhaust. *Why can't these wretched men turn off their bloody motors? And why didn't I ever bother to speak to the boy or ask him his name?*

It was already seven-thirty, and Kesh would be pacing the house wondering where she was. Meena riffled through her purse for her mobile phone, but came up short. Her husband would be furious. If only he had made some friends. The only exception was Madhav. But what kind of friend would hire a foreigner to design the community center when he could call on one of the best architects in the country? Madhav wanted Kesh to be the junior member of the design team. The local architect. Now there's a recipe for disaster!

Vendors were popping up, hawking cigarettes, evening newspapers, and *paan,* betel leaves filled with areca nuts and spices. A boy wandered around with an oversized aluminum teakettle, calling out, *"Chai garam,"* hot tea, while a barber worked his trade in the shadow of a banyan tree.

Reconciled to a long wait, Meena opened her briefcase and dug out a report on Indian women and dowry law. But the sentences were long and obtuse; her mind seemed frozen, unable to navigate beyond images of her angry husband and the dead boy. It was as if her head were stuck in a traffic jam of its own.

A good hour passed before the lorry was cleared and cars began to move. She finally pulled into the driveway of their lime-green bunga-low. Kesh kept promising to call the painters, but never seemed to get around to it. But he's never too busy to pour himself a drink and watch another cricket match! She entered the front door, unfastened the straps of her low-heeled sandals, and placed her briefcase and car keys on the side table.

CHAPTER 2

"What took you so long?" Kesh barked. "You're two hours late!" Meena walked into the dining room, cringing at his sharp tone. Her husband was already seated at the dinner table, puffing a Gauloise and nursing a bourbon. With a deep frown, he leaned against the tall back of the wooden chair carved with frolicking elephants, their thick trunks wrapped around blossoming trees. Dressed in a white kurta embroidered with flowers around the neck and sleeves, Kesh was beginning to look like his late father—the former maharaja of a small princely state tucked into the Himalayan foothills.

"Sorry, Kesh, there was a terrible accident on M. G. Road. I wanted to call, but I left my mobile at the office." She planted a kiss on his cheek and headed to the bathroom. "A young boy was hit and killed by a lorry—"

"Which swerved to dodge a goat," Kesh added.

"Pardon?"

"A goat," he called after her. "There are more goats than people in

Sompur. The ratio is twelve and a half to one. I read an article by a Professor Billy Gotra at Sompur Technical College. Get it, *Billy Goat-ra*? Anyway, what else do I have to do in Sompur, the armpit of the world? My office in Delhi seems to be running just fine without me."

"Sorry, dear," Meena called out as she dried her hands, "what did you say?"

Kesh raised his voice. "I said, what else do I have to do in this armpit of the world? Well, I suppose India's got a lot of armpits, since every bloody deity has ten arms."

"No, something about goats?"

"Forget it."

Meena emerged, patting her cheeks with a towel, only to find Kesh's face hidden in a cloud of smoke. She seated herself across from him. "Kesh," she said, hoping for a little sympathy, "I've just come from the scene of a terrible accident. Remember the shop where you bought me that *Banarasi* sari for our last anniversary?" She took a deep breath and lowered her head slightly.

"A. J. Kalbarta & Sons. How could I forget? You must have taken two hours to pick it out!"

"Someone said the poor boy was bringing chai to customers. I can't stop thinking it was that sweet child from the sari shop. The one who always served me when I'd bring in a new resident to buy her a sari. I remember you talking to him."

"Sorry 'bout the dead kid."

Kesh's eyes wandered to the servant, who entered with a dish of rice and a bowl of egg curry. At fourteen, she had been forced to marry a forty-four-year-old gold trader. Two years later, she ran away and ended up at Behera House with a deep scar on her cheek and burns on her arms. Kesh snuffed out the cigarette and fingered the soft blue pack for another.

"Please," Meena pleaded, "not at the table."

"Last one, promise," he said and fired up.

"You really shouldn't be smoking at all." Kesh looked like a coal-fired power plant with jets of smoke streaming from his nostrils. Meena thought this was rather ironic for a man who wanted all new buildings to run on solar power. "Remember Doctor Chakraborty saying how all this smoking is giving you hypertension?"

"Hypertension is a sign of distinction for a man in his mid-forties." He popped out of his chair and marched to the liquor cabinet. "In any case, a spot of bourbon will offset any bad effects." He ripped the plastic seal from a new bottle of Jack Daniel's, positioned his glass underneath, and turned the bottle upside down, as if he were pouring apple juice.

"So, Meena dear," he said, plopping back into his chair. "Shall we continue our discussion on the phone this morning?"

Meena didn't respond.

"Why do we need a bloody Western starchitect? I'm not good enough for your victims of violence? Your burned and battered brood? Sorry if it sounds like I'm talking about a batch of overcooked pancakes." He looked exceedingly pleased with himself.

"Was that supposed to be funny? These women are suffering and this is my life's work. I know you didn't mean what you just said. If you could only hear yourself, Kesh!"

"Sorry, dear. You know I respect you and am *exceedingly* proud of the way you bring succor to those unfortunate women."

"That's better."

"In fact, I idolize you, my one and only goddess."

Meena's blood was reaching boiling point, but she tried to stay calm. Kesh would be better in the morning when the alcohol was no longer streaming through his veins.

Kesh pulled the serving dish close, scooped a mountain of rice onto his plate, and, with his fingers, molded it into a giant doughnut. "It's just that I've become so damn frustrated living in this rathole eight hundred miles from my office. Five fucking years! Last month we lost that commission for the new airport in Goa. Had I been in Delhi, maybe, just maybe, I could have . . ." He shook his head. "And now this blow from Madhav." Kesh helped himself to two eggs and thick yellow sauce. He stuck two fingers through one egg to break it apart, twirled a piece with rice to produce a gooey ball, and popped it into his mouth.

"I keep telling you to spend more time in Delhi," Meena said, picking up her fork. "You've made a huge sacrifice shifting to Sompur for my job, but that doesn't mean you can't travel more often. We could even take money from your father's inheritance and buy a small flat there. You need more face time with your colleagues. Spending weeks on end all alone with your computer isn't good for you, Kesh."

"I know."

It was hard for Kesh to be far from his company, where he reigned over twenty-five employees—most young architects in awe of his talent and forever seeking his advice when they weren't fetching him a mug of coffee or a pack of Gauloises. Working remotely was no way to feed the insatiable tapeworm lodged in his ego. Especially now, as more architects brandished their green credentials and were beginning to win major competitions.

"Sometimes you act as if you no longer head up one of the top architecture firms in the country," Meena continued. "Still, you can't expect to win every commission." She took a sip of water. "You really must get a grip."

"Get a grip, you say, when Madhav wants to hire a bloody starchitect. He said he wants the center to wow people like the Bird's Nest, the national stadium under construction for the 2008 Beijing Olympics. Fine, that's one hell of a project, I admit! But then the bastard turns his back on me."

"Kesh, you just won an award for that new art museum in Rio—your first international success. The *Financial Times* critic praised it as one of the top ten designs of 2004, and he wasn't limiting himself to green projects. Why can't you internalize your successes? Forget the community center. There will be other opportunities just as good or better. Didn't you tell me the Taj Group was about to commission a new hotel in Udaipur and that you were invited to submit a proposal?"

"Yes, I suppose."

"What do you mean *you suppose?*"

Kesh slammed his glass on the table and a few golden drops flew onto his hand. He chugged down what remained and, tilting the glass, tapped the bottom a few times to retrieve any lingering drops.

"No veggie tonight?" he asked, glancing toward the kitchen.

"It's coming. *Arre,* Indu, the *subzi* ready?"

"*Hai,* memsahib, *aarahi hai,*" came a voice from behind the door, indicating they were on their way.

The servant emerged with a large bowl of palak paneer. Kesh stole a glance at the young woman's dark midriff, punctuated by a deep navel. Indu quickly adjusted her sari and turned away. Kesh spooned the spinach and cheese mixture onto his plate and scooped some up with a piece of chapati.

"Everyone knows you're one of the best," Meena said, "but we've been over this before—Madhav is calling the shots, not me. And why not? He's the one shelling out a gazillion rupees to build the new campus. Go argue with him if you don't like it! Actually, don't—just get over it, Kesh. You're going to have to work with a Westerner. You should be happy he wants you on the design team at all."

"Here we go again," Kesh grunted, "worshipping any fat slob with a white face. Why are we Indians so goddamn insecure, as if we all had small penises?"

"Pardon?"

"This bloody country worships the lingam, the holy sausage!" He held the empty glass in the air as if to make a toast. "To the millions of peckers—in every temple, under every banyan tree, in every home. Long ones, short ones, fat ones, skinny ones, even cold ones like the natural ice lingam in Amarnath. Now that's original, huh, an ice-cold hard-on!"

"Are you finished?"

"I suppose."

"Now, can we *please* have a normal conversation? I told you I've had a hard day."

Kesh placed the glass on the table and scooped more curry onto his plate. A drop of yellow sauce spattered onto the new placemat. Meena cringed but held her tongue.

"You know, Meena, we've become too sluggish. I mean, as a country." He mixed more curry with rice. "Isn't that why every nation has been able to invade us and suck the tit of Mother India dry? Greeks, Huns, Scythians, Kushans, Lodis. Then the goddamn Moghuls and Brits with their mince pies and custard tarts. Well, at least the Russians had the good sense to stay away. Imagine eating stuffed cabbage leaves every day for lunch!"

Meena wondered if the Hindu Democratic Party was finally getting to him with their endless ranting about how India was too weak, how we needed to reclaim the "good old days" before the Moghul Empire.

"Just look at how we keep kowtowing, mimicking every Western fad, from rap music to Christmas!" Kesh said.

"Christmas?"

"Yes, I went into a store the other day and saw poor Krishna hanging on a plastic Christmas tree."

"Kesh, please!"

"No, my dear girl, it's time we Indians unite and stand tall with our whim-whams erect. After all, are we not the land of Shiva, the ithyphallic god? Of course, the way Indian men adjust themselves every fifteen minutes, you'd think we were the land of the *itchy* phallic god!"

"Kesh, that's disgusting." She chewed her lip, knowing what was coming. Her husband's soliloquies were the first tremors of a massive volcano, with boiling magma about to flow her way. She thought of yesterday evening, when a pleasant dinner conversation morphed into a lecture on how Hindus discovered the decimal system and could have invented the personal computer if they hadn't been standing on their heads for the past three thousand years. "If you don't want to have a proper conversation, let's just eat in silence."

"I'm damn serious!" He reached for a napkin and wiped his mouth. "I've been designing sustainable buildings for thirteen years, long before some white dick with an MBA from Harvard figured out he could toss a bunch of ancient design practices into a box, tie a ribbon around it, and sell it as some fancy-sounding green building certification. LEED. Well, LEED, SCHMEED! As if sustainable architecture were a fucking box of corn flakes."

"Aur pani lao!" Meena called to the servant for more water.

"Why the hell should I have to play second fiddle to some foreign dickhead? Madhav is my personal friend. We have lunch every second Friday of the month. I have no problem telling him we don't need any blue-eyed boy to design a world-class building. *I* can give him his Bird's Nest, if that's what he wants!"

"Look, Kesh, Madhav's no dummy. He knows you are top notch. But he probably thinks hiring a famous Western architect will bring visibility to our cause. Stop taking it so personally. This isn't just about you!" She feared her words slammed down like a gavel.

"Now you're siding with Madhav?"

"All I'm saying is the women who come to Behera House have been beaten, raped, and some nearly burnt to death. The new community center should be welcoming and comfortable. Sure, we'll have bamboo floors and cisterns to collect rainwater. But we're not going to sacrifice comfort just to be green. And is it a crime for a businessman to demonstrate his latest cooling system when it's his money funding the project?"

"So that's what it's all about—air conditioning! You don't trust me, do you? You think I'd design a building that's so bloody green it won't have air conditioning? Is that why you're siding with Madhav? Well, why didn't you just marry a fucking HVAC engineer? No backtalk. No hot air! Life would have just been a cool breeze."

"Go to hell, Kesh!"

Meena threw her napkin on the table and stormed out. She marched upstairs to the bedroom, slamming the door behind her. The quilt on Kesh's side of the queen bed was pulled back and the curtains drawn. Was he now napping during the afternoon? She changed into sweat pants and a T-shirt, then stretched out on the bed. Why even engage with him after he's had so many drinks? Then the dam broke. After crying a few minutes, she leaned toward her dresser to grab a tissue and caught a glimpse of a photo taken twelve years ago on their honeymoon. They were standing in front of the famous Meenakshi Temple in Madurai. Kesh looked so debonair. At thirty-three, he was clean-shaven with a shock of thick black hair.

Meena recalled the first night of their honeymoon as they sat on the steps of the famous Meenakshi temple. Her new husband described the "green" elements India's architects deployed over ten centuries ago: how large slabs of stone around the temple inhaled the cool nighttime air and exhaled it during the hot day, as if the goddess were cooling the feet of her devotees with her own breath. That night, Kesh likened the clear rays of the autumnal moon to drops of milk. He recited an ancient Sanskrit poem about Soma, the moon god, whose nectar was supposed to bestow never-ending life. He turned to her and whispered how the ambrosia from her lips was all he needed to ensure his immortality; and that she, Meenakshi, was his private temple, since her body would confer its blessing on him night after night. No, it wasn't hard to fall in love with a man who made green-building strategies sound like love poetry and compared her young, insecure body to one of India's holiest temples.

———◆———

Kesh remained at the dinner table, stewing. He shook some salt on the table and was trying to balance the saltshaker on its side when Indu entered to clear the dishes. Her swarthy feet bore heavy metal anklets. An open crack along the side of one foot looked like a groaning mouth. How he would love to chain her to his bed with those shackles and fuck her in the ass!

She shot him a poison glance, as if she had read his mind. He put his hand to his heart and whispered the words from his favorite Jimi Hendrix song: "I have only one burnin' desire, let me stand next to your fire." Then he shook his head violently, trying to rid it of his fantasies.

She turned toward the kitchen, revealing an arm disfigured with burn marks. Kesh cringed. How could a husband be so cruel? He stuck his finger into a pack of Gauloises and felt one last cigarette hiding in the back, as if it, too, were afraid of him. He fished it out and crushed the pack in his hand. Then he lit up and flung the lighter on the table. It slid clear off the edge.

Indu returned for the remaining dishes and saw the lighter on the floor. Would she pick it up? She did, bending down slowly. The top of her sari fell from her shoulder and revealed her *choli*, the upper garment, which seemed too small for her ample breasts. She adjusted it and took hold of the lighter with two fingers, placing it gently on the table. *It's not a fucking landmine.* Or was it? Could the lighter have conjured up painful memories?

"*Shukriyan,*" Kesh said, but his word of thanks vanished in the air like the smoke from his mouth.

He meandered into the den. Above the TV hung a drawing of Durga sitting sidesaddle on her tiger. The independent goddess who never married. Her ten arms formed a perfect circle around her body, like a spinning wheel. He pursed his lips and blew a smoke ring onto her fleshy cheeks. For a brief moment, it looked as if a lasso had caught her around the neck. Then the smoke dissipated and she was free again.

He sank into the couch and picked up a book of Indian miniatures from the coffee table. The cover showed a husband fallen on his knees, supplicating his wife after he had returned home from a tryst. The man's lip bore his mistress's teeth marks, and his chest was smeared with the sandalwood paste that once adorned her breasts. Ripened mangoes bent the branches of a fruit tree in the background.

Kesh had read enough Sanskrit love poetry to know how the story would end. The wife would feign anger and the husband would demand she punish him with a kick. Affair, anger, punishment, forgiveness—wasn't that the ancient formula? *If only Meena would give me a good hard kick and fall into my arms.* But she didn't even notice his affairs, much less feign anger. He stubbed out his cigarette and bit off a torn hangnail on his thumb. Soon his cuticle was bathed in blood.

CHAPTER 3

New Delhi, six weeks later

United 451 landed at Indira Gandhi International Airport at 1:45 a.m. with a thump. By the time Simon reached the Maurya Sheraton and checked in, it was almost 4 a.m. He set his watch alarm for 9:30, swallowed ten grams of melatonin, and crawled under the crisp white sheets. In the morning, after a quick shower and shave, he threw on khaki slacks, a white button-down shirt, and a blue blazer. He longed for a tall mug of very strong coffee with each step to the elevator.

In the center of the lobby stood an abstract ice sculpture. A figure appeared to be trapped inside. As he approached it, he thought of Lin Yang outside the new MIT library waiting for her boyfriend on that cold day in February. A chill shot down his spine. He pictured the massive sheet of ice crashing onto her head, killing her instantly. Everyone loved his award-winning project—until the accident.

He took a deep breath, then scoured the room for a man with black owlish eyeglasses. Someone who might belong to what he called the ICSA, or International Club of Smug Architects. Nobody stood out. He made his way to an empty couch, still thinking about the figure shrouded in ice. It was a rude reminder of the lawsuit, an indelible stain on his career.

The soft leather was so comfortable he almost fell asleep. He ordered coffee from a waiter wandering around the lobby and again thought of Lin Yang, the smart, beautiful graduate student in neuroscience. After six weeks of haunting litigation, his firm had been exonerated. The accident was deemed an *engineering* error. But that decision could not undo her tragic demise or the damage to his reputation. Simon knew Lin Yang's death marked the end of an era. Maybe the *New York Times* architecture critic was right after all: it was time for Simon to move beyond the sharp angles that had characterized his award-winning designs for almost two decades. Maybe the commission in India would provide fresh ideas.

He had long admired the Moghul period, which produced some of the world's finest architecture. The central dome and rounded minarets of the Taj Mahal, the scalloped archways of the small mosque in the Gardens of Babur, the hierarchy of domes of the Hagia Sophia in Istanbul. Shortly before his trip, Simon had picked up a book on Hindu temple architecture. At first, he found the temples overly designed, even fussy. After some time, they began to grow on him, especially the Kalinga temples of Orissa, with their gently curving towers. They reminded him of hands coming together in prayer.

The coffee arrived. Simon drank it, ordered another, then craned his neck to view the lobby's domed ceiling. Arched beams divided the half sphere into segments, each painted with a different scene of urban or rural life. His eyes fixed on a Hindu temple in the form of a chariot with giant wheels to ferry the sun god across the vault of sky. He imagined climbing in and flying across the subcontinent, gazing down at three thousand years of architectural wonders.

Just then a stunning woman passed by, shaking him back to the present. Tall, a river of black silky hair twisted around a long, sensuous neck. Skin the color of milky tea, the proverbial high cheekbones, ruby lips—the works. And that sexiest of Indian outfits: the *salwar kameez*—a long orange and turquoise tunic hanging over skintight pants bunched up around her delicate ankles, one adorned with a silver thread.

"A Strad, na?" came a man's voice from behind. "Enjoy the music, but no plucking the strings!"

Simon wheeled around.

"And she probably snores, so don't get your hopes up."

A stocky middle-aged man in an impeccably tailored navy-blue linen suit sailed around the couch and stood over Simon. A yellow sports shirt flashed under the jacket. The full break of his cuffs gently grazed the tops of soft leather shoes.

"Mr. Bliss, I presume?"

"Yes, Mr. Na—"

"Keshav Narayan. I'm terribly sorry to be late, but I had an early morning meeting—a commercial real estate developer from Singapore—which took longer than expected."

Simon wedged his way to a standing position and stepped to the side. At six feet two, he found himself gazing onto a scalp barely covered by thin, graying hair. Dandruff decorated the shoulders of Narayan's jacket, and his beard looked like Celtic salt—his wife's latest whim.

"Skittles?" Narayan reached into his pocket and held up a small pack of candy. "They can make even grumpy cats smile. At least that's what the ad says."

"Oh, no thanks." *Do I look grumpy?*

Narayan popped a few of the flat spheres in his mouth and drew a silk kerchief from his breast pocket. "Call me Kesh," he said, wiping his hands, "since you Americans have a love of the monosyllable, which, I might add, is rather seditious when you consider that English is a bona fide member of the Indo-European family, whose languages include Sanskrit and German, where no noun compound is too long. Sure you don't want a Skittle?"

"No, I'm good."

"The sad truth is, I once knew an American who turned my name into *Ketchup*. Now, don't get me wrong, old sport, I love the stuff, although I would not go so far as to deem it a vegetable. Anyway, I trust your flight from Washington was decent enough?"

"Yes, long, but uneventful." A silver hair poking out of the corner of Kesh's right brow looked like a snapped tungsten filament.

"Well, that's good. It's so nice to meet you, Simon. And what a lovely surname, Bliss!"

Simon was about to say it was originally *Bleis* from Normandy, but Kesh didn't give him a chance.

"Even sensuous, if not downright *blissful*, the way the back of the tongue forms a thin channel to focus the stream of hissing sibilants."

What's with this guy? It was as if Kesh's brain had two left hemispheres.

"So, Simon—may I call you Simon?—how about some breakfast? You must be famished!"

They walked to the coffee shop, where they were shown to a table facing a lush garden. At the buffet, Kesh helped himself to a *masala dosa*, the extra-long crepe filled with spicy potato. It stuck out several inches from both sides of his plate. He joked that the restaurant should provide little red flags with the words *Caution, Wide Load*. Simon took an omelet, a slice of smoked salmon, and fresh fruit salad.

"I'm thrilled at the prospect of collaborating on the community center with a man of your stature," Kesh said as they settled into their seats. "Really, I am honored to work with the man *Time Magazine* hailed as a world leader in sustainable architecture, the first green architect to join the ranks of I. M. Pei, Frank Gehry, and Zaha Hadid."

"I'm not so sure about that," Simon responded. He was embarrassed, but also delighted his reputation had preceded him all the way to India.

"However," Kesh continued, "I do think the author went too far when he talked about how sustainable architects are a different breed. What did he say—that they don't feel the need for recognition, since their satisfaction comes from knowing they design morally superior edifices?"

"That's not all," Simon added. "Remember that nonsense about how green architects have turned sustainable design into a religious quest, the Holy Grail being the zero-carbon building?"

"Yes, it was all rather over the top." Kesh complimented Simon on one of his latest projects, the new Museum of Modern Art in Geneva. "It reminds me of a favorite project of mine—the extension to the Denver Art Museum by Gio Ponti. I admire the way Ponti dispensed with traditional angles in favor of something bolder. The lines give the viewer a feeling of being among the peaks of a mountain range. Having grown up in the foothills of the Himalayas, I like the way you and Ponti are pushing the envelope, so to speak."

Simon was relieved. *Somebody* still appreciated his angular designs.

"But going back to that article, what was that rubbish about you looking like Pierce Brosnan in his younger days?"

Simon rolled his eyes. He was sick of being compared to James Bond. Kesh removed his glasses and stuck his nose into Simon's face like a dermatologist searching for cancerous moles. Simon jerked to the side.

"Well, there is a strong resemblance, down to the blue eyes. But that wooly Irishman doesn't hold a candle to you, at least in the eyebrows department. God, how I envy you those thick brambles."

Simon's brows were extraordinary. He sometimes joked how they shaded his eyes like the metal canopies he incorporated into the façades of his green buildings to block direct sunlight. Alisha, his wife, once likened them to the flaw purposefully woven into Persian carpets so as not to offend their God.

"So, what about you, Kesh? Tell me about your work."

"Most of my commissions have been here in India. For example, I recently completed a 2,600-seat concert hall in Mumbai. The design is expressionistic in that I tried to evoke some of the feeling one gets listening to an early morning raga. May I show you a photo?"

"Yes, please."

Kesh whipped out his laptop, typed something, and swung the computer around. "There, top right. What do you think?"

"It's remarkable, Kesh, sort of like a cluster of caves, isn't it?"

"Yes, I was inspired by Ajanta, a series of Buddhist rock-cut caves that date back to the second century BCE. I'm proud of the fact that we were the first firm in India to design sustainable buildings." Kesh closed the laptop. He tore a piece of the *masala dosa* with one hand and dipped it in the thick, dark tamarind sauce. "But being the first in India, well, that's a bit like bragging about being the tallest midget in the room, since you *Amurricans* invented sustainable architecture and LEED, the green building rating system."

"Granted, LEED certification is a product of the US Green Building Council, but haven't Indians been practicing sustainable architecture for centuries?"

"Spot on, old chap. I could not have said it better, and I have to confess my remark was something of a sting operation. But you didn't take the bait. Instead, you quickly challenged me."

O-k-a-y.

"Much of my time these days is spent on lobbying the government to mandate higher energy efficiency standards in commercial buildings and promoting LEED for government-funded projects, such as the Technocities. That's a mega-project to attract foreign IT companies to India. I'm also actively engaged in the India Green Building Association, and in January will take over as chairman, if all goes my way."

"Congratulations."

Soon the men were chatting over a bottomless thermos of coffee. Simon listened politely as his host sermonized on everything from Indo-Saracen architecture to the pre-Indo-European origins of the wheel. Simon praised Kesh's new art museum in Rio, which he had read about in *Architectural Digest.* Kesh described its unique ice storage system for cooling. But before long, he continued to veer from one subject to the next, reminding Simon of the taxi ride from the airport. Cars didn't even pretend to stay in their lanes, if there even were any.

"Well, enough of this empty prattle," Kesh said finally. "I've just noticed the time, so I'd like to present you with two choices. To be more precise, one choice, which, of course, *is* two options."

Simon raised one brow and feigned a smile.

"We can repair to Sompur on the one o'clock flight as planned or spend the day touring the capital, in which case we would take the first flight out tomorrow morning. I'll put my prejudice squarely on the table and table the idea, in the English sense, that we postpone the trip in favor of a little sightseeing. So, what does Simon say?"

Simon's mood quickly lightened. He'd always wanted to see the capital of the British Raj, designed by Edwin Lutyens. And he longed to stand on top of the massive Red Fort built by Shah Jahan. What architect wouldn't? And wasn't sightseeing the perfect opportunity to start culling new design concepts—ideas that might help him reboot his career?

"Excellent!" Kesh exclaimed, without waiting for an answer. "So, here's the plan: we'll head straight for the old city, winding our way through the centuries and following in the footsteps of all those marauding tribes, beginning with the Afghan invader Mohammed Ghori in 1192. So, how about it—a thousand years of history in one afternoon—sort of like your theater, what's it called, the one that performs *The Complete Works of Shakespeare (Abridged)* in an hour and a half."

"Are you sure Ms. Kaul won't object?" Simon asked, fishing in his pocket for her email outlining the week's agenda. He did not want to disappoint his client.

"Not at all. In fact, Meena, who happens to be my lovely wife, actually suggested the idea, since some urgent business has brought her to Mumbai."

"Wait—you're Ms. Kaul's husband?"

"The one and only, at least, to my knowledge. You never know in India. In the *Mahabharata*, Draupadi had five husbands. But seriously, we are married. I think it's been twelve years now. You look surprised."

"Oh, no. I mean, I suppose, a bit. You have different last names."

"India is a land of extremes, my friend. On the one hand, we have a growing number of feminists, who won't even take their husbands' surnames. On the other, women who follow their dead husbands into their funeral pyres."

Simon's face disintegrated. Judging from her photo on the Behera House website, Ms. Kaul was no less dazzling than the woman who passed him in the lobby earlier that morning. The Strad. Ever since Simon received Meena's letter inviting him to bid on the commission, images of Behera House's executive director flew in and out of his head like barn swallows. He knew it was wrong and felt guilty, but he couldn't stop it.

"So, here's the plan," Kesh said. "First, we'll test your mettle in Old Delhi—a non-Euclidean world where no straight line goes unpunished. But come lunchtime, we shall be rewarded at Karim's, whose juicy *seekh* kebabs were the favorites of Moghul emperors since Akbar the Great. In fact, they're so succulent, you'd swear they've been marinating since the emperor dined there four hundred and fifty years ago. So, shall we make a move? I suggest we change into more comfortable clothes and meet in the lobby in fifteen minutes."

Simon agreed and practically danced to his room.

CHAPTER 4

Mumbai, the same day

Behera's limo pulled up the moment Meena exited Mumbai's domestic airport. She felt like a little girl as she climbed into the plush leather back seat. Meena was no stranger to luxury, having grown up in a large house in Golf Links, one of New Delhi's wealthiest neighborhoods. As an only child, she was spoiled rotten by her father, a successful barrister. But family wealth had always been an embarrassment. And marrying the son of a former maharaja only made her more self-conscious of her privilege.

As the car passed Mumbai's endless shantytown, she wanted to hide from the scrawny waifs who clustered around the car window at red lights. *Why didn't I tell Madhav I'd take a taxi?* At one stop, a teenage girl approached with a baby nestled into her side. Big brown eyes pierced Meena's heart, right through the bulletproof glass. She reached into her pocketbook for a few rupees and the bag of peanuts she carried for such occasions. Then she opened the window and was hit by a gust of hot air. She handed the money and peanuts over with a smile. The light changed and the limo sped away.

The Mercedes snaked through cramped neighborhoods before finally turning onto Marine Drive. She cracked the window and was comforted by the cooler, salty air blowing in from the Arabian Sea. The Oberoi Hotel loomed in the distance. She thought about her last meeting with Gita, who wouldn't stop ranting about the Hindu Democratic Party. *What right did those Nazis have to announce a partnership with Behera House? What right this, what right that, how dare they this, how dare they that. As your deputy, I'm not going to let the HDP turn Behera House into a pawn in their political game. Over my dead body.*

It was all so dreadful.

The car entered Mumbai's business district and stopped in front of Behera Towers. Meena rode the elevator to the top floor, glancing in the tinted mirror at her shoulder-length hair, a new look. After five years in Sompur, she had decided to dispense with the traditional braid she'd worn to better identify with the young women who landed at her doorstep. She stepped into the reception area and cringed at the oversized gold letters: THE BEHERA GROUP.

A woman sat behind the reception desk, staring into space. The corners of her mouth were turned upward into a faint smile. She looked like a computer on sleep mode, ever ready to light up at the press of a key. Sure enough—her face broke into a big smile at the sight of Meena.

"Morning, Meena, how are you? Please go on in. I'll tell Saumya you're here."

The chairman's personal assistant greeted Meena and asked her to have a seat, since Mr. Behera was on the phone. Saumya offered her a cold drink or tea. Meena smiled and shook her head. After exchanging pleasantries, Meena glanced at the *Financial Times* on the coffee table. "Behera Group to Invest $100 Million in Joint Venture with US Giant Cisco." The article announced that the new company would manufacture mobile networking devices. It described how the enterprise was positioning itself to serve the communication needs of IT companies going into twenty-five new "Technocities," a massive government-backed project.

"Meena, how wonderful to see you," Behera said, emerging from his office. "Come in."

"Hello, Madhav." Meena gravitated toward a photo of an attractive young woman seated at a Steinway piano in a formal dress, prominently displayed on the cadenza. "This wasn't here the last time I visited. Who is she?"

"My niece. She was a brilliant musician."

"Was?"

"Yes. Sarita was one of the twenty-three innocent civilians gunned down by Muslim fanatics at the Reserve Bank of India five years ago. Actually, five years, three months, and, let's see, four days. It was just weeks before I met you."

"I'm so sorry," Meena said, turning toward Behera. She remembered that tragic day, as did everyone in India. But she had no idea Behera's family was personally affected. She didn't even know he had a niece. "You've never mentioned her to me."

"I'm sorry, Meena, but I've hardly talked to anyone about Sarita. The whole damn thing is just too painful. It's taken me five years to dust off the photo and set it there. I still feel like killing those bastards."

Behera's niece had been in the lobby of the bank waiting to meet a friend for lunch when four masked men broke in, armed with AK-47s. Eight minutes later, twenty-three dead bodies lay strewn across the floor.

Sarita took seven bullets in her chest. It was just two days after she'd made her debut with the Bombay Chamber Orchestra playing Mozart's second piano concerto. The *Times of India* hailed her performance and named her one of the country's top ten musicians under twenty-five. The organization that took responsibility for the grisly act was an Indian affiliate of Al Qaeda, with ties to the ISI, Pakistan's intelligence agency.

"You know, Meena, not one person was ever indicted. Goddamn Congress Party. You wouldn't see the HDP standing around twiddling their—oh, forget it, you didn't come to Mumbai to hear me rant about the bloody Nehru dynasty."

A boy entered with two cups of chai and biscuits. Behera gestured to the couch.

"So, you're unhappy about A. B. Dey's announcement at the HDP rally in Mumbai last week?"

"Unhappy?" shot Meena, lowering herself to the edge of the sofa. She hoped Madhav wouldn't notice the slight tremor in her hands. "How dare the head of their charitable foundation announce a partnership with Behera House? You promised not to accept any grant money before hearing me out. Were you just placating me? No, I'm not unhappy, Madhav. I'm furious." Meena bit her lip. "I'm sorry. It's just all so stressful." She fumbled in her purse for a tissue. "Anyway, weren't we supposed to meet that industrialist friend of yours about now?"

"Oh, Dhole," Behera said, referring to a businessman with black money growing out of his ears. Behera and Meena had planned to solicit him for a major contribution toward the new campus. Dhole was not one to shed tears for abused women, but he was always on the lookout for ways to cozy up to the country's top business tycoons. "He called an hour ago and apologized. Said he had to fly to Dubai to rescue a deal. I wish I'd known a few hours earlier; I could have spared you the trip, since we're meeting that American architect the day after tomorrow in Sompur. Bliss, this time, right? That's still on, isn't it?"

Meena nodded.

"Now, before we get down to this HDP business," Behera said, "I have a small favor to ask of you."

Meena raised an eyebrow.

"It's come to my attention that Kesh is, well, how should I put it, out of sorts?"

"Is this about the Technocities?" Meena was proud of Kesh for having successfully lobbied the government to require all new construction within the proposed IT cities to be LEED certified. *Business India* described the project as hotter than the Indian sun in May. The mandate meant IT companies would have to design buildings with smaller cooling systems. She wondered whether Madhav was concerned that his company's chillers would not make the grade.

"No, it's not about that. Yesterday I read an article in the *Financial Times* saying your husband had tabled a proposal to change the whole goddamn LEED rating system. A change that would affect every LEED project, not just the Technocities. You know about this?"

Meena nodded.

Behera walked over to his desk and rummaged through a pile of papers. "Here," he said, grabbing the *Financial Times*, "on the second page. 'LEED Goes After Construction Industry.' Kesh is quoted . . . where the hell is it . . . here we go. 'If elected chairman of the India Green Building Association, I will table a referendum to abolish a loophole in the rating system' . . . blah, blah, blah, okay, get this . . . 'the change would require all LEED projects to be at least twenty-five percent more energy efficient than the industry standard.'"

"Madhav, I already know about his—"

"Wait, there's more. 'I also propose to reserve LEED Platinum for projects that are carbon neutral.'" Behera lifted his head. *"Carbon fucking neutral! Excuse my French. Meena, do you know what that means? It could sink my plan for the community center."*

Behera explained that he was investing in the center to position his company, Himco Air Conditioning Ltd., for the twenty-five Technocities. If IT companies knew that India's first LEED Platinum building had installed a Himco cooling system, they would be more likely to choose Himco for their factories and office buildings. But Kesh's proposal threatened to tank Behera's plan for the flagship building of the new campus. The Himco chiller was better than most domestic products, but not nearly as good as those manufactured abroad. To achieve carbon neutrality and secure the LEED Platinum certification, companies going into the Technocities would opt for foreign chillers with higher energy-efficiency ratings. Meena listened with half an ear, since she already knew Behera's motive for investing so much of his own money in the project.

"Meena, I'm a firm believer in climate change. But your husband's idea is, well, too radical. All I'm asking is that you talk to him. Explain that it's in everybody's interest to postpone his proposal for another year or, even better, two. He's already got one major victory under his belt—that all projects in the Technocities be LEED certified. Just urge him to hold off on this carbon neutral thing, at least until the center's finished and the goddamn LEED Platinum plaque is nailed to the bloody wall."

Meena heaved a sigh.

"Look," Behera continued, "the world's been spewing billions of tons of carbon dioxide into the atmosphere since the industrial revolution. It's not like one more year is going to bring on a biblical flood."

"So, what do you want me to do?" she asked, averting her gaze.

"A little triage might work—the old one-two punch. I'm having lunch with Kesh next week. I've already told him that Himco is coming out with a new energy-efficient chiller called GreenChill. It will be able to compete with any foreign product. But development is behind schedule by about nine months. I need more time, that's all, and so I'll ask Kesh to back off. By the end of 2006, GreenChill will be ready for the market and we'll have a decent chance at—"

"Madhav, please don't drag me into this."

"This isn't just about my business, Meena. Keeping Himco competitive will help restore our domestic economy. Do you know multinational companies expatriate most of their profits?" Behera rattled on about how stopping Kesh was in the national interest. Meena was waiting for him to say Kesh was preventing India from sending a rocket ship to the moon.

"Madhav, the truth is I have no control over my husband when it comes to the India Green Building Association. And even if I did, how could I? India is burning far too much coal. And please don't tell me the problem is cows passing gas or belching methane." Meena dropped her head. "I'm sorry, Madhav, I didn't come here to lecture you. But even if I wanted to help, I'm utterly useless when it comes to Kesh and the IGBA."

Behera walked over to a cadenza and poured himself a whiskey. "Okay, then, will you join me for a drink?"

"No thanks."

"Not even a chardonnay?"

"Maybe later."

"All right, let's talk about A. B. Dey's announcement."

Meena took a long deep breath and held it, as if she were about to dive into a pool.

"I know you're thinking a grant from the HDP has strings," Behera said. "But the funds for the new campus would come from the foundation, not the political party. There's a big difference. The foundation is a separate, nonpolitical organization funding anti-poverty programs, rural education, women's health—that sort of thing."

"Nice pitch, Madhav," Meena replied, her voice cracking. "But I'm not buying. It's been less than a week since the stock market crashed and you reneged on half the funding. The HDP Foundation doesn't approve grants in three or four days. Especially grants the size we're talking about. For God's sake, we haven't even submitted a proposal! Dey's announcement was political and you know it."

Behera gulped his whiskey and gazed at her with widening eyes.

"Madhav, I'm sorry that you've lost money, and I understand why you can't cover all the costs of the new campus. But what on earth is going on? You called me saying there was a *possibility* the HDP Foundation would step in and asked my opinion. I said I needed time to think, since there could be repercussions. And you promised to hear me out before taking any decision."

"Okay, guilty as charged. I did meet with the HDP leader and we discussed the funding gap. Ganesh Shukla is a dear friend, and he agreed to talk to Dey about a grant to cover half the construction costs. I thanked him, but I swear, I was just as surprised by that announcement as you. Believe me."

"Madhav, I wasn't born yesterday. This is an election play to win women's votes and you know it. The HDP wants to make us their poster child for women's rights. It's no coincidence that this announcement came just days before Professor Bhattacharya's op-ed appeared in the *Times of India*."

"Meena, the national election is in May 2006. That's thirteen months from now. There's no election play."

"I beg to differ. The HDP is clever; their leaders are thinking ahead."

"It's a little warm in here, isn't it?" Behera remarked. He walked to the thermostat, pressed the down-arrow button three times, and turned to Meena. "You said it yourself. The public announcement came *before* the op-ed. The two have got nothing to do with each other."

"No, I'll bet there was a leak. Someone high up in the HDP must have known the op-ed was coming. The announcement of a partnership was crisis management—preemptive crisis management, if you will." Meena fell silent and steeled herself, as if she needed time to reload a rifle. "The whole country is talking about Professor Bhattacharya's piece. People are up in arms after learning the HDP leader once said *sati* is an important part of Hindu culture. That young women throwing themselves into a funeral pyre is an ennobling act! And you want to take money from this party? Some of the young women who commit sati are so young they haven't even gone to live with their husbands. They're children, Madhav! No woman should have to do such a horrible thing, young or old."

Behera began to fidget with his pen.

"Look," Meena continued, "I'm not judging you for supporting the HDP—you must have your reasons." She glanced at the photo of Sarita. "But if you accept this grant money, women's groups and progressives all over the country will write us off. It will hurt our cause, maybe permanently. Behera House will be the laughing stock of—"

"The HDP is not the goddamn Taliban," Behera interrupted. "Ganesh's quote was taken out of context. And it was something he said twenty-five years ago." Behera tilted his head and stared at Meena, as if giving her an invitation to respond. But she didn't, and so he pushed on. "You're wrong in questioning HDP's commitment to women. Last year the foundation gave away more than 3.5 crore rupees to organizations working on women's health and literacy. I know. I'm on the board and voted for these grants. We can take their money without any quid pro quo. Believe me." Behera cracked his knuckles. "Well, maybe a few public appearances."

"A few public appearances where I have to get up in front of TV cameras and say how grateful I am to receive a grant from an organization whose leader once said it was an ennobling act for teenagers to turn themselves into human torches?" Meena sprang to her feet, folded her arms, and turned her back on Behera. "No, thank you! It's your decision, Madhav, but I can't promise to stay on as executive director if you insist on taking their money."

"Meena, calm down, please. Soon after the op-ed hit the street and the hullabaloo started up, Ganesh made a public apology. He went on record strongly condemning sati. You're getting all worked up for no reason. Would you reject a grant from the Ford Foundation because Henry Ford fought against labor unions a hundred years ago, or because the company now sells SUVs? Even your climate-crazy husband drives one of those gas-guzzlers!"

"And what about recent editorials linking the HDP to those paramilitary groups responsible for the communal riots in Tulsipur?" Meena snapped, recalling TV coverage of Hindu youth tearing down an ancient mosque. "That ended with hundreds dead. And the train bombing in Mumbai just three weeks ago?"

"Meena, I don't know where all this is coming from, but you must believe me when I say the HDP has renounced violence. The party's platform clearly affirms its commitment to a secular society where different religions can coexist with mutual respect." Behera leaned back and folded his hands behind his head, as if contemplating a corporate merger. "Okay, what if Ganesh agreed to forgo any mention of a partnership? The money would be a grant, nothing more. Would that satisfy you? I want to make you happy. You're like a daughter to me."

Here we go again, playing the daughter card.

"And no mention of the grant at political rallies?" she asked.

"Well, I don't know, but I can ask."

Meena turned toward the window. Two pigeons were perched on the sill looking in, as if anxious for Behera's reply.

"Okay, done!" Behera exclaimed. He rose from his seat as if to shake hands with the head of a company he had just acquired.

"Madhav, please sit down." Meena clenched her fists. "I am certainly grateful that you founded Behera House with your own money, and I respect that you are the chairman of the board. But in the world of NGOs, it's general practice that executive directors have control of the grants that are solicited and accepted."

"I respect that," Behera said, "but—"

"No, please, let me finish. This whole business has become much too stressful. I don't know how much more I can take. Gita is threatening to quit. And I'm deathly afraid of the response I'll get from the heads of women's organizations, people I greatly admire. My role models!"

"Please pull yourself together. I've made a reservation at Vetro. They have the best selection of French chardonnay in Mumbai. We'll have dinner and then head over to the National Center for the Performing Arts. The American cellist Yo-Yo Ma is performing the third Bach Suite for Unaccompanied Cello. It's part of a new multimedia series. Tonight, he's playing with a dance troupe. The program is called 'Falling Down Stairs.' It's sold out, but I have box seats."

"That's appropriate," Meena sneered. "I feel like I've been pushed down a few flights of stairs."

"Come, Meena, get a hold of yourself. After the concert I'll drop you at your hotel."

"All right, but if you accept the grant and HDP doesn't play by the rules, I'm going to publicly denounce the . . . Madhav, you're smiling!"

"You're a strong woman with deep convictions. I've always liked that about you." Behera raised his elbow. Meena hesitated, then took his arm.

CHAPTER 5

New Delhi, the same day

Simon changed into a navy-blue polo shirt and swapped his cordovan loafers for Teva sandals. He glanced over his shoulder to make sure the hems of his khakis didn't scrape the floor before heading to the lobby. Stepping out of the elevator, he hardly recognized Kesh, who was now wearing a homespun cotton kurta over crisp white pajama bottoms. The outfit was as flawlessly pressed and starched as his linen suit. He seemed shorter, having traded his leather shoes for Indian chappals. Any pounds lost in height seemed to have been redistributed to his girth.

After they settled into a hired SUV, Kesh ordered the driver to take them to Lahore Gate, the entrance to the Red Fort. They passed through New Delhi toward the old city. Imposing government buildings, built with heavy limestone and sandstone, spoke of the British Raj's imperial authority. The car made a short stop at Rashtrapati Bhavan, the president's house. Simon admired the Pantheon-like dome of the grand mansion, the home of Mountbatten and every British viceroy.

"Now gird your loins," Kesh said as they headed for Old Delhi, "for we'll soon be in Chandni Chowk." The car sped into a roundabout, practically throwing Simon into Kesh's lap. "What was once a grand boulevard flanked by stately mansions has fallen into a state of dilapidated shops, dank Sufi tombs, and crumbling tenements. But, like everything in India, these buildings are stubborn and refuse to hit the dust. Sometimes I think God has not only forsaken this place, but taken gravity with him."

Simon wondered if Kesh preferred the rough-and-tumble old city to New Delhi, since he seemed to revel in his own chaotic state of mind. But there was little time to think about his host as they entered a bazaar teeming with women draped in colorful saris. It looked like a mass of rainbows had fallen into the market. Simon cracked the window and delighted in the singsong calls of hawkers.

"So, old chap," Kesh said, "would this be a good time to tell you my theory of domestic violence? After all, you've been short-listed to design a center for unlucky lasses whose husbands mistake their wives for punching bags."

"Actually, Kesh, I'd rather you tell me why an Indian business tycoon is willing to fork out 25 million dollars of his personal fortune on a shelter for battered women? Isn't that rather unusual?" He felt a sting of guilt as the B-word slipped from his lips—he could almost hear his wife's accusing voice: *they're not battered women, but women who've survived domestic violence.* But he quickly relaxed. Alisha was seven thousand miles away.

"Behera House is far more than a shelter, but you'll see soon enough. Sometimes we refer to it as an institute, at least in English, since its scope is so, well, institutional."

"Sorry. But doesn't Mr. Behera own one of India's largest air-conditioning companies?"

"The largest."

"So, is he really going to let us design a building that's so green it won't need AC? Or, at least not much."

"Good question," Kesh said, as the car swerved to avoid a bullock cart. "So far, Madhav has only said he wants the center to be the first building in India to achieve LEED Platinum, the highest rating of the IGBA, that's the India Green Building Association. Not a bad feather to stick in one's proverbial cap, wouldn't you say? Of course, you don't need more feathers, Simon; I dare say your cap already looks like a Native American headdress."

Was that a jab?

"Actually," Kesh continued, "he's trying to position his air-conditioning company for a massive government-funded project which, due to my lobbying efforts, will require all new construction to be LEED certified. But that's a topic for later. Suffice it to say, you should be honored to be short-listed for this commission. After all, wife beating is a national pastime in India, sort of like your NBA. Joking aside, and I admit, that was a bad one, the community center is important and will attract attention. If you don't mind, allow me to give you some background."

"Background?"

"On domestic violence."

Simon agreed, but begged Kesh to keep it short.

"At the risk of sounding dolefully Viennese, the roots of this scourge go back to the primordial mother. You see, for three thousand years every Indian woman has had the same résumé. It starts with a simple goal statement: to have a son or, better yet, a brood of sons and no daughters, thank you very much!"

Before long, Kesh was talking about Freud's Madonna-whore complex. Simon spent most of the time observing the scenery, trying to ignore the lecture. When he did look at Kesh, he noticed the man hardly blinked. Not only did Kesh's jabbering seem to be one run-on sentence, but his eyes, too, appeared to lack punctuation.

Cars, motor scooters, auto-rickshaws, and bicyclists wove in and out of the smallest spaces, snorting and bucking as drivers tried to avoid pedestrians and various four-legged creatures.

They finally stopped at a crowded intersection. Kesh ordered the driver to park and wait for them. He hired a bicycle rickshaw, better suited to negotiate the narrow streets of the old city. The air hung heavy with dust, and black clouds belched from delivery trucks. Simon reached into his pocket for a handkerchief and held it over his mouth and nose. They climbed onto the red plastic seat of the metal carriage fixed to the back of a bicycle. Kesh graciously took the side where coir padding pushed its way out of a hole. The *rickshaw-walla*, a pile of bones, wrapped a dirty rag around his head and began to bear down on the pedals with all his weight, which couldn't have been more than a hundred pounds.

"India has no shock absorbers, old sport, so hang on tight."

Simon wished Kesh would quit referring to him as *old sport* or *old chap*. He was in India, not an F. Scott Fitzgerald novel. As the rickshaw gained speed, he grabbed the metal rim of the carriage. This was not the cozy tour of Indian architecture he had expected. But it was exhilarating. He managed to tune out most of Kesh's chatter as the streets, flanked by bustling shops, turned into thin, twisted gullies, and the world around him squeezed into smaller and smaller spaces. A canopy of tangled electric wires provided some shade from the unremitting sun. Still, Simon's sweaty back stuck to the plastic seat cover. Every now and then he pushed forward to unglue himself.

As they inched along the cramped lane, people squatted everywhere:

men smoking *beedis*, boys playing marbles, women sweeping the hot pavement. Even the once stately mansions looked like they were sitting on their haunches. As far as Simon could tell, Kesh was dead wrong about God abandoning the old city and taking gravity with him. He felt the urge to sit up and lengthen his spine, lest he be pulled down like everything around him.

"Do you hear that?" asked Kesh as pretty young girls piled out of a middle school in green uniforms and headscarves.

"Yes, it's lovely—the sound of children."

"No, not the children—men . . . chanting."

A Nissan Jeep advanced toward them. Its sides were covered with wooden cutouts to make it look like a chariot. Painted red, yellow, and green, it could have come straight out of a comic book. Inside, two Hindu priests were squeezed between larger-than-life idols of Lord Ram and Sita, his wife. The vehicle passed without incident but stopped at the next street corner, blocking traffic. Then a mob of protesters led by two bearded men in saffron robes surged toward the rickshaw. Some waved flags with swastikas; others brandished placards depicting a sacrificial fire. A pack of boys bearing lighted torches took up the rear, dancing to the beat of drums.

Jai Ram ji ki, jai Ram ji ki, victory to Ram, victory to Ram!

"What's going on?" Simon blurted.

"*Vaapus chalo!*" Kesh yelled, ordering the rickshaw to turn back. But there was no way out. The chariot blocked the road behind them; in front, another wave of protesters poured toward them. The rabble-rousers moved like jellyfish, undulating this way and that.

"Goddamn it!" Kesh thundered, shaking the driver's shoulder. "*Taraf se chalo*, move to the side and let the buggers pass!"

Simon felt vulnerable in the open vehicle. Kesh swung his head from side to side in search of an escape route. Then a voice, blaring from a megaphone.

Ladies and gentlemen, motherland is suffering. India will not survive unless we unify ourselves around Ram Raj, righteous governance . . .

"What the hell are these ruffians doing here?" Kesh cried.

Simon's mouth felt dry and gritty, as if he had chewed a mouthful of uncooked spinach.

Fellow citizens, we are not against any religion. The Hindu psyche is all embracing. But there should be no toleration for policy that makes Hindus underdog. Friends, in Ramayana, Sita is kidnapped by demon Ravana. Today, Sita is none other than Mother India herself. Demon is secularism, which is sapping our great country of her strength, her manliness as nation. Time it is to stop useless pandering to minorities . . .

Fists shot into the air.

"Goddamn HDP," Kesh roared as several protesters with long bony faces shuffled past them.

Sita Ravan se vaapus lao! Take Sita back from demon! Take back Sita!

A wall of men marched toward them with a banner spanning the entire street: ENACT UNIFORM CIVIL CODE.

"Is there any way out of here?" Simon shouted. Ignoring him, Kesh tried to light a cigarette. His hand trembled, and it took a few seconds before the flame stayed with its target.

Pandering rok lo! Stop the pandering!
Allah-wallas Pakistan ke liye vaapus bhej! Send Allah-wallas back to Pakistan!

The swarm of demonstrators finally passed and the rickshaw moved on. Simon took a few deliberate, slow breaths. He asked if the protesters were Hindu fundamentalists. Kesh wagged his head ever so slightly, like a quarter turn of a screw.

"Was that a yes or a no?"

"Yes, they're goddamn fundamentalists—members of the Hindu Democratic Party. And by May of next year, these zealots may be ruling this bloody country!" Ash fell on his white pajama pants. "Damn it! And Madhav, our patron saint, supports these hooligans," he said, brushing the ash off.

"What? Why?"

"He's fed up with the Congress Party, like most people in this god-forsaken country."

Simon felt his muscles wrap around his bones, as if hugging them for protection. How could his progressive firm take on a project funded by a man backing an ultra-right-wing party? How would it look to his colleagues? His reputation had already taken a blow—this was no time to take risks. He felt an urge to bail out even before meeting Meena and Mr. Behera. Then he thought of the pile of invoices from his law firm.

"Ah, the holy *jalebi!*" Kesh shouted with glee.

A street vendor hovered over a giant vat of boiling oil. His enormous belly could have been the original mold for the cauldron. Kesh's face turned into a giant smile, as if the protest were a thousand miles away. He ordered the driver to stop. Bright orange sweets looked like radioactive pretzels floating in some kind of cosmic soup. With a giant slotted spoon, the vendor fished out a handful for two children. Kesh stepped off the rickshaw and introduced the man as the Aga Khan of *jalebi-wallas*. The merchant handed Simon a few of the iridescent sweets wrapped in newspaper, which was soon stained by oozing oil.

"Come, have a few," Kesh insisted. He brushed away a fly that had landed on one. "They're made from fermented lentil and flour. You won't die."

Simon, still sitting in the rickshaw, looked anxiously at the sweets in his hands.

"Go on, they're deep-fried, dead as a doormat."

Should he insult his host by refusing to eat them or risk spending the next twenty-four hours on a toilet, if he could even find one? He decided to brave it and cautiously raised a jalebi to his mouth. The second he bit down, a loud explosion ripped through the air, as if he'd set off a bomb.

People screamed and scattered like frightened mice. Birds screeched and flew high into the sky.

"SHITFUCK!" Kesh screamed. "Quick, we've got to get the hell out of here!" He grabbed Simon's arm and yanked him off the rickshaw. The jalebis dropped to the ground. Kesh stuffed a few bills into the rickshaw driver's hand and started pushing Simon through the frenzied crowd. Then more screams and a second blast. Kesh pushed on, almost ramming Simon into the side of a woman shrouded in black.

A naked toddler, wailing alone in the middle of the street . . .

Glass shattering . . .

Howling cats . . .

Sirens . . .

Plumes of smoke rising in the distance . . .

"There's a shortcut back to the car," Kesh yelled. "But we'll have to negotiate a ravine. You game?"

Before Simon could answer, Kesh tightened his grip on Simon's arm and started to jog.

A pack of young HDP recruits rocked a car in front of a sign, KHAN'S BUTCHER SHOP—HALAL MEATS, as police moved in with clubs. A protester hurled a chair against the pole that supported an open tent, where Muslim women offered free drinking water to Hindu demonstrators.

Simon was clenching his teeth as Kesh dragged him through an alleyway. A cow rummaged through a smelly heap of composting food scraps and wilted flowers. A boy was kicking a tin can down the lane as if nothing were happening. A paved lot, strewn with used automobile parts and heaps of old truck tires. A tannery. Thick, black effluent spurted from a pipe down a steep hill into a dark, bubbling creek.

"Watch out!" shouted Kesh. "The ground's slippery."

Simon thought he could make it past the streaks of motor oil but soon landed on his side, breaking the fall with his forearm. Swearing, he got up, his elbow scraped and bleeding. Oil stained his new khakis.

"Oh God!" Kesh cried. "Are you okay?"

"FUCK NO!"

"Oh, dear. I mean, I'm terribly sorry, but we don't have far to go now."

Simon looked down the steep embankment to the creek, bubbling with thick brown sludge. It stank like an open sewer. Several old tires floated on top.

"Come on, old chap!"

"Don't *old chap* me."

"Follow me, Simon."

"You're joking—we're going down *there*?"

"No choice," Kesh said, starting to descend. Simon reluctantly followed, alternately stepping and sliding as he almost gagged from the stench. Halfway down, the effluent turned the earth into wet clay and he couldn't stop. Prickly shrubs scratched his arms as he flew down the hill, clutching branches as best he could, until he skidded to the bottom and landed in the stinking mud. A leech crawled out of the muck. For a brief moment, he felt a strange sense of freedom, as if he were a kid again. Without thinking, he slapped the wet earth with both hands and laughed.

Kesh removed his sandals and mounted a fallen tree that formed a bridge across the creek. Extending his arms like a tightrope walker, he scurried to the other side. "Come on, Bliss!"

Simon unstrapped his sandals and climbed onto the tree. Halfway across the slippery trunk, one foot lost its grounding, tossing him into the ravine. Any sense of childhood abandon was gone as drops of stinking, brown goo splashed into his face, stinging his eyes.

"FUCK!" Simon waded through the open cesspool toward the other side. Something sharp pierced his heel. Each step hurt like hell. He imagined every parasite on the subcontinent boring into the open wound.

"Hang in there," Kesh hollered, "the worst is over."

The far side was not as steep, but Simon struggled to keep his punctured heel from touching the ground. As he limped up the hill, he remembered a similar event from his childhood. He and his buddies used to slide down a steep incline behind their junior high school. The ground was often muddy from water that leaked from a broken fire hydrant. They would ride on round snow sleds, which inevitably threw them off, or they'd curl into a ball and roll down, amassing layers of mud.

Kesh led Simon to a public spigot where a woman squatted, filling a clay water pot. When the men approached, she quickly removed her vessel and stepped back. Kesh motioned for Simon to go ahead and wash himself.

Simon advanced and scrubbed his feet with a small gritty bar of green soap that lay on the ground. Within a few minutes, a crowd of young boys had gathered. They stood around and giggled as Simon tried to balance on one foot while scrubbing the other. When he had finished, an old bearded man approached, his head covered by a round knitted cap. The man waved the boys away and, with a bowed head, extended an orange towel with both hands as if it were a prayer shawl. Simon thought of his mother. She would always hand him a fresh, clean towel as he headed to the shower after a muddy escapade with his friends.

They finally made it back to the car, where the driver lay stretched out in the backseat snoring, his mouth wide open. Kesh kicked his leg. As they drove back to the hotel, Kesh apologized profusely for taking the shortcut. "Bad judgment call," he muttered time and again. "Goddamn Hindus holding a rally in the old city. Just asking for a fight so they can blame the Muslims."

Simon listened with half an ear. Alternate thoughts of the unfortunate afternoon and his carefree childhood were crisscrossing his brain like pedestrians in Times Square at rush hour.

"And I'm really sorry we never made it to our destinations. I especially wanted to give you a tour of the Red Fort. Maybe after you've finished up in Sompur." Kesh lit a cigarette. "Too bad you don't smoke. One Gauloise would kill any parasites you might have missed during your little scrub-down." Simon didn't react and Kesh apologized, insisting he was only trying to inject a little humor into a tour gone amuck.

When they arrived at the hotel, Simon made a beeline to his room, ripped off his clothes, and stepped into the shower. He scrubbed his legs and arms until they were pink. He used half a small bar of soap on his feet alone, occasionally pushing lather into the wound. Then he slipped into the crisp, white robe hanging in the closet, plopped into the reading chair, and let out a roaring laugh.

It was the best worst day of his adult life.

He glanced over at Meenakshi Kaul's letter, which lay open on the side table: a grayish-white envelope sported a row of stamps showing Mahatma Gandhi spinning cotton. The letter was crumpled, as if it had gotten caught in the Mahatma's spinning wheel.

You should plan to come to India for discussions with key stakeholders and a visit to the project site. I encourage you to make the trip as soon as possible, since the advent of the monsoon in June makes travel difficult.

His eyes slowed at the word *monsoon*, like a driver rubbernecking at the sight of a crash. How his mother loved to tease him, saying he had been through a monsoon without even making a trip to India. He thought about the accident shortly after his fourteenth birthday. He was mixing chemicals in his basement lab, when the batch suddenly exploded in his hand. His mother rushed him to the hospital, where he was drugged and placed on a metal stool in a shower for twelve hours. Hour after long hour, water pounded his body to flush out the chemicals. From that day, his mother joked about his *monsoon treatment*.

He grabbed his drawing pad and began to sketch ideas for the community center. The first few attempts—variations on the rendering he submitted for the commission—were marked by sharp angles, as if decades of muscle memory were guiding his hand. What kind of building would he want if *he* had suffered repeated abuse? What was *his* idea of a refuge, a safe place? He closed his eyes and soon fell asleep.

He was sailing with his mother on a sunny day. It wasn't the familiar daysailor they used to rent during summer vacations, but rather a vessel made of white marble. The sail, filled with wind, mimicked the contour of the Taj Mahal's central dome and provided ample shade from the punishing sun. He moved close to his mother, her hand firmly gripping the tiller, and snuggled his head into the soft curve of her lap.

CHAPTER 6

Kesh ushered Simon into the window seat and sat down next to him. Simon felt trapped. He took the airline magazine from the seat pocket and opened to a story about Deeg, the old capital city of the Jat kings of Bharatpur in Rajasthan. A large photo jumped out at him. It was of a structure that looked like a small palace built on the side of a reservoir, with two layers of scalloped archways and a rooftop that resembled an upturned boat sitting comfortably on gold facades. The caption read, "Sawan Pavillion, Deeg Water Palace." The article explained how the pavilion had a unique cooling system, which took water from the reservoir to produce "monsoon showers." The enchanting palace could have been a golden pearl fallen from heaven. He quietly tore out the page and stuffed it into his pocket.

Just as he was about to pull down the shade and nap, Kesh plunked a document in his lap. It was Meena's draft mission statement, intended for prospective donors. Kesh urged him to read it before they landed in Sompur.

Behera House was established in April 2000 with funding from Shree Madhav Behera, president and CEO of the Behera Group. The House is more than a refuge for women who survive domestic violence. The average stay is three weeks. We offer psychological counseling, skills training, and help with job placement. Most important, we teach residents that the violence they have suffered is not their fault. Our goal is to instill in them a sense of self-respect and confidence. They learn to stand up for their rights under the law. . . .

Simon shut his eyes and tried to imagine how a new community center could relieve such terrible suffering. The Deeg palace came to mind—a gold nugget sitting calmly in water. He imagined the palace floating on a lake and fell asleep.

The plane landed at nine-thirty. As soon as they exited the airport, Kesh said he had to attend to some urgent business, but not to worry, he had arranged for a car and driver. He promised to swing by Behera House at twelve-thirty to take Simon to the site of the future campus, about an hour's drive. He led him across a parking area to a clunky black car with a driver who spoke little English, shoved a tourist map into his hands, and vanished into a crowd.

The car was soon plodding through unruly traffic. A thick yellow haze hung stillborn. He asked the driver whether they were headed to Behera House or the hotel.

"Yes, sir, it is very good place," the man responded, pounding the horn, which worked only sporadically, as if it too refused to live by any rules.

Kesh had drawn two big circles on the map—one around the Grand Savoy Hotel, the other around Behera House. If they were going to the hotel, Simon should see the Shenyang Normal University (India Branch) and Saint Albans Hospital. If they were headed to Behera House, there would be a roundabout with a large statue of Mahatma Gandhi.

But there was no university, no hospital, no Gandhi. Just road after noisy road clogged with traffic. It was as if the same dreadful street had been replicated over and over through some kind of DNA sequencing. Here was a country where more than a billion people were slotted into rigid castes and sub-castes, yet the streets seemed positively egalitarian. The auto-rickshaws, the crowds, the beggars, the hole-in-the-wall shops—it was an architect's worst nightmare. Even the banyan trees repeated themselves, each spreading roots downward to become another banyan and then another. He reached into his pocket for a breath freshener and felt the folded pages Kesh had given him on the plane. He pulled them out and read on.

> *Behera House has developed a network of more than fifty nongovern-mental organizations (NGOs) across northern India. Each NGO, in turn, has forged relationships with dozens of medical clinics and police stations, as well as select faith healers and holy men. These organizations and individuals receive a small fee for informing affiliated NGOs of potential threats to women. Since there is money to be earned, even the police . . .*

Unable to read, he set aside the pages, closed his eyes, and thought of Alisha. As the car lurched forward, he pictured his wife's lovely face, her flaming red hair and dimples. Then the burning accusations. Suddenly, the car seemed to be moving smoothly and without the cacophony of horns. He opened his eyes and was surprised to see a wide street with hardly another vehicle in sight. They passed a grassy park. Men and women walking briskly around the perimeter path lined with blossoming trees. Healthy-looking kids in pressed whites playing cricket. Farther on, single-family homes and well-manicured lawns. He cracked the window and the scent of jasmine filled the car.

"Here vee are," said the driver, turning into a semicircular driveway. "Behera House."

———◆———

Simon marveled at the three-story mansion built in pink sandstone. Custard apple motifs adorned the second- and third-story trim along with balustrades sculpted into blossoming pomegranate flowers. Scalloped archways of mustard yellow divided the building into sections. Potted bougainvillea with red, yellow, and white blossoms surrounded Behera House like a fresh garland. It looked like something out of a fairytale.

A young woman holding a pot scrambled into the house. As Simon got out of the car, a thin woman emerged from within holding a garland of marigolds, her slight figure wrapped tightly in a brown cotton sari. Simon bent his head as she placed a garland around his neck. Then she joined her hands in front of her heart. "*Namaste*, Mr. Bliss Sahib, you will be pleased to follow me. Memsahib is just coming."

Simon placed his briefcase on the ground, drew his hands together, and smiled. She returned the smile, if only for a second, and swung around, exposing a nasty scar on her cheek. She couldn't have been much older than Sara, his sixteen-year-old, but she looked as if her life blood had been drained out of her.

They moved inside, where Simon was shown a wooden bench. Two women sat on straw mats under a blossoming tree in the courtyard. One wore a sari with a pattern of pink flowers. She picked at one with her nail, as if the flower had fallen from above and stuck to her garment. The other woman, stiff as a board, sat clenching her fists.

"Mr. Bliss," a voice called out. Simon stood and turned around. A woman in her mid-thirties approached with a brisk stride. "Meena Kaul," she said, extending a thin but strong arm. "I'm so pleased to meet you, and thank you for coming to India at this dreadful time of year."

"It's a pleasure to meet *you*, Ms. Kaul," Simon answered, momentarily transfixed by the diamond in her nose. She was taller than Alisha, five ten or eleven, and thinner, but with a larger bust. Her face, an Indian version of one of his favorite paintings—Botticelli's "Portrait of a Young Woman." Another Strad, sculpted by the violinmaker from Cremona? Kesh's wife, *really*?

"Please call me Meena, and do forgive me for not coming to Delhi to welcome you. I had to put out a fire. I do hope Kesh took good care of you."

"Oh, yes, he was quite the host," Simon replied, imagining himself falling into the ravine.

"Now, shall we have a quick tour of the house before we settle down to business? Being an architect, you must be curious about this building. So, how about it—a short tour before heading up to my office?" Her Indian accent was flavored with hints of Oxbridge.

"Yes, perfect," Simon stuttered, noticing a gap between Meena's two front teeth. Was this her Persian carpet, her single flaw implanted with care so as not to offend her god?

"Come, follow me." As she turned, the pleats of her green sari shimmered like seawater rippling against a coral border.

"The house," Meena said as they started down a long veranda facing the inner courtyard, "was built in the late 1930s by Abhishek Behera, the father of our current chairman."

A slip of a girl appeared with a glass of fresh mango juice.

"Don't worry," Meena said, "the water for the ice was boiled for twenty minutes."

Simon smiled.

"The Behera Group started out as a small mining operation back in the 1800s. Today it's a conglomerate, with interests in power generation, oil refineries, mining, and more recently manufacturing, mostly IT equipment."

"Yes, I read it's the country's fourth largest industrial house."

"Third, actually," Meena said with a hint of pride.

Some of the worst industries polluting the environment, Simon thought. But from her fulsome lips, it was as if all the bad stuff had been filtered out. He told himself to get a grip.

"Oh," she continued, "there is also a plan to build a five-hundred-megawatt coal-fired power plant in Patna. There have been protests for the last two months, so the project's stalled. Kesh has been lobbying Madhav, that's Mr. Behera, to put his money into a solar electric plant instead."

Simon imagined billons of tons of carbon dioxide being pumped into the atmosphere every year. What would his colleagues say? His firm didn't even accept clients that manufactured cigarettes or brewed alcohol. Coal-fired power plants were not just bad: they were the devil incarnate.

"Anyway," Meena continued as a worker rushed by carrying two heavy pails, "the business started here on the outskirts of Sompur, Madhav's ancestral home, but now the Group's facilities are spread all over the country and Southeast Asia. There's also a factory going up near Shanghai." She patted her hair. "Something to do with computer networks. Madhav divides his time between Sompur and Mumbai, the company's headquarters."

"The house is charming." Simon eyed the winding staircases with mahogany handrails at both ends of the courtyard. "I can't imagine why you'd want to leave."

"We don't really, but we've outgrown the place."

Simon nodded.

"The mansion is an exact replica of Rabindranath Tagore's house, only a third the size. The Tagores were among India's first feminists, but that's a topic for another time—that is, if you're interested. Most of the rooms on the ground floor are used for skills training."

Simon poked his head into one. Straw mats covered the floor and handlooms were arranged along the far wall.

"You'll like the site for the new campus. It's quiet and not far from one of India's oldest temples, which sits on the Bay of Bengal. Shifting to the country will give us more than five times the floor space and, of course, some breathing room. Quite literally. The city air is wretched!"

"Do you want to retain elements of this house in the new community center?" Simon asked.

"Oh, Simon—may I call you Simon?—you're getting way ahead of yourself. But as long as you've asked, the answer is *no*." She gently fixed the end of her sari, which was sliding off her slender shoulder. "The house is a pearl, but the new campus should have its own character. Especially the community center. Madhav wants a world-class design. Well, I'm sure you've figured that out, since, as I said in my letter, he's budgeted a hundred and fifty crore, almost twenty-five million US dollars! For some reason, he always uses the example of the Bird's Nest."

"The Bird's Nest?"

"Yes, the national stadium going up in Beijing for the 2008 Summer Olympics. But don't be thrown off. He simply means the center should draw international attention. You know how much publicity *that* project is getting. Quite extraordinary, that a country with so few birds would call its Olympic stadium a bird's nest!"

A staffer approached and whispered in Meena's ear. She excused herself and Simon sat down in a cane chair facing the courtyard. He leaned back and closed his eyes. Meena's mention of the Bird's Nest unsettled him. He started to fidget with his wedding ring. Soon, he recalled a biting exchange with his wife only days before his trip.

One of Alisha's friends had returned from Harbin and happened to mention she hadn't seen a single bird during the entire six months she spent there. She told the story of how Mao once declared sparrows "enemies of the state," since they were devastating the grain harvest. The supreme leader demanded that farmers across China bang trees with sticks so the birds would fly out. The farmers were ordered to keep up the racket until the birds—with no place to land—dropped dead of exhaustion. It was a ridiculous story, but Alisha couldn't stop laughing. Simon's feelings were crushed. His wife seemed to get a perverse satisfaction from beating up on his beloved China. For months after his mother's untimely death, when he was only fifteen, Simon would sit on his bed and stare at a book of Chinese temples with their clean simple lines, curved roofs, and thick lacquered columns. He imagined himself in the temple courtyards, protected by high walls, and could almost feel the embrace of the golden arms of their gilded Buddhas.

Meena returned, brushing a fly from her cheek. Her skin was the color of white pine, which he associated with old sailboats. Her eyes glistened like the ocean on a sunny day. They continued down the wide veranda. It was unusually quiet. Meena explained that most of the residents were on a field trip to an artisan's cooperative. "Two young women stayed behind." She gestured to the women still sitting under the tree in the courtyard. "Priya, on the left, arrived about three weeks ago from a village in Bihar. She was married at thirteen, though she didn't go live with her husband until the ripe age of sixteen. Less than six months later, her husband accused her of sleeping with their landlord. He beat her every day. One night he came home drunk and tried to strangle her."

Simon gulped. "Was the husband arrested?"

"No. The bastards rarely are. He made up some story about how he was possessed by a *bhoot,* that's an evil spirit. Malati has only been here a week. Her husband is an electrical engineer with a good job. One day, Malati caught her husband fondling their eight-year-old daughter. When she tried to leave, he threatened to douse her face with acid. She was too scared to make a move. But the threats only got worse—I'll spare you the details. Long story short, she ended up here with her child. Both are now safe."

They neared the end of the hallway. Simon was still thinking of Malati when Meena said, "It's a frangipani."

"Excuse me?"

"It's a frangipani—the plant in front of you."

He took notice of the delicate white and yellow petals.

"The flowers attract sphinx moths at night, when the scent is strongest. But the moths hover without alighting on the petals. They are thought to be servants of Lord Krishna, and the frangipani is said to be Radha, his beloved. As servants, they shouldn't touch their master's beloved!"

They took a few more steps. "That one is called Pink Ice," Meena said, pointing to a potted plant. The shiny magenta petals looked like colored icicles.

"One of the residents said its flowers reminded her of a hundred arms praying. Now everyone calls it the praying tree."

"What's with the red strings tied to the branches?"

"Once it became known as the praying tree, some residents started tying strings as prayers. The practice caught on. So, these days we keep a supply of red strings next to the plant so they can tie one whenever they like. It may sound rather silly, but it gives them peace of mind."

"No, it doesn't sound silly at all."

"Oh, you dear man, you must think I'm absolutely potty with all these myths and rituals. Come, follow me."

They climbed the left-hand stairway to her corner office. Inside, an old woman squatted with a long grass broom, gliding from side to side like a hermit crab. She scurried out of the room as soon as they appeared. Meena pointed to a sitting area with two rosewood chairs and a small couch with orange cushions.

"I'm sorry we don't have air conditioning," she said, turning on the overhead fan. "You must really take off your blazer. You're in India, for God's sake, and it's forty degrees! That's what, something over a hundred Fahrenheit?"

"104," responded Simon, who had been following New Delhi's rising temperatures in *The Washington Post*. He removed his blazer and settled into the couch. Meena sat on a chair, her legs tightly crossed. Her back, neck, and head were perfectly straight, as if she had undergone multiple spinal fusions. Behind her desk, a cloth painting depicting a local deity with a black face and large discus eyes. Flames rose from all sides of the god's head. He looked like a cast-iron cooking pot in the middle of a campfire. A large cloth painting hanging on another wall caught Simon's attention.

"That's Krishna and his consort Radha." The dark blue god was dripping with jewelry and garlands.

"Our residents love that one, probably because it shows a happy couple. You know, Simon, the women who land up at Behera House have gone through terrible times. They crave role models—strong women in good relationships. Fortunately, Hinduism offers plenty of examples, and there's no happier couple than Radha and Krishna, although he can be quite the rascal."

"Really?"

"As a boy, Krishna pinched curds from the kitchen cupboard, and later, as a young man, he snitched the clothes of young milkmaids who were bathing naked in the river!" A young woman appeared with tea and biscuits. "The god is incorrigible when it comes to beautiful women, but his exploits are always playful, never cruel."

Simon drank the sweet tea and stared at the wall hanging. The blue god looked familiar. Then it hit him. Raj—Simon's neighbor growing up—had the same wall hanging, or at least one very similar. Simon hadn't seen Raj since he was fifteen. Simon recalled his mother's stormy affair with Raj that ended when his neighbor took a job in Mumbai. His stomach tied up in knots; it wasn't long after Raj's departure that Simon found his mother lying dead on her bed—the result of drugs and alcohol.

Meena began to review the day's agenda, jolting Simon back to the present. The plan was to have a general discussion of the community center that morning; at noon Kesh would swing by to take him to the project site, with a stop for lunch. Time permitting, Kesh would bring Simon to the local temple, the only tourist attraction in or around Sompur.

"And you?" Simon asked. "Will you be joining us?"

"I'm afraid not."

"Another fire?"

"No." She smiled. "Just too many unanswered emails."

Simon sucked in his lips to hide his disappointment.

"Then back to the hotel to rest," Meena continued. "By late afternoon, you should be thoroughly exhausted. This evening, Kesh will take you to his favorite restaurant. The food is divine, and you'll be entertained by tribeswomen dancing with pots of flaming fire on their heads. It's all rather daft, but good fun. Unfortunately, I have another commitment."

Simon sucked even harder. Then a young woman poked her head into the room. She was in her mid-thirties with a plump, round face framed by short curly hair.

"Have you read today's paper?" she asked, ignoring Simon.

"Gita, I'm in a meeting. Come and let me introduce you."

Gita walked over to Simon, shook his hand without making eye contact, and asked if he could spare Meena for a few minutes. The two women stepped into the hallway. Gita swung the door behind her, but it stayed open a crack and their voices carried.

"So, did you speak to Behera about Renuka Bhattacharya's op-ed?"

"Yes, and we came to an understanding."

"An understanding? Okay, but don't expect me to change my mind. If you decide to take money from the HDP, you can find yourself another deputy."

"I know. You've already said as much."

"Is this Shukla's idea of women's liberation, giving teenage girls the freedom to throw themselves on their husbands' funeral pyres? There's no way we can take money from a party whose leader once said it's a woman's right to roast herself in a human barbecue pit! If Behera can't foot the entire bill for the new campus, so be it—we'll find an alternative."

"I see you're upset, and I understand, but I need to get back to Simon. I'll come by your office later. Kesh is picking him up at twelve-thirty. We can talk over lunch."

Simon could hear Gita stomp off. Meena returned and produced a twisted smile. He asked if everything was all right.

"Yes, just a little hiccup—nothing we can't sort out."

It didn't sound like a hiccup. Simon suddenly felt hot, his hands clammy. Meena's blue-green eyes that glistened like the ocean no longer worked their magic. Images of Behera and his bevy of dirty industries flashed through his mind. Then a clanking sound, reminding Simon of buoys tossed around by the sea. Meena said it was the *gas-walla* bringing cooking-gas cylinders on his bicycle. Her eyes seemed grayer, as if a storm were brewing within.

CHAPTER 7

Simon sat on a bench in the entrance to Behera House waiting for Kesh. On a console table, an oil painting of a young woman. A fresh garland of marigolds hung over the gilded frame and a *tilak* of red powder was smeared on the glass directly over the woman's forehead. He had seen garlanded photos in the shops of Old Delhi, but they looked like oversized passport photos. This was different—not only was it a painting, but the woman was young and beautiful. She wore a gold necklace and cast a sultry, somewhat flirtatious look, with a long braid twisted around her shoulder. Under the photo, a small brass plate: *In Loving Memory of Lalita Devi, 1948-1970.* He made a mental note to ask about her. Then, with no sign of Kesh, he booted up his laptop and was delighted to see an email from Tina, his twelve-year-old.

Hey Dad,
How are the sacrid cows? Eat any recently? Just kidding. Remember

the conversation we had at dinner before you left? I said I wanted to become a vegatarian because they don't kill animals. Remember? And mom said it's not necessary cause we eat organic meat—happy cows that roam around and eat grass. Reeeemmeeemmmber? Well, she's wrong. #1) if they're happy, we shouldn't eat them, right? We should eat the unhappy cows! #2) I asked if the happy cows suffer when there killed and you said organic farms use electric prods that are newer and cleaner so the cows die quicker, so there's less pain. Well, I DON'T CARE! An ELECTRIC PROD IS AN ELECTRIC PROD! So I'M NEVER EATING MEAT AGAIN! And as for what you said, that I could become a non-practicing vegatarian, well dad, I think that's stupid, no offense. Maybe Cathalics can sin and still be Cathalics— isn't that what you said?—but I don't see how a vegatarian can eat meat and still be a vegatarian. Please EXPLANE!!!!!

Love Tina

P.S. And I still don't get what you meant when you said just look at me, I'm a non-practicing hedonist!

P.P.S. If India's vegatarian, do the cows look happy?

Simon chuckled. He'd never seen such sickly bovines in his life.

"Good day, Bliss Sahib," Kesh said loudly as he approached in a rust-colored kurta and crisply ironed white pajama bottoms. He led Simon to a Range Rover and turned the ignition key, which seemed to rev up the cylinders in his mouth as much as the car. As they drove off, Kesh railed about the destruction of Indonesia's forests, a story he'd watched that morning on CNN. "The bogs are spewing billions of tons of carbon into the atmosphere, giving the climate a damn good drubbing. If they have to burn the stuff, you'd think they could at least make a good scotch."

What to make of Kesh? One thing for sure: the man was never dull. Unlike those buttoned-up therapists whom Alisha invited to dinner last week. Her colleagues argued forever about the merits of emotionally focused therapy. What therapy isn't emotionally focused?

Kesh drove through the countryside as if he were prepping for NAS-CAR. Simon tugged on the seatbelt strap to make sure it locked. After twenty minutes, they pulled into a truck stop, where lunch consisted of fatty mutton korma, slimy okra, and yellow dal. No cutlery. Simon asked Kesh about funding for the new campus. Gita's flare-up outside Meena's office was still ringing in his ears.

"It's the stock market, which has been plummeting south for the last week."

Simon wanted to say things don't plummet in any other direction. He decided it would not only be rude, but could lead to one of Kesh's longwinded etymological mudslides.

"Madhav," Kesh went on, "is pleading poverty and says he can only cover the design phase and *half* the construction costs. But don't worry, Simon, it'll get sorted out."

Simon's brain was bristling with questions, but Kesh was intent on pushing the conversation elsewhere.

"So, here's the program. First stop, project site. After that, we'll head to the local temple, a thirteenth-century masterpiece where feminine beauty is carved in stone. Now, if you'll excuse me, I have to make a quick trip to the loo."

Kesh's words brought back a bitter exchange with Alisha.

"Go to India for your goddamn project," Alisha had said as the lines on her forehead deepened into long narrow trenches. "But don't forget to take a moment to visit one of those erotic temples. You might learn something!"

"Come on, Lish, that was below the belt."

"Well, I wish our sex life was below the belt! For the past year, it's been one long rain check!"

Simon heaved such a heavy sigh that another customer turned around to look. Kesh returned. Simon picked up the mutton shank with his right hand, searching for a bite with less fat. Then he scooped up some dal with his chapati, only to find his mouth on fire. He reached for the glass of water, but Kesh stopped him.

"Wait!" Kesh asked the waiter for a fresh-lime soda without ice, then proceeded to describe the temple. "The friezes are replete with beautiful women standing and sitting in various positions. But don't think *Hustler*, my boy. If you must, you may picture Gauguin's Tahitian women."

Simon's whole mouth was burning. He looked around for the waiter. Where was his fucking soda?

"It's a chance for you to see how women were portrayed in ancient times." Kesh paused, then added in a strong Indian accent. "So much beauty is available!" He looked like he'd just bit into a lemon.

The soda finally arrived, and Simon drank up. He asked Kesh what was with his lemon face.

"That's because I'm talking about beautiful woman."

Kesh launched into a full-blown imitation, repeating the words *so much beauty is available*. Yes, he was a certified nutcase, but genuinely funny. Simon couldn't remember the last time *he* was funny. His father used to call him "Serious Simon." His college roommate, an incorrigible teaser, called him "Serious Bliss."

"And, if you believe the HDP," Kesh continued, scooping dal over his rice, "lovely women are the antidote for domestic violence and one reason the nationalist party wants to rebuild the temples."

"What?"

"You see, my friend, the party says this canker on our society could be managed if we could only get back to our roots, which they define as a time when women married and made babies, well, male babies. They pine for the days when the fairer sex dressed in saris, cooked chapatis from morning until dusk, and massaged their hubbies' stinking feet when they came home from work. None of this trotting off to Bangalore for IT jobs in tight jeans and men's kurtas."

"Sounds like the HDP is blaming the victim," Simon replied.

"Not only that, those maniacs know better—it's politics as usual." Kesh broke off some of the mound of rice on his *thali*, mixed it with dal to form a ball, and popped it into this mouth. "Most, though not all, domestic violence happens in the villages and among low-caste city-dwellers. It's generally not the college grads in Bangalore who are getting clobbered over the head with iron skillets."

"You may be right, Kesh, but in my experience domestic violence doesn't discriminate when it comes to class. One sees it in rich families as well as poor ones."

"Good point," Kesh said, now gnawing at the bone to retrieve the very last bit of meat. "My experience is limited, based solely on the rural women who land up at Behera House. In any case, I have a better idea than the HDP's harebrained plan of turning back the clock. I say we move the clock forward, with genetic engineering."

"What?"

"Genetic engineering. Let modern science do the job."

"Do what job?"

"Get rid of all the domestic *vee-o-lance* in this bloody country. I say we give women a few genes from randy elephants and, if they don't grow trunks, they'll be stronger than bulls. Hubbies won't dare pick a fight."

"Well, there's a politically correct solution!"

"Who cares, so long as it works? Do you have a better way to stop millions of men who have nothing better to do than beat their wives into pancake batter or, worse still, throw acid in their pretty faces?"

How to respond? Kesh seemed to really care about the issue, but his solution was, well, asinine. Still, Simon was beginning to detect a pattern. Kesh would babble on about some serious topic, just as he did about the peat fires in Indonesia, and top it off with a joke, often one in very bad taste. Or, as in this case, he would just come up with some extraordinary statement, however politically *in*correct. Was Kesh's humor a coping mechanism? A way to deal with the ugly realities of life in India? Just maybe, underneath all the shit was a man truly tormented by the suffering around him.

They finished lunch and drove on to the project site. As soon as the car reached a terrifying speed, Kesh started in where he'd left off.

"In Sanskrit court poetry, women's tapering legs are often likened to elephants, so we're already halfway home."

"Pardon?"

"The elephant gene. Genetic engineering—remember?"

"Come on, Kesh, get real."

"Listen, 365 million years ago some wretched fish had a stunted fin, which got passed on genetically and eventually led to the development of land-dwelling creatures with limbs. A hellbender or some slimy thing-amajig. Anyway, a few seconds later, in evolutionary time, we humans pop up. We're all just a bundle of gene mutations. So, what's so bad about manipulating another gene or two, if it's for the good of mankind? Well, actually, womankind."

"You're not kidding, are you?"

"Sure, it sounds like we're treating women like cattle—well, pachyderms, actually—but if it stops the violence, who cares? Then take the millions of dollars flowing to India from USAID and other donor organizations to end domestic violence and use it to fight climate change. It's a win-win, as you Amurricans say, and if you go one step further and do a little breast enhancement while you're at it, well, it's a triple win, at least for us men!"

"And just out of curiosity," asked Simon, "have you run your idea by Meena?"

"OMG, don't you dare utter a word of this to my wife. She'd have my head on one of those aluminum thali platters we just ate off of. And, yes, of course I'm kidding, although I wish there were a simple solution."

Simon took a deep breath. "Well, that's reassuring." He looked out the window as the car cruised through the countryside. A woman standing on the flat roof of her two-story cement house was hanging clothes on a line. A gust of wind poured into a red and yellow sari, causing it to billow like a spinnaker. Then a herd of she-goats with bulging udders meandered onto the road. Kesh stopped the car and sat, nervously drumming his fingers on his thigh until they passed. After fifteen minutes, they approached a metal fence with a large sign: PRIVATE PROPERTY, DO NOT ENTER. Kesh leapt out of the SUV and unlocked the gate.

A maze of rusty catwalks barely connected to a heap of crumbling silos. Was this godforsaken place the project site? One of the ramps had collapsed into a pile of metallic rubble, a tangle of corroded corridors, staircases, and chutes. On the ground lay a beat-up sign with the letters BEH RA CEMEN CO. L D. Where were the rolling hills and blossoming trees he had imagined? As Simon stepped onto the moonscape, a gust of hot air hit his cheeks like a blowtorch. He reached for his sunglasses, only to realize he was already wearing them.

"The factory went belly up when cement prices dropped about five years ago," Kesh said. "Don't worry, the site's really better than it looks.

Which, I admit, is sort of like saying Wagner's music is better than it sounds."

Simon scanned the site and his spirits sunk even lower.

"The winds come from the Bay of Bengal." Kesh pointed to his left. "Problem is, they're brutal during the monsoon and then nada for the rest of the year. So, don't get any bright ideas about wind power."

Kesh led Simon a few hundred yards toward a knoll, where the air was salty and refreshing. At the top, a cluster of thin trees with oblong leaves and large yellow-pink flowers. Simon ducked underneath the canopy to escape the sun's punishing rays, which felt like needles pricking his neck.

"These are *sal* trees," Kesh explained, "indigenous to the area. They're sacred, but, of course, everything in India is sacred, even the profane."

A flock of birds raced overhead.

"The *sal* is supposed to burst into bloom at the kick of a young maiden. Especially if she's naked or wearing one of those sexy girdles you'll soon see on the temple statues."

Here we go again!

Kesh walked over to one of the trees and gave it a kick. "I guess it doesn't work for dirty old men."

Simon admired the pattern of dappled light as the sun's rays filtered through the trees. Then he noticed gently rolling hills to the east and his mood lightened.

"The best site for the community center is over there." Kesh pointed north. "The area is flat and there's plenty of shade. By the way, it wasn't long ago that shipbuilders used the resin of *sal* trees as caulk. It's also used as a binder in new construction. And it's local and non-toxic, so I'm already smelling some gooey LEED points."

LEED, SCHMEED! Please don't start counting LEED points, Simon thought. He wanted to say he was an architect, not a bookkeeper who tallies LEED points to get projects certified. That too many green architects have begun to design by numbers: highly reflective roof, check; radiant floor heating, check; waterless urinals, check. But he kept quiet.

"Hear that?" Kesh asked.

"What?"

"The ocean." Kesh pointed east. "It's just a few hundred yards that-a-way."

The sound of waves lifted Simon's spirits. They climbed to the crest of the hill, from which point they could see the water. In the distance, a schooner. Below, a fishing village.

He sat on the ground, removed a drawing pad from his backpack, and started sketching: the grove of trees, the rolling hills to the east, the flat area to the north, and the ocean below. He made a line across the sky to indicate the arc of the sun and, after questioning Kesh, drew arrows to indicate the direction of the wind in different seasons. On another sheet, he sketched a rough design. Kesh approached and glared over his shoulder.

"As I've said, I'm a great fan of your work, Simon." Kesh reached into his pocket for a small silver case. "I've spent a good deal of time studying your designs, which are magnificent. But in so doing, I've observed your proclivity toward the sharp corner, the jagged edge. Not to say you don't make good use of the hexagon, the pentagon, and, well, all the other –gons."

Simon stiffened. It was bad enough that he'd been raked over the coals by some of America's top critics; quite another thing to be criticized by an Indian architect.

"Now," Kesh continued, "for the new center, how about something softer, with more curves?" Kesh opened the case's tiny latch, withdrew a diamond-encrusted platinum toothpick, and began to wiggle it between two teeth. "After all, we're talking about a place of refuge for women who've suffered repeated bouts of violence."

Simon was about to explain how angles create large, open spaces filled with natural light when Kesh started in again.

"Assuming you win the commission," Kesh said, wiping the toothpick with a monogrammed handkerchief and returning it to its case, "ought we not consider something more, well, feminine?"

"Do you have something in mind?"

"How about a taste of India? Think Taj Mahal, which is not just the pinnacle of world architecture, but the textbook example of how to build sustainably. Walk into the Taj on a scorching summer day, and you'll feel refreshing, cool air rising from the thermal mass of marble. It's a gem of sustainability, if you don't mind a few leaky roofs. Not a single BTU has been sacrificed as a burnt offering, no pun intended."

Mention of the Taj Mahal stung harder than the sun's scorching rays. Not long after his mother died, Simon was flipping through one of her cookbooks when a photo fell to the floor. His mother and Raj were locked in a passionate kiss in front of the crown jewel of Moghul architecture. The image had been engraved in Simon's mind ever since.

"In my opinion," Kesh said, "buildings must speak to our highest aspirations and sacred bonds. And what's more special than the relationship between a man and a woman or a mother and son? That's what makes the Taj so special. Built by Shah Jahan for his wife who died in childbirth, it is nothing less than a monument to love."

The Taj *was* a monument to love, thought Simon. But the *wrong* love. He wasn't angry at Raj for betraying his father, an ice-cold utility engineer. Nor did he begrudge his Indian neighbor for taking his mother on a tour of India. But why did he have to leave her, to move to Mumbai, if he loved her? Was the job offer from Colgate India more important than his mother? Right or wrong, Simon blamed Raj for his mother's overdose only months after his departure. Asking Simon to make the community center look even remotely like the Taj Mahal was as good as asking him to design it in a shape that foreshadowed his mother's death.

CHAPTER 8

As they drove away from the project site, Kesh gave Simon a short history of their next stop—a thirteenth-century temple dedicated to Lord Jagannath.

"The temple is in the Kalinga style, where each major element represents the body of the cosmic man, Prajapati, who, by sacrifice, created the world. It is also an idealized version of the human body, whose nervous system is said to contain the universe. The *shikhara* or tower, which rises above the inner sanctum holding the deity, is curvilinear, with the diameter of the top being half that of the bottom. The tower, or trunk, is divided into horizontal tiers, *bhumis*, each marked off by fluted disks. These echo the ribbed cushion or *amla* that crowns the spire."

After describing other architectural features, Kesh quipped, "For centuries, dozens of priests have doted on the god, feeding him five meals a day. Another dozen follow up with Pepto-Bismol." He looked over to Simon. "That was a joke, Bliss, you're supposed to laugh."

"Ha, ha."

"Now, if you don't mind, a word about the head priest, Upadhyaya, who's mad as a bedbug. When Upi—that's what friends call him; to his enemies he's Uppity—isn't chanting the Vedas or poking the god's ears with Q-tips, he can often be found reciting erotic Sanskrit poetry."

Simon was beginning to feel tired, jet-lagged. Or was it Kesh's diatribe?

"In his former life, Upadhyaya was P. R. Srinivasan Professor of Sanskrit at Banaras Hindu University. In 2003, the former priest of the temple was hit on the head by a falling boob, rendering him quite dead. It's an occupational hazard for those working at ancient stone temples."

An image of Lin Yang.

"When the former priest died, Upi was recruited. Our patron saint, Madhav Behera, is an old friend of his and helped him get the job by making a significant donation to the temple. The appointment was controversial, not only because Upadhyaya came from academia, but because of an article he had written a few years earlier. He argued that Sanskrit poets used a simple linguistic device to transform secular love into devotional poetry. What I mean is, they turn their human lovers into goddesses through a kind of literary alchemy. Needless to say, his was not your traditional résumé for the head priest of a temple. Do you want to know more?"

"Do I have a choice?"

"Normally, I would say yes. But today's lesson is too important; it's sort of like an SAT prep class, guaranteed to improve your chances of winning the commission."

Simon braced himself for the worst. Did he even want the commission?

"Seriously, Simon, the reason I want you to hear Upi's backstory is because his theory has been hailed by leaders of the HDP as the antidote to domestic violence."

"Sorry, what's the HDP again?"

"The Hindu Democratic Party. One might say our good priest's theory has been elevated to national policy—well, more like stuffed into the party's campaign platform."

"I thought HDP's answer to domestic violence was to make sure women don't wear tight jeans and trot off to Bangalore for IT jobs."

"Ah, you are a good student—remembering what I said earlier. Yes, that's part of it. But the other part is how we men must shift our thinking about women. Instead of treating them as mere lovers or wives, mortals with bad breath and weak bladders, we must see the goddess in them, just like the poets of yore. After all, if bloody cows are sacred in this country, why not women?"

"What are you saying? That Indian men need to worship women before they'll stop dousing them with gasoline and lighting matches?"

"Spot on."

"Gee," Simon said sarcastically, "that sounds like a real feminist approach to the problem! You don't stop beating, or worse, burning your wife not because she's human and deserves respect and love, but rather because she's morphed into a Hindu deity. Does she grow ten arms, too?"

"Very funny, ten points for that one!"

An accident ahead. Two crushed vehicles blocked the road, and an ambulance crew was busy tending to trapped passengers. Without slowing down, Kesh veered off the road and whizzed by the smoldering wreckage.

"As I was saying, our priest's theory intrigued certain HDP leaders because it showed how easy it was for a poet to turn a mere woman into a divine being worthy of male adoration. They thought this sort of alchemy might be transferable to the population as a whole, since, as you'll soon see, it's rather simple. You don't have to be a Sanskrit poet. In fact, any peasant with half a cow could work this magic! Now, you might ask, *how did* those poets transform their beloveds into goddesses?"

"I might, but I'm not going to."

"Simply by changing the way they *referred* to their women."

"What?"

"You see, my friend, in Sanskrit poetry lovely women are usually denoted by colorful, descriptive compounds, such as 'she whose face is the moon,' or 'she whose legs taper like an elephant.' Now, when we read such an epithet, we know we're swimming in the waters of profane love. Why?"

"Let me guess—because a goddess doesn't have elephant legs. At least, I hope not."

"Actually, in India some do, but let's not go there. The point is, such a reference would *limit* her. If she were a 'woman with elephant legs,' she wouldn't be a woman with, say, the legs of a goat. If she were a 'woman with almond eyes,' she would not be 'a woman with eyes like pistachio nuts,' right?"

"If you say so."

"So, what does the poet do when he's so besotted that he begins to think *beyond* his beloved's elephant legs, almond eyes, or chapel pegs? He throws those fancy compounds out the literary window and resorts to the humble pronoun, *sah*, which rhymes with the exclamation *ah* and simply means—are you ready?—'she.'"

"Kesh, what on earth are you talking about, and what in God's name does all this have to do with the commission or me?"

"Just hang in there, my friend, I'm almost done." Kesh pulled a cigarette from his pocket and stuck it in his mouth.

"Would you mind not smoking in the car?"

"Oh yes, of course. By referring to his beloved as *she*, the poet suggests that the old girl cannot be limited, just like God. Have you read Maimonides or heard of apophatic theology—the idea that God can only be described in negative terms? Well, the ancient Indian poets did something similar by using the simple word *sah*. At least according to Upadhyaya, who, I'm told, stole the idea from a Ph.D. thesis of a Harvard graduate student back in the '70s, but that's another story. So, then, the Indian poets stripped the mortal attributes of their beloveds by substituting the word *sah* for the usual descriptive compounds. Just imagine, yanking those barefoot and pregnant women out of the kitchen and turning them into goddesses by the mere use of the low-caste personal pronoun!"

"Look, man, I'm an architect, not a philosopher or poet, and I'm feeling quite jet-lagged. Let's talk about something I can understand. Why don't you tell me more about the temple we're going to?"

"So, what's the lesson learned? The bottom line? The Cliffs Notes summary?"

Silence.

"Come on, Simon, we're almost there."

"OK, let me guess—if the HDP is elected, the whole country will be forced to start putting garlands around their wives' necks and coconuts at their feet? Well, let's hope they don't get elected. I can't think of a more offensive and ridiculous solution to reduce domestic violence. Well, aside from inserting elephant genes into women's butts."

Suddenly, four magnificent stone towers loomed ahead. Each façade consisted of vertical ribs curving inward and culminating in a mushroom-like stone cap. Deep horizontal spaces cut across the ribs, giving the impression that the tower was made up of a thousand sheets of paper, each suspended by a thin layer of air.

Kesh pulled into a parking area. A mossy wall separated the temple from the outside world. Atop the wall, on the far left, a golden-haired langur monkey squatted, picking lice from the heads of its young. At the other end, seated at the foot of the wall, a holy man sat cross-legged in meditation. His matted hair was burnt orange, the color of the monkeys' coats. A deep crack in the wall ran from the top left, where the monkeys sat, all the way to the yogi below. It reminded Simon of a timeline one would see in a museum of natural history—as if the monkeys and yogi were scions of the same evolutionary family.

"Sea salt brings out the flavor in food," Kesh said, "but wreaks havoc on stone temples. So be careful. You don't want to get clobbered by a falling breast, like the late priest."

As soon as they entered the temple complex, Simon started to scrutinize the façade of the first tower like the monkey examining his young for lice. Sensuous female figures danced gracefully or played musical instruments. A particularly voluptuous woman, naked except for an ornamental girdle circling her swollen hips, captivated him. Her torso leaned to one side while her hips were thrust to the other. She looked like she had swallowed a snake. Then he stepped back and again took in the towers, gently stretching toward the sky like hands in prayer. He made a quick sketch, but soon felt a hand on his shoulder.

"Come now, the priest is expecting us."

CHAPTER 9

Kesh led Simon into the first of four temple structures. They were greeted by a short, pot-bellied man naked from the waist up. His lower half was wrapped in a simple *lungi*. A full head of shiny silver hair was meticulously parted on the left, as if he'd used a ruler. His nose took an unfortunate dip in the middle.

"Keshavji, my dear friend," the priest gushed. "It's so good to see you. And this must be the famous American architect you told me about."

Kesh introduced Simon. Then Upadhyaya ushered them to a side room where Gita was sitting cross-legged on a thin cotton dhurrie. She wore a brown kurta over jeans.

"Gita," Kesh blurted. "What a surprise! I see you've come to spread your good cheer."

She threw a frosty glance at him, a sharpened flint.

"Has memsahib come to learn more about the National Temple Revitalization Program?" Kesh continued.

Gita's face turned to a solid block of ice.

"Still trying to find some dirt under the holy dhurrie, old girl?"

"As deputy director of Behera House, it would be remiss of me not to look into the HDP's signature project. That is, now that the *Hindu* party has offered us a sizable construction grant. And who better to put my mind at ease than your friend Shree Upadhyaya?"

Kesh leaned toward Simon and explained that the HDP had hatched a scheme to renovate or expand thirty-three of the largest temples across India. Upadhyaya had been designated to head up the temple program, which would also bring back temple dancers—an ancient tradition outlawed since British times.

"The young women are not just dancers," spat Gita, who had overheard Kesh. "They're devadasis."

"Ah yes, the attribution *temple dancers* may be a misnomer," Kesh said. "Gita subscribes to the *devadasis-are-nothing-more-than-teen-sex-slaves-masquerading-as-the-wives-of-the-Lord* school of thought, propounded by liberals and feminists alike."

"As well as most educated Indians," Gita added. She shot Upadhyaya a glance so prickly it could have drawn blood.

"Guruji," Kesh said, "please put Gita's mind at rest. Tell her the temple program is above board."

Simon was confused. Until now, Kesh had nothing good to say about the HDP.

"It's one hundred percent above board," Upadhyaya said, fiddling with his sacred cord, a piece of twine worn by Brahmins across their chests. His belly was perfectly round and slightly bluish, as if he'd swallowed a giant blue exercise ball.

Gita started to ask if by that he meant the devadasis would not be having sex with patrons outside the temples, but Kesh cut her off. "Simon has come to India to propose a design for the community center of the new campus of Behera House."

"Architecture!" Upadhyaya exclaimed. "I thought of making architecture my field of study. It's incorporating so many disciplines: art, math, engineering, and now green missionaries, na?"

Simon leaned over to Kesh. "Green missionaries?"

"*Machineries*, like geothermal heat pumps."

"Actually," the priest continued, "uncle-ji was chairman of architecture department in Banaras Hindu University only."

Simon marveled at the way he pronounced the final syllable of the word *actually*. It began on a high pitch, dipped down an octave with a distinct glissando, and then slid up to end mid-octave. It was as if the word had taken a ride on his rollercoaster nose.

"Mr. Simon, did you know that Keshavji's firm designed the new Film and Television Institute at Banaras Hindu University? It was the first project in India to receive the LEEDS."

"Guruji," Kesh said, "that building is in Pune."

"Oh, yes, of course. How could I get so mixed. Anyway, as I was saying, me and my uncle are agreeing disagreeing on so many projects." The priest adjusted his hearing aid. "Like London pickle."

"Do you mean the *Gherkin*?" Simon asked.

"Yes. Uncle is big fan. For me, pickle is Himalayan eyesore. You say what, Mr. Simon?"

"I'm not particularly fond of Norman Foster's design." Simon leaned toward Kesh and whispered, "By the way, how should I address him?"

Upadhyaya overheard. "Call me Guruji only, like your friend Keshavji. Or, if you prefer, you can call me Upi. I am not minding. You are American, so no rules are applying."

Gita's nostrils widened as if she were about to exhale fire.

"You know, Mr. Simon," Upadhyaya continued, "I am thinking reviewers are afraid to say emperor is wearing no clothes, or should I say no dhoti! I am trusting your projects are very beautiful. No pickles or other condiments!"

"No, no pickles, sir. I like to think my designs are intrinsically beautiful, functional, and, of course, sustainable." He used his arms to lift his butt and relieve the pressure on his aching back.

"Inno*way*ion should be like salt bringing flavor out of food," continued the priest, "not dish itself. Mr. Simon, many Indians are calling the Gherkin London's 'Shiva lingam'!"

"Gentlemen," Gita interrupted, fuming. "I've come to discuss the devadasi program, not to hear a discourse on phallic architecture." She stood up to leave.

"Please be seated, Miss Gita. Just one or two minutes and I promise to be getting back to your good self." Gita acquiesced, then excused herself to go to the bathroom. Simon yearned to follow her and walk around the temple.

"You are also having very good architects in America," Upadhyaya said, turning to Simon. "I like Lebanese *woe-man*. Zaha ... Zaha Hadid, isn't it? And what a beautiful name, like a mantra only. One could even chant it, I am thinking. Shall we give it a try?"

The priest closed his eyes, extended his right arm with his palm facing up, and started chanting, "Om Zaha, Zaha Om." His voice was deep, relaxed. Soon he was reciting his new mantra at full stentorian throttle, and the words morphed into *Zah-aum*.

Simon was at first startled, but soon felt his limbs relax. He noticed his breath slowing and forgot about his aching back.

"*Zah-aaauuummm . . . Zah-aaauuummm*." The chant lasted a few long minutes.

"You are liking meditation on Zaha Hadid?" Upadhyaya finally asked, opening his dreamy eyes.

Simon smiled gently.

"Her name is like actress, Zsa Zsa Gabor, isn't?" They laughed. "Now tell me, Mr. Simon, which you like better, Zaha or Zsa Zsa?"

"Zaha or Zsa Zsa . . . well, that's a strange question. I mean, Zaha is an architect and Zsa Zsa was an actress."

"Try, please."

"I don't know. They're so different. It's hard to compare them."

"You must be trying, please."

"Well, I guess I like both."

"*Shabash!* Mr. Simon, well said! And why you are liking both?" The priest placed both hands on his paunch as if he were about to throw the medicine ball to Simon.

"Why? I don't know. Zsa Zsa is beautiful, as are Zaha's projects, like the MAXXI in Rome. It's architecture at its very best."

"Is it sublime?"

"Sublime? Well, I don't . . . I guess so, sure."

"And would you say there is something sublime in beauty of Zsa Zsa?"

"Uh, well, I never thought of it. I suppose."

"Oh, Mr. Simon, you have struck a bingo! Both Zaha and Zsa Zsa make you feel good, even sublime!" Upadhyaya leaned toward Simon and whispered, "What you are saying, this is very profound. In both cases, the secular is turning into sublime. Or, if you prefer, sacred and secular are existing in same thing, maybe even coming together as one being, like Shiva in form of half man, half woman."

Simon had lost the priest somewhere along the road. But he didn't care; a sense of calm resulting from the meditation lingered on.

"Now, tell me, what does our foreign architect think of Sompur Jagannath temple?"

"I like it. It's graceful," Simon replied. He suddenly realized Gita was still missing. "To be honest, I was expecting something quite different."

"What expecting?"

Simon looked at Kesh, who nodded, as if to say *go ahead, speak your mind.* "Well, please don't take this the wrong way, sir, but I was expecting something busy, even a bit overwhelming."

"The opposite of, say, a Chinese or Japanese temple?"

Simon pictured the Forbidden City, with its majestic temples and perfect sense of proportion. Even the country's name in Chinese, the Middle Kingdom, suggested symmetry. And so clean.

"Why, yes," Simon answered. "But I don't feel overwhelmed, at least not in a bad way."

"Mr. Simon, possible is it you are feeling overwhelmed in good way?"

"I suppose, yes."

"Ah, that what you are saying is very profound, this overwhelming. You see, Mr. Simon, our ancient temples are meaning to overwhelm, like ocean waves rolling over devotees."

Meena's eyes flashed before Simon.

"I see it as my job to increase *good* overwhelming. You asked earlier what to call me. So how about chief overwhelming officer! COO for short!" Upadhyaya laughed so hard his belly bounced. Simon feared the exercise ball was going to pop out.

Gita reappeared with a bottle of water. "You gentlemen seem to be having a jolly good time," she said, unscrewing the cap. "Now, can we talk about the temple program? In particular, the devadasis?"

"Yes," the priest replied, wagging his head. "It is good idea."

"I've read that you plan to install four hundred devadasis among the thirty-three participating temples. That's a bold plan."

"Yes, Miss Gita, you are right. In fact, so much boldness is there that people are calling me sexiest, exploitative. Oh, my, so many of names they are hurling. But I say to myself—Upi, even Vishnu had a thousand names, isn't it, though they weren't the bad ones."

"I think you mean sexist," said Gita frowning.

"A journalist for your *Time Magazine,*" Upadhyaya said, turning toward Simon, "wrote an article suggesting how I am bringing prostates in guise of temple dancers only."

"Prostitutes," Kesh said. He suggested the priest talk in Hindi with him translating.

"I'm sorry, but what again are devadasis?" Simon asked.

"Temple dancers," Upadhyaya continued in English with a wolfish smile. "Sacred wives of Lord Jagannath, who are dedicated to temple, sometimes at tender age. But trust me, Mr. Simon, devadasis are having so much of status in Indian community. They are enjoying full benefits of married woman, but never are stigmatized as widows." He stretched out his arm, with palm up and his index and middle fingers outstretched. Making Kesh's bitter lemon face, he asked, "How can they be widows when Lord Jagannath, their husband, is never dying?"

"Then how do you respond to accusations that devadasis were innocent young women who were turned into sex slaves by priests like you?" Gita asked.

"Truth is there, Miss Gita, that in some states devadasis were having outside patrons, but no sex slaving is there."

"Okay, so what is *your* plan for the devadasis, assuming the HDP comes to power and is able to rescind the laws that now forbid them? I've read op-eds saying you intend to use the devadasis as prostitutes to raise money for the HDP."

"Gita memsahib," Upadhyaya said with a patronizing smile, "devadasis are being brought back for one reason only: to honor Hindu tradition." He turned to Simon. "Mr. Simon, India has become weak nation. We are needing to become strong like America. For this, HDP wants to rouse people around a simple idea. And what better idea is there than old fascist Hindu way?"

"Excuse me?" Gita said, her eyes bulging.

"*Old-fashioned*," Kesh said, shaking his head in frustration. "Please, Guruji, speak in Hindi and I'll translate."

"You know, Mr. Simon," Upadhyaya said, again in English, "some Hindus are forming militia and promoting rifle clubs to drive out Muslims and Christians. This is not true Hindu way. And it is not HDP way. Strengthening of nation must be there through love only, not violence. Devadasis are women of beauty, like Zsa Zsa. They are dancing before Lord Jagannath, inspiring love and devotion in hearts of disciples. This is Gandhi's approach to nationalization. Nonviolence only. So, return of devadasi is progressive, and this temple in Sompur will be getting first devadasi this summer only, although delay may be there. It will be like reunion with beloved after long separation."

"But," Gita said, "you'll be breaking the law."

"I have cut a loophole, my dear Gita. Before HDP leader is sitting comfortably in prime minister's house and said laws are rescinded, devadasis will not be dedicated to Lord. Mr. Simon, that means no marriage ceremony will be there. And without marriage, the girls will not be devadasis, technically speaking." The priest took a handkerchief tucked into the fold of his *lungi* and blew his nose. Then he asked Kesh to fetch him a glass of water, as well as bottled water for Simon. When Kesh returned, Upadhyaya held the glass high, tilted it, and drank without letting it touch his lips. He mopped beads of sweat from his forehead. Simon took an antiseptic wipe from his knapsack, opened the bottle, and cleaned the rim.

"Mr. Simon, are you wanting to see some friezes carved for temple addition? As Kesh may have told, Sompur temple is getting first renovation, even before national program is launched."

"Yes, I'd love to."

"*Chalen*, let's go to the workshop."

Kesh asked Upadhyaya to first recite the *sah* poem for Simon before heading off to the workshop.

"The *sah* poem?" Simon asked. Kesh explained that this was a famous Sanskrit poem which Upadhyaya often recites to explain his theory.

The priest wagged his head in agreement, closed his eyes, and extended his right arm with his palm facing up. His thumb, index, and middle fingers pointed out, while his ring finger and pinkie remained pressed into his palm. Soon sibilants were rolling off his tongue. Simon had no idea what the words meant, but the man's face looked particularly anguished, as if he'd eaten one of Kesh's bitter lemons. When he'd finished, the priest's eyes, cheeks, and mouth were drooping, as if gravity was tugging at the corners of every muscle.

"*Kyaa baat hai*," Kesh gushed.

Upadhyaya offered a translation—

On the porch, she, and in all directions, behind she, she in front.
In bed she, and on every path of me sick from separation.
Alas, oh heart, here is no other entity—she she
She she she she in the whole wide world. Why talk of non-duality?

"It's just like every other half-witted Sanskrit poem I've heard." Gita said. "Here we go again—another verse where some useless man turns his beloved into a bloody goddess. Since men in this damn country can't handle real women, they raise them onto pedestals so high up in the air there's no oxygen and they suffocate!"

Ignoring Gita, the priest turned to Simon. "Gita is right, Mr. Simon. You see how easy is it to turn beautiful *woe-man* into goddess?"

"I've had enough," Gita said and started to collect her things. She looked like the Queen of the Night, ready to break into a riveting aria condemning the dark temple program.

Upadhyaya smiled, folded his hands in front of his chest, and bowed his head toward Gita, who stomped off.

"Now, shall we repair to the workshop, where love is being chiseled in stone?"

The three men walked to a wooden building. Inside, white marble dust filled the air like snow. A half dozen men sat on the floor carving statues from large blocks of stone. Some looked like the weathered statues that adorned the façade of the seven-hundred-year-old temple. A few men held the marble with calloused feet as they carved away. Others squatted, with the stone blocks propped up on wooden crates. None wore protective gear, although dirty handkerchiefs hung loosely from a nose or two. A large rat scampered along the wall.

"We don't mind rat in India," said Upadhyaya, turning to Simon. "Rat is Ganesh's vehicle. Every Hindu god has vehicle. Like Shiva, who rides bull. Our gods are very good role models. No need for SUV—no carbon footprint!"

Simon noticed a scorpion crawling on the leg of a female statue. He jumped back and pointed to the creature. One of the workers rose cautiously and picked up a brick. He tiptoed to the statue and tapped it, hoping the insect would land on the nearby crate. But the scorpion flipped onto the statue's breast instead. The man slowly extended his arm until the brick was within an inch of the deadly insect, now perched on her nipple. Then he thrust it forward, crushing the critter. "*Shabaash*," yelled a few workers as the nipple fell to the ground.

Upadhyaya bent down and picked it up. It was gooey and bore a small piece of the scorpion's claw. He turned to Simon. "Maybe we glue it back on. She would be really poisonous, a femme fatale, isn't it?"

Kesh thanked Upadhyaya for the tour, and the men took a final walk around the temple complex before heading to the car. Simon wondered how such a man had ever become the priest of a temple, much less the head of a national temple program of a major political party. It was nearly six o'clock and Simon's stomach was grumbling. Before long, they arrived at Kesh's favorite restaurant. Seated outdoors under a large, colorful tent, they savored the tastes of Northwest Frontier cuisine: mutton korma, the tender meat simmered in creamy coconut milk with chickpeas, onions, and potatoes; *seekh* kebabs, ground beef marinated in yogurt with garlic, ginger, coriander, and lime; and *murgh malai tikki*, chicken with ginger, green chili, cream, and cardamom.

In the course of the evening Kesh knocked down three double bourbons. Within an hour, he was lecturing about how Indian men were all useless mama's boys who marry their mothers. As an encore, he sang the famous lines from *Peter Pan*.

I won't grow up, (I won't grow up)
I don't want to go to school. (I don't want to go to school)
Just to learn to be a parrot, (Just to learn to be a parrot)
And recite a silly rule. (And recite a silly rule)
If growing up means . . .

———◆———

As Simon lay in bed that evening, the strange visit to the temple played over and over in his mind. Kesh and the priest were surely carved from the same stone. Upi was like a busy Hindu temple, teeming not with erotic friezes, but with wild notions and erotic poems. Just as the temple's busy architecture was meant to overwhelm its devotees, Upi himself overwhelmed. A chief overwhelming officer indeed.

Simon looked for a mini-fridge. But Sompur's Grand Savoy was no Maurya Sheraton. In fact, this hotel was one starless night. He dug into his knapsack for a pack of roasted tamari almonds he'd taken from the plane. As he munched away, thoughts of the project site flashed through his head, and he was soon overcome with self-doubt. What did he know about this mad country? He eyed the pitcher of water, then called room service for a beer.

How different India was from his beloved China, where temples expressed a universal beauty and harmony. The *emptiness* of Buddhism. How could he possibly design a community center for Meena's women? How could he express the Hindu sense of life's *fullness* and still convey peace and tranquility? A healing quality. *A sense of being overwhelmed in a good way.*

Room service arrived with a sixteen-ounce Taj Mahal beer. Simon sat in the reading chair nursing the drink. He recalled Kesh saying, "In the end, fullness *is* emptiness." Kesh had invited Simon to imagine a child drawing black lines on a sheet of white paper with a thick crayon. The kid goes nuts, frantically scribbling more and more lines until the paper is all black. Then Kesh asked, "Now, Simon, do you see emptiness or fullness?"

He finished the beer and thought about Upi making that ridiculous bitter lemon face when he recited the love poem *sah!* And didn't Kesh say the lotus, India's national flower, literally meant "born in the mud"? And what did Kesh say Indians do when moved to tears by raga? *Kyaa baat hai,* "what's the matter?" *When one's heart fills with joy, something's the goddamn matter!*

This was not a world of happy sunflowers growing in American cornfields. Indians seemed to express the human condition differently. He recalled Kesh saying there was a word in Sanskrit that meant both *beauty* and *salty,* since salt brings out the flavor of food. Beauty came with a bitter face, a salty taste. Were Indian women never *sweet*hearts? And things seemed to easily morph from one thing to another. By some linguistic magic, poets turned their lovers into goddesses. Temples with fussy façades suddenly felt like peaceful sanctuaries. Vishnu reincarnated himself as a giant fish. And hadn't Meena's glistening eyes turned into a gray, stormy sea?

He squeezed his eyes shut and tried to imagine a Hindu temple becoming so busy that it became a tranquil sanctuary. It didn't work—he was an architect, not an alchemist. There was no way in hell he could design a women's center in a country where *busyness* overwhelmed in a good way. As soon as he got back to Washington, he would turn the project over to Anand. His colleague grew up in Pune and was far better qualified to figure out if a piece of paper could be so full it was empty, or so empty it was full. Simon ordered a second beer. As he waited, he felt empty inside. An emptiness with no hint of fullness.

CHAPTER 10

Ash-hadu alla ilaha illallah Ash-hadu anna Muhammadan rasulullah . . .
Yes, God is great, now can I sleep? It was four in the morning. But the call to prayer ended, and Simon fell back asleep. Waking at seven, he noticed the empty Taj Mahal beer bottle from the night before. But Raj and his mom were absent from the label. No passionate kissing in the foreground. He stared at the minarets, arched façades, and balloon dome of the mausoleum—features he'd never really focused on.

He flipped through *Fodor's India,* as he had done many times before the trip. But this time he looked at the temples, palaces, forts, and mosques with a different eye. Some of the architectural features intrigued him, but none inspired him with new ideas. He closed the book and remembered something Meena had said—that Mr. Behera wanted the center to be like the national stadium under construction for the Beijing Olympics. The Bird's Nest. He imagined a songbird breaking out of its egg in a cozy nest.

Simon dressed and waited outside the hotel for Meena's driver. A car pulled up at nine and drove him to Behera House, where he was escorted to Gita's office. Meena's deputy was slumped behind her desk sucking an ice cube, which she proudly displayed as soon as their eyes met. Her orange kurta was wrinkled. The room was sparsely furnished. On one wall, a poster: *Well Behaved Women Rarely Make History.* Behind her desk, a cadenza with photos. One showed Gita and a taller white woman, her arm around Gita's hip, both smiling. In another, Gita and the same woman stood atop a mountain wearing shorts and hiking boots. The woman's arm rested on Gita's shoulder.

"Sit, Simon." Gita hissed the words like an old radiator. "Meena had to go out for a meeting, so you're stuck with me."

"But I thought Meena and I were having lunch with Mr. Behera today?" Simon assumed his best poker face to hide his disappointment.

"Don't worry. She'll be back."

Gita extended a manila envelope without a word, as if she were handing over a court summons. Simon opened it: *Design Intention for Community Center of Lalita Devi Center for the Advancement of Women.*

"Lalita Devi Center for—"

"We couldn't exactly call the new campus Behera *House,* now could we?"

Simon held his tongue and flipped through the pages. After a few minutes, Gita began to outline four main functions of the center (administration, dining, training, and recreation), the number of people involved in each activity throughout the day, and the rooms needed for each. She spoke without emotion, as if reading from a shopping list.

Simon rattled off a series of questions. Were there special requirements for the kitchen? Did residents eat at tables or on floor mats? How would the women respond to an enclosed, air-conditioned atrium instead of a courtyard? Gita answered as briefly as possible, as if each word cost her a hundred rupees. At the end of every response, she exhibited the ice cube in her mouth as if it were a period.

"I get it," said Simon, inserting the document into his briefcase. He leaned forward and spoke in a low voice. "I couldn't help overhearing your conversation with Meena yesterday. In the hall. Something about the HDP leader saying it's all right for a woman to throw herself into her husband's funeral pyre."

Gita's jaw tightened, cracking the ice.

"Would you mind telling me what this is all about?" Simon asked.

"You've got sharp ears."

Simon was suddenly shaken by a loud screech, as if someone were being strangled.

"Relax, it's just a peacock in the garden. They cry like that before the rains. It's their mating call. Peahens have it a lot better than women in this country, but that's another matter. Now, regarding our funding, the stock market's in the dumps. Behera's personal wealth consists largely of shares of his company, which are down thirty-some percent. So, our patron saint is pleading poverty . . . says he can only fund the design phase and half the construction costs of the new campus."

"So, what, the HDP is stepping in?"

"Behera is a big supporter of the Hindu party. He's twisted some arms to get a mega-grant from their foundation. But you shouldn't worry. We'll find an alternative. There's no way in hell we're taking their dirty loot, at least not while I'm here. It's an ultra-right-wing cabal. If elected, they'll destroy whatever progress we've made on women's rights over the last hundred years. There's even talk that the HDP would rescind laws banning sati, one of India's most important contributions to world civilization. Do you even know what sati is?"

"Yes, I think so. Widows throwing themselves into their husbands' funeral pyres."

"Well, *being pushed* is more likely. Anyway, it's a nasty business, but not your problem."

"But it does trouble me. I don't know much about Indian politics, but—"

"I'm reassured that the idea of women being turned into roasted mutton troubles you. It doesn't seem to bother half of this godforsaken country. By that I mean nearly a hundred percent of the male population." She removed the cracked piece of ice from her mouth and put it in a bowl on her desk. "Listen, Simon, I've got this thing under control. I'm researching alternative sources of funding and have a few leads. But if, in the meantime, Behera takes the HDP's grant, well, quite frankly, I'm out of here."

"Well, me too! My firm doesn't even take clients who make cigarettes or alcohol, not to mention companies that build coal-fired power plants or engage in mining and other extractive ind—"

"Are young women turning themselves into French fries on your no-go list?"

Simon felt blood rushing to his face. "Gita, were you serious yesterday, I mean at the temple, when you accused Upadh . . . the priest of turning the HDP's temple program into a giant harem? I mean by using those darvi—"

"Devadasis, the so-called temple dancers. Hell, yes—I don't trust that worm for a second. I'm sure his National Temple Revitalization Program is nothing more than a scheme to raise money for that Nazi party. There have been rumors to that effect. Quite clever, that priest, if one can call him that. He designs a program to rally Hindus to the party before the national election; at the same time, he's planning to use the devadasis as an underground money-printing machine . . . with him taking his cut, of course. Unfortunately, we may not know the truth until it's too late."

"What do you mean?"

"I mean, nothing will happen until the national election. If the HDP wins and forms a government, that's when the shit will hit the fan. As of now, the tradition is outlawed. Upadhyaya's hands are tied, well, almost—he's got his little loophole, but that's not going to get him very far. So, it's all speculation."

"Just curious—have you spent time in the States?" Simon was surprised by her use of American slang.

"No, but I have an American girlfriend."

"Oh, I see." Simon paused. "So, does Meena have the same fears? I mean about the HDP?"

"Meena, I love her dearly, but she trots around like a thoroughbred with blinders. She says we shouldn't worry until there's hard evidence of a crime. But how could there be evidence when these snakes aren't in power yet? Look, the temple program is a bloody can of worms, and I don't need a can opener to prove it. Anyway, a can opener wouldn't do me much good right now. As I said, the goddamn program can't even get off the ground unless these crooks win the national election." Gita reached into her kurta and pulled out a pack of cigarettes. "Which is highly likely, given that India is like a car with one gear, reverse." She extended her hand with the pack. "Smoke?"

"No, thanks."

"I figured," she said, firing up. "Well, then, any more questions about the center?"

The ice in the bowl had melted. *This woman is all fire and ice.*

"I said, any more questions?"

"Well, yes, one more. What's in it for Mr. Behera, I mean throwing all this money at a new building for, you know, your women?"

"Look here, the GOI, that's the Government of India, is planning a project to build twenty-five new IT cities. From scratch." She took a long drag. "Twenty-five Technocities across the country, creating a whopping one billion-dollar demand for cooling systems. Yes, that's US dollars. It's the largest single construction project ever proposed by the national government. And thanks to Kesh's lobbying, the government is requiring all new construction within the cities to be LEED certified. Behera is funding the center so he can showcase his chiller in what he hopes will be the greenest building in India. 'Dark green'—his new mantra."

"Okay, but why choose a community center for women survivors of abuse, and, if you don't mind me asking, why Sompur, when he could showcase his new chiller in, say, a five-star hotel, like the Grand Hyatt going up in Mumbai. Who comes to Sompur? I mean, he'd get so much more visibility if—"

"It'll be clear when we get to the lobby. Are we finished?"

"Yes, I suppose so."

Gita snubbed out the cigarette and escorted Simon to the main entrance. She pointed to the garlanded painting of the young Lalita Devi propped up on the console table opposite the door.

"She's the reason we're here," Gita said. She poked her head outside to see if Behera's car had arrived. "Madhav—that's Behera—was in his twenties when he took a liking to Lalita, a young sweeper who worked in his office. The relationship wasn't sexual, but it was still highly unusual, since she was a Dalit—that's, quote, untouchable. You see, Madhav considered himself an amateur painter, and every so often, he would pick an employee, usually a woman, to come to his office and sit for him—with her permission, I'm told. What's wrong? You look puzzled."

"Only that she doesn't look like a sweeper. I mean, with that silk sari and gold necklace."

"It doesn't hurt that she's knockout gorgeous. Behera dressed her up and did a pen and ink drawing. It was later, after the incident I'm about to tell you about, that he made the oil painting you're looking at."

"Mr. Behera did this painting? It's quite good."

"Yes. So, one day he noticed burn marks on Lalita, who was sweeping the area outside his office. He felt sorry for her and asked her what happened. She told him her husband burnt her arm with cigarettes. Behera was horrified and took an interest in this woman. Before long, he was asking her to come to his office to sit for him."

"God, she's beautiful," Simon said, staring at Lalita's face. "Sorry, go on."

"Behera gave Lalita the sari and the necklace, saying they were gifts for all the time she sat for him. I don't know why he didn't just give her some cash, which would have been more practical. Anyway, the necklace turned out to be a time bomb. A week later, she didn't show up at the office. Behera feared the worst. But he didn't have a clue how to find her. Naturally, he'd never been to her hut, and companies that hire servants like Lalita don't take addresses. They're employed in what's euphemistically called the informal sector. Read, *no rights*. So Behera asked her co-workers if they knew anything. Eventually he got an answer and it wasn't pretty. Are you sure you want to know?"

"I think I can guess."

"That's right. The husband found the necklace." Gita stuck another cigarette in her mouth. "Doused her with petrol and lit a match."

"Jesus Christ!"

"That's not all. Some say his mother stood by and watched. Didn't lift a finger. She was convinced her daughter-in-law had an affair with Behera, which wasn't the case. Lalita's mother-in-law believed her son, who insisted Lalita was screwing the big boss. In the mother's mind, Lalita had not only committed adultery, but she had crossed a caste boundary. This wretched pecking order has been with us for three thousand years. It's like a poison that, with every century, seeps deeper and deeper into the hearts and minds of us Indians, even the Dalits, who have internalized their own inferiority, at least until fairly recently. In lying with Behera, Lalita would have brought shame to *her* family. If the story is true—I mean, about Lalita's mother-in-law just standing by—she was trying to protect the family's honor. I know, it's very hard to understand. Even for me."

"Was there any justice?"

"No. It was chalked off as just another kitchen accident. Business as usual. The only silver lining is this place. Behera felt enormous guilt and vowed to build a home for women who've survived such atrocities. It only took him thirty years."

"What's *Cikaidi,* there, in quotes, below her name?"

"That was her nickname. It means 'chickadee.'"

CHAPTER II

The Polo Club of Sompur looked like a darker, dustier version of the Harvard Club of New York. Walls papered with portraits of dead white men. White privilege. The manager led him through a long corridor plastered with photos of men playing polo. The largest showed the Maharaja of Jaipur and Prince Philip in 1965 mounted on horses in full regalia.

Simon reached the entryway to the formal dining room and was greeted by a maître d' wearing an elaborate silver headdress with pleated ends protruding on two sides. The man shot Simon an apologetic glance, as if to say, *Yes, sir, I am fully aware that it looks like a flying saucer has landed on my head, but there's not a whole lot I can do about it.*

The dining room looked like nothing had been touched since the British quit India almost sixty years ago. Dusty chandeliers gave off a dim, yellowish light. Tables were set with gold-rimmed Wedgwood china, darkened with hairline cracks, and sterling silver flatware. Wafer-thin men with hollowed cheeks scurried around with large silver trays. Simon wondered if the waiters had stopped eating in 1947 to protest the end of the British Raj. Mr. Flying Saucer led Simon to a table where a bald man with an unusually round head sat reading a newspaper and sipping whisky.

"Bliss," Behera exclaimed as Simon approached. The business tycoon stood up and gave him one of those Fortune 500 handshakes, the kind that would squeeze the life out of a competitor and foreshadow his fate.

Behera was stocky and shorter than Simon had imagined. Large bags hung from anthracitic eyes. But, as Kesh had pointed out, he was not without a sense of humor; the industrialist liked to joke that the pouches under his eyes were for carrying toiletries he needed to get through those all-nighters at the office.

"How very nice to meet you!" Behera said with a smile so polished it could have been run through one of his auto plants.

Simon returned the smile and waited for Behera to loosen his grip. Just then Meena strode in wearing a green *salwar kameez*. The ends of her bright yellow *dupatta* scarf flew behind her like rays of sun that refused to part with such a lovely woman at the entrance.

"Sorry to keep you gentlemen waiting."

"Waiting for you is like doing *puja*," Behera said. Meena had warned Simon that the businessman's flattery was over the top, although perfect-ly harmless.

"Oh, you silly man," Meena replied.

A waiter approached and they ordered drinks. Behera compliment-ed Simon on the new library in Berlin, his project recently featured in the *International Herald Tribune*. After a few minutes of sizing each other up, the businessman suggested they look at the menu. When they had ordered food, Behera asked if Simon's short stay in India had given him any new ideas for the center, which seemed like an odd question, seeing that he had arrived only two days ago. Simon said he was struck by the many temples and mosques with curved spires and domes. Behera didn't seem satisfied with the reply, so Simon reeled off typical features of green buildings that could be incorporated into the design: a vegetated rooftop, an atrium filled with natural light, shading devices to reduce summer heat and manage glare, and natural ventilation.

"And what about air conditioning?" Behera rocked his glass back and forth and watched the scotch splash up the sides, as it were a game to see how close the drink could get to the rim without spilling over. "How will a LEED Platinum building affect the air-conditioning load?"

"Taking everything into consideration, I think we could reduce AC demand by twenty-five or thirty percent without adding to the capital cost." Another stock answer. "Of course, if you want deeper cuts, we—"

"Twenty-five percent, that's perfect," Behera exclaimed, removing his hand from the glass. The whiskey settled. "Now there's a balanced approach. Balance is what we need, isn't it, Meena?"

Two waiters rolled a food cart to the table. Giant tandoori prawns for Simon, a vegetarian thali for Meena, and, for Behera, a thick chateaubriand accompanied by three sickly spears of asparagus, which looked like they were fulfilling an affirmative action requirement.

"Well, *bon appétit*," Behera said as he picked up the steak knife and began to cut away. A few drops of blood invaded the lifeless vegetable. Behera asked about the green building movement in America. As Simon talked, the businessman seemed preoccupied with his meal, letting out an occasional grunt to indicate he was listening. He finished his steak, leaving the asparagus untouched, and looked at Simon with needle-sharp eyes.

"Mr. Bliss, do whatever it takes to get LEED Platinum. The center will be the first building in India to receive the India Green Building Association's highest rating. I want it to be a world-class design. It's my legacy, so there's no need to skimp." Turning to Meena, he added, "We wouldn't want those poor girls to be uncomfortable, now would we?"

An image of Lalita, Behera's chickadee, popped into Simon's head.

"I don't mind paying a little extra for all those green products you mentioned earlier. In fact, bring 'em on!"

"Sir, in my opinion, LEED Platinum is of course a worthy goal. But I would hate to see it become more important than the project itself. What I mean is, some architects are so obsessed with LEED that they'll ruin a design, heaping the project with green strategies and technologies just to rack up points. More LEED points don't always make for a greener building. I'd hate to see the community center sacrifice good design just for the sake of achieving LEED Platinum."

"You're right, replied Behera, distracted by two businessmen entering the restaurant. "Keep it simple and don't let any personal agenda take over. *Like too much natural ventilation.* The girls need to be comfortable with a proper air-conditioning system. I like your approach, Bliss. It's more balanced than Kesh's." He turned to Meena. "No offense, dear, but am I wrong?"

Meena grimaced.

"Twenty-five percent reduction," Behera repeated. "Now that's balanced." He finished the whiskey, wiped his mouth, and tossed the napkin on the table. "And let's move quickly, Mr. Bliss. Now, you'll forgive me, but I've got to make a move. Please don't get up. Enjoy dessert. I've already signed the chit. I recommend the nutmeg custard tart." He squeezed Simon's hand, this time even harder, pecked Meena on the cheek, and disappeared.

Simon's face crumbled. Had Behera heard anything he'd said? And what about this "let's move quickly"? Had he already won the commission? Meena seemed lost in her own world. Few words were exchanged as they drove back to his hotel. He felt like a kid being dropped off at daycare by a mother with a high-powered job.

Simon spent the remainder of the day holed up in his room. He watched part of a Hindi movie. In one scene, the two lovers were singing and dancing in front of a marina filled with boats. He flipped through the pages of *Fodor's India* again, but the photos lost their magic. He thought of Lin Yang, the budding neuroscientist whose life was cut short because of his project. Lin's unfinished dissertation was on the topic of the teenage brain and risk-taking behavior. *Why not take a risk myself?* He began to sketch buildings with features of sailboats. But each attempt looked like a ship washed up on dry land. He flung himself on his bed and pictured Alisha. Tears welled up in his eyes and the room became blurry. He noticed a water spot on the ceiling and fixed his gaze on it. Through his watery eyes, he saw exactly what he was looking for. It was right there, above his head: the perfect design. He closed his eyes and tried to flesh out the concept. But within minutes, he had fallen asleep.

CHAPTER 12

The Muslim call to prayer blared at the same god-awful hour, waking Simon. What airheads build a hotel a block away from the city's largest mosque? Simon remembered the watermark on the ceiling—the blurred image that inspired him with an idea for his design. He looked up and squinted, batted his lashes, and widened his eyes. But all he saw were dried-up mineral deposits.

He tried to recreate the image from memory, but without luck. No design ideas, no Meena, no Kesh even! She was too busy, as always, and he had to travel to his ancestral home for some personal matter. Simon took his laptop from his briefcase and began to scroll through emails. Ten or eleven from his office, which he answered, and one from Alisha. She went on at length about how Sara was having anxiety attacks over her final exams. What could he do seven thousand miles away? He went to Safari and typed *www.beherahouse.org*. There she was, a black braid cascading past the mast of her neck. An old photo, when Meena's hair was long. He sat admiring her statuesque features and golden, honey skin from which every impurity had been strained.

Simon stepped into the shower. As the warm water poured over his face, he recalled the look on his wife's face the moment he first mentioned the India project. She lectured him on why going to India might be a good idea after all. How his inner child needed to get out of his beloved China, where everything was aesthetic and harmonious, and over to India, where he could learn to embrace his inner chaos. How this, how that. Always the goddamn therapist! How he had wished she would just hand him the hundred-forty-dollar invoice and end the session. The pulse in Simon's neck began to throb. Yes, he was married to his work, and no, he was not the best husband or father. Guilt morphed to sadness as he dried off.

Then he paused. Was she right? Was chaos the answer? He thought about the nutty priest, how Hindu temples, with their intricate designs and carvings, were meant to overwhelm, and how Upadhyaya said Simon could call him the temple's chief overwhelming officer. It was as if the priest and Alisha were both telling him to let go. And was Kesh part of the same cabal? *I've observed your proclivity toward the sharp corner, the jagged edge. Not to say you don't make good use of the hexagon, the pentagon, and, well, all the other —gons.*

A car picked Simon up at eleven-thirty. The driver did the usual dance in and out of the traffic, eventually stopping in front of the Jubilee Mission Hospital. Meena and a frail young woman wearing a teal sari with the corner pulled tightly over her head stood waiting at the entranceway. Asha was not much older than Sara, but she looked as if the spirit of life had been drained out of her.

"*Namaste*, sahib," Asha said in a soft voice. Her eyes were fixed on the ground as she held her hands pressed tightly in front of her chest. Simon returned the gesture. Meena guided them to a path at the side of the hospital, where wooden treads led up a steep incline.

The hilltop restaurant was a simple room with walls painted deep blue. An opened barn door offered patrons a breathtaking view of the city below. Behind the cashier hung a picture calendar of Krishna playing a bamboo flute, his skin the same saturated blue. Three ceiling fans made a whistling sound that could have come from the god's instrument.

———◆———

They took a table overlooking the city. Meena insisted Simon sit facing the view, while she and Asha sat opposite him. A waiter approached with bright yellow pumpkin flowers deep-fried in chickpea flour. Meena could hardly stop looking at Simon. His blue shirt brought out the blue of his eyes and matched Krishna's skin. She wanted to tell him, but worried he might be embarrassed. Instead, she handed him a pumpkin flower. Asha's arms were folded tightly around her flat chest. Meena invited her to begin her story.

"I come from a poor family in Bihar," she said in her local language with Meena translating. Her eyes were glued to the table. "We are Dalits. My father married me off when I was twelve, but I didn't go live with my husband until I was fifteen. His family was rich, at least for a Dalit. Ram, my husband, is tall and handsome."

Asha looked at Meena, who nodded approvingly.

"In the beginning, we were happy. He called me *sweet rose* and would sit with me when I ate dinner after him. But he lost his job at the sawmill. He said it closed because foreigners protested the cutting down of trees."

Asha took a sip of water and looked up at Meena again. Meena smiled and gave her a pat on the shoulder.

"Ram started drinking from early morning."

Meena glanced over at Simon. He was listening so attentively, unlike her husband.

"If Ram found a rat in the house, he smiled and killed it with his bare hands. I protested, saying it was Ganesh's vehicle. But he didn't listen. When I asked what was wrong, he said he wanted a boy and that I was a useless wife. He started to beat me and burn holes in my arm with cigarettes. 'Tell me if this hurts,' he would say, as if it were a game." Asha shivered. She took hold of the edge of her sari wrapped around her head and pulled it over her forehead, as if it were a theater curtain she could drop at any moment to cut the show short.

"Ram would stay out half the night and come home drunk as a monkey. He would hit me until I was black and blue. 'Barley and millet improve by adding salt,' he would say, 'but women only get better by being beaten with a pestle.'"

Simon wrung his hands together. They were strong hands with long fingers, Meena thought. She took a sip of water and vowed to concentrate on translating Asha's words.

"Ram accused me of sleeping with his father." Asha started to weep. "'Why would I sleep with him, when you are my lord?' I'd ask. Even if I wanted to sleep with the old man, how could I when I'm up at four in the morning and work all day in the paddy fields? What time is there to be screwing his pockmarked father when I don't even have a chance to sit down and enjoy a cup of chai?"

Asha started to cry just as the food appeared. Simon looked pale when he saw his fish smothered in fresh coriander. Meena pretended not to notice him scraping it off. Asha wiped her eyes and stared into the goat curry under her nose.

"But he didn't believe me," continued Asha, without touching the food. "He whipped me with his belt, even after I told him I had a fever and my bones ached." She raised her narrow hand and squeezed the end of her sari, crushing the fragile reeds and wild grasses embroidered on the border. "I was rolled up on the floor and wanted to die. He went into the corner of the room and knocked down my altar. Durga was also lying on the floor, just like me. I grabbed her and prayed to Mother Earth to split open and swallow me, just like it swallowed Sita."

Meena urged Asha to eat while she told Simon how the earth opened for Sita, wife of Lord Ram, after the goddess refused to endure a second ordeal to prove her chastity to her disbelieving husband. Asha took a bite, then started in again.

"One day I got pregnant and he stopped beating me. Ram was happy until we went to the clinic and the doctor said it was a girl. From then I suffered his belt every day of my pregnancy. After I had the baby, I grabbed her and ran away to my sister's house. Things were good until her husband raped me. He said I was making eyes at him, which was a lie. I never even looked at the stinking man. But my sister wouldn't talk to me. So, I went back home. Meanwhile, Ram was messing with every girl in the village. The bastard would come home every night smelling like coconut oil. When I accused him of being with another woman, he'd take off his boot and hit me over the head. 'Who are you to tell me I've been with another woman?' he'd say and call me a useless slut."

Meena noticed Simon cringing.

"We were broke," Asha continued, "with nothing to eat, so I went to the ocean to drown my baby to spare her this miserable life, but I couldn't do it." Asha pressed her thumb on her wrist, causing the vein to bulge. "I kept thinking of *ardhanarishvara,* Lord Shiva as half man, half woman. If only God had made us like that, there would be no misery.

When man and woman are separate, that's when trouble begins!" She scrunched her eyes to hold back tears, but a few drops oozed through the corners.

Meena thanked Asha for her courage and insisted she finish lunch. Asha ate half the meal and said she wasn't hungry. Meena asked her to tell Simon what she planned to do after leaving Behera House.

"I am faithful, like Sita. I want to go home."

"To that son-of-a-bitch?" Simon whispered to Meena.

"Yes," Meena replied, "I know it's very hard to understand."

"But I won't take shit. I have rights. If he starts to hit me, I'll tell him he's a coward, because real men don't beat their wives. If he doesn't stop, I'll go to the police. I am a woman. I am strong, like Durga, even though I picked Sita as my protector."

Meena explained that each Hindu resident of Behera House was encouraged to pick a goddess as her special protector against her husband's violence—one different from the goddess she normally worships. Then she asked Simon if he wanted to say anything.

"I'm so sorry," was all he could manage. After a long pause, he asked what she would like to see in the new center.

A hesitant smile broke through Asha's face, like a flower pushing through a crack in the pavement. Her torso straightened and she relaxed her hand, although she was still fingering the printed border of her sari. It seemed like even the crushed reeds were coming back to life. "A large kitchen, a movie theater, a sewing room, and a shelter for saving sick birds."

Meena turned to Simon. "What do you think? You seem far away."

"No, I'm right here. I'm just thinking about what Asha just said—that the center should have a shelter for saving sick birds." He pointed to the pumpkin blossom. "Didn't you say these were fried in chickpea flour?"

"Yes, so?"

"*Chick*pea flour," he repeated. "*Chick-pea. Chick-adee!*"

"What?" Meena asked.

"The other day you said Mr. Behera wanted the center to be like the Bird's Nest, the national stadium going up for the 2008 Olympics."

"Well, yes, but I wouldn't make too much of that. He just means he wants a signature design. Something special that would attract international attention, like all those showy projects popping up in Beijing."

"No, not at all."

Meena did a double take.

"He may want a signature design all right, but there's more to it. His reference to the Bird's Nest is brilliant, really."

"What's brilliant?"

"He means *the community center should be a bird's nest*, metaphorically speaking. What is a bird's nest, after all? It's a place where mothers give birth and nurture their chicks." Simon raised his hands, as if he were about to conduct an orchestra. "Gita told me about Mr. Behera and Lalita, the young sweeper whose nickname was *chickadee*. How the husband found a gold necklace that Behera had given her and . . . well, you know."

Meena felt like the stupidest person on earth. How could she have missed Madhav's reference? She turned to Asha to translate and was searching for the right words when Simon broke in again.

"This project is about giving Lalita Devi, Mr. Behera's chickadee, a nest. Coddling her, symbolically, of course." Simon turned to Asha. "Through you, Asha, and the other living residents. He wants to create a place where you'll all feel safe, *like newborn chicks*."

Meena again turned to Asha and translated. Asha smiled gently and wagged her head ever so slightly.

Simon signaled for the waiter and ordered a coffee.

113

"The community center will not only have a shelter for saving sick birds, as Asha wants, it will be a shelter for protecting all of Behera's chickadees, so to speak. It should be designed with soft lines," he said, fingering the curved petals of the pumpkin blossom. "Sure, there will be natural daylight, but the building shouldn't be flooded with light. It shouldn't be an extension of the outside world. We must be careful not to add green elements just to score LEED points. This center is about the residents, not certification. It is about a home that nurtures and heals."

"So, you're going to design a bird's nest?" Meena asked.

"Yes, I am, at least in spirit."

For the next few minutes, Simon talked of the need for contained spaces with soft lighting, where the residents could feel safe, as well as bright spaces, where they could begin to blossom again. Meena tried to get him to slow down so she could translate, but soon gave up. He was like a truck pushing other vehicles and pedestrians off the road. She became frustrated, since she didn't know how to translate half the words into Asha's dialect. Simon finally stopped and leaned so far back in his chair that it almost tipped over.

Asha excused herself and went to the bathroom.

Meena reached across the table with one hand and laid it on top of Simon's. It was warm, alive, and his eyes seemed to glow with a passion for the project. In the distance, a sudden roar of laughter. Simon quickly withdrew his hand.

"Don't worry. It's just the Sompur Laughing Club—a bunch of octogenarians who sit in a circle in a park near the hospital and laugh until they're blue in the face."

"What do they laugh about?"

"Nothing. They just laugh. It's a kind of therapy. Laughing yoga."

"Hmmm."

Then Asha returned and they descended the wooden stairs. Asha first, then Meena, followed by Simon. Meena sensed he was looking at her. She swung around and, without thinking, pressed her mouth onto his. It was rash, violent. But she didn't care. Yes, it was unprofessional, but she couldn't help herself. And, it seemed, neither could he. A cloud—the first to appear all week—positioned itself directly above them, blocking the stabbing rays of the sun. It seemed to hold still for the duration of the kiss, as if offering its blessing.

CHAPTER 13

Kesh tossed and turned all night. He could not stop thinking of the fortune he missed out on when his father sold their ancestral home to the government so they could turn it into a luxury hotel. *Our royal palace, now the property of the Government of India—what a joke!* The idea that the government would convert his home into a five-star hotel was sickening. Kesh had no hope of earning the two percent profit from the business to which he was entitled as heir. The crooked bureaucrats would find a way to swindle him out of any revenue. He wouldn't see a single rupee.

A year after his father's death, Kesh was still upset that he wasn't consulted on the deal. He looked at the letter he had received last week from the Ministry of Home Affairs stating that the conversion of the palace had begun. He decided to make a trip to Gond, the small province his family had ruled for three hundred years. It was his last chance to wander through his ancestral home as he knew it.

As the first rays of daylight entered his room, Kesh stumbled into the kitchen. He made a pot of coffee and scratched his itchy scalp furiously, producing a cloud of dandruff on the black T-shirt he'd worn to bed. After dressing and packing his satchel, he headed for the airport to catch an early flight to New Delhi. From there, he caught a flight to Dehra Dun, nestled in the foothills of the Himalayas. He rented a Jeep Wrangler and was at last toiling up the mountain. He drew back the canvas top. Invigorated by the cool air, he began whistling songs from his childhood as he negotiated the tight switchbacks.

After an hour, he pulled into a local truck stop for chai. He sat outside on a bench and was entertained by a rufous-necked hornbill crossing the road. Two Tibetan monks in maroon robes were seated to his left sipping tea. The bird, with its brownish-red beak and neck, looked like it had joined the religious order.

He finished his drink and continued up the mountain, savoring the brilliant red and blue wildflowers, which peeked out of the conifers. The pine trees were so tall and straight, unlike the gnarled banyans in the city. He switched on the radio. Hindi film music. He fumbled in his satchel for a Rolling Stones CD, shoved it into the slit, and cranked up the volume.

> I see a red door and I want it painted black
> No colors anymore I want them to turn black
> I see the girls walk by dressed in their summer clothes
> I have to turn my head until my darkness goes

Kesh was shouting the words, jutting his lips out like Mick Jagger, when he noticed a black Audi in the rearview mirror careening toward him at a terrifying speed. The road was too narrow for the car to pass.

Hoping to get some distance between them, Kesh slammed on the accelerator.

I look inside myself and see my heart is black
I see my red door and it has been painted black

Soon he was driving around the switchbacks at an alarming speed with his eyes fixed on the rearview mirror. There was no railing and the drop was over a thousand feet.

Maybe then I'll fade away and not have to face the facts
It's not easy facing up when your whole world is black

The asshole, still on his tail, was now honking furiously. But what could he do? He switched off the CD player and imagined the Audi ramming into his Jeep as he rounded a hairpin curve. The perfect crime. Nobody would ever find him down in the valley, the end of the earth.

Kesh noticed the road widening ahead. There was a shrine and space to stop. He pulled over and the wanker whizzed by. After a few minutes, he regained his composure and started up the mountain again. There was less snow than a year ago, when he had come for his father's funeral. It was as if the mountain's white cap had shrunk in a dryer. *These glaciers,* he thought, *are the water tower that feeds two and a half billion people—a third of the world—and they're going down the goddamn drain, literally.*

It was mid-afternoon when Kesh pulled into the driveway of his ancestral home, a two-hundred-room mansion modeled after Buckingham Palace. It could have had two thousand rooms given the gilded mirrors adorning half the walls. Kesh sneered at the sign at the entrance: THE OBEROI GOND, FIVE-STAR LUXURY HOTEL, GRAND OPENING—

OCTOBER 2006.

How cheeky of the government! How déclassé. As if this palace were just another Grand Hyatt with rows of NordicTracks and chefs serving ham-and-cheese omelets. He cringed at the thought of his childhood home being overrun by oversized Americans chugging sixteen-ounce bottles of Coca-Cola and poker-faced Chinese businessmen slurping shark-fin soup. *Five stars, my ass. This place is the goddamn Milky Way!*

In front of the main entrance lay an assortment of picks, shovels, and wheelbarrows. To the side, a trampled, weed-choked garden. A few men sat on string cots sipping chai from saucers, while others poured cement onto the path.

As he entered the palace, the noise of power saws accosted his ears. There were no guards checking visitors. The place seemed to be under siege. If only he had come earlier, before this ragtag army of workers started hacking the mansion to pieces.

Kesh's eyes fixed on an ivory-inlaid table directly under the drawing room's soaring dome. *What are all these heirlooms still doing here? The crew should have put everything into storage before these marauding hordes diddled me out of my inheritance.* His blood was boiling when he remembered that all the furnishings conveyed with the palace. *Why didn't my father convey me, too, the bastard? Isn't anybody fucking in charge around here?*

Kesh stared at the table. On the front side was a carving of a bearded Zeus wielding his thunderbolt on Mount Olympus. On the backside, Sarasvati, the Hindu goddess of learning, seated on a lotus with her *veena*. He and his sister would steal cigarette butts from his father's ashtray, light them, and stick them in the carving's crevices. One time a lighted butt fell onto the seventeenth-century Isfahan carpet and burnt a hole. What an awful trouncing he suffered!

Kesh thought about how his father loved to dazzle visitors with that carpet. The silk rug depicted a daytime hunting scene. After showing it, the man would light the carpet from the other side, exposing a nighttime scene with two lovers under a crescent moon. Kesh would while away whole afternoons sitting on the magic carpet pretending to be whisked away to Shangri-La.

He walked to the southern wall of the drawing room, which was covered with formal oil paintings of his ancestors. Tears began to well up as he approached a large portrait of his mother. At first, she seemed to smile at him, however faintly. But as he stepped to one side, her face changed, just like the Persian carpet. There was sadness and disappointment. What a wretch he had become. An insatiable womanizer, with thinning hair and a bulging waistline. Where was the cute, plump boy she suckled for four years? He thought of Iago, his favorite Shakespearean character. *From some vile germ or atom I was born . . . I am wicked because I am a man, and I feel the primeval slime in me.* He sneered as he walked past the portrait of his father, wrapped in the fine silks and jewels.

Kesh peeked into a parlor where he and his mother watched parrots sing the Indian national anthem while riding small silver bicycles. He picked up his pace as he passed his father's study, grimacing at the leather couch and the antique Safavid carpet where the maharaja lounged with his half-naked courtesans. The old Remington typewriter still sat on the ivory-inlaid desk. He wiped dust from a large gilded mirror at the far end of the drawing room and peered into it. But all he saw was his father.

He climbed the winding staircase to the second floor. French doors led to the master bedroom. Above, a shiny brass sign: MAHARAJA'S SUITE. He rolled his eyes and pushed through. On the fireplace mantel, a golden peacock, a gift of the maharaja of Udaipur. Its tail was studded with precious rubies and emeralds. He could almost hear the otherworldly shrieking of live peacocks in the garden. To the left, a Louis XVI vanity. Kesh picked up the jeweled box his father used for his collection of tongue scrapers. He looked around and quickly stuffed it into his pocket. He was soon overcome with a deep sense of loss. The palace, with all the bejeweled gifts from other maharajas, the Louis XVI furniture, and the ancestral portraits, would soon be a commercial hotel. It was as if he himself had died and could see his own organs being readied for transplant into the body of a used car salesman.

A broomstick of a man wearing striped pajama bottoms and a New York Yankees baseball cap bolted through the doors. A knockoff Rolex slid down his gangly forearm like a woman's bangle as he lifted his hands and joined them in front of his heart. "I'm Sonny, assistant construction manager," he announced, proudly displaying a gold-plated tooth. Other teeth were stained red.

"I'm Keshav Narayan, son of—"

"Sahib," interrupted Sonny, "don't you think I know who you are? I hail from Gond only." *Paan* was tucked into one bulging cheek.

"Right," replied Kesh. "Well, Sonny, why haven't my family's possessions been safely stored before all these workers arrived? Who's in charge around here?"

"Sahib, I tell you, everything is topsy-turvy. The moving vans were supposed to come last week only, before the workers, but there was strike. What to do? But a new company is now hired and they are coming day after tomorrow to put everything in the storage. In meantime, sahib, I am checking every worker leaving premises to make sure no thieving is there."

Like hell you are!

Sonny explained that Mr. Oberoi himself insisted everything be preserved as is, including the twenty-four-inch floorboards made from Himalayan deodar trees. It was a huge challenge, since workers had to install air handlers underneath hundreds of rooms.

Kesh was about to take his leave when a short Sikh entered, no more than five feet two inches. Sikhs were supposed to be tall and muscular, like bulls; Yashbir Singh looked strong, but with the smooth physique of a well-toned ballet dancer. Kesh gazed down at the top of his head. He'd never had an aerial view of a Sikh's turban before. Yashbir introduced himself, and then asked Kesh to wait a moment. He left the room and returned a few minutes later with a box.

"We found this box hidden under the floorboards of the master bedroom," Yashbir said, handing it to Kesh. Metal studs formed three squares on its top. In the middle square, an inverted swastika with a dot between each bent arm. "Mr. Oberoi wanted it returned to your family. I was going to send it to you, but since you are here, you may have it." Kesh took the box, thanked Yashbir and Sonny, handed each a hundred-rupee note, and left the palace. He walked to his car and opened the box.

Holy shit!

There, couched in red velvet like a goddess curled up in satin sheets, was an ornamental girdle made of glittering diamonds. Braided silver threads fastened the large centerpiece. He wondered how long the girdle had been hidden under the floorboards. A light seemed to come from within. Like an ascetic, he thought, who accumulated a storehouse of psychic energy through years of silent meditation and abstinence. He lifted the girdle and held it up to the sky, as if making an offering to Surya, the sun god. Then he pulled out the velvet bed on which the girdle had lain. Underneath was a note: *For Kesh, my beloved son.*

CHAPTER 14

New Film City, an Indo-Taiwan Enterprise, had opened two months ago with much fanfare. Gita discovered the 1.5-kilometer perimeter path was perfect for her early morning power walks. It led past a Moghul garden, a eucalyptus forest, a man-made lake, and various landmark buildings, including a full-size replica of the Chinese Luihe pagoda, complete with blossoming cherry trees, the Empire State Building, and the Eiffel Tower. From certain points, one could see fabulous movie sets, including the White House, complete with the South Lawn, and, a little farther on, the Kremlin, and Tiananmen Square. If lucky, a visitor might chance upon a famous Bollywood star or American actor. *The Hindu* reported that Jack Nicholson and Nicole Kidman were spotted there two weeks ago.

Meena pulled into the parking lot. She was happy to find a space shaded by a cork tree. It wasn't even seven-thirty in the morning, but the late-April sun was already working overtime. Just as she was about to take the key from the ignition, a voice on the radio caught her attention. It was the HDP leader, Ganesh Shukla.

Even the great German philosopher, Johann Herder, demonstrated that the roots of all human civilization go back to India. He claimed Sanskrit to be progenitor of all Indo-European languages. But look at us now! We say the same thing and the Congress Party calls us Hindu fundamentalists, right-wing extremists, even terrorists . . .

"Idiot!" She got out of the car, slammed the door, and headed to the visitors' kiosk. She scanned the area for Gita, nervously rocking on her heels. Her mind veered back to last night. She was still reeling from Simon's kiss when Kesh burst through the front door brandishing a diamond girdle. He pranced around the house like a tribesman wielding a talisman.

Her deputy appeared wearing a magenta kurta over baggy white pajama pants and Nike running shoes. "You're going to walk in those?" Gita asked, pointing to Meena's low-heeled sandals.

Meena shrugged off the question and the two women started down the path. She wasted no time in sharing the story of Kesh's trip to Gond and the diamond girdle.

"So?" Gita said.

"Gita, you don't understand. Kesh immediately called Madhav, asking if he'd buy it. Madhav collects antique jewelry—he was ecstatic. He offered to buy the damn thing and to lend it to the priest until the national election."

"You've lost me. Why would the priest want a diamond girdle and what does this have to do with your husband? Oh, I get it—that crooked priest wants it for his devadasis. But what does that have to do with

Kesh?"

"I'm coming to that. Not long after Kesh talked to Madhav, he gets a call from Upadhyaya, who was so pleased that he offered Kesh unlimited access to the hundreds of devadasis he's installing in the temples."

"Access?"

"Yes, you know what that means!"

"Oh, dear God, you mean your husband is essentially trading a diamond girdle for a lifetime of sex with those teenage temple dancers?"

"Well, Madhav is paying him for the wretched girdle, but he's getting so-called access to the devadasis as a kind of sweetener. Oh, Gita, it's all so dreadful! Thank heaven he's leaving tonight for Delhi. His firm is rushing to submit a preliminary design for a new World Trade Center in Chengdu. He'll be gone all week. Hopefully, immersing himself in his work will bring him to his senses."

"Men!" Gita bellowed, as if a three-letter word could embody all that was wrong with Indian society.

A woody scent from the eucalyptus grove gave Meena a moment's relief.

"Madhav's quite clever," Gita said. "He's not just lending Upadhyaya the girdle, but he's convinced the crooked priest to let Kesh screw his precious devadasis so he'll fritter away his time in the arms of those temple dancers. It's Madhav's way of diverting Kesh from his crusade to change LEED."

"Shit, you're right."

"Madhav's out to protect his air-conditioning business, isn't he?" Gita continued. "He doesn't give a shit about your marriage." She stopped to tie her shoelace. "Madhav's no dummy. He knows Kesh is like one of those suicide bombers who crashed into the World Trade Center—happy to die for seventy-two virgins and a king-size bed."

"Oh, Gita, to think of my balding husband with his middle-aged paunch crawling all over those helpless . . ." Meena shivered. "It's nauseating!"

"Well," Gita responded, "if nothing else, this goes to show the HDP's true colors. As I've long suspected, Upadhyaya is nothing more than a pimp in a priest's dhoti. If he's willing to give Kesh a free pass at hundreds of devadasis in return for a few glittering rocks, he certainly has bigger plans for those girls than just marrying them to Lord Jaga-*face*. For all we know, the whole National Temple Revitalization Program is just one big National *Harem* Program—a racket to fill HDP's coffers!"

Gita's words sapped Meena's energy. They approached a mango grove and sat on a bench. The branches, bent with ripe fruit, seemed to empathize.

"Behera's one hell of an operator," Gita said. "He's appealing to Kesh's insatiable libido to distract your husband from changing the green building certification system. At the same time, he's helping the HDP raise money."

"What do you mean?"

"Think about it. If Upadhyaya is planning to sell his darling devadasis to the highest corporate bidders, Madhav has just raised the stakes. Don't you see? Those stinking rich businessmen will shell out more money for those dancing girls when their gyrating hips are loaded with diamonds the size of Swedish meatballs. That means more loot for the HDP. And for Mr. Uppity. I'm sure he gets his cut. Why else would a priest want a diamond girdle?"

"This is all too much for me. Madhav and his scheming, Kesh and that wretched girdle, the slimy priest, and this so-called partnership with the HDP!" Meena unstrapped her sandals and started to rub her left foot. "I don't know how much more I can take."

Two workers hobbled by carrying a gigantic bronze sculpture of Shiva performing his cosmic dance to end the Kali Yuga, the current age of corruption. Gita offered to massage Meena's aching feet, but Meena demurred and they started down the path again.

"Do you sometimes think the world would be a better place without men?" Gita asked as they approached an artificial lake with swans.

"Sure, I think about it every time a woman walks through our door with scars or arms riddled with cigarette burns."

Lord Ram and Hanuman, the monkey god, lumbered past them. Ram was laughing as he sipped a Kingfisher beer and adjusted himself. Hanuman carried a Pepsi in one hand and fondled his fluffy tail with the other.

"Will we ever tire of making films based on that ghastly epic?" Gita snapped.

"It's not ghastly, Gita. I love the Ramayana, even though some scenes are a little hard to understand given our modern views of women."

"A little hard to understand? All right. But isn't two thousand years of Sita having to prove her chastity by walking through fire enough? Sometimes, I just want to rid this goddamn country of men. They're bloody Neanderthals. Even Sanskrit poetry, our highbrow literature, is so fucking patriarchal—the way Kalidasa and those ancient poets objectified women. Our mango breasts, plantain thighs, and pomegranate lips. You'd think we're just piles of fruit stacked up in a vegetable market! Men—what vermin!"

"Well, it sounds like you're ready to call an exterminator. Anyway, Kesh is not in the same category. Sure, he has his faults, which include an overactive libido, but—"

"But? But what?"

"*Everything* about Kesh is overactive. But no one said it was easy trying to save the planet."

"With his prick," Gita growled. "I'm sorry, Meena, that wasn't fair. But I stand by what I said about men in general."

Meena felt sick. She came for advice, or at least some empathy, not one of Gita's weekly tirades about men. She was about to mention that Kesh just completed a preliminary design for a new HSBC bank in Hong Kong. The project would be carbon neutral, generating one hundred percent of the electricity it used. But there was little point in defending Kesh to Gita.

"Face it, Meena. Indian men are babies. They run off to prostitutes because they can't handle liberated souls, like you and me. And you know what goes on under those red lights. We're not talking scenes from Romeo and Juliet. Men, four and five times their age, tie those poor girls up and fuck them in the ass. Twelve- and thirteen-year-olds—innocent kids, sold into the sex trade by their parents. They're forced to do it five times a day. It's rape. Worse than rape, if that's even possible. And do you know—"

"Enough!" Meena shouted. "I know how rotten men can be—I see the damage every day. But at least we're doing something about it."

Gita rolled her eyes, as if to say, *Meena, you just don't get it.* Then she started in again. "I was twelve when my uncle told me about sati. How Hindu scriptures praise women who follow their husbands into the funeral pyre—they say these good women, satis, live in paradise with their husbands for thirty-five thousand years. My mother wrote it all off as an ancient custom, like not eating beef. I chalked up everything sick about India as a religious custom. It wasn't until I was older that I realized sati is just institutionalized murder by misogynous men. A grotesque custom whitewashed by the paintbrush of history and glorified in holy books written by men."

Meena had her eye out for the kiosk; she wanted to be done with Gita as soon as possible. But the path seemed to go on forever, with no end in sight. They came upon a few moving vans parked in front of one of the studios. "Come," Meena said, hoping to distract Gita, "let's peek in and see what's happening."

Inside, Ram—the actor they had passed earlier—was demanding Sita prove her chastity after being kidnapped by the demon Ravana. Then Sita spoke, "Oh, my lord, I am as pure as fire. Hence I will prove the purity of my character by passing through the raging fire flames." Flames burst up from the studio floor, and the actress lifted the bottom of her sari to step in.

"I'm going to puke," Gita said.

"Enough!" Meena snapped.

By the time they reached the kiosk, Meena felt worse than when they had started out. She gave Gita a polite hug and scurried to her car, where she burst into tears. After a good cry, she thought about the excursion she had planned for Simon that afternoon. She pictured the dark lonely Panchavati caves with their shadowy niches. Her limbs loosened. She placed her hand between her legs and felt herself. Soon goose bumps appeared all over her arms. Yes, it was a bold plan, but why not? It was Simon's last day in India. Her last chance.

CHAPTER 15

Simon paced the entryway outside the Grand Savoy Hotel, nervously watching for Meena's car. What kind of *secret* excursion did she have up her sleeve? Her car pulled into the driveway. She stepped out and offered a quick peck on his cheek. Earthy musk perfume, woody. He savored her outfit: tight jeans hugging her thighs and calves, a turquoise belt hanging loosely around her crisp, white, untucked shirt, and matching turquoise sandals with a low, slender heel. Large sunglasses rested on her hairline, Bollywood style. Her hair seemed shorter, leaving her exposed neck vulnerable to his stares.

"So, where are we going?" he asked, struggling to get both legs into the front seat of Meena's pint-size Maruti Suzuki. He pushed the seat back as far as possible but still had to rest his legs to one side so they wouldn't press against the dashboard.

"To the Panchavati caves," she replied, smiling coyly.

"Hmm."

"Don't worry," she continued, "no ghosts or goblins, but plenty of gods and goddesses. Well, Shiva and his wife Parvati mostly. They were carved into stone twelve hundred years ago, so they're rather harmless."

"And where is this ghoulish place?"

"Not far. It's under an hour to the coast, then we'll catch a ferry to a small island called Alaka."

"I feel like I'm being kidnapped."

Simon caught Meena smiling. His spirits were flying when he noticed an odd figurine suctioned to the dashboard. It looked like a primitive mother goddess with gigantic breasts, one red and one black. He imagined her popping out babies like one of those old PEZ candy dispensers. Her chest was made of a separate piece of plastic so that her breasts changed positions with each bump of the car. Red, black; black, red.

"What the heck is this?" Simon asked, giggling.

"Oh, a present from Gita—a local deity who's supposed to protect drivers. Well, more like a silly spoof on the deity. Gita stuck it there one day after I complained that navigating traffic in Sompur would be the end of me." She tore the figure off the dashboard and handed it to Simon. "Please put it in the glove box."

Simon obeyed, but couldn't resist the urge to give the divine bosoms one last twirl.

Meena was unusually quiet. Yesterday's kiss sat between them like an unwelcome third passenger. Sparse conversation was followed by long periods of dead silence—it reminded Simon of a concert he'd been to last month: a performance of John Cage's composition *4'33"*—three-movements of crushing silence punctuated by audience sounds of coughing and shifting in seats. Meena finally pulled into the ferry terminal, where a group of Indian and foreign tourists crowded around the ticket counter. She parked and turned toward him.

"Simon . . ."

Ah, the moment of truth. Not necessarily a declaration of love, but maybe, just maybe, an admission of some feeling for him, a reassurance that their kiss after yesterday's lunch was more than a fleeting impulse. But he quickly realized something was on her mind, not in her heart.

Meena started talking about Kesh's trip to Gond. First, she gave Simon the backstory, since he knew nothing about her husband's royal background. Without dwelling on his princely childhood, she simply said he was the son of a former maharaja and grew up with a silver spoon in his mouth. Or, as she joked, an entire set of gold cutlery.

Simon listened politely, trying not to show his disappointment. Had their kiss not found even the smallest nook in her heart? After all, she initiated it. He longed to talk about *them*. Or better yet, not to talk at all, but to drink her lips. Still, he knew listening was the order of the day, at least the price of another kiss. And for a *passionate* kiss, he'd have to show empathy, which normally would not have been difficult, since he really did care about her. But today was different. He was impatient. Right or wrong, he craved her.

By the time Meena finished telling him about Kesh's escapade and the crooked priest's offer, tears had smudged the kohl around her moist green eyes, as if a hurricane had swept across the ocean. She flipped the visor down and wiped her eyes in the mirror. As they headed for the ticket counter, she launched into an explanation of how Kesh spent half the night at his computer calculating the carbon footprint of his royal family since 1712, the beginning of the Narayan dynasty in Gond.

"Whenever Kesh feels guilty about his background, he obsesses about the damage his ancestors have inflicted on the environment."

"Wait, tell me again, why was he feeling guilty?"

"Because of the girdle. He longs for it, but at the same time the wretched thing brings back memories of all the stinking wealth he grew up with. He has a love-hate relationship with his father. On the one hand, he's embarrassed by the maharaja; on the other, he secretly pines for the lifestyle of the man who passed his days fondling naked courtesans. It's as if he has a need to out-maharaja his own father."

Why is she telling me such intimate facts about her husband?

"Then there's Kesh the environmentalist," she continued. "The man who is pained by how much carbon has been pumped into the air by his ancestors. As you can imagine, it takes the better part of a coal-fired power plant just to keep the lights on in a two-hundred-room palace."

"Two hundred rooms?" Simon recalled Kesh talking endlessly about environmental degradation at their breakfast in New Delhi. Every problem loomed over civilization like a guillotine. *Plant and animal species are vanishing . . . fish are dying . . . rainforests are disappearing.* He spoke most passionately about global warming. *The planet is heating . . . glaciers are melting . . . the sea is rising.* Every verb was in the continuous present. Simon had felt like checking his watch to see how much time was left before they needed to evacuate the restaurant for higher ground.

"Last night," Meena continued, "Kesh swore he would live without electric power for at least six hours a day. It was a token gesture, his way of atoning for the sin of owning the girdle. But his vows never last. Next week he'll buy the forty-eight-inch HDTV he's got his eyes on! He'll swear off red meat one day and feast on chateaubriand the next. There was a time he vowed to wear only homespun cotton for the rest of his life. A week later he spent fifteen hundred pounds on a tweed suit from Harrods!"

They reached the sales counter. Meena bought the ferry tickets, and they proceeded to the dock.

"There's more," she said as they lined up behind a stocky middle-aged couple speaking German.

Ah, she is upset about the kiss. He anxiously boarded the ferry and followed her to the uncovered front section. But his heart quickly tanked. It was not talk of yesterday's kiss that emerged. Rather, she told him about a phone call she'd received from an HDP operative. The caller had given her an ultimatum: accept the grant so that Ganesh Shukla could announce it at an upcoming news conference in Mumbai. If not, be prepared to kiss the HDP funds goodbye. Forever.

"This whole thing is absurd," Meena said as the boat's engine went into high gear and the ferry began knocking through the water. "I haven't even submitted a grant proposal and these bastards are showering their dirty money over me like confetti!" Simon strained to hear her over the noise of the engine. "In the end, Madhav is going to do what's best for him. I just wish he wouldn't pretend my views counted."

She fell silent and looked at Simon, presumably for a response. But what could he say? What did he know about Indian politics? What did he care, at least at that very moment? Her upper lip was slightly curled, revealing the seductive space between her teeth. He wanted to crawl in without uttering a word, but he knew the entrance fee.

"I'd accept the money and let Shukla make the damn announcement."

"Really?"

"Listen, I've heard a lot of accusations, especially from Gita the other day at the temple. She lambasted the priest for the HDP temple program. All this stuff about how he's bringing in temple dancers to raise money for the party. But it was all speculation as far as I could tell. Has your deputy come up with one iota of evidence that the darvidisee program is a scam?"

Meena laughed. "They're *devadasis.*"

"Whatever. Maybe that shyster, Upa, has offered Kesh a deal that involves those deva-whatevers, but that doesn't make the whole program a farce. And all this speculation that the HDP would turn the clock back on women and bring back sati—come on, Meena, it's 2005! I just don't buy it."

"You're right! There's no evidence, so why shouldn't we take the grant? For all we know, it's the Congress Party spreading nasty rumors. They're feeling the heat, now that the HDP is gaining traction."

"Look," Simon said, "if Gita turns out to be right, you can give up the grant and denounce the party. You just return any money that hasn't been spent. By then, who knows, the campus may already be built and the bills paid. Nobody can force you to give back a grant once the money's gone. Especially if it's been used to fund a campus for women who've survived terrible abuse. It'd be political suicide for the HDP to even insinuate that you should return the funds. And if Gita is *wrong* about the HDP, what harm is there in taking their money?" Simon straightened up, feeling quite pleased with himself.

Meena drew closer. Suddenly, the ferry slammed into a wave, showering them with salt water. What if his colleagues could hear him tell Meena she should take money from an ultranationalist party? A party whose leader once endorsed sati? For a project *his firm* would design? He could hear Gita's sarcastic laughter when he said his company had a policy of not accepting clients that manufactured cigarettes or alcohol. *I'm reassured that the idea of women turning themselves into roasted mutton troubles you. It doesn't seem to bother half of this godforsaken country.*

Meena snuggled up to Simon. "If I agree to the HDP's demands, do you think I can convince Madhav that it's not in his interest to give that wretched girdle to the priest?"

The girdle was squeezing the life out of her. "Sorry, Meena, but your question is above my pay grade. I've been in India only four and a half days."

"No, I'm the one who should be sorry for dumping my problems on you. So, what about the commission?" She stroked his arm. "It's yours, if you want it."

Simon froze.

"I talked to Madhav about your idea for the center. He was thrilled and wants you to design your bird's nest!"

Silence.

"Well?"

"I'm flattered, but the truth is, I'm not sure I could pull it off."

"But you were so excited yesterday . . . during our lunch with Asha."

"I was, I mean, I am. But then I hear Kesh's voice and I begin to doubt myself. He went on about how the roots of domestic violence go back to Indian mothers who are sexually frustrated and transfer their sexual impulses to their male children, who begin to fear women and—"

"Oh, dear God." Meena let out a long sigh. "My husband has been chewing your ear off with his Freudian psychobabble!"

"To be honest, most of what your husband said went straight over my head. But it got me thinking how presumptuous it is to parachute into India to design a center for women like Asha. People so totally different from me. From anyone I've ever known! It just seems so damn arrogant."

"It's not arrogant, and, frankly, I'm tired of hearing Kesh blame mothers for everything wrong with Indian men. I wish men would take responsibility for their actions. It's high time they grow up and society hold them accountable." She uncrossed her legs and crossed them the other way. Her light brown foot, long and narrow, glittered from the latest splash.

"I didn't invite you to bid on this commission because I thought you were an expert on India's social ills. You're an architect, and a very good one. Your job is to come up with a sustainable design. This many rooms for classes, this many for offices, a kitchen, and so on. Fill the building with natural light and all that pizzazz you green architects talk about. You had a brilliant idea about creating a bird's nest. Honestly, I don't know why Kesh has to drone on and on with his psycho-gibberish! It's not your job to worry about this inscrutable land. The women who come to Behera House are hurting. They need a place to congregate, to learn new skills and heal. That's what matters." She paused. "And if being coddled by one's mother is so terrible, why didn't Jesus turn into a wife-beating madman?"

"He didn't have a wife, unless you believe Dan Brown," Simon joked, noticing the top button of her shirt had come undone. She was breathing quickly, and her breasts gently rose and fell like the tides.

"It's hard for me to admit," Meena continued, "but Kesh is really talking about himself when he goes on about Indian men being mama's boys. The man was nursed until he was four years old! Yes, he's a rock star with prostitutes, but when it comes to his wife, well, let's just say . . ." She hid her head in her hands. "I'm so sorry, Simon."

Simon looked pensively over the water. In the distance were two tankers. Were they moving toward or away from each other? He couldn't tell.

"Maybe I'm the problem," Meena said. "Kesh is fond of telling me I'm such a cold fish and married to my work. I guess I'm not a very good wife."

"So, you're not a sati?" Simon again tried to inject a little humor into the conversation. "Isn't that what sati means, literally?"

"Oh, God, no! I mean, yes, it does, but I'm certainly no sati in *any* sense of the word!" She moved closer to him and asked him to lean forward. She placed her index finger on the back of his shirt. "Can you guess the letter I'm writing?"

"P?"

"That's right. Now what about this?"

"L?"

"Very good. And this?"

"E?"

"Indeed. Can you guess what's coming next?"

"A, and then S and E?"

"Bravo. *Please*."

"Please what?" *Kiss me?*

"Please take the commission."

He would have preferred a different invitation, but that wasn't on the table. After a long silence, Simon spoke up. "Do you want to know the idea I've been toying with?"

She smiled and nodded.

"I've been thinking of designing the center in the form of a ship."

"I thought it was going to be a bird's nest—now it's a ship?"

"I don't mean to say it would look like a real ship, but it could have elements of one so the residents *feel* like they're crossing water." He noticed the small island in the distance. Dominated by two hills, it looked like a giant camel sunbathing in the ocean.

"What's wrong with the bird's nest?"

"Birds' nests are about nurturing and healing; but they are stationary, whereas ships move. The center, I'm now thinking, should be about healing *and* moving on. My ship would include a bird's nest, which would be like an inner sanctum of a temple, deep within. But, conceptually, the overall idea would feel like a ship moving through the waters, delivering the residents to the other shore."

"A bird's nest in a boat! Simon, I think you've spent too much time in Disneyland."

"Look, the campus will be near the sea, and even the rolling hills look like waves. Ships take people to greener pastures, better lives. Odysseus sailing home from Troy. Noah, saving the human race by building an ark."

"Oh, dear me, you're going to build an ark?"

"Looking at it, you won't say, 'Wow, this is an ark!'"

"Sure, Simon." Meena stroked his arm. "I'm fully on board. Maybe we can import a few giraffes and kangaroos from Australia." She laughed.

"Actually, there are no giraffes in Australia," he said.

"Smarty pants!"

"Kesh told me there's a Hindu myth similar to the Noah story. Something about how Vishnu turned himself into a giant fish to save the Vedas. Knowing his dive from heaven could cause a deluge, the god asked a man named—I think it was Satyavrata—to build a ship to save the human race."

"You've clearly been paying more attention to Kesh than I have." A fly landed on Simon's cheek. She brushed it off with the back of her hand. "Let me think about it," she whispered into his ear. Her lips barely touched, tickling him.

"In any case," Simon said, "where there's a ship there's water. And where there's water, there's an oceanic feeling. The womb and all that rubbish, as Kesh would say. So maybe this idea has some legs? The ark, I mean. At least nobody would say it's too angular!"

Meena looked at Simon quizzically.

"Kesh said my designs are too angular, that they've got too many rough edges. It's something I've been hearing a lot lately."

"He's one to talk about rough edges!" Meena grimaced, then perked up. "I'm a Pisces. So, if I'm riding in your ark and get thrown overboard, I suppose I'll be in familiar waters. But if I do start to drown, you'll save me, won't you?"

"Nobody will fall out of my ark." He stroked her hand. "Not you or Asha or anyone." The ferry slammed into the dock with a jerk, practically throwing Meena into Simon's lap. She didn't move, and he locked his arm around the curve of her waist. They sat like that until the last passenger had left the boat.

CHAPTER 16

The miniature cog train chugged up a steep hill to a landing area. Simon and Meena pushed their way through a gaggle of beggars and vendors hawking postcards, bangles, cigarettes, and cheap souvenirs. Soon they were climbing an endless flight of stairs in the blazing midday sun beside throngs of tourists.

Only mad dogs and Englishmen go outside in the midday sun, Meena thought, but she didn't seem to mind the heat. Her worries about Kesh and the HDP seemed to melt in the presence of Simon. At one point, the tip of Meena's sandal caught the edge of a stone and she stumbled. Without thinking, she grabbed his arm. Fate seemed to be on her side. She regained her balance, but did not pull away. Their hands soon joined and stayed clasped until they came to an immense stone portico, which served as an antechamber to the caves.

Meena overheard a tour guide saying that the dozens of chiseled pillars, which looked like intricately carved wood, seemed to support the heavy stone roof. But it was an illusion, since the roof didn't need support. Simon stood staring at circular capitals atop the pillars. He pulled out his drawing pad and sketched the capitals. Pointing to them, a British woman asked her friend if she thought they looked like giant meditation cushions.

Meena led the way into the caves. At the far end stood a colossal torso with three heads conjoined in the middle. One looked straight ahead, while the others faced either side. Each head was adorned with a tall stone crown. The central face portrayed the god deep in meditation, his eyes gently shut, oblivious to the heat and smell of bat poop.

"I shan't bore you with clichés about the different forms of Shiva," Meena said, lifting her elbow to cover her nose. "I'm sure you're up to your eyeballs in Indian philosophy after two days with my husband."

A different guide emerged with a crowd of tourists; Meena recognized several from the ferry, including the German couple. The man wore shorts exposing legs as white as a bathtub. Below, black socks and Birkenstocks. *Extraordinary!*

The guide waved to the stragglers, beckoning them to come close, before launching into his stock speech. "These caves were modeled after famous caves near Mumbai called Elephanta. In fact, artisans tried to make exact replica only. Look now at three-headed Shiva. The face on the left is god as Bhairava, the terrible one who is raging with fury. At the end of each cosmic cycle, it is he only who destroys the world with flames from third eye, leaving ashes. Even moustache is twisted in anger. The right face is feminine aspect of Shiva. See his youthful appearance and sensuous lips. Main face is meditating god. *Dekho.* So much peace is there."

"Well, *dekho*, there you have it!" Meena said, poking fun at the guide's dramatic finale. She took Simon's arm, gently pulling him away from the gawking tourists. They turned a corner and walked into a second, cooler wing of the cave. But relief was brief, and Meena wondered if the seeming drop in temperature was caused by the change of light. They stopped to admire a relief showing Shiva standing next to Parvati, his wife. The god and goddess looked like young newlyweds. Meena, anxious to be as far from the tourists as possible, nudged Simon toward the next frieze: Shiva as half man, half woman.

"It's sagging, the heavy stone," Simon said, looking up, "and it looks as light as a fishnet—I've never seen anything like this."

Two freckled teenagers skipped up to the androgynous form of Shiva.

"Wow," the girl shouted, "he's got half a mustache!"

"And one boob," added the boy, laughing.

Above the youthful giggles rose a long, shrill scream followed by a heavy New York accent. "My pearls! They're missing. Someone's stolen my pearls!"

Everyone turned to look—Meena and Simon, the tour guide, and his entourage, many of whom were busily matching the statues in the cave with the photos in their guidebooks. The piercing words came from a wiry, middle-aged blonde with an aquiline nose and bright red lipstick. Clad in a tank top covered with gold sequins, a thick red belt, and tight blue pants, she could have been related to the Costa Rican macaw.

"Madam," said the tour guide, feigning a smile, "please, no worry. I am most certain they must have just dropped off by themselves only, somewhere along our way." He waved his flashlight back and forth across the sculpted rock relief. Lady Macaw stood as motionless as the statue behind her, one hand glued to her chest where the necklace once hung.

The guide told everyone to relax while he searched the cave. He went from one relief to the next, painting the stone floor with his light. After a short time, he cried out, "*Arre baba*, there they are, just as I was telling." His head was wagging as he walked over to the thick stone slab that framed the panel showing Shiva and Parvati as a young couple. Shiva's wife was naked except for an ornamental girdle loosely framing her wide hips. The guide picked up the pearls, which were wrapped into a neat ball between Parvati's feet, and delivered them to the lady.

An old man in a white kurta-pajama outfit must have thought the pearls popped out of Parvati's private parts. He raised his arms to heaven as if he'd seen a miracle. Then he prostrated himself before the goddess. Parvati, gently smiling, seemed amused by all the fuss. But this was no miracle for Lady Bird. Rather than expressing her gratitude to the guide for returning her necklace, she grew more enraged and soon found a target for her anger.

"There's the culprit!" Her voice bounced off the walls like a Greek chorus. She pointed a claw-like fingernail at the dark outline of a young woman skulking in the shadows of a relief. All heads turned. The figure appeared to hold a broom of long oriental grasses.

"No, not possible, this thing," said the guide with a patronizing smile. "It is not like that. You have your pearls. Now everybody is happy."

"Nobody's happy," the woman snarled, still pointing. "When she heard me yell out, she must have panicked and tossed the necklace."

The mother of the teens turned to the crowd and urged everyone to move on. But the crazed lady demanded the sweeper be arrested. A uniformed guard lumbered over to the group, clearly irritated that his tea break had been interrupted. Just as the guide started to explain what had happened, the lady wrested the flashlight from him and shone it on the young woman. Still crouched in the nook, she looked like one of Shiva's dwarf attendants.

"Get her, for God's sake!"

In the commotion, she slipped away. The guard pulled a flashlight from his broad black belt and began to scan the area. By this time, most tourists had dispersed. Simon indicated that he had had enough, but Meena insisted they stay. "If they find her," she warned, "it's all over for the young thing. There is no justice for a penniless sweeper."

The guard beamed his flashlight to the frieze of androgynous Shiva, the half moustache, then the lone breast.

"She's not hiding in his boob," the lady shouted. "Look behind him, her, whatever it is! She's got to be here, somewhere."

The beam illuminated the diamond girdle wrapped around the feminine half of the statue's hip. Meena froze.

"There, behind the penis!" The crazed lady strutted toward a ten-foot lingam, the gold sequins on her chest fluttering. She wrapped both arms around the thick, phallic stone and started patting and rubbing the symbol of Shiva as if she were searching for a secret door where the young woman could be hiding.

The teenagers burst out laughing. But not all were amused. "I hope the lingam sprays its divine sperm all over her," the father said. His wife turned to him with a face that looked like the wrathful form of Shiva.

"The girl must have climbed the penis!" Lady Macaw screeched, pointing to the top of the lingam. "I order you to go up and get her. She's probably hiding in the hole."

"What hole, madam?" asked tour guide.

"The hole in the penis, you moron. Doesn't your god pee?"

"Madam, this is lingam only. It is symbol of Shiva, not real penis. There is no hole, at least to my knowledge."

"I just saw something move up there, on top of his *thing*! Go on, climb up and bring her down."

"Madam," the guide replied, "we cannot be climbing Shiva's lingam. This is eighth-century carving and very sacred."

"Well, *she* climbed it!"

"Madam," the guide continued, "I will wait here until the cave closes if necessary. If she is up in lingam, then she must be coming down only.

You are not to worry your good self."

"This is absurd," Meena snapped. "Someone has got to put an end to this nonsense!" She started toward the guard, who pulled a small pad from his pocket and began to write.

"No, let me," Simon insisted. He swaggered over to the guard. "Sir, put your pad away."

"And who are you?"

"I'm Senator Bliss from the United States Congress, here on official business. And if you charge the young woman, I shall call our ambassador and have the US Embassy allege police misconduct."

"Senator Bliss, did you say? I am a guard, not a policeman, and who said anyone was being charged? But since you've stuck your neck out, why don't you tell me what you saw."

"I saw an elderly woman find the necklace on the ground, pick it up, and place it on the stone slab. It probably fell off *her* during the tour." He pointed to the accuser.

"He's lying!" she squawked.

"Madam," the guide said, "unless proof you are having that the girl took the necklace, there is nothing he can charge her, even if he were an officer of law." He and the guard exchanged a few words in the local language. Then the guard announced that he was closing the cave for one hour. A chorus of groans issued forth from the few remaining tourists.

Meena grabbed Simon's hand and pulled him across the stone floor into a pitch-black corner. "Let's wait until the tourists have left," she whispered. "When the coast is clear, the young woman will emerge. I want to make sure she gets out safely and isn't accosted by that psychopath."

"*Chalo, chalo*, go on, go on," the guard said, herding everyone toward the entrance. The guide lingered to make sure everyone complied. Meena and Simon crouched, as still as the figures carved in the friezes. They watched nervously as the guide's flashlight made slow strokes, scanning the surroundings. Simon's back was against the wall with Meena pressing against him. She could feel his member as a beam of light landed on the couple. It paused for a few seconds before disappearing into the darkness. They were finally alone, but the heat was unbearable and the air stank.

"Senator," said Meena, turning around, "you were magnificent." She patted the sweat from his forehead and smoothed back his damp hair. Simon said he needed to get out of his crouched position before his legs fell off, and they both stood. She planted a forceful kiss on Simon's mouth. She pushed her thin body tightly into his. Her embrace was violent, almost desperate. Simon responded by lifting her by the waist and sweeping her around, then pressing her whole body against the stone.

Her chest heaved as she wrapped her legs around his hips. He kissed the conch shell of her ear. "I hear the ocean," he muttered. His hand slipped under her shirt; she felt it creeping up her back. Panting, she untucked his shirt and dug her nails into his moist skin. The heat seemed more intense. She imagined them in a furnace, their bodies melting together like Shiva as half man, half woman. She felt Simon's hand on her breast and threw her head back. Her body was on fire. Suddenly, a bat swooped within an inch of them and she instinctively pulled away.

"Let me down," she whispered. She wanted more, but this was not the place. She stuffed her shirt back under her belt and tried to smooth out the wrinkles. Simon bent down and handed her a sandal, which had fallen from her foot. She ran her fingers through his thick locks, pulling his head between her legs. Then, letting go, she raised her hands to her nose, pretended to scratch an itch. The smell of their bodies lingered as they headed toward the entrance.

Meena eyed the statue of androgynous Shiva. The god seemed to shoot an approving glance. They reached the portico, where the guard sat on a folding chair and blocked tourists who were yelling to be let in-side. Seeing the couple, he dragged his chair away from the entranceway. The crowd shoved into the cave like a juggernaut of inebriated devotees. The sunlight pierced Meena's eyes. Squinting, she held onto Simon's up-per arm as they moved away from the entrance. It was firm and muscular, unlike Kesh's.

"Senator, wait please!" The guide's voice from behind.

"Damn it," Simon said, "he's going to give us shit for not leaving the cave."

The guide smiled, joined his hands in front of his heart, and bent down to touch Simon's feet—a gesture of deep gratitude. Meena no-ticed the young sweeper crouched behind him like a shadow. She looked frightened, but seemed to be holding a smile deep within.

"My new bride," the guide said, pulling her slim body up.

Simon looked confused and uncomfortable. "What's going on?"

Meena understood immediately. The guide had indeed seen them stacked together in the niche as he scanned the area with his flashlight. But he wanted them to have the cave to themselves. It was his way of thanking the senator for defending his beloved bride from the harsh ac-cusations of the awful bird woman.

Meena and Simon started down the wooden stairway without utter-ing a word. But this was not the awkward silence of the car ride there. A puffy, white cloud appeared out of nowhere and hovered over them. It seemed to follow the couple down the hill like a living canopy, offering its shade—a blessing from on high.

———◆———

Simon gazed out the window as the jet broke through the clouds on its way to Washington. Soon, he was sound asleep. He found himself walking through the Panchavati caves. But instead of depicting various forms of Shiva, the stone friezes were the shapes of his projects: the Hangzhou international airport, the Berlin municipal center, the new library in Cordoba. He stopped in front of the MIT Art Museum, set in an alcove of its own. Long icicles hung from the roof. One by one the icicles broke off, frightening him. He worried about Lin Yang, expecting one to come crashing down on her like a dagger. Suddenly, the icicles were all gone. He looked up and the angular roof morphed into a giant meditation cushion. It billowed, like an ocean wave. Then he saw her, Lin Yang, alive, sitting cross-legged on top, smiling.

Meena woke up several times that night—alone, since Kesh had gone to Delhi. She lay in bed trying to recreate that precious moment in the cave; she pictured them crouching like children as the guide scanned the area with his flashlight. *Two lovebirds huddled in a nest.* Had she only known him for five days? Then thoughts of Kesh. Who was he? The romantic husband who called her a poem on their wedding night? The country's premier green architect fighting global warming? The bush-man, who pranced around the house brandishing that wretched girdle? Or, all three?

She rolled over and glanced at the alarm clock. Ten to seven. Simon would be landing soon. She slipped into her bathrobe, made a cup of tea, and called Behera to say she had no objection to his taking the HDP grant. Then she spotted the World Wildlife Fund calendar on the fridge and counted the weeks until mid-September, when Simon would return to present his preliminary design. She imagined him sailing back to India in the boat that would become the new community center. Her eyes fixed on the photo above the calendar: the heads of two baby swallows peeking out of a bird's nest perched on a tree.

PART II

JUNE–SEPTEMBER 2005

CHAPTER 17

Washington, D.C.

Throughout the summer, Simon labored over the design of the center by himself. Kesh had withdrawn from the project soon after Simon left India in April, saying his firm had won a major commission in Chennai—one that would consume all his time. Simon's colleagues expressed little interest in his concept and claimed to be too busy with their own projects.

As Simon worked, the scene in the Panchavati caves replayed in his mind like a video clip in a never-ending loop; he scrutinized each frame to find some sign that those few precious moments with Meena were more than an aberration, a typo she would white out.

He passed many weekends in the bowels of the Smithsonian, poring over large tomes on Indian art and architecture. He made two trips to Boston to see the permanent India collection at the Boston Museum of Fine Arts. Despite his single-minded devotion to the project, he managed to carve out time for the family. One Saturday he took his daughters to the IMAX at the Natural History Museum to watch a 3-D film, *Night of the Living Dead*. On a sweltering weekend in July, the family drove to New York City to see *Wicked*. After the play, he argued with Alisha, who seemed far more villainous than the witch.

On August 29, Hurricane Katrina narrowly missed New Orleans. The ensuing storm breached the levees, unleashing torrents of water. Boats and casino barges rammed into buildings and landed in the middle of the city. Bridges collapsed, roads were blocked and utility lines cut, trapping people in the dark, wet world. The TV news showed tens of thousands of the city's poorest residents streaming into the Superdome as if they were escaping hungry wolves. Bloated corpses floated in rivers of water everywhere. The worst hit were the elderly and the bedridden. In the days that followed, hundreds of bodies were recovered from homes, or what was left of them, especially in the city's Lower Ninth Ward. The coastal towns of Mississippi were also devastated.

On the third day of rampant destruction, the *New York Times* published a letter to the editor by Keshav Narayan of New Delhi. He asked readers to imagine a world where a Hurricane Katrina happened in tens of coastal cities every year. This, he insisted, would be the effect of a six-foot rise in the ocean if nations did not start converting to cleaner fuels and institute green building construction practices immediately. He backed up his claim with computer forecasts from the Intergovernmental Panel on Climate Change.

Simon's concept of an ark seemed especially timely. As Kesh once said, *if you're going to save the planet, you gotta start somewhere.* Simon read Genesis for God's instructions to Noah, but soon tired of the details: the ark must be built three hundred cubits long and fifty cubits wide, etc., etc. And what the hell was gopher wood anyway? He gave up after a

Google search that yielded a few renderings of the ark. They looked like old Vermont barns with the head of a giraffe or elephant sticking out of a window.

Nevertheless, the biblical story fascinated him, though attempts to share his excitement with his family fell on deaf ears. Alisha was especially dismissive. One evening he cornered Tina, his youngest, and told her how Noah, after eleven months in his ark, sent out a mourning dove to see if it could find dry land. "Great story, Dad," she blurted. Then she flew into the kitchen and grabbed a Dove Bar from the freezer.

Simon spent days searching the Internet for a ship on which he could model the center. He found himself being drawn to schooners: relatively small, intimate boats with a tapestry of sails of different shapes and sizes. He studied and sketched them with the same intensity he brought to drawing Chinese temples the year after his mother died.

One day he came across a photo of the *Alma*, a gaff-rigged schooner built in San Francisco in 1891. The shorter foremast was equipped with a triangular sail, followed by two square sails, the rear one twice the size of the middle. The *Alma* also flew a small trapezoidal topsail above the larger rear sail. He collected dozens of photos of the vessel, which he plastered all over his office. He would sit for hours squinting at them, trying to imagine how the *Alma*'s hull could be transformed into a stationary façade without looking like it belonged in Disneyland. And he labored to find a way to turn the trapezoidal topsail into a photovoltaic array. The key was subtlety. Connotation rather than denotation.

As the weeks passed, he found himself taking risks, softening an angle here and an angle there. For inspiration, he posted a photo of Salvador Dali's melting clocks over his work area. Below it, he scribbled the sage advice of his favorite grad school professor: *Don't be afraid to sail close to the wind.* The final version was like nothing he had ever done before. In an email to Meena, he joked that his design was the result of a one-night stand between a building and a boat. One of Simon's colleagues swore he'd smoked too much weed in India.

One day Simon searched the Internet for a photo of a pirate ship peopled with scrubby, unshaven ruffians in dark eye patches. On top of the mainsail he photoshopped a picture of the severed head of Blackbeard, the notorious English pirate. He emailed his creation to Meena, saying it was his best shot at a preliminary design. She didn't miss a beat. She thanked Simon and promised to forward it to Mr. Behera without delay. For a split moment, he panicked.

When Simon wasn't poring over photos of schooners, he visited websites and blogs on domestic violence in India. It wasn't a pretty picture. Every year hundreds of beautiful faces were horribly disfigured in acid attacks. Sometimes, for refusing a man's marriage proposal, other times, for threatening a divorce. Often a jealous husband would lash out with no proof of infidelity. Women were tortured, beaten, and burned for failing to produce a male child. In-laws greedy for a second dowry—a scooter or refrigerator—doused their daughters-in-law with cooking oil and lit a match. Each story turned his stomach, but also pushed him on, like a trade wind blowing against the sails of his beloved *Alma*.

In mid-August, the family took their vacation on Martha's Vineyard. On sunny days they trotted off to Lambert's Cove Beach, where Simon would set up a large umbrella and two beach chairs. Sara and Tina splashed around in the water while Alisha, like half the people on the beach, devoured Dan Brown's *Da Vinci Code*. Simon tried to make conversation with Alisha, but was usually rewarded with a grunt. Feeling ignored, he buried his nose in books on Indian architecture. From time to time, he would look up and gaze at sailboats circling the Elizabeth Islands. But whatever he was doing, visions of Meena gatecrashed his head. Simon repeated her name so often it began to sound like a mantra. *Meenameenameena.* If Zaha Hadid could be "OM-ed," why not Meena?

What was it about India that so captured his imagination? Soon after Meena's original letter, Alisha had said a visit to India would help him find closure so many years after his mother's death. Simon had always assumed his wife was thinking of something concrete, like a trip to the Taj Mahal. That he would see the monument for the building it was and not as a backdrop of the photo that had been gnawing at his heart for so many years. Or, that he would find some kind of Holy Grail—a letter, a key, a coded document—something physical, real, which would free him from the trauma of his mother's untimely death.

As he sat in his office churning out sketch after sketch, Simon realized something *was* happening. There was no Holy Grail, as far as he could tell, but his hand was freer and his designs softer with fewer sharp angles. Was Kesh's humble curve his Holy Grail? He remembered events that he had not thought of in decades. Especially small moments with his mother. The day they played tag in the ice-cold Maine lake after their Sunfish capsized. The time he was stung by a bee as they picked blueberries— the berries went flying and landed on her head, leaving blue patches in her hair. When, at nine, he trotted off to Macy's with eight dollars in his pocket to buy his mother a dress for Mother's Day. In these passing moments, he would hear his mother's voice, feel the touch of her hand, sometimes even smell her skin.

One night a thought hit Simon hard, like the sheet of ice crashing on Lin Yang's head. Was his proclivity for designing buildings with sharp angles his way of turning his back on that painful photo he found after her death? The photo of Raj and his mother kissing in front of the Taj— that monument of grand domes, round minarets, and curved archways?

As Simon sketched, he began to reclaim the deep feelings he once had for Raj. His Indian neighbor was no longer the evil adulterer who destroyed his mother's life by leaving for Mumbai. He was the neighbor Simon once loved more than his own father, a retired engineer for Long Island Power Authority. He recalled his aunt once saying Simon's dad had the emotional IQ of a step-down transformer.

Simon remembered how his Indian neighbor would regale the family over dinner with wild stories about his homeland. There was Megasthenes, the ancient Greek traveler, who went to India and wrote about its winged scorpions, gold-digging ants, and men without mouths. Once Raj returned from a trip to India with a hundred-year-old nutcracker. A naked prince was carved on one of the handles and an unclothed princess on the other. Raj brought along a bag of walnuts and gave Simon the job of cracking them. Every time Simon cracked a nut, he and Raj would watch the royal couple join together and shout, "Boom boom!"

One night lying in bed, Simon recalled his thirteenth birthday. His mother had given him a ventriloquist's dummy and suggested the name Rich Kidd. What a goofball with his mop of red hair, bright blue rolling eyes, and those silly eyebrows, which popped up and down. Simon would dress Rich up like a preppy college student: plaid pants, a green sports jacket, a crisp white shirt and checkered bow tie. He taught himself how to throw his voice and was soon making money entertaining at children's birthday parties.

As he lay in bed, Simon tried to recreate his favorite skit, which Raj had written for him. It began with Rich babbling about how he just got back from India, where he had picked up a parasite. Rich asked Simon to feed him a nut wrapped in a green leaf in his jacket pocket. "After all," the dummy said, "I might be a Rich Kidd, but I'm still a dummy and can't move my arms!" The kids howled as the young Simon reached into the dummy's pocket and held up a leaf in the shape of a triangle.

Rich explained it was *paan,* a combination of betel nut, lime juice, and spices that killed parasites. Simon pretended to put it in Rich's mouth. Then the dummy explained that everyone in India chewed the stuff and how it turned saliva red. Before long, Rich was spitting red water, which looked like blood. The kids howled even louder. Simon would grimace and say sternly, "Mr. Kidd, behave yourself! You know it's not polite to spit, especially at a birthday party!" The dummy apologized, but a few seconds later a four-foot tapeworm came crawling out from between his lips. By this time, the kids were rolling on the floor! What was it about India that had unleashed such vivid recollections? He felt like someone had poured a can of Drano into his head, dislodging memories that had calcified decades ago.

CHAPTER 18

Mumbai, September

Kesh was in good spirits when he picked Simon up at Mumbai's Chhatrapati International Airport. He lost no time in boasting that he won the India Green Building Association election by a landslide and would take over as chairman in January.

The men drove to the Grand Hyatt Mumbai, where the IGBA annual conference was in session, and went for a late-night dinner at Soma, the hotel's elegant Indian restaurant. As they drank beer and munched on crispy papadum, Kesh turned the conversation to his prized girdle. In describing the treasured piece, Kesh was soon performing the kind of verbal trapeze act Simon had come to dread.

"The piece I found in my ancestral home is a bejeweled girdle, traditionally worn by courtesans to show off the female zone, no pun intended, since this girdle is also a zone, from the Greek *zona*, meaning a geographical belt. To feminists, including my dear wife, it is a reviled garment, or better yet, a non-garment, since its purpose is to reveal rather than conceal. Now I prefer to say it is maligned rather than reviled, or, to be more precise, *misaligned*, since alignment is not a virtue when such a zone is worn by a courtesan in her birthday suit, that is, if the intention is to show off her private assets, which, biologically speaking, are centrally located."

Kesh was telling Simon that he sold the girdle to Madhav, who, in turn, lent it to the priest, when a waiter approached with a cart full of dishes that perfumed the air with wonderfully contrasting aromas. The waiter was dishing out the food when Kesh spotted a friend and excused himself.

Sitting alone, Simon thought back to a conversation with his wife on the day he had received Meena's letter inviting him to bid on the commission. When Simon showed it to Alisha, her face turned to stone. "Go to India," she snapped and then proceeded to say how much *she* had always wanted to visit the subcontinent. "But did I even mention the idea? No, I've always bagged it thinking a trip there would be torture for you—a Guantanamo with chicken tikka. To a therapist, India is paradise, a place where every neurosis is hanging out to dry. A Costco of symbolism. Ganesh with his elephant head and thick, phallic trunk; Shiva sitting in meditation with the Ganges falling onto his matted hair; Durga, the goddess with ten arms who wears a necklace of skulls and dances on a male demon. Hey, what professional woman with young kids wouldn't want a few extra arms?"

Kesh returned to the table and invited Simon to come back to Sompur after his presentation to Mr. Behera and Meena. There, Kesh said, the two men could enjoy some carno-spiritual pleasure at Upadhyaya's temple. "Our esteemed priest has recruited his first devadasi-to-be and—"

"Kesh, stop where you—"

"Let me finish, please. The girl's name is Amrita and a second young angel is on her way as we speak. Yours for the taking. We'll have a roaring time. Think Gatsby, old boy. You really shouldn't pass up this opportunity. After all, it's a gift from the priest in return for the girdle."

"Wait, I thought you said you sold the girdle to Mr. Behera."

"Yes, I did. And he lent it to the priest, who offered me free access to his four hundred devadasis, as soon as they're installed, that is. I suspect the idea came from Madhav, who is trying to distract me from my mission to tighten the energy requirements for projects going for LEED certification. He's nervous for no reason at all, since the community center has already been approved for Platinum. I can't change that. In any case, Madhav's got another thing coming if he thinks a few sexy girls can stop me. Anyway, what the hell can I do with four hundred devadasis at my age? That's a bit much, even for a horny old chap like me. I'm happy just knowing the priest will arrange an occasional tryst with Amrita, the first girl he's recruited to become a devadasi. She's about all I can handle." He bit into a leg of tandoori chicken.

"What in God's name would a priest want with a diamond girdle?" Simon asked.

"To adorn the hips of the lovely devadasis, the temple dancers," said Kesh, his mouth still full. "So, how about it, a little carnal pleasure at the Sompur temple?"

"No thanks," replied Simon, savoring scrumptious pieces of lamb cooked in coconut milk.

But Kesh's peripatetic tongue was not about to give up. "And remember, what happens in the temple stays in the temple. We shall recline on soft pillows like Roman senators as the lovely ladies whirl and twirl on lotus feet reddened with henna before taking us into their arms and, if we're lucky, their sweet-smelling mouths. Vishnu reclines, as does the

Buddha, so why shouldn't we? Never trust a religion without a reclining deity, that's my view. So, what does Simon say?"

Biting into a flatbread stuffed with spicy potato, Simon wanted to reply that the only carno-spiritual pleasure he longed for involved Kesh's wife. But since that was impossible, he simply said no thanks and asked Kesh what he planned to do with the money he got for the girdle.

"I'm going to start my hundred-solar-school program. I figure I can outfit more than a dozen schools with solar systems. After the program is launched, I'll solicit corporations for contributions, both here and abroad. I won't stop until I get one hundred schools outfitted and totally off the grid. That will give it some real traction, which I'll use to lobby the national and state governments to include the program in their budgets. I want kids to think of themselves as part of the solution to climate change, not part of the problem. As of now, the electricity for over ninety percent of all schools in the country comes from coal-fired power plants."

"That's very generous of you, Kesh."

"Well, Madhav gave me close to a million dollars for the goddamn girdle. I'll use half for the program and keep half for myself—a square deal. I've been wondering for a long time how I was going to find seed money."

Simon was impressed and asked questions as he tore off pieces of chapati to scoop up shrimp curry and black dal. As Kesh talked about his solar-school program, his eyes widened and his speech got faster. Buried beneath all the bravado and swagger was a decent man. A very decent man. Which made Simon feel guilty about his running after Meena. It was so much easier when Kesh was just a misogynous bastard.

After dinner, Kesh escorted Simon to a crowded lounge, where some of the IGBA leaders were enjoying a nightcap. Present were G. S. Mitra, the outgoing chairman; R. S. Varma, the chairman of Kalyan Industries, a diversified conglomerate; Anjali Sachdev, the newly appointed director of the Jaipur Technocity; and Tom Rice, the US Green Building Council's vice president of international programs, who had been invited from Washington as a guest speaker. They all welcomed Kesh, complimented him on his presentation, and greeted his distinguished guest.

"So, tell me, Mr. Bliss," asked Varma, the industrialist, "how do you like India? Most people love it or hate it, but few are indifferent."

"Many foreigners love to hate it," quipped Mitra, the outgoing chairman.

"Well, Mr. Varma," Simon replied, "it's the first day of my second trip, and my first lasted all of five days. But my first impressions are very positive. India is a colorful country and people have been very kind to me."

"Not too chaotic?" asked Sachdev.

"Well, yes, I suppose it is, but by some miracle it all seems to work and not spin out of control."

"As if a centrifugal force is keeping everything in orbit!" Varma said.

"No," Mitra joked, "it's the Himalayas that hold everything together. They're like a giant paperweight." A few guarded laughs.

"So, Simon—may I call you Simon?" continued Varma. "Do you think the green building movement is here to stay, or is it just another American fad? I ask because I've been approached by a US company that wants to form a joint venture to manufacture insulated concrete forms."

"ICFs, an excellent product!" shot Rice, the US Green Building Council's VP, who could always be counted on for a glib comment.

"The idea," Varma continued, ignoring him, "is to manufacture the ICFs for the local market and use India as an export base to supply the Middle East and Africa."

"I don't know about India or those other regions," Simon said, "but in the US, the movement toward sustainable architecture has reached a kind of tipping point. I don't believe there's any going back."

"Ah, the holy tipping point, where there's no going back!" Kesh exclaimed with one arm in the air and eyes scanning the room for a waiter. "It should remind us all that the glaciers are tipping right into the warming oceans, which could rise a full meter by the end of the century." A waiter appeared and took drink orders. "Now, Simon over here has got the right idea. He's designing an ark, but I'm afraid this one is only for a handful of abused women. I don't think men will be allowed on, much less kangaroos and swine with cloven hoofs."

"Kesh," Simon piped up, "is referring to my preliminary design for a community center. The preliminary sketches have some nautical elements." He was about to explain his concept further when Sachdev, director of the Jaipur Technocity, jumped in to compliment Kesh on his keynote speech. She liked the fact that he had urged Indian architects to look to the natural world for building solutions.

Kesh's Jack Daniel's arrived along with Simon's beer and a bowl of mixed nuts. Kesh took a swig, grabbed a handful of nuts, and proceeded to lecture the group about the African scimitar-horned oryx, which used its horns to conduct intense desert heat away from its body. The example was clearly intended to impress Simon, since everyone else had heard his presentation. He described how the animal's form was designed to keep it cool: the long legs, which raised its torso far above the hot sand; the white belly, reflecting the ground heat; and the muzzle, which contained blood vessels to flush heat from the core of its brain.

"As long as you green architects don't start adding horns to your buildings!" Varma joked.

Kesh downed his bourbon and started discoursing on the stupidity of humans. "Why do we continue to design the same buildings in ice-cold

Kashmir and sweltering Delhi? Animals are far smarter. For example, we've known for centuries they've evolved shorter appendages to reduce surface area and minimize heat loss."

Simon glanced at his watch. He would be meeting Behera and Meena in only eight hours. He wondered why Meena had not wanted to join him for breakfast. He pictured her long legs swathed in a silk sari. Would she be wearing a bindi on her forehead? How would she greet him after four long months? With a namaste or a peck on the cheek? Or, would her glossy lips linger on his cheek for a delicious moment?

"Kesh," Varma blurted, shaking Simon out of his reverie, "if you're so smart, why don't you come up with a green technology I can manufacture and sell here in India? I don't care whether you steal your idea from an oryx, a toucan, or a flea on a donkey's ass. They can't sue for patent infringement! I'll even give you an equal share of the company."

Simon slipped into another daydream. Was there a plan for the afternoon, following the presentation of his preliminary design? Would he have any chance to be with her alone? Would she suggest they take a trip to Elephanta, the cave temples in the Mumbai harbor? And what about the evening? Would she come to his hotel for a late-night drink? Then guilt. How could he even think such thoughts after hearing about Kesh's plan for the money from selling the girdle! *Get a grip, Simon!*

Then Sachdev leaned over to Kesh and spoke in a low but firm voice. "You had better be careful. I overheard a group of manufacturers bitching about the election results. I know at least one chap was from Trane. They were scheming ways to thwart your plans. Maybe even put you out of commission, if you get my drift. You'd be smart to watch your back." Kesh dismissed her with a shrug, turned to Varma, and started proposing ideas for a new company.

Simon didn't get to his room until after 2 a.m. He dreamt he was sailing across the ocean in an ancient vessel. But the figurehead at the ship's prow was Meena with a torrent of black hair flying behind her. The wind coursed through the gap between her front teeth, making a whistling sound that attracted a flock of birds. Suddenly, the birds were hovering around her mouth building a nest.

CHAPTER 19

Meena savored the panoramic view from the penthouse of Behera Towers. On one side, Mumbai's bustling business district; on the other, the vast Arabian Sea. She looked down at the street to see if she could spot Simon, but pedestrians were as small as ants. She brushed her hand over the pleats of her sari, a deep burgundy.

A peon entered the conference room with a plate of oversized chocolate chip cookies. Meena wondered if they were meant to make Simon feel at home. She could almost feel her arteries running for cover.

Behera and Simon marched in together. Simon, a head taller than Behera, looked stunning in a dark-blue suit. She hoped Madhav would get an urgent phone call so they could be alone. But there was no phone call, and Meena suffered through the usual exchange of pleasantries.

"Well," Behera said finally, "how about we get the show on the road? Or, should I say, launch this boat? The sooner we're done, the sooner we can head to Peshawri for a tasty lunch of grilled meats smeared with exotic spices. What do you say, Simon?" He rubbed his hands together and gestured toward the thick teak conference table.

While Simon unpacked his laptop, Behera pushed a button under the table and the wall behind him gave way to a giant white screen. The industrialist invited Simon to take his place at the head of the table.

"So, Meena tells me you designed a ship! Something about Noah's Ark saving our young ladies from the flood. So, tell me."

"It's not really a ship, sir," Simon replied, "but the design is meant to *suggest* certain nautical features."

The first computer rendering showed the two-story building from a northern orientation: the view from the gate of the cement factory. The overall impression was of a ship with overlapping sails of different shapes and sizes. But the design was elegant, Meena thought. No Disneyland here, thank heaven. She glanced over at Behera, who offered a quick but approving wag.

Simon directed his laser pointer to the lower half of the façade, a honey-colored wood. It could have been a soft pine hull and was punctuated with small windows reminiscent of portholes. He described each element: the top perimeter consisted of a thin clerestory, which would draw in natural light. From inside, residents would see the sky but no land, creating the sense they were cruising on the ocean. But the height of the clerestory limited the light; it would not penetrate the deep interior. Meena tried to conceal her joy.

Next, Simon pointed to the upper story, which consisted of a simple glass curtain wall. He explained that the transparent façade suggested an open deck where natural light would bestow a feeling of freedom, in contrast with the ground floor, which offered a protective, womb-like space. He explained that the idea of incorporating both wood and glass came from Indian architecture. He clicked the remote and Old Delhi's

Jama Masjid, India's oldest mosque, flashed on the screen. White marble domes loomed over the red sandstone enclosure wall. Another click and Rashtrapati Bhavan, the presidential palace, appeared next to the mosque. Heavy red sandstone topped with off-white limestone.

"Well done, Simon!" Behera exclaimed. "Some people say the layering of stone is a metaphor for how the British Raj was built on the shoulders of the Moghul Empire." Simon agreed, but pointed out that the idea of a two-toned façade long preceded the British. Out of the corner of her eye, Meena saw Behera's mouth twist.

The next slide showed the southern orientation, which faced the ocean. An imposing, blue rectangular structure above the second story dominated this view. It swept across the outside of the building, starting high above the upper floor and ending in the middle of the lower hull-like façade. A much smaller but similar structure hung over it.

Simon focused the beam of light on the two structures, dark blue as a moonless night. He explained they were photovoltaic arrays that produce electricity. He clicked again and a photo of the *Alma* appeared. There was no mistaking that the overlapping structures reflected the mainsail and jib of his beloved schooner. He explained how the solar "sails" hanging over much of the glass façade would block the harsh summer sun, prevent glare, and lower the inside temperature. The ten-degree tilt would maximize the sunlight that could be turned into electricity. His inspiration, he said, came not just from the schooner, but from Hindu temples with their overhanging eaves. Meena sneaked a look at Behera, who was smiling.

Another click revealed the center from the same southern orientation, but farther away. "Observe how the solar arrays, or sails if you wish, are attached to a feature that suggests a mast." Simon pointed to the slightly rounded end of the eastern side of the southern wall. "See how it bulges out and extends up, beyond the top of the building? As with all good architecture, form follows function. What you are looking at is actually hollow inside. Think of a chimney. It sucks up hot air, which exhausts out of a hole in the top. This creates a low-air-pressure zone, pulling in the cooler air from the ground and creating what's known as the 'stack effect.'"

"But you're not cheating me out of my air-conditioning system, are you?" Behera asked, arching his brow like an arrow ready to shoot.

"No, sir. Natural ventilation won't work from June through August, when humidity levels are extremely high, so the building will require a full-size chiller."

Behera lowered his brow.

Simon pressed the button on the remote and a slide showed the solid gold canopy of the Peacock Throne, built by Shah Jahan. Next, Simon projected the Hall of Audience at Fatehpur Sikri, whose roof was adorned with four domed pavilions. Simon pointed out that such elements were inspiration for the slight curve in the roof on the upper story.

The residents will feel like royalty, Meena thought. She looked over at Behera. Would he take offense that Simon was inspired by the throne of a Moghul emperor? Thankfully, the industrialist didn't react.

"I like it," Behera said. "Now, what about those waterless urinals I've been reading about?"

"Now, there's a brilliant idea for a women's institute!" Meena chided.

"We'll certainly have one or two in the men's room," Simon added to lessen any embarrassment on Behera's part. "For male workers and visitors, of course."

"And now the moment you've been waiting for," Simon said with a smile. He clicked the remote. "The bird's nest."

Meena clenched her fists in anticipation. This feature would either impress Behera like nothing he'd seen before or fall flat on its face.

A small, round room appeared on the screen. The walls were covered in deep-blue velvet. The floor looked like a giant cushion. Simon kept pressing the remote and, one by one, streaks of light started to emerge from inside the walls. Going in every which direction, they looked like twigs illuminated under a full moon. Simon continued to click, and the number of lines slowly multiplied until the entire room resembled a bird's nest under the moonlight. All of a sudden, a constellation appeared on the ceiling. It was Sagittarius, Lalita Devi's sign. Meena looked over at Behera, whose mouth had dropped in awe.

"This room is deep within the ground floor of the center," Simon said. "Here women can sit comfortably in total darkness or, using a remote, they can illuminate the walls and create their own nests."

Behera scrunched his eyes, as if fighting back tears.

"This bird's nest is the sanctuary," Simon said, "a sacred place, like the inner sanctum of a Hindu temple. It is a place of comfort and healing."

"I'm speechless," Behera said. Meena heard him muttering *my dear chickadee* under his breath.

The next slide revealed a rooftop garden.

"Go back," insisted Behera. "Please."

Simon reverted to the previous shot.

"Do it again, Simon. Go from the dark room to the twigs—you know, the way you built the nest before." Behera watched, mesmerized. When the nest was fully illuminated, he covered his eyes with his hand. After a few moments, he gave Simon permission to move on.

The roof garden covered about half of the roof, starting with the chimney "mast." From that point, residents could look out over the sea, as if they were standing on a ship's bow. The computer rendering showed an outdoor café, where women in saris were seated at tables drinking from cups, while others milled around the deck-like space. Large potted plants lined the perimeter like a garland. One, situated slightly apart, was a small tree adorned with red strings.

"Oh, dear me, it's the praying tree!" exclaimed Meena.

Simon smiled. The final slide showed the southern lawn, modeled after a Moghul garden, with computer-drawn women relaxing on benches under a blossoming tree. Simon explained that he'd substituted indigenous grasses and plants to conserve water.

"Well, there you go," he said, holding his hands in front of his chest.

"Very impressive." The tips of Behera's fingers came together in a polite applause that grew louder after a few seconds. Meena followed, but her claps were soon drowned out by Behera's.

"Thank you," Simon said. "It seems to me that Indian architecture is like a tapestry woven with threads from Hindu, Muslim, and British traditions. I've tried to create a design that weaves elements from each of these in a way that will best support women residents like Asha." He looked straight into Behera's eyes, but the industrialist—the patron saint of the ultra-right Hindu party—didn't take the bait.

"A ship and, within, a bird's nest," Behera mused. "Very, very clever. Brilliant, really. It's exactly what I wanted. A bird's nest, yes. Perfect. You know, Simon, when I said I wanted a signature project like the Bird's Nest in Beijing, I didn't realize what I was saying. Did you, Meena?"

"No, me neither."

"But you did, Simon. It's brilliant. The girls will feel safe in the nest. Protected. And the boat, ship, that's good, too. They're moving. Going somewhere better. It's good, Simon, very, very good." He smiled, slowing wagging his round head.

Meena could hardly contain her enthusiasm.

"And there shouldn't be any problem getting LEED Platinum?" Behera asked.

"No, sir."

"Do we get any points for building an ark? After all, we're saving humanity!"

"Only psychic satisfaction," Meena countered.

"Well said, Meena," Behera replied. "And now that I'm facing retirement, I could use a boat myself—a lifeboat!" Behera let out a nervous chuckle. Coming from one of India's richest business tycoons, the remark fell flat.

"So, Simon," Behera asked, "how long will it take you to complete the design? I'm willing to pay a premium to get this project up and running as quickly as possible! Shall we aim to start construction in three or four months, say by the New Year?"

Simon gasped. "We can get through the design development phase in three months, but after that, it will take another three months to complete the construction documents, at least. I don't see how construction could start before March or April, earliest."

"No, no. Listen, I've hired a local architecture firm that will replace Kesh's. It can do the scut work fast. If you finish design development by mid-December, we can have the construction docs done by end of February. That means breaking ground by March 1. As long as we can have our ship in the waters by October, we'll be okay. Yes, that'll work, won't it? Now, how about some grub?"

———◆———

Red Bukhara carpets and copper pots hung from the walls of Peshawri, Mumbai's highest-rated restaurant for Northwest Frontier cooking.

A host led them to a rough-hewn wooden table and handed out wood-en menus, which looked like they belonged on a pirate ship. Behera ordered drinks—a bottle of French chardonnay, a double Glenlivet for himself—and enough food for the Indian army: dal Bukhara, black len-tils cooked overnight in a tandoor oven with tomato puree, butter, and cream; Sikandari *raan*, mutton leg marinated in ginger, garlic paste, chili powder, lemon juice, and rose water, then grilled for two hours in a wrap of roti bread; *burrah* kebab, lamb infused in a yogurt sauce of red chili, mace, nutmeg, cloves, cumin, raw papaya, malt vinegar, and other spices; giant tandoori prawns; *murgh malai* kebab, tender chicken kebabs rubbed with cardamom, garlic, and ginger paste, then soaked in a mixture of cheese, cream, coriander leaves, and green chilis before being grilled on bamboo skewers; and an array of vegetarian dishes. "That should get us started, what do you say, Simon?"

Behera praised Simon's design, then suggested that a waterbed should be sunk into the top floor near the rooftop garden. Simon was appalled. He argued against the idea, but to no avail. Meena watched as Simon's whole body collapsed like a failed soufflé. When they were done eating, Behera insisted Meena take his limo and give Simon a tour of the city. The boss would taxi back to the office.

Meena and Simon were soon ensconced in the plush leather back seat of Behera's car. She moved to the middle, leaning slightly into his side as the driver headed to the Gateway of India. As they walked around the monument, she took Simon's arm and put it around her shoulders. When they stopped to admire the ships moored in the Arabian Sea, she mustered up her courage to execute her plan. She asked Simon if he'd like to see the Gateway from a lounge on the top floor of the neighboring Taj Mahal Hotel. She took his hand and led him into the lobby, through the reception area, up the elevator, and to her room. She kicked the door shut with her foot, grabbed hold of his tie, and pulled him onto the king-size bed. The bunch of pleats holding her sari in place seemed to untuck themselves.

CHAPTER 20

Sompur, the same day

As soon as Kesh returned to Sompur, Upadhyaya called and said he had arranged a rendezvous for him with Amrita that evening. *Thank you, girdle*, Kesh said to himself, before retiring to his home office. After reviewing a few designs sent to him from his colleagues, he walked to the closet and pulled out a leather suitcase that once belonged to his father. Everything inside was just as he'd remembered: a silk Nehru jacket richly embroidered with flowers; a turban strung with semi-precious jewels; a black sari made of raw silk and brocaded with gold threads; a vest strung with the finest pearls from the Persian Gulf.

By six that evening, Kesh was practically exploding with anticipation. He rifled through his dresser for a wad of hundred-rupee notes and counted out ten, trying to avoid the gaze of Gandhi on every bill. *Screw you, you holier-than-thou Mahatma with your vow of abstinence and your cold baths. You were seventy-seven when you were sleeping naked with your teenage nieces, so don't you look at me like that!* He strapped the suitcase to the steel rack of his Harley. But the hook didn't catch and snapped back, striking him in the middle of his forehead. *Fuck me!* After wiping a spot of blood, he mounted his bike.

Kesh snaked through the narrow streets until he arrived at a small city temple that was also under Upadhyaya's jurisdiction. The priest greeted Kesh and led him next door to a concrete house surrounded by a cement wall. Amrita, his "devadasi-to-be," was newly arrived, and he joked that the Sompur temple now had a leg up on all the other temples recruited for the national program. Upadhyaya reminded Kesh how lucky he was to have recruited Amrita well in advance of the national election. The priest didn't seem to care that the HDP might lose, in which case there would be no temple program, much less devadasis dancing around the temples.

The front door of the house was framed by pink and purple bougainvillea. A girl of about fifteen led them to the living room. Two black and white striped cushions in the shape of zebra heads were strewn on a hot pink faux-leather couch. In one corner stood a rabbit-ear TV. In another, two musicians sat cross-legged on a straw mat. The ribs of the half-naked tabla player protruded so far out that it looked like he had swallowed an oval basket made of bamboo. Using a silver hammer, he tapped the cork tuning pegs strapped to the smaller of his drums until the sound *dha* rang out with pristine overtones. To his side sat a butterball of a woman playing a harmonium.

"I thought you might like a dance performance to cut up the ice," Upadhyaya said.

"That's very thoughtful of you, Guruji."

The wafer-thin girl appeared with two huge bolsters. She looked like a giant ant with two gigantic purple eyes. The priest sat cross-legged, leaning slightly on one, while Kesh lay on his side, propped up by his elbow.

The music started and Amrita glided into the room. She wore a sizzling gold sari draped in the style of Odissi dancers. Its sequined pattern looked like cobra scales. Her dark eyes flashed like bees hovering over a flower. A silver ornament hung onto her forehead from the center part of her hair, which formed a bun laced with jasmine flowers. Silver bells dangled from her ears. Her hands were joined and raised over her head. Two small lotus flowers were painted in the centers of her shaved armpits.

As the pace of the music quickened, Amrita slinked this way and that, guided by her folded hands. Kesh's eyes roamed up and down her body like a scanner, occasionally resting on the diamond shining in her navel. She extended her elbows until they resembled a snake's broad hood. Her tongue gently slithered in and out, the tip occasionally curling into a fork.

Red henna designs spread over her feet, as if she were wearing soft Chinese slippers. As the drumbeat got faster and faster, her feet turned into hammers, pounding the floor. She opened her hands wide to reveal two large circles on her palms—the eyes on the cobra's hood. Moving toward Kesh, she slid one hand down and the other up, as if the snake's eyes were shifting to track him—her prey. She unfastened the clip on her head; a waterfall of black silk cascaded to the floor, releasing jasmine flowers like snowflakes. As she danced, her feet crushed the petals, sending spurts of sweet fragrance to Kesh's nostrils.

Upadhyaya's right hand was outstretched with his palm up. He used his thumb to count the sixteen beats of the rhythmic cycle, one knuckle at a time, starting with the bottom of his pinkie. The corners of his mouth were turned down as he shook his head in pure ecstasy. The music crescendoed into an orgasmic fury. Then it stopped. A few dying notes dribbling this way and that.

Amrita approached Kesh. "You like my dancing?" she asked, panting.

"Magnificent. You speak very good English."

"I also sing. But to hear me, and you must come into my bedchamber. I cannot sing with zebras staring at me." She pointed to the striped throw pillows. "They get too excited," she giggled. She took Kesh's hand and led him into a small bedroom lit by an oil lamp. Kesh's eyes immediately fixed on an antique Victrola with a giant cornucopia horn.

"Upi Sahib bought it at an auction," Amrita said. "It belonged to the governor of Bengal."

Kesh flipped through a stack of records below the phonograph.

"That my favorite." She pointed to the cover in Kesh's hand. It showed the smiling face of the American singer Frank Crumit holding a ukulele. Kesh slid the black vinyl out of its jacket and placed it on the green velvet pad. A scratchy noise preceded a high-pitched voice:

I wonder why I am always lonesome
And what the trouble can be
Most fellows find their dates
But it just seems my fate
Has made a monkey out of me . . .

"I brought you something to wear," Kesh said, lifting the needle off the record. "A gift of sorts. Wait here." Kesh scurried out of the room and returned with his suitcase. He opened it and invited her to take one item.

Amrita's eyes widened as she rummaged through the clothes. "But this is a man's *achkan*," she said, holding up a full-length Nehru jacket. "Did you think you were going to meet a man? I hope I don't disappoint you!"

"No, I'll wear that. I thought it would be fun to dress up as a maharaja while you played the courtesan."

"But I *am* a courtesan, at least until Shree Upi's party wins the election and changes the law. That's when I will be dedicated to the temple and married to Lord Jagannath. Then I shall be a devadasi!"

"Sorry," Kesh replied, "but today you must stay a courtesan."

"It's not fair. I want to be someone else!" She stomped her foot like an angry teen.

"Who, then?"

"I want to be Texas."

"You mean a Texan?"

"Yes, with a cowboy hat and a guns." She pointed to the suitcase. "You have a guns?"

"I'm afraid not. Anyway, why would you want to be a cowboy?"

"Because they are free! And they shoot bad men."

"How do you know all this?"

"Gita told me. She says it's good for woman to own a guns."

"Gun, not guns. Anyway, Gita who?"

"Gita Sen."

"For God's sake, how in the world do you know her?"

"She comes to me sometimes to learn about devadasis. I think she does some research. She's very curious about my job in the temple. After a few times, we become friends. Sometimes I even start chewing ice, just like her!"

"Bloody hell!"

"So, if I can't be Texas, why not I am Pocahontas?"

"Pocahontas? But she's Indian. I mean, American Indian."

"Yes, and she falls in real love with Mr. John Smith. Will you be my

Smith?"

"How about we play Pocahontas and John Smith next time, since I don't have the proper costumes? Today I'll play a maharaja and you play his favorite courtesan. These garments and jewels belonged to a real maharaja's family." Kesh rummaged through the suitcase and pulled out the pearl vest. "Here, this would look lovely on you."

"Okay," Amrita said, resigned. She snatched the garment and disappeared behind a sandalwood screen.

Kesh could barely control himself as he dove into white *churidar* pants, which bunched up at the bottom. The embroidered Nehru jacket was tight, but he struggled into it after leaving a few buttons undone. He squeezed into his father's silk slippers, lined with pearls, and crowned his head with a fanned turban trimmed with a jeweled brooch. He picked a rose from the vase on the nightstand and stuck it into his lapel buttonhole. Then he took a mirror from the suitcase and applied a thick line of kohl to his tired eyes. He looked like his father with a rounder, puffier face.

Amrita whirled into the room wearing the vest, which was not fastened in the middle. Pearls seemed to drip down her dark chest. As she moved, the silver clasp shook, looking like a comet struggling through the Milky Way. Around her hips, the glittering girdle, which did little to conceal her sacred space.

"Shree Upi said you like the bourbon." She turned to reach for a bottle of Jack Daniel's, revealing the full moon of her buttocks. "So, he bought this just for you only!" She poured a glass, which Kesh guzzled. "Guruji said it's one of your feelings. I hate man with no feelings. They are too dull."

Kesh motioned for her to come close. Her inner thighs shone like polished copper. He grabbed her waist, then the two globes of her buttocks.

"This is one of my failings—I mean, feelings," he said laughing as his fingers looped toward her crack like inchworms.

Amrita swung around with a jerk. "You naughty maharaja," she scolded, feigning anger and pelting him with a toy lotus.

"Punish me," Kesh said. "Whip me with your lotus, or better yet, with your lotus arms." He sat up on his knees, snuggling his head into the space between her breasts. "Did you know that a woman's breasts should be just so big that no more than a single lotus stalk can fit in between them?"

"Who said that?"

"It's a stock image from Sanskrit poetry."

"What's a stock image?"

"Never mind. Now, I can fit my head between yours with no problem, but I'm hardly disappointed." He rubbed his unshaven cheeks against the soft sides of her breasts, then licked the underside until his tongue reached her nipple. There it fluttered, like a hummingbird over a crest of sugar water. After a few moments, he opened his mouth and lunged forward, as if he were about to swallow her. She jumped back and waved her finger at him.

"Bad maharaja!"

"*Aree*," Kesh said, "do you know the story of Urvashi, the celestial nymph who propositions the young Arjuna, but is rejected?"

"Of course. I'll dance it for you, if you promise to be good."

Kesh wagged his head.

Amrita's body shimmered as she took on the role of the seductive goddess. Then, changing parts to play Arjuna, she turned her head away from Urvashi to indicate he would not have sex. Her face grew hot with anger; she sliced her hand through the air and cursed the mortal who scorned her. When the dance was finished, Amrita approached Kesh, who was still sitting on his knees at the edge of the bed.

"Bravo. Now, in the version I know, Arjuna tells Urvashi he can't have sex with her since he thinks of her like a mother. She must have been much older than him, don't you think?"

"How can a goddess be older?" Amrita asked. "They're immortal. Like me. I'm immortal, since my name is *amrita*, undying." She laughed. "Goddesses like me don't grow old."

"I don't know, but I'm with Arjuna. I wouldn't want to have sex with my mother. Now you, on the other hand, are a courtesan, the very opposite of a mother." He grabbed her buttocks and thrust his finger into her. Amrita's whole body jerked forward and up. She shrieked and pulled away. Kesh laughed so loud a gecko sputtered up the wall.

"Bad boy! Didn't your mother teach you to go slow with girls? Now go wash your hand like a good little maharaja, and I will give you a treat."

Kesh obeyed and returned to the bed.

"Now close your eyes and open your mouth," she said, placing something on his tongue.

Kesh savored the crunchy betel nut, mixed with lime paste and fennel, then opened his eyes.

"Upi Sahib tells me you are green architect. At first, I was afraid you were really green."

"I am green, but in a different sense."

"What you mean?"

"I design green buildings."

"What's green buildings?"

"Buildings that are good for the planet and don't damage the air and water. They use less energy and so don't warm the planet. The heating is causing the oceans to rise. We wouldn't want humans and other species to drown in a massive flood, now would we?"

"I love species, too," she said, climbing on the bed. "Especially chili peppers."

"Yes, that's terrific, Amrita. So now, why don't you come onto the bed with me?"

She climbed on and sat with her legs pulled tightly to her chest. Kesh put his hands on her knees and drew them apart.

"I have many talents besides dancing," she said, oblivious to the fact that her yoni was now on parade.

I'm sure you do.

"Like playing the glasses."

"The glasses?" Kesh repeated, staring at her.

"Yes. I fill different-sized glasses with water starting with the little one and rub a wet finger around the edge. I can play ragas and Western songs, like 'Jingle Bells.' Even 'Star Sprangled Banner.' Gita taught me."

"Gita, Gita! Can you please stop talking about Gita? And it's Spangled, not Sprangled."

"I also learned some of the arts of the *Kama Sutra*, like how to make potions. I know one that will put me under your spell forever."

"*Bapre bap!* I'd like that!"

"I cut up sprouts of the *vajnasunhi* plant and dip them in a mixture of red arsenic and sulfur, then dry them seven times. Finally, I rub the mixture on your sea monster with some honey."

"Oooh, that sounds yummy," said Kesh, lighting up. "Hey, I hear a voice."

"Ah, that's just Pinkie." Amrita jumped up and pranced over to her dresser, where she lifted a black cloth covering a wooden cage. Sitting on a bar was an overweight parrot. "She must have just woke up. Good morning, Pinkie. Sing a song for our little maharaja."

"I'm as lonesome as a raindrop!" the parrot shrieked. "I'm as lonesome as a raindrop!"

They laughed. When Amrita returned to the bed, Kesh stroked the high arch of her narrow foot. Then he raised it, bent over, and started kissing her inner thigh.

"Upi says you're a son of a real maharaja."

"Yes," Kesh muttered, lavishing kisses up and down her leg. "And I am also a priest, and you are my sacrifice. Your lap is the sacrificial altar, your pubic hair the sacrificial grass. Your skin is the press used to make the ritual *soma* drink, and the lips of your delicious yoni are the sacrificial fire."

"Are you off your tree? Who ever heard of a maharaja-priest?"

"I am also Kama, the god of love. My standard is the sea monster. Would you like to see my sea standard?"

"Oh, dear Kama, I fear I have no choice." She tugged the drawstring of his pants. Kesh lifted his butt and pulled them off.

"Oh, Kama, I am struck with admiration. There is no doubting you are the god of love." She dipped down and began to caress his member. Before long, she took him into her mouth. Kesh drew in his stomach and arched his back.

"Ouch! Be gentle, girl! You don't want to break my royal scepter, do you?"

"Oh, no," she said, coming up for air. He swiveled around until his head reached her vagina. He sucked her, whispering that her yoni was the conch shell that must be blown to ensure the sacrifice was properly executed. After that, he tossed her onto her back and climbed on top.

"Now," he whispered, "my member is *Mandarancha*—the mountain Vishnu used to churn the cosmic ocean." He plunged into her and his hips began to gyrate. "Soon the ocean will produce *amrita*, the nectar of immortality!" He licked the salty sweat from her skin and nestled his face in her breasts, which were smeared with fragrant sandalwood paste. "Kama is getting tired," he panted, spinning onto his back and tossing her on top. "Now you play the man and I shall be the woman! Mount me, my lord, and do to me what you will."

She bowed her head and started to pump her body up and down. Her loose hair caressed his chest and a jasmine petal fell onto his face.

"Now *I* am a tiger," Kesh shouted, "and you are Durga! Ride me, goddess, ride me hard!" Her hot breath poured onto his face. But this position was not satisfying, so he flipped her over and was again on top. As he ground his hips into hers, his heart throbbed. His nostrils widened, and he snorted like a wild pig.

"Easy, man, you're hurting me!"

"Oh, my fucking God!" Kesh howled like a wild beast before collapsing onto her.

"Please move. You squishing me."

Kesh slid off her, his chest heaving. Amrita turned toward him and stroked the long hair that grew from his brow like a weed. "Maharaja, why you don't snip this off?"

"Shush," Kesh whispered, trying to catch his breath. After a few minutes, he lifted his head slightly. "Did you hear that?"

"Hear what?"

"A voice."

"Pinkie?"

"No." He rolled off the bed and leaped to the window. Outside a crowd was milling about. A man draped in a saffron shawl was yelling into a megaphone from the back of a truck parked in front of the main entrance of the temple compound.

We Hindus are not violent people, but there can be no toleration of this Muslim slaughterhouse within fifty feet of our temple, home of Lord Jagannath. This is too much of insult to our Lord. For one month now, we have done our level best to negotiate, to reason, without—

An explosion ripped through the air.

"Burn it down, burn it down!" the protesters chanted.

The speaker raised his hands to quiet the mob, but the chanting only grew louder and angrier.

"What's happening?" Amrita asked, picking up a nail file.

"It's the goddamn HDP. Upi warned me about this demonstration. There's a Muslim slaughterhouse not far from the temple. It's a cause célèbre, since they're butchering cows."

"A what?" Amrita said, filing her nails.

The temple wall blocked Kesh's view, but he could see banners and lit torches gliding in the direction of the slaughterhouse. They moved past a majestic banyan tree, its aerial roots like aged sentinels powerless to stop the protesters.

"Listen," Kesh said, "this could get ugly and spill into the temple compound. You should get dressed and come with me."

"No, maharaja," she said, sauntering behind the screen to change. "I stay here, you go."

"Please, it's not safe."

Amrita started singing. "Oh, say, can you see . . ."

"If that's what you want. But I wouldn't go outside until the coast is clear."

Another blast and a cloud of smoke rolled toward the window.

"They've set fire to the goddamn slaughterhouse. Shit! Hand me the vest!"

Her voice from behind the screen, "But you said that was my gift."

"Okay, but it is a gift that you must earn over time."

Kesh spotted the bottle of Jack Daniel's and took a swig. Bourbon dripped down his shirt. "Remember what I said—don't leave the house until it's quiet out there." Then he jogged out the door, hopped onto his motorcycle, and tore off.

Kesh sped through the small streets of the old city, past Sompur Technical College, crowded with students milling all around; he flew by the Ganesh temple, where devotees lined up with trays of coconuts and marigolds; then down the street that cut through the Bhandarkar Agricultural Institute. He soared past a row of butcher shops with carcasses hanging out to dry and chickens clucking in cages; next, he sped through a gaggle of narrow gullies lined with jewelry shops. He rounded a corner at Sardar Vallabhbhai Patel Chowk and whizzed past D. D. Gadkar's Printing and Copying Co. Ltd. He raced past Saint Joseph's High School and United Coffee House. The fourteenth-century Sufi shrine was the last thing he remembered.

CHAPTER 21

Gita swung open the front door of the hospital, hitting a peon who was squatting against the wall smoking a *beedi*. She offered a quick apology and strode to the reception desk, cutting the queue. The nun in charge looked as stiff as the crucifix around her neck. She cast a disapproving look, as if Gita's behavior were grounds for excommunication.

"I'm looking for Mr. Keshav Narayan."

The nun glanced down at her book and flipped the page. "Room eleven. First floor, turn right."

Gita climbed a flight of stairs and stood in front of Kesh's room. The door was closed, but she could hear voices inside.

"Where am I?"

"You're in the Saint Francis Xavier Memorial Hospital. I'm Sister Alphonsa. You were in a road accident and, thank the good Lord, are still alive. You suffered a concussion and your right arm was broken."

"Dear God! So, you are Sister Alphonsa. Wasn't the good saint known for performing miracles? Curing clubfeet and that sort of rubbish? Maybe you can do one better and get me the hell out of here."

Silence.

"Well, if you're not going to answer me, can you kindly tell me what day it is?"

"Sunday."

"And my Harley? Where's she?"

"Who's Harley?"

"My goddamn motorcycle!"

"Please do not use the name of our good Lord in vain. And I wouldn't worry about a motorcycle if I were you. You should be grateful you're alive."

"I am. Now, does my wife know I'm here, alive and grateful?"

"We called her—thank the good Lord you were carrying identification. She's flying back this morning from Mumbai. Unfortunately, we weren't able to get hold of her last night. Her phone had been turned off, but we left a voice mail."

A knock on the door. "Ah, maybe that's her now. Come in, darling."

"Gita!" he groaned in pain, trying to pull himself up from a lying position. "What are *you* doing here? And with flowers?" The nurse walked past Gita and nodded as if bestowing a blessing. "They're gorgeous. Are you here to confess your love for me? Oh, not-so-slender woman with tapering legs like a baby pachyderm and lips as red as the ketchup plant—"

"Go to hell, Kesh," Gita growled. "They're from Meena, who asked me to visit, since her flight doesn't get into Sompur until later this morning."

"What was she doing in Mumbai?"

"Don't you remember? She went to meet Behera and Bliss, the architect. He presented his preliminary design for the center yesterday."

"Bloody hell, I completely spaced. I saw the bloke last night at the annual India Green Building Association meeting. Or, was it two nights ago? Never mind, let's give her a tinkle, shall we?"

Gita took her mobile from her handbag and dialed. "Voice mail, she's probably in the air."

Kesh grabbed the phone and pressed it against his ear. "Honey, it's me. I died, but kind and gentle Gita was kind and gentle enough to come visit and awaken me from the eighth ring of the underworld. She is now my Virgil, escorting me to Paradise. Or was that Beatrice? Anyway, she's giving me the most delicious foot massage, so take your—"

Gita snatched the phone back. "Meena, it's me. As you can tell, Kesh is very much alive and as cheeky as ever. And no, I am not giving your husband a foot massage. Please hurry."

"Cheeky?" blurted Kesh. "I'm not cheeky. It's the nun who's cheeky. I guess Jesus likes 'em that way. I prefer big tits, myself."

"Kesh, shut up."

"Seriously, did you see how that habit squished the nun's face? She looked like a chipmunk ready to blow out birthday candles. Or maybe the good Sister Alphonsa stores Alphonso mangoes in her cheeks. So, when can I get out of this prison?"

"Six months."

"What? You've got to be kidding!"

"I am, although the world would be a safer place. At least for womankind."

Kesh groaned as he used his good arm and feet to pull himself up.

"So, what happened?" asked Gita. "Do you remember anything?"

"No. Well, yes, I remember speeding through the city on my motorcycle. That's all." He started telling Gita about the SUV that nearly ran him off the mountain road on his way to Gond. Gita reminded Kesh that that incident took place five months ago. The motorcycle accident happened yesterday in Sompur. She said Meena asked her to see if there was an accident report. There was, and she found something in common with the first incident. A witness reported seeing a black SUV trailing Kesh just before he crashed.

"So," Gita said, "maybe you were pushed off the road."

"But who'd want to hurt me?"

"God, you're naïve. You are the chairman of the IGBA and everyone knows you're on a crusade that's going to make life hell for a lot of entrenched businessmen. Just think about all those corporations that stand to lose millions if you succeed in changing LEED. Like all the air-conditioning companies that want to continue selling their monster chillers to real estate developers going for certification."

"Well, I suppose. But am I such a threat that they'd murder me?"

"I wouldn't put it past Himco or any one of them."

"Well, it can't be Himco. That's Madhav's company, and he's my dear friend."

"Kesh, grow up. A plot to take you out wouldn't necessarily even get to the chairman. Maybe it was the president of Himco or one of a dozen other companies like Trane or Hitachi. Maybe it wasn't an air-conditioning company at all. Think about those big-time commercial developers who flip their projects right after they're up and running. Many of them want LEED, but they get nothing by investing higher capital costs in green buildings. They don't care how much energy their buildings use, since they won't be paying the utility bills. If LEED projects have to be twenty-five percent more energy efficient than the industry standard, they're screwed."

"Gita, darling, don't take me for a half-wit. I've been giving presentations and writing articles about this bloody subject since you were snoring in your crib. Or, were you masturbating?"

"Then don't be so naïve about all those corporate thugs who would love to send you off a mountain or drive your precious Harley into the nearest chai shop."

"Maybe it was a soda company like Campa Cola!" exclaimed Kesh. "After all, when it's hot, people drink up! They've got to be rooting *for* climate change. Or should I say root-beering?"

"Kesh, joke all you want, but I'd say there's a bull's-eye on your back."

Kesh let out a big groan as he tried to look over his shoulder at his back. "Okay, okay. I get your drift. But how's murdering me going to change anything, except create a temporary dip in the stock price of the Jack Daniel's Company?"

"Do you think there's anyone at the IGBA who has half your passion to turn the whole construction industry on its head?"

"Maybe not," said Kesh, adjusting his balls. "Well, if I'm going to die, it probably doesn't matter if I thin my blood with some aqua vitae. If the nuns object, we can always invoke the name of the good Saint Patrick, who—"

"Kesh, you're on a morphine drip. Don't be insane."

"Go to the window, my quick-footed one, and tell me if you see a house of spirits. I'll be indebted to you for life. I'll even sleep with you!"

"Don't be disgusting! And there's no drinking in a hospital, especially one run by nuns. They'll throw you out by your ears."

"All the more reason."

"N-O!"

"All right. Then why don't you come over here and let me kiss the deep orifice of your navel?"

"Get lost, Kesh!" Gita stood up to leave. "I realize you're drugged to Timbuktu and don't know what the hell you're saying. Still, I've had enough."

"No, don't go! I'll be a good boy, I promise."

"Okay, but one wrong move and I'm out of here."

Kesh joined his hands together in a gesture of supplication and bowed his head.

"So, where were you going yesterday in such a hurry?" Gita asked. "Let me guess: to the temple to meet with Amrita."

"Actually, I was not going, but rather returning from a tryst *majeure* with the First Lady of the Sompur Temple, who, I'm told, is now a friend to whom you are teaching American ditties like 'The Star-Spangled Banner.'" Kesh began to sing. "Oh, say, can you see, by the dawn's early . . . what was I saying? Ah, yes, the lovely Amrita, whose eyes are like lotuses, the flower that opens during the day and closes at night and is thus not to be confused with the low-caste water lily, which closes during the day, although it may be said that Amrita has been known to open up at night, in a manner of speaking, at least for me. Oh, shit, my arm itches like hell!" He began to bang the cast against the side of the bed. Sister Alphonsa rushed in and asked if everything was all right.

"Yes, sister, my beloved Gita here was just hitting me over the head. What's the hospital policy on domestic violence, anyway?"

Gita rolled her eyes and assured the nun that everything was fine. The nurse left in a huff.

Gita turned to Kesh. "I hear you cut a pretty good deal with that old goat of a priest and are getting Amrita's services free of charge."

"I am actually very generous with the girl. When I left her yesterday—was it just yesterday?—I deposited a few hundred rupees on her dresser. Even the wife of the Lord must earn her keep in these modern times. Is it not the age of the two-income family and all that rubbish? Times are tough, even for the Jagannath family."

Gita rolled her eyes.

"But at least our young woman of ambrosial lips has the good sense to conduct her business in a proper way—that is, with a man, and, if I dare say, one of good standing or, if you must, good lying, such as my good self—and, unlike your good self, cannot be accused of breeding a nation of independent Durgas who scorn the male gender."

"Kesh, the morphine is talking. I would advise you to keep your mouth shut before you put your foot in it any farther."

"Gita," responded Kesh, swinging his good arm toward her foot, "I'd rather put your not-so-tender foot in my mouth. Anyway, do you deny that your good self and your boss, my good self's dear wife, exhibit an unabashed proclivity toward misandry, which, according to the anthropologist David Gilmore, is a neologism, since the misandrist really reserves his or her—well I think it's fair to just say *her*—hatred for male traditions, the culture of machismo, and not for any specific individual, who—" Kesh stopped short and grasped his chest. "My fucking ribs!"

"I have no clue what you're talking about," Gita said, rising to leave.

"Sit, please, and answer me. Do you not deny that you are engaged in a mission to rid the good subcontinent of men? Your India shall be called *Durgadesh,* the land of Durgas. It shall be a country where men hurl themselves into their wives' funeral pyres out of blind devotion. A kind of reverse sati, if you will."

"Kesh, you're so full of shit, if you'll excuse my French."

"You are indeed frank, Gita, or should I say Frankish? But if you insist on speaking French, then speak it, for God's sake. I believe the expression is *plein de merde.*"

"You are incorrigible. If you could only see yourself as others see you!"

"Pray tell, dear Gita, whose name is a song, how might that be? Sing it to me!"

"The truth is, you are just like all the sexist men in this country. You're afraid of high-powered women who don't genuflect when you come home from work. That's why you turn to prostitutes and devadasis. You can't stand your wife's success and all the national attention she's getting. That she spends her time reconstructing lives that have been torn apart by men like you, instead of slaving in the kitchen making chapatis and washing your stinking maharaja feet when you come home."

Kesh leaned forward and pretended to sniff his feet as Gita walked over to the window and opened it, then lit up and blew a smoke ring.

"I fancy the smoke around your sweet-smelling mouth is a swarm of bees hovering for a free lunch. Or does the smoke issue forth because your tears, caused by my cold words, are redirected inward and fall onto the burning embers in your heart? Oh, shy Gita, you mustn't cry, for I have not meant to spurn your love."

"Oh, dear God, Kesh, you're sick. I'm leaving!"

"No, Gita, don't go. I command you by the authority vested in me as the husband of the co-founder of the sovereign state-to-be, Durgadesh, to stay and comfort this love-challenged creature of broken heart and limb. If you go, I shall die in this prison of morphine drips." Kesh held the tube running into his arm across his face, as if it were a steel bar.

"If I stay any longer, I'll say something I might later regret."

"Oh, do!"

"Like predicting that you will leave Meena."

"But you already predicted I'd be bumped off by a not-so-green corporation. So, which is it? Am I to be struck down by a flying air conditioner, or shall I leave my lovely wife?"

"Very funny. Do you want to know why you will leave her?"

"Not really."

"Not because you don't love her—I know you do—but because you are not man enough to be with a successful woman."

Kesh put his hands over his heart and pretended to cry. "That is deep, Gita. Very, very deep! Since when have you honed such sharp analytic skills?"

"You can joke all you want, but that's the truth. You're the kind of man who needs a prostitute, someone you can dominate. It's like that Freudian babble of yours. How Indian men are not able to sleep with their wives so they resort to whores or the young women Upadhyaya is recruiting for the temples. Like Amrita, who's now being made to gyrate her hips for you in that ridiculous G-string that belonged to your family."

"If you don't mind, I prefer to call it by its Sanskrit term, *mani-mekhala,* but if that is too difficult for you to pronounce—since you may have swallowed one or two of those bees from my earlier metaphor, or was it a simile—you may simply refer to it as the diamond zone, from the Greek *zone* or Latin *zona*, which my etymological dictionary defines as 'a geographic belt' or 'celestial zone.'"

"Fuck you, Kesh. Goodbye."

"Oh, Gita, I have to tell you that it excites me when you hurl invectives in my direction. Please, abuse me; you may even whip me. Indian men love to be assaulted by their wives, whom they spurn since they think of them as their mothers. It helps relieve the guilt arising from their sexual transgressions."

"I'm not your wife, and what's more—"

"Don't be so literal. Of course you aren't, but you are taking her place at this church of healing. *In situ* wife art thou. Or, art thou more like an owner's rep?"

"Kesh," said Gita, snuffing out her cigarette and lighting up again. "I'm going, but first let me tell you something."

"And, if you like, I can ask Sister Alphonsa for some rope, which you can use to tie me to my bed. I shall lie naked, and you can prick needles into my flesh. Better yet, you can even crucify me! I shall ask the nun for long nails and a hammer! What nun doesn't like a good old-fashioned crucifixion?" Kesh's eyes closed and he let out an awful groan. "Gita, please push the button for the nurse."

As Gita reached over Kesh for the button on the far side of the bed, he grabbed her wrist and pulled her on top of him.

"Let me go!"

"I refuse to live in a country where the women wear the pants!" yelled Kesh. "They should wear *no* pants!" He slipped his hand under her jeans and reached for her buttock.

"Let me go! Now! Or I'll yell 'rape'!" She tried to reach for the buzzer, but he stopped her.

"Gita, relax, and tell me, do you want to live in a country like America, where women grow hairy armpits and leave their young ones with aliens from El Salvador, people who can't even make a good chicken tikka?"

"If you do not let me go this second, I will take this cigarette and stick it in your ear!"

"Oh, Gita, you're exciting me again!"

She tried to free herself, but his grip was too tight. So, she touched the tip of the cigarette to his earlobe.

"Ouch!" Kesh reached for his ear, freeing Gita, who leapt to her feet.

"Kesh, I could charge you with rape, but I won't, because you're the husband of my boss, who happens to be a good friend. But I'm leaving. Go run away with your teenage fantasy. You can pass your days just like your father, the maharaja of Gond, or should I say Gond-orrhea?"

"Good one, Gita!"

"Go fritter your life away smoking opium and fondling young breasts. You're no different from your father: insecure with a pin-sized dick."

"I beg your pardon," replied Kesh, pulling up his smock to reveal a thick, erect penis.

"Gross! Put that disgusting thing back!"

Kesh threw the smock over his member. "Sorry, my love, I didn't mean to offend you. Are you a Vaishnavite, a worshiper of Vishnu who does not pay tribute to the holy lingam?"

"Don't *my love* me. And no, I'm not a Vaishnavite or any other –vite, but I am someone who hates a country where women are enslaved. They walk behind their husbands, eat after their husbands, trudge for miles to fetch water for their husbands—oh, forget it!"

"Gita, my head is spinning and all I hear is a squawking goose."

"Go to hell, Kesh. Or better yet, go diddle away your life reading Sanskrit love poetry. Why don't you try living in the real world, where women laugh and love, cry and grieve, just like you men—at least the normal ones? Go to your devadasi, and when you see the first wrinkle on her face, throw her away like a Muslim. Just say, 'I'm done with you, I'm done with you, I'm done with you.'"

"That's only Sunnis, not Shi'a Muslims."

"Or, throw her in a vat of boiling oil and call it a Hindu rite. Then find someone younger who'll suck your dick even harder."

"Is that an offer?"

Gita stomped out of the room. But as soon as the door slammed shut, she poked her head back in. "By the way, there's a new product on the market you might want to look into. It's called deodorant. If you're going to rape somebody, try not to smell like a skunk." Then she slammed the door even harder.

Kesh slouched in his bed. He reached for a glass of water, but suddenly felt a stabbing pain in his arm. His whole body jerked, knocking down the stand that held the morphine drip. He stared at the tube taped to his arm, then buried his face in the pillow.

PART III

MAY–OCTOBER 2006

CHAPTER 22

May 2006

Only weeks after the HDP's landslide victory, tens of thousands of saffron-clad HDP supporters swarmed into Puri for the launch of the National Temple Revitalization Program. On a platform built outside the famous Shree Jagannath Temple, priests from thirty-three participating temples sat cross-legged chanting verses from the Vedas. Prime Minister Ganesh Shukla gave a speech in which he claimed to have restored Ram Raj, the age of good governance. He announced that parliament would be rescinding the 1934 Bombay Devadasi Protection Act and other provincial laws that had banned the devadasis, and listed, one by one, all of the temples that agreed to rededicate young women as devadasis.

It didn't take long for the controversy to flare up. Editorials in the *Times of India*, the *Indian Express*, and other liberal newspapers denounced the program, often using language that harkened back to the reformists of the late 1800s. They questioned the HDP's motives for launching the program. Journalists, like Gita before them, speculated that the devadasis would become sex slaves to rich patrons so the HDP could fill its coffers. The headline on the front page of the *Times of India* read, "HDP Brings Back Devadasis, Turns Clock Back on Women." The author denounced the practice as modern-day slavery.

Gita promised Meena she would not quit her job unless there was hard proof of wrongdoing. She suspected the temple program would eventually explode in the party's face, but *eventually* wasn't good enough. She needed a scandal to justify cutting ties with the party before the inauguration of the new campus, scheduled for October 1. Otherwise, the national media would use the event to play up the HDP's connection with the Lalita Devi Center. If a major scandal were to break after the inauguration, the new center could suffer irreparable collateral damage. Gita imagined hundreds of skeletons falling out of temple closets, burying their dreams.

Gita called Sanjeev Mainkar, an investigative journalist she had known since college. Sanjeev was young and ambitious, hungry for a story that would catapult him into the national limelight. Gita shared with Sanjeev her suspicions about the temple program and urged him to investigate. To her surprise, Sanjeev had already seized on the idea and had even come up with the name *TempleGate* for the scandal he hoped would establish him as India's Bob Woodward, who broke the Watergate scandal. He said he was lining up photographers to stake out ten of the most prominent temples. They would take photos of all men entering or leaving the devadasis' living quarters and, whenever possible, record activities inside the devadasis' bedrooms. He had already staked out the Sompur temple, since Upadhyaya had recruited Amrita as a devadasi-in-the making. Unfortunately, he needed to wait until other young women were installed in temples to start a full-fledged investigation.

Gita was too impatient to sit back and wait for Sanjeev to act. She was desperate for the shit to hit the fan, and relished the idea of being the one to plug the fan into the socket. She decided to pay a visit to Uta Fischer, a German graduate student researching the devadasi tradition for a Ph.D. dissertation at Berlin's Freie Universität. Uta was the key to learning about the rituals involving devadasis as far back as the tenth century. After all, Gita couldn't engineer a scandal if she didn't know what was scandalous.

Gita steered her car onto Chakra Tirtha Road. She passed a shrine under a sprawling banyan tree. She took a left onto Loknath Road, which bordered the temple, then drove through a crush of pilgrims, rickshaws, bullock carts, scooters, and four-legged beasts until she arrived at Manikarnika Sahi Road.

She stopped in front of an apartment building. Air conditioners jutted out of windows. An old bicycle secured by a rope hung from one balcony. A woman was hanging bedding across a railing. Another shouted to an apartment across the street. The number above the front door read D-212. She drove a short distance looking for D-254, only to find that the street ended with D-232. She asked a young boy if he knew where D-254 was, but he shook his head. But when she asked if he knew where a German woman lived, a white *farangi*, he pointed to where Gita had just come from. She turned around and eventually found Uta's place next door to the apartment house where she had first pulled over. The sign to the left of the gate read: B. K. DUTTA, PH.D. FAILED.

She parked and climbed the outdoor staircase to the roof, from which she could see the imposing towers of the Puri temple. On the very top, Vishnu's disk-like weapon; above that, twelve flapping red flags indicating the god was home. Uta lived in a wooden studio built on the flat rooftop. Gita walked across the roof to the door and knocked. An open padlock hung from the rusty metal shackle.

"*Einen Moment, bitte.*"

"It's Gita."

"*Ja, gut,* just a minute."

Gita was excited to meet the woman who had spent years traveling the country interviewing former devadasis, most old women now. It was hard to imagine she would soon be face to face with the only Westerner who succeeded in prying open an ancient tradition of esoteric rites and sexual practices undertaken in the dark inner sanctums of some of India's most important temples.

The door opened. "Gita, come in," Uta said in a heavy German accent.

Uta's face was framed by muddy brown hair streaked with gray and parted in the middle. She wore white kurta pajamas—no jewelry, no makeup. A pair of worn Birkenstock sandals lay near the door. She could have been a hospital orderly.

Gita scanned the large room. In one corner, a narrow bed covered with a colorful Indian bedspread printed with elephants. A wooden crate served as a side table, supporting a lamp and a few books. On the other side of the room, under a window, an oversized wooden desk strewn with open dictionaries and papers. What the woman lacked in jewelry, she made up for in books: piles of them lay in neat stacks against each wall, most with plain cloth bindings. The sweet voice of a German tenor issued from a boom box on the floor.

"Do you prefer Indian music?" Uta asked.

"No, this is lovely."

"Yes, but you come to talk, so I turn it off." Uta reached for the machine, but Gita asked her to translate a few lines. Uta smiled for the first time.

"He says, *Wenn ich in deine Augen seh*—when I look in your eyes, all my sorrow and pain disappear; but if I kiss your lips, then I become wholly well. If I lie upon your breast, a heavenly happiness comes over me; but if you say 'I love you,' then I must weep bitterly." She pressed the off button. "It's Schumann's *Dichterliebe*. You take chai or café?"

"Coffee, if you don't mind."

Uta went to the kitchen, calling out that she had recently brought back a genuine Italian espresso maker from Berlin. Gita approached a pile of books near the bed. The Sanskrit title of the top book was long and obtuse. Underneath, a rust-colored cloth book with gold letters entitled *Sexual Life in Ancient India*, and, below that, a large blue tome with faded letters: *Eighteen Principal Upanishads*, Volume I, by Limaye & Vadekar. She walked over to a pile on the floor. *Der Rig Veda*, Harvard Oriental Series. 1951. She flipped to a random page in the middle of the book and slowly read the first line out loud, *"Hell flammend wie der Buhle der Morgenrote . . ."*

"You read German?" Uta called out, emerging with two espresso cups and a plate of Parle biscuits.

"Ein bischen. I had two years in college."

Uta told Gita that she was able to buy so many books because the Indian government gave German scholars Indian rupees as a way of paying back German aid. She described the bookseller as a leathery octogenarian whose skin was as tough as his bindings. "Mr. Sapre lives in the heart of the old city—a rundown apartment with no address. He is selling mostly to foreigners. Indians don't care about Sanskrit anymore. They're all busy studying computer science, engineering, and business: the holy trinity." She joked that the average age of most Sanskrit professors was dead. "The only reason my Sanskrit pundit was willing to teach a female farangi like me was because Indians no longer give two shits."

Gita asked if she could go with Uta to meet the bookseller sometime.

"*Ja*, come, but be prepared for a lot of dust. Before Sapre hands you a book, he is pounding it with his fist and a giant cloud is filling the room. Sometimes I think that's how he determines the price. The bigger the cloud of dust, the rarer the book, and more he charges. Sorry, I forget to ask, you take *Zucker*?"

Gita nodded and Uta hurried back to the kitchen. Gita followed her. It was traditional, with a stovetop connected to an LNG cylinder, a vintage GE refrigerator, and an aluminum sink deep enough to be a village tube well.

"First, thank you for seeing me," said Gita as Uta picked up a bowl of large gray crystals. "I imagine you're very busy."

"Not so busy." Uta shrugged, reaching for a pack of cigarettes and lighting up. "I'm becoming very Indian." She wagged her head. "I don't believe time exists anymore. But now, with the HDP in power, I think maybe I go back to Germany. Funny, *na*, Germany a safe haven from fascists in India!"

They returned to their cushions, and Gita scooped a teaspoon of sugar into her espresso. "Uta, as I mentioned on the phone, I work for—"

"I know, Behera House."

"We're expanding and building a new campus. The HDP Foundation has—"

"*Ja, ja*, I hear. The HDP gives you a big grant. Be careful, dear. Did you read the interview last Tuesday with Home Minister Tewari?"

"If you don't mind me asking, how do you know about the grant?"

"I have connections to the home minister—spies! You must be careful about this man. His ministry adds many staff to enforce Section 377 of the Indian Penal Code, which makes homosexual acts punishable. It's just one example of his backward thinking."

Gita wondered if Uta was fishing, but ignored the comment. The German grad student was not her type. "Uta, I know nothing about the temple dancers, except that their presence in Hindu temples is as old as the Huns and that the devadasis became somewhat of a cause célèbre for Christian missionaries."

"Old as the Huns—I like that." She lit up. "Those Christian missionaries know nothing about India," Uta said, drawing her lips so tight they looked like they would snap. "The devadasis were an integral part of temple rituals."

"Did they have sex with the priests?"

"You don't waste your time, do you, Miss Gita?"

"I'm sorry. I didn't mean to—"

"It's okay," Uta responded, gulping what remained in her cup. "It's just this HDP rattles my nerves. They want to bring back the devadasi, fine, this is good. But I don't believe they do it for the right reasons." She lit a cigarette and sucked on it. "Gita, the rituals performed by the devadasis, they are very clearly prescribed. The HDP don't care; they do with the devadasis what they want."

"Can you give me an example of a traditional ritual?"

"Okay, I tell you about *Candan Jatra* or Sandalwood Festival, which take place in the inner sanctum. There, in total darkness, the devadasis entertain Balabhadra, the elder brother of Lord Jagannath. As they sing about the coming of the white clouds of the monsoon, the young women are taking off their upper garments and pretending to seduce Balabhadra, who represents Shiva, the ascetic, and therefore he only wears a loin-cloth. This ritual is taking place twice a day for forty-two days during the hottest time of the year. Three Brahmins, who sit on platforms and fan the gods, are witnessing this action."

Total darkness, my ass, thought Gita, imagining dirty old priests glowering at the half-naked young women.

"The devadasis represent the dry, barren earth. They are seducing the ascetic to stop his austerities, which produces heat. In this way, the ritual symbolizes the breaking of the hot season to usher in the cool, fertilizing rains. That's the nutshell. You see, Gita, the ritual is about bringing forth the rains; it is not having anything to do with sex."

"I know I'm treading on thin ice, but do the Brahmin priests ever have sex with the devadasis?"

"Gita, people who tread on thin ice fall into ice water!" Uta dragged on her unfiltered cigarette until it disappeared; all one could see was a glow between her fingers. Then she threw the remains into a glazed turquoise bowl brimming with miniscule butts. Her right index and middle fingers were stained a deep yellow. "You are just like a Westerner and will never understand."

"Please, Uta, I beg you." Gita smiled seductively.

"Okay, I tell you, but only because I like what you do at Behera House and I think you should know the truth so you cut your ties with the HDP. Sometimes the priest makes sex with the devadasis because he needs her sexual fluid, what is called *rajas*. It is auspicious and a necessary ingredient of a ritual to bring about the monsoon after the hot season. So, he doesn't have sex with the devadasi for pleasure, but as part of a ritual to usher in the monsoon rains. To make the land fertile again."

Gita was horrified, but she kept a poker face lest Uta throw her out by her ears.

"You think this is very strange. I know you're Indian, but you're Western-educated, so you're like a foreigner. You never understand."

Gita pleaded for more details, saying her only goal was to expose the HDP temple program as a scam. Uta finally agreed, but spoke in such a hushed tone Gita strained to hear.

"Well, there are different times of day when the devadasis dance. One is taking place in the afternoon during the Royal Meal or *rajopacara*. The devadasi becomes the goddess Shakti and is dancing in front of the devotees. Her movements produce a fluid."

"A sexual fluid?"

"*Ja und nein.* But the devadasis do not get excited. The fluid is caused by the movement of their bodies. This fluid is very auspicious. Devotees come up afterwards and roll on the floor of the dance hall so the fluid sticks to their bodies. In Sanskrit, this fluid is also called *shakti uchhista*, 'what's left over from the goddess,' or just *uchhista*, meaning 'leftovers' or 'what remains.'"

"I don't get it, Uta. You mean young women are having orgasms as they dance?"

"*Nein!*" Uta shouted. Gita practically jumped out of her seat. "*Du versteht's gar nicht! You don't understand!*"

"Uta, with due respect, I don't see how they can secrete fluid without having orgasms."

Uta stood up and her body stiffened. Her face looked like the picture of Kali taped to her fridge. "Westerners like you *kann's nicht verstehen!*" she belted. "You never understand! *Niemals!*"

"I'm sorry, Uta. I didn't mean to upset you. Really."

"Then don't be so stupid, so American. Devadasis are not having orgasm!"

Uta strutted around the perimeter of the room several times bobbing her head, as if circumambulating a temple. Was this the end of the interview? She finally sat back down. Her face was still tight, and her voice sounded like it was being pushed through cheesecloth. "Of course, excitement is there. You call it pre-orgasm fluid if you must. But it's really not that either. Stop using Western thinking. Indian religion is not science."

"But you said earlier that something was left on the dance floor—something with physical properties. What is it if it's not sexual? Aren't they wearing underwear?"

Uta shook her head. "Underwear, this is a Western invention."

"Are they naked?"

"*Um Gottes willen,* no!"

"The devadasis are not supposed to have sex outside the temple, isn't that right?"

"*Völlig verboten*—absolutely not! Gita, you are crazy. These women are married to Lord Jagannath."

Gita had a hundred questions, but thought she'd better quit while she was ahead. What the hell was this *rajas,* and how was it produced? Did these young women touch themselves as they danced? Uta had clearly thrown Western biology out the temple window, so there was no point in pressing on. She stood up to leave.

"Sit," Uta ordered like a Nazi commander.

"It's okay," said Gita. "I can see my questions have upset you."

"*Ja,*" said Uta, cracking her knuckles. "I am telling so you understand the HDP temple program is a scam. You must know the truth so you can cut with those insects. Otherwise, you are feeding the beast. Behera House is doing good works. You can't be seen eating off the same thali, so to speak. It would be total ruination of Behera House, and worse, it would be seen as an endorsement of those creeps."

"You know something, don't you?"

"Look," said Uta, sitting down and lighting another cigarette, "last week I get a call from a reporter. He says he will be investigating the devadasis. You know, since the HDP is making such a big deal about them. Like you, he is wanting to interview me. And like you, he is smell-ing rotten fish in the water."

Gita lowered herself back onto the cushion. *Sanjeev!*

"He tells me he's had an eye on the Sompur temple, since it is the only one to have some girl already there. And that he's uncovered something very damaging to HDP. He suspects this will be just *die Spitze des Eis-berges*, how you say . . . the top of the iceberg. Since hearing him, I am stunned, but also happy because someone is confirming my suspicions."

Gita bit her lip. *Why didn't Sanjeev tell me?* "You say he's uncovered something big?"

"*Ja, sehr* big. If he's right, I eat a broom if this crooked government don't fall within a month."

"You'll eat a broom?"

"Sorry, it's an idiom. What do you say in English?"

"I'll eat my hat?"

"*Ja*, I'll eat a broom and a hat! Well, only if they're made of dark *Schokolade*. I shouldn't joke about this. The matter is *sehr Ernst*."

"Very serious?"

"*Ja.*"

"Tell me, please."

Uta inhaled her cigarette. Deep trenches formed on her forehead. "The Sompur priest has dishonored the Lord. He breaks every rule in the book. He's . . . *Scheisse*, what's the English word . . . *kuppeln* in German?"

"Pimping?"

"*Ja*, pimping the young thing. I am sorry, Gita, but I promise him I don't repeat the name. Not to anyone. He doesn't want any leakage be-fore all facts are in."

"I know who it is," said Gita. "It's Kesh Narayan, my boss's husband." *The creep.*

"No, a much bigger man."

Gita did a double take, then pleaded with Uta, who finally gave in.

"He's H. C. Tewari, the home minister."

Gita felt nauseated. The thought of that sleazebag groping Amrita turned her stomach. She asked Uta for a smoke. Uta extended the pack and rolled a blackened thumb over the metal wheel of the lighter. Her thumbnail was bitten so far down it made Gita shudder.

"He's got photos," Uta said, holding the cigarette up as if it were a torch, "but he suspects the minister will be picking one flower from every meadow, so to speak. We wait and see when all the devadasis are installed. Maybe every week he picks a different temple and a different young woman."

Gita spit out a flake of tobacco. *I've got 'em, the goddamn HDP!*

"Also," continued Uta, "the journalist is wanting to see if other ministers will also be picking the flowers. Maybe even the prime minister. He plans to have spies crawling all over the temples once the devadasis are installed. We know soon enough. But patience is required. Now, you must go. I need to finish an article I write for *Die Zeit,* a German magazine."

Gita thanked Uta and left. She crossed the roof terrace to the open staircase. On the way down, she glanced at the looming temple and felt sick. She fumbled for her cell phone. She leaned against the railing and started to dial Sanjeev. But her hands were trembling and the phone dropped, falling to the pavement and shattering the screen.

CHAPTER 23

Four months later

Kesh steered his motorcycle into the Sompur temple compound. The new addition, the first to be funded by the HDP's temple program, was a smaller version of the ancient temple. Workers were busy setting the last few statues of semi-divine ladies into the niches of the façades. The figures were bustier than those of the adjacent ancient temple—proof to Kesh that civilization progressed with time. A speck of dust flew into his eye. He was blinking like hazard lights as he dismounted and stumbled past a large banyan tree to the wooden door of the one-room workshop.

He pulled the latch and pushed the door open. *Creeaak.* Where was she? And why the hell did she suggest they meet in a goddamn godown rather than Upadhyaya's cottage in the city temple, their usual place of rendezvous? It was more a question than a concern, since Kesh would have gone to the moon to bask in the glow of Amrita's young body. But this meeting was special: their first since Amrita had been formally dedicated to the temple. *Such a blazing offense,* he mused, *making love to the wife of Lord Jagannath. How delightfully sinful! Where is my little angel anyway? And where is the fucking bed?*

The room was nearly empty, with workbenches pushed to one corner. An opium pipe and small oil lamp lay on a wooden chair. On the floor, the Victrola, plugged into a thick orange extension cord.

Vast sheets of burlap stretched across bamboo scaffolding against the longest wall. Kesh lifted one and was startled to see dozens of marble statues set on rows of wooden planks. But these were no Muslim women hiding behind a burqa. He ogled the voluptuous Hindu dancers with their jar-like breasts and wondered why there were so many statues when the new addition to the temple was virtually finished.

His eyes fixed on a young woman leaning against a blossoming tree. A string of jewels barely concealed her private parts. He touched her breast. It was hard and cold. Some enterprising young entrepreneur could make a good business embedding electric heaters in these knockers, thought Kesh. They could even be made to look like veins!

Four workers barged in bearing a queen-size bed covered with silk sheets and colorful cushions. A supervisor ordered the men to place the bed under the scaffolding. The workers monkeyed up the sides of the bamboo structure and lifted the burlap all the way to the top, throwing it over the backside, revealing the statues.

"You're early," came a velvety voice from behind.

Kesh felt like he'd been tickled on the neck with a feather. He swung around. Amrita looked like the Ganges in her shimmering silk robe. She lifted her thin arm to remove a barrette and shook her head. Thick black hair tumbled to her slim waist.

"I thought you might like to do your business in front of all these naked ladies," she said, casting a roguish glance at her patron. "Isn't that what turns you men on?"

"They're lovely," said Kesh, removing a silver cigarette case from the pocket of his kurta and lighting up, "but a tad cold to the touch."

"They're all rejects," said Amrita, tiptoeing to a naked figure playing a four-stringed tambura. She pointed to a crack in the statue's breast. "Men don't like women with broken tits, do they? Just one blemish and we become outcastes. Untouchables! So cruel are you men." She picked up a busty statue with a missing arm. "Look at this one. Quite a rack, isn't it?"

Kesh bit his lip as Amrita pulled her robe down to reveal a shapely breast.

"Much bigger than mine," she said with a smile.

"With your dark skin and silky white robe," Kesh replied, "you make the confluence of India's two sacred rivers look dull in comparison."

"What did you say? *Confluz*?"

Kesh repeated his awkward attempt to compliment her.

"Oh my, I knew you were an architect, a maharaja, and a priest," she said, taking his hand and placing it on her breast, "but I had no idea you were also a poet."

Kesh closed his eyes to relish the warmth from within.

"Now I've been called many things, but never a *confluz*. What is a *confluz* anyway?"

"Confluence. It's where two things come together. The Ganges is said to be white and the Yamuna dark. Where the two rivers meet is a very holy place. It's in Allahabad. I personally prefer *Prayag,* the ancient name of the city. May I call you Prayag?"

"Prayag?"

"Yes. It actually means 'place of sacrifice,' for it is believed to be the spot where Brahma offered his first sacrifice after creating the world."

"So, I am a place of sacrifice? Well, if that's the case, you must be the sacrificial victim." She blushed with a twinkle in her eye.

"Oh, I do like that!" blurted Kesh, rolling her nipple between his thumb and index finger. "And you shall also be Durga, the slayer of Mahishasura, the buffalo demon. I'll be the beast and you'll slay me!"

Amrita smiled and pulled up her robe, exposing the full length of her thigh.

"Oh, Durga," he panted, "destroyer of demons, do not waste my time." He fell to his knees and rained kisses onto her leg. Kisses soon turned to licks.

"Are you a dog?" she asked.

"Yes, a rabid one!" Kesh barked and licked more furiously, inching up and inward. Soon his head landed between her legs. "Now this is the sacred confluence I like best!" he mumbled as his tongue reached its target. He grabbed hold of her panties with his teeth and started to pull them down.

Amrita gasped and pushed him away.

"Sorry," Kesh said, "but this doggie has a bad case of restless head syndrome."

"You are Mahishasura, the buffalo demon," replied Amrita, "not a dog. So, play by the rules."

"And what might they be?"

"Well, first I must dance for you. I may be a *confluz* and even Durga, but first and foremost I am a true devadasi now, a temple dancer."

Amrita pranced to the corner of the room like a young doe in the woods and disappeared behind a screen. A minute later, she floated out unclothed except for the girdle that belonged to Kesh's ancestors, drawing Kesh's eyes to her hips and groin. Glittering strings of diamonds sparkled against her dark skin; she looked like a starlit sky after the monsoon rains had given the firmament a good scrubbing. One of her arms was lightened with sandalwood. She sailed over to the Victrola and placed the metal arm on the edge of the vinyl. Kesh sunk onto the bed as the downy tones of a bamboo flute swelled throughout the room. Then came the tabla, adding rhythm.

Dhira kita taka dhira kita taka dha
Dhira kita taka dhira kita taka dha
Dhira dhira kita taka
Dha thira kita taka

"My left arm is the Yamuna and the right the Ganges," she said, waving one dark and one lightened limb like undulating rivers. Her eyes darted like black birds above the water. Her neck and torso swayed as her feet, reddened with henna, tapped to the complex rhythms. As the beats got faster and faster, the diamonds of the girdle looked like comets streaming across the night sky of her body. Her hands, joined together, pointed to her vulva, as if her loins were Prayag, the holy city where the two sacred rivers converged.

Kesh picked up the pipe, which contained a piece of dark gooey opium. He held the oil lamp under it and inhaled the vapors. Something was different about the taste. Within seconds, his body felt lighter, almost weightless. The cold workshop turned into a warm and cozy den. Even the marble statues seemed to glow from within, as if they were yoginis generating psychic heat. Amrita's arms flailed and crossed like intertwining streams. Her arm-waves rushed toward him.

The tabla thundered as she screamed, "Prayag!" shooting her arms out as if punching the air.

The Ganges and Yamuna were crashing toward him. He became

frightened. His head spun and body tingled. A tsunami. He felt like ducking. Then something crawling up his thigh. He tried to shake it off, but it was too late. A sharp sting.

Fuck!

His limbs quickly turned numb.

He couldn't swallow.

His tongue swelled, thick as a cow's.

He gasped for breath.

He started to salivate like a rabid dog.

"*PRAYAG!*" she cried. "*I AM PRAYAG!*"

Her arms looked like whips, striking this way and that.

A voice. "Oh, Mahishasura! I am Durga and I drown you, demon buffalo, in the torrent of my gushing waters!"

Her head shook so fast it turned into the multi-headed goddess.

"Soon I slay you!"

Scores of goddesses were spinning around his aching head.

Hundreds of searing eyes and arms brandishing swords and nooses.

Garlands of freshly severed heads, dripping blood.

"WHAT THE FUCK!"

"Now I burn you to ashes, you stinking demon buffalo!"

He opened his eyes and tried to focus on Amrita. Something was different. She seemed heavier. Where was the thick black hair, cascading down her back? Suddenly, the room was quiet. His hands and feet began to jerk uncontrollably. He saw his own face on each severed head of her garland. Sweat poured from his hot flesh. He ripped off his shirt and struggled to open his eyes. A shadowy figure moving away from him. Then fire, encircling him. He lay down and felt his body melt away.

Amrita fled from the burning building and watched the flames consume the workshop like tongues of ravenous wolves. The heat was unbearable, but she did not flinch. It was nothing compared to what her sister must have felt the day her husband doused her with gasoline and lit a match. But this was not the time for painful memories.

She sprinted to the bush where she had hidden a bag of clothes. She unhooked the diamond girdle, stuffed it in the bag, and pulled out a pair of jeans and a man's shirt. She quickly wrapped her hair in a bun and covered it with a Sikh's turban and fake beard, complete with the gauze netting. Finally, she replaced her gold bangles with a steel wristband, grabbed the bag, and sprinted to the hole in the temple wall. She crawled through and slipped into the passenger seat of a car, which was waiting with its motor idling.

"*Chalen!*" she sighed. "Quick, let's go!"

The driver smiled, and the vehicle sped into the night. Amrita sighed. Her life as a sex slave was over. The false smiles. The cute dances. Those fat, grimy bodies. Never again, she thought. Never again.

———◆———

By the time the fire trucks arrived, the workshop was little more than a jumble of burnt wood and ash. Three firemen hosed down the smoldering rubble. Police arrived soon after and joined in the search for bodies.

"Found something!" shouted a policeman, pointing to a charred hand poking out from a heap of white marble statues. Two firemen tiptoed over mounds of rubble, their arms outstretched like tightrope walkers. They carefully removed the statues covering the victim. There was no need to feel a pulse.

Kesh was stone dead, buried in a mountain of hips, breasts, and tapering thighs.

The left side of his face was virtually obliterated. The stench of burnt flesh was sickening, and the workers covered their noses with handker-chiefs. A burning ember lay next to his neck, and smoke seemed to flow out of his ear.

"Here's the culprit," one of the firemen said. He lifted a statue of a dancing girl that lay near the top of Kesh's head. "Must have come crashing down on the poor sot's head." He pointed to a blood mark on the statue's forehead. The marble lady was clad in an ornamental girdle. The right side of her face was cracked, mirroring Kesh's disfigured face. The fireman handed the statue to the policeman, who placed it in a large plastic bag and sealed it with tape.

It was 9:27 p.m. when the deputy commissioner of police arrived with his assistant. A. J. Kulkarni towered over the firemen. The DCP was well built with a mop of black hair, a gray thistle-brush mustache, and razor-sharp cheekbones. Epaulets on his tan uniform bore two metal stars under the state emblem. He made his way to the body and poked the embers with his boot, shaking his head in disbelief.

"What a bloody mess!" Kulkarni blurted as his assistant took photos. Afterward, one of the firemen used a shovel to scoop up body parts, which were carefully deposited on a stretcher and carted off. Upadhyaya was standing on the sidelines, stunned, as motionless as one of the statues. The DCP walked over to interrogate the priest. Weeping, Upadhyaya confessed that he had allowed the workshop to be used for a rendezvous by the devadasi and Kesh, but insisted the idea was Amrita's.

"Keshav Narayan, the husband of Ms. Kaul, the director of Behera House?" Kulkarni asked.

"Yes, sir," the priest replied.

"Shit!"

Kulkarni ordered the firemen to scour the temple complex for the young woman, but there was no sign of her. Upadhyaya sobbed uncontrollably, sputtering occasional words about his good friend Kesh and the lovely devadasi. His double cowlick collapsed, as if in sympathy with both.

The young policeman handed Kulkarni the evidence bag. The DCP donned a pair of white gloves and removed the statue. The thin line of dried blood on its forehead looked like a misplaced vermilion streak worn by married women in the part of their hair. Although her face was chipped, she displayed a half smile, as if she were pleased with her day's work.

"What the hell are you running here?" Kulkarni asked. "A temple or a goddamn brothel?"

Upadhyaya lowered his head.

"Don't leave the temple. I'll be back tomorrow to interview you." He mopped his brow, ordered his assistant and the firemen to carry on, and strutted off.

CHAPTER 24

Meena sat on the living room couch tinkering with the draft agenda for the inauguration of the new Lalita Devi Center. October 1, the big day, was fast approaching—a short ten days away. She stood and opened the window to let in the cool night air. Thoughts of yesterday's meeting with Madhav and the head of the HDP Foundation distracted her, and the humming cicadas had a hypnotizing effect. She pondered A. B. Dey's offer of 1.5 billion rupees for a second Lalita Devi Center in Mumbai. He even talked of funding a third center in Kolkata.

But, as usual, there was no free lunch. Dey had said the prime minister wanted to use the upcoming inauguration to announce a ten-year partnership to combat "the national epidemic of domestic violence." Meena recalled the time Tewari got up at a political rally and declared a partnership with Behera House. It was eighteen months ago, before Meena had even agreed to accept the original grant. With Madhav's help, she had found a way to accept the money and avoid any embarrassing publicity.

But everything was about to change. The HDP had made sure every major media outlet in the country would be on hand to cover the upcoming inauguration.

Meena walked to the *tulsi* plant by the window. She tore off a leaf and chewed on it. The thought of becoming the HDP's poster child for their disingenuous campaign against domestic violence turned her stomach; she felt like a viper was trailing her, nibbling at her heel. And Madhav was useless, blinded by his commitment to the nationalist party.

In ten days, the whole country would know she had sold out. Every progressive she admired since college would shun her and speak ill of the Lalita Center. She would be called HDP's puppet, the right-wing party's pawn.

She stared at the agenda. A low buzzing from outside sent a chill down her spine. She walked over to the window. The sound grew louder, triggering a memory of when she was six years old. She and her mother had gone to Mumbai to visit her aunt. They were walking near the Parsee Tower of Silence when a vulture let out the same throaty noise before dropping a half-chewed human hand. It landed a foot away from Meena's little nose, causing nightmares for months.

She slammed the window shut, turned on the window air conditioner, and tried to focus on the agenda. Was H. C. Tewari really the right person to introduce Madhav? Should Kesh present the LEED Platinum plaque before or after the home minister's speech? Could she get those bloody politicians to limit their speeches to five or ten minutes?

Then Gita's voice, like a phantom. *Sanjeev's got hard evidence the national temple program is a national prostitution ring.* He claimed to have photos of three cabinet ministers and some of the country's top industrialists entering and leaving the residential quarters of the newly installed devadasis in Puri, Madurai, and Tanjavur. And of one minister in the act! But he said he needed more dirt to bring the party to its knees. He refused to hand anything over until he caught every last stinking HDP fish in his net. That would take time, and he predicted his article would come out no sooner than mid-October. His reputation was more important than her inauguration. Too bad.

Meena had confronted Madhav with the hearsay, but her boss dismissed any accusations as vicious rumors spread by the opposition. She cursed Sanjeev, who refused to let Gita see the photos until he had finished his job. "Trust me," his mantra.

Meena's eyes were fixed on the agenda, but she didn't see the words. Instead, images of the burned and scarred bodies of Behera House residents flashed before her like pictures on a deck of cards. *Why can't that damned journalist break his story before the inauguration?* More than anything, she wanted the scandal to surface so she could tell Tewari and his HDP to take a long hike. *If Sanjeev can finish up in three and a half weeks, why can't he bust his whippersnapper ass and be done in ten days? Can two more weeks really make that big a difference?*

She tried to convince herself that any criminal activity at the temples was confined to one or two individuals. But deep down, she feared the problem was not just her husband or a few bad apples, but crates of them. She bristled at the idea that the HDP Foundation grant, which funded half of the construction costs, might have come from the priest pimping those young temple dancers. But she remembered the devadasis were recruited more than a year after the HDP funding had been dispersed. A small consolation.

Meena gazed into space. Sanjeev's head is filled with rubbish. All his talk of becoming India's Bob Woodward was playing games with his mind. *That's why he keeps telling Gita he needs more time—he doesn't have anything!* And all those talking heads blabbering on about how the HDP wants to bring back sati—*where's the evidence?* Just one article the prime minister wrote twenty years ago in college?

After she had made a few minor changes to the agenda, her mind boomeranged back to the HDP. The party operatives were trying to turn the ceremony into some outlandish Vedic rite, complete with chanting priests and a sacrificial fire. Feeling a sharp pain in her neck, she reached for a vial of Tiger Balm. She rubbed the ointment into her neck and thought about Simon, who was in Japan receiving an award. "He needs another award like he needs a hole in the head," she said under her breath, amused by the expression she'd recently heard from Gita.

Suddenly, a loud knock on the front door. She glanced at her watch: 11:30 p.m. What the hell?

"Who is it?" she called out.

"A. J. Kulkarni, deputy commissioner of police."

Had the prime minister changed his mind about making an appearance? Or, better, had he agreed to postpone the inauguration? Most likely it was some idiotic security issue. Without opening the door, she reminded the DCP of the time and asked him to come back in the morning. But Kulkarni insisted. She sighed deeply and told him to wait a minute. She scurried to the bathroom, washed the papaya mask from her face, and rushed back to the front door.

Kulkarni entered and suggested Meena take a seat. He wasted no time in relating the tragic news: her husband's body was discovered at the Sompur Jagannath Temple at 8:05 p.m. Mr. Narayan, he explained, was being "entertained" by Amrita, the devadasi, in the temple workshop. The coroner put the time of death between 5:00 and 7:30 p.m. The DCP tried to describe the circumstances of Kesh's death, but Meena kept interrupting, insisting he had the wrong person. Her husband had gone to New Delhi for a business meeting. Kulkarni had to repeat three times that the body was identified by the priest, who had arranged the assignation.

Meena froze like a glacier, which soon melted in a flood of tears. After a long silence, she started to squirm in her seat. She reached for a glass of water and almost lost her balance, as if the glacier were slipping into the sea. She caught herself, stood up, and started pacing the room like a sleepwalker.

Kulkarni's words were tactful, but there was no hiding the fact that her husband was in the temple workshop for sex. The DCP finally described the godown and offered his theory: Kesh or Amrita must have bumped into the massive scaffolding and knocked it down. A statue struck Kesh on the head, inducing a concussion or even death. The burlap curtain cover fell onto the oil lamp and caught fire, igniting the sheets and mattress, along with everything else. Kesh was probably unconscious before the fire broke out. Thus, his death was most likely quick and relatively painless. There was no evidence of foul play. The DCP offered to take Meena to the city morgue, but he warned that her deceased husband was not a pretty sight. She declined and Kulkarni took his leave.

Meena lay down on the couch and began to sob, at times choking with spasms and unable to breathe. She did not want to see Kesh's charred body, she thought, squeezing her soaked handkerchief. Not that night, not in the morning. And what would she tell her parents and relatives, Kesh's colleagues and friends? That he was struck dead by an avalanche of marble statues of naked dancing girls?

She dragged herself into the bathroom to pee. But she couldn't hold it, and a few drops trickled down her leg. It seemed like every part of her was weeping. She splashed water on her face and gazed into the mirror. Her eyes were as red as overripe tomatoes oozing juice.

Meena called Simon at his Tokyo hotel, waking him. Her words gushed out like water from a broken main. Simon kept asking, "Who's Shesh?" She repeated his name three times before he understood it was

Kesh. He promised to catch a flight to India the minute the award ceremony was over. Unfortunately, the Tokyo event was pushed back a day on account of a powerful earthquake, whose epicenter was three hundred miles southeast of the capital. So far eleven bodies had been recovered; organizers decided it wouldn't look good to be handing out an international award for architecture before the search for bodies was complete.

Meena hung up and wondered if Kesh's death could have caused the earth to tremble as far away as Japan. He was such a force of nature! She sat on the kitchen stool with her legs crossed, frantically jiggling her foot. A sharp cramp arose in her stomach. Was she getting her period? No, she just had it. It took ten minutes for the pain to subside. Then more worries. She would call the DCP first thing in the morning and insist he not speak to the press. But what about the priest—could that maggot keep quiet? My dear God, Kesh hammered by an erotic statue. And probably wearing one of those blasted girdles! The symbolism was not lost on her. She recalled how Kesh recently accused her of being cold as marble. It was as if she were the cold, hard statue that crushed him. She began to reflect on the sorry state of their marriage, but her mind was soon flooded with memories of their younger days. Kesh's passion for the environment. His unstoppable zeal to change the country's construction industry. His recitations of Sanskrit love poetry.

It was nearly three in the morning when Meena lay down on her bed. She managed to get a few hours of sleep. At dawn, she made a strong cup of tea and steeled herself to call her parents and close friends. She invited them to a cremation ceremony on Sunday. However, she decided Simon should stay away, lest his presence fuel speculation about their relationship. He could join the funeral gathering at her home, which would follow.

CHAPTER 25

Family and friends welcomed each other with tearful embraces and the customary greeting: *ifonlyweweremeetingaftersuchalongtimeunderhappiercircumstances. Ifonlyifonly* . . . The ceremony lasted less than an hour: just what Kesh would have wanted. "Life's a one-act play," he liked to say. "A tragicomedy. When I go, I'm gone. Don't fuss over me, don't waste money on priests who croak like bullfrogs in a muddy pond, and, for God's sake, don't crack my skull open to liberate my soul. I like my head just the way it is, thank you very much. And, of course, make sure I'm cremated in an electric crematorium. Solar-powered, if possible. If even one tree is cut down for a funeral pyre, I'll come back as the Lorax to haunt you."

Following the cremation, everyone piled into cars and drove to Meena's house. Her parents, Satish and Kiran, who had arrived from New Delhi; Lok Narayan, Kesh's uncle, a retired four-star general, and his wife Rekha, who sings ragas from morning until night, had driven in from Kolkata; Kesh's younger sister Happy (who wasn't) and her husband Harsh (who was), managing director of Central Railway Information Systems, had flown in from Mumbai. Also, from New Delhi was Ramesh, Kesh's deputy; and, from Baroda, Jitendra "Whispers" Shah, Kesh's oldest childhood friend, who believed the only way to get attention in a noisy world was to speak so softly that nobody could hear him.

After a few swigs of scotch, Harsh, Kesh's brother-in-law, turned to Meena and asked, "So, tell us again how Kesh actually died?" Meena kept the explanation simple, if not entirely truthful: he was in the temple workshop with Upadhyaya, his longtime friend and head priest, when the scaffolding bearing marble statues accidentally toppled over, causing a fatal blow to Kesh's skull. Somehow, the priest managed to walk away unscathed. To avoid questions, Meena quickly disappeared into the kitchen.

"Was the poor chap hit on the head by one of those naked *yakshis*?" Uncle Lok chuckled. "Those mythical earth spirits?"

"She didn't say they were naked!" scolded his wife, Rekha.

"Come on, girl," snapped Lok. "What temple statues in this bloody country aren't naked? It's our ancient porn." He lit a cigarette. "And those *yakshis* with their wide hips and overripe boobs—they're the worst! Well, it's tragic, all right, but an apt ending for dear old Kesh. I mean, if he had to go."

Rekha, who never drank, smoked, or ate an egg, looked appalled. She was demanding an apology when a teenage girl came around with a tray of sweets. She eyed them cautiously before taking a *ladoo*, a marigold-colored ball made of gram flour and enough sugar to fill her handbag. She hesitated, then added a *rasgulla*, a spongy sweet made of buffalo milk.

Uncle Lok started talking about how Kesh was just like his father, the infamous maharaja of Gond "whose libido had no off switch." As soon as Meena emerged from the kitchen, everyone hushed up and smiled as if posing for a photograph. Then Happy, Kesh's sister, regaled everyone with a story about the time Kesh, at fourteen, blindfolded his pet elephant and set it loose in the women's quarters. The boy laughed his head off as his father's courtesans flew out of the *zenana* half naked. Meena smiled politely, but, unable to stand the chatter, soon escaped to the backyard. She sat under a *Gulmohar* tree, which seemed to be burning with fiery red blossoms, and wept.

Lok turned to Simon. "And how well did you know my nephew?"

"Not well at all, but I admired Kesh for his big ideas and sense of humor, although I have to admit half his jokes were lost on me."

"Big ideas," Aunt Rekha repeated scornfully. "Don't worry, Simon. Nobody understood him, especially after he'd had a few drinks."

"There's nothing wrong with a drinkie once in a while," Lok quipped, casting an admonishing glance at his wife. "In fact, I'd rather like another whiskey myself." He snapped his fingers to get the attention of a boy circulating with drinks. "Anyway, Kesh was a teetotaler compared with my maharaja brother, the mad bugger!"

"Poor Kesh," Rekha wailed. "His own father never had any time for his only son. Sending him away to Eton like that."

"Nonsense!" Lok shot back. "Nothing wrong with a boarding school to whip a young boy into shape. And Eton's not just any boarding school."

"Yes, but at such a tender age." Rekha cringed. "No wonder he ended up like that."

"Like what?"

"I don't know. Like someone who's always, you know, not having children and ignoring his beautiful wife."

"Kesh wasn't—" Lok stopped in mid-sentence when Meena suddenly appeared, as if his mouth had short-circuited. Meena sat on the couch between Simon and her mother, who asked where Kesh wanted his ashes scattered.

"In the Himalayas," Meena replied. "But when I once asked him, 'Where in the Himalayas? It's a big place,' he just smiled and said, 'Surprise me!'"

Everyone laughed with a collective nod, as if to say, *yes, that was Kesh, all right!*

The conversation turned to Kesh's work. Ramesh, dressed in a starched pink shirt and bow tie, mentioned Kesh's scheme to have twenty-five percent of the country's train stations outfitted with hybrid solar-wind energy systems by 2010.

Meena kept blanking out, alternating between visions of Kesh engulfed in flames and priests enacting ancient fire rituals at the upcoming inauguration. She thought of the burnt faces of some of the residents at Behera House. She wanted to escape the gathering, to crawl into a hole and die. Without thinking, she leaned her head on Simon's shoulder, but her mother nudged her to sit up. Happy was telling everyone how she and her brother used to chase peacocks on the vast lawns around the palace when the doorbell rang. Meena excused herself again.

"Oh, how Kesh would carry on about this and that subject," Rekha groaned. "I doubt he ever took the time to just be quiet and listen to his inner voice."

"He was a good conversationalist, dear," Lok replied. "Nothing wrong with that!"

"Happy, here, thinks Kesh began talking so much to cover up that ghastly twitch when he was a boy," Harsh said. "She would say how the left corner of his mouth would hike up every thirty seconds. On the dot—you could have timed your soft-boiled eggs to that damn twitch!"

Happy elbowed Harsh as Meena crossed the room with a bouquet of flowers and disappeared into the kitchen.

"He could be so damn funny," Lok said. "I'll never forget the day when we were watching a cricket game on TV and one of the cricketers adjusted himself right in front of the camera. Kesh joked about how Indian men are always doing it in public."

"Please don't," interrupted Rekha, gripping the end of her sari and pulling it over her head.

"Don't *please don't* me," Lok snapped, holding a whiskey between his legs as he lit another cigarette. "It's what Indian men do. So, we're watching this cricket game and Kesh is going on and on about how politicians are the worst of the lot. He swore they adjusted themselves in public not because they needed to, but in order to bond with their male constituents—like George Bush wearing that daft cowboy hat to show he's just a regular dude."

"What rubbish," Rekha said, pulling the end of her sari further over her face.

Lok continued, quoting Kesh. "'So, a politician's campaigning at a rally and it's 2 p.m., so what does he think? Time to scratch my balls. It's probably the only thing that's done on time in this bloody country.' Man, oh, man, was he funny!" Lok slapped his thigh. "'If an Indian politician loses an election,' Kesh says, 'I'll bet the first thing his campaign manager tells him is, *Babaji, what I tell you. You should have scratched on the half hour too, or at least adjusted only!*'"

The men howled, while the women started talking among themselves, pretending they weren't listening. Meena returned with the bouquet in a purple vase and the laughter evaporated into the smoky air.

"Simon," Ramesh asked, "did you know Kesh has started a scheme to have one hundred schools outfitted with solar panels? He had negotiated a deal with Reliance Energy—that's one of our biggest private utility companies—to own and operate the systems. The schools would only pay for the electricity. He wanted to make schools living labs, where students would learn about renewable energy. He said students should feel like they're part of the solution to climate change, not part of the problem."

Meena's cell phone rang. She answered it and cupped her hand over her ear to block out the noise. Then she walked into the study where it was quiet. A minute later she reappeared, looking frazzled, as if she'd put her finger into an electric outlet.

"That was Madhav's personal assistant," she sputtered. "Madhav, I mean Mr. Behera . . . he . . . he suffered a massive heart attack. This afternoon, playing golf . . . at the Bombay Presidential Golf Club in Mumbai. He, he died three hours later at Breach Candy Hospital." Meena's eyes closed, and she dropped to the floor.

"Oh, my God," Rekha yelled. "She's fainted!"

Simon rushed over to her. In an operatic performance, he loosened the tucked-in pleats of her sari, raised her legs above her heart, and cradled her limp body in his arms. Everyone looked on in amazement.

CHAPTER 26

Meena tossed and turned all night. She dreamed she was giving a speech at the inauguration when Upadhyaya snuck up from behind and pushed her off the dais. Suddenly, she was falling down a chute toward a raging fire. The phone rang just before her alarm was set to go off at 7 a.m.—a moment before she was about to plunge into the blaze.

It was an HDP operative. In a voice sounding like Marlon Brando in *The Godfather*, the caller warned Meena to abandon any thought of ditching the HDP before the inauguration, only six days away. *How do these morons know what I'm thinking?* If she tried to cut ties with the HDP, the government would accuse Gita Sen of murdering Kesh. He made a special point of saying how such an indictment would destroy the reputation of the new Lalita Devi Center. When Meena countered that the idea was ridiculous—*it was an accident; why in the world would Gita want to kill Kesh?*—the man assured her the HDP was perfectly capable of staging a trial that would result in her deputy's conviction, guilty or not.

After hanging up, Meena sat in her easy chair and wondered why she shouldn't ditch the Hindu party, since the campus was built and paid up, especially now that Madhav was gone. She reached for a jar of English Breakfast tea and thought more about the caller's threat. Blaming Gita for her husband's death was absurd. But it could strike a fatal blow to the Lalita Devi Center if the lie stuck. Those bastards are clever. *They know full well I wouldn't jeopardize the reputation of the institute, much less betray my deputy.* The thought of Gita rotting away in some godforsaken prison for a crime she did not commit was unthinkable.

The teapot started to whistle just as the phone rang again. She hurried to the stove and turned off the heat. By the time she got to the phone, the caller had hung up. It rang again. She let it ring five or six times before picking up. It was Kulkarni, who wanted to know if Simon would come to the police headquarters for a brief discussion. The DCP had questions about the green building industry and LEED certification—questions that might shed light on Kesh's death. Kulkarni added there was new evidence. He was no longer ruling out murder.

Murder?

Meena sat down again and sipped her tea so slowly she could have been rehearsing for a Noh drama. The only part of her body that moved was her right arm—from her lap to her mouth and back again. She eventually called Simon, but she didn't speak for a few seconds. He kept asking if anyone was there. She finally identified herself, but then forgot why she called. It took the better half of a minute to say the DCP wanted to see him.

———◆———

Simon was unable to find a taxi, so he boarded an auto-rickshaw. It rattled through the lawless streets to the police headquarters. He was relieved to get away from his shabby hotel. And from Meena, whose sadness wrapped around her like a second sari. But his mood soured when the rickshaw drove over a speed hump and he banged his head on the metal bar supporting the canvas roof. He slouched the rest of the trip, occasionally fingering the bump on his scalp.

The vehicle passed four men carrying a litter bearing a shrouded corpse. Simon thought about Kesh. How he had said, "Surprise me," when Meena asked where in the Himalayas he wanted his ashes to be scattered. His mind veered to the story about Indian men adjusting themselves in public. Simon laughed out loud. Why wasn't *he* lighthearted and witty like Kesh? Simon couldn't remember the last time he made a joke or a funny remark out of the blue.

Envy quickly morphed into guilt. What the hell was he doing running after Meena when her husband hadn't been dead a week? Surely, he could wait, if not abandon his quest altogether. But for how long? Two weeks, a month, a year? Then he felt guilty that he felt so little guilt, about either wanting Meena or betraying his own wife. Had his heart run out of batteries?

The auto-rickshaw passed a cinema. A long line had formed below a giant billboard. It showed a mustached soldier who looked like evil personified pursuing a woman whose breasts resembled two anti-aircraft missiles. *Now that's pure and unadulterated lust,* Simon thought, trying to console himself. His desire for Meena was somehow different. Purer. Wasn't it? And weren't both their marriages faltering or, worse, in an advanced state of decay?

He began to ponder how to win her affection. The ticket to Meena's heart, he concluded, was helping her defuse the time bomb the HDP planted under her feet. It was ticking away, set to go off at the inauguration in six short days. But what could he do? He might be a starchitect, but his star didn't shine in the treacherous skies of Indian politics. The rickshaw jerked to a stop.

The reception area of the police headquarters looked like it hadn't been painted in a hundred years. A calendar advertising Rajendra Prasad's Auto Service hung on the wall. Insects dashed against a humming tube lamp. Below, a bright green gecko stood motionless. Simon announced himself and was asked to take a seat. He settled into a wooden chair and overheard two middle-aged women seated across from him.

"Did you read about the young boy who fell into the construction site in New Delhi?" the thinner one asked her rotund friend. "In Golf Links, such a nice, quiet neighborhood, too. And now they're ruining it with that glitzy hotel."

"No, tell me."

"The boy—I read he was only six—fell into the foundation and hit his head on a bulldozer. Poor little thing! He died immediately." The gecko suddenly sprang into action, scurrying across the wall. "How tragic, isn't it? And that poor mother, who was working as a day-laborer for a few measly rupees a day!"

"Yes, very sad," replied the rotund woman, making the bitter lemon face and wagging her head.

"By the way, what's LEEDS?" the thin woman asked. "It's plastered all over the wall around the construction site." The woman pulled a newspaper from her bag and turned a few pages. "There," she said, handing the paper to her friend.

"LEED? I don't know. It must be the name of the five-star hotel going up."

Simon's head began to ache, as if *it* had hit the bulldozer. The two women were called into a meeting with a junior police officer. Simon moved to a seat closer to Kulkarni's office, where he could hear

Kulkarni's angry voice.

"And call the new Ministry of Construction, *whatshisname*, Bhandari, R. K. Bhandari, who's in charge of energy efficiency. Find out what Narayan was up to. Whether he'd been lobbying the government to require LEED for government projects. I mean other than the goddamn Technocities! And find out if Himco has any hope in hell of selling its chillers to those IT companies . . . Yes, the ones moving into those bloody Technocities. I mean, now that they need to be LEED certified . . . What do I mean? I mean whether Himco's chillers are good enough for LEED, damn it! . . . I don't care; consult an HVAC engineer if you bloody have to!"

A young uniformed man exited, shutting the door behind him. A few minutes later the door opened again. Kulkarni emerged and welcomed Simon into his office. It was a large room furnished with two wooden chairs facing a metal desk. Stacks of pink and green binders, each neatly tied up with colored string, covered most of the surface. A peon appeared with two cups of chai. Simon couldn't imagine what his triglyceride level would be after just a week in India. *What nonsense, Kesh jabbering about how the national taste is bitter lemon. It's sugar.*

The deputy commissioner of police thanked Simon for coming and remarked on the strange coincidence of events that took the lives of both Kesh and Behera within the same week. Then he asked Simon to treat everything he said as confidential. Kulkarni was under strict orders not to investigate Kesh's death. It was to be written off as an accident, pure and simple.

But the DCP said he wasn't buying the goods, and he treated Simon to his speculations. According to the priest, there was nothing to explain why the scaffolding would have come crashing to the floor. Either someone snuck in during their tryst and pulled the massive structure down, or the devadasi did it herself. If someone snuck in—or was hiding in the workshop all along—why hadn't it landed on both Narayan and the devadasi? But there was no second body. As the police officer talked, he kept pushing his lower lip up over his upper lip, as if he were trying to touch his nose.

"So, it was the devadasi?" Simon asked, raising his eyebrows.

Kulkarni reached for a pack of Gold Flake and shook it. Three or four cigarettes popped up. He pulled the top one out, flung the pack onto the desk, and walked over to the window, the unlit cigarette hanging from his mouth. He struggled to open it. "Goddamn thing's always stuck." He gave it a hard yank and the window jerked up with an awful screech. He lit up and sat back down.

"That's what I thought at first, since she, the devadasi, seems to have run away. But where's the motive? I mean, why kill Narayan?" Kulkarni flicked some ash into a red plastic ashtray with the words *Drink Campa Cola* printed across the edge. "No, I don't think it was the devadasi, unless, of course, she was paid to do it."

"Well, then, who *do* you suspect?"

"I'm getting to that. We found a half-empty pack of cigarettes. Four Squares. Narayan smoked Gauloises. Four Squares is a popular brand—there must be a hundred million men in India who smoke them. Now Upadhyaya doesn't smoke, and it's unlikely that his workers would smoke a brand like Four Squares, which is pricey. And I doubt the devadasi smoked anything, except maybe an occasional *beedi*. So, I'm guessing the pack wasn't in the workshop prior to the rendezvous."

Why is he telling me all this?

"There were fingerprints on the pack, but we haven't been able to identify them yet. But a phone number is scribbled on the back of the aluminum wrapper." Kulkarni reached into a box on his desk and pulled out two plastic bags with large white labels: *CASE 144W: Specimen A* and *CASE 144W: Specimen B*. One bag contained a pack of cigarettes. The other, an empty glass jar with a red and white checkered top. Simon felt like he had walked into the wrong club. It was all very interesting, but why was the DCP confiding in him, an American architect, as if they were buddies?

"We've traced the number—it belongs to a Mr. Arun Gupta, who is an advisor to the president of Himco, Behera's air-conditioning company. As far as I can tell, he's the only one with a motive."

"Which is?"

"To stop Kesh from pushing his proposal to change LEED, that green building certification. So, tell me something, Mr. Bliss," Kulkarni asked, sitting back in his chair. "I know LEED buildings use less air conditioning than those merely built to code. But what are we talking about?"

Was the DCP implying a Himco advisor killed Kesh to protect his client's air-conditioning business? But would someone murder for that? Simon started to explain how various green building strategies reduce air-conditioning loads by different percentages under differing conditions, but the DCP was in no mood for an academic lecture. He was looking for a ballpark figure. After several false starts, Simon stated, "LEED buildings are so tightly constructed they require smaller chillers."

"How much smaller?"

"Typically, they have twenty to forty percent less air conditioning capacity." Simon explained that many projects accumulate LEED points through cheaper measures that don't affect the energy load, such as incorporating recycled materials or bathroom fixtures that use less water. He emphasized that the rating system was very egalitarian: one LEED point was as good as any other LEED point—a fact that drove Kesh crazy. "Kesh once told me LEED should be more like India and institute a caste system. Energy points would be the Brahmins and should be required, since they're morally superior."

"Morally superior?"

"Yes, Kesh's words. His point was that all LEED projects should be required to use less energy than what's mandated by code. This, Kesh thought, should be nonnegotiable."

"Okay," replied Kulkarni. "Now let's consider what would have happened if Kesh had succeeded in closing that energy loophole. Would Himco be at a disadvantage selling its cooling systems into projects going for LEED? What I mean is, would Himco's systems be efficient *enough* for LEED?"

Simon confessed he knew nothing about Himco's products, but said most energy savings came from better design strategies and not from cooling systems. A project using a less efficient chiller might still have a chance of getting certified under a revised rating system. He launched into a sermon on the merits of improving a building's thermal envelope.

"Please, let's keep this simple, Mr. Bliss. Let's assume Marriott is building a five-star hotel in Mumbai and wants it to get LEED certification. Would Marriott be less likely to go with a Himco chiller if it had to reduce the building's energy demand to twenty-five percent *below* the industry standard? Wasn't that the magic number Narayan was going after?"

Simon explained that hotel companies like Marriott don't build hotels—they are contracted to manage buildings after construction. That being said, he expressed doubt whether an international real estate developer looking to have his building operated by a hotel company like Marriott would incorporate a Himco chiller, whether the project was going for LEED or not. He explained that big hotels depend on the absolute reliability of these systems for their business. They don't take chances with local brands. Moreover, big international real estate companies have worldwide procurement contracts with foreign brands like Carrier and Trane. Simon didn't think Himco had a shot at selling cooling systems to the likes of a building that would be managed by Marriott. He added that chip manufacturers moving into the Technocities were even less likely to go with a Himco system, since they depend on high-performance air-conditioning systems for their production process. Simon didn't want to speculate about domestic firms, especially those that just assemble computer parts for foreign companies, like Dell or IBM.

Kulkarni listened attentively. The tips of his long fingers touched each other lightly, forming a steeple. When Simon was done, the police officer pulled the empty jar from one of the plastic bags. "This was also found at the scene."

Simon leaned forward and stared at the label. *Bonne Maman: Wild Blueberry. Product of France.*

"Now, I'm not an expert on sexual dalliances," Kulkarni continued, "but I doubt Narayan and Amrita were eating a lot of French bread with jam that evening. Do you see the dry white powder inside?"

"That chalky stuff?"

"Yes. I'm sending it off to forensics. It's probably nothing, but you never know." The DCP returned the jar to the bag. "So, the question I'm asking myself is, how did this jar get into the workroom?"

"Mr. Kulkarni, do you mind telling me why you were ordered not to investigate the case?"

"Mr. Bliss, you're an American and can't be expected to understand the ins and outs of Indian politics. Let me just say the ruling party has a vested interest in the success of Ms. Kaul's institute. Behera House has an impressive track record of helping women who have suffered domestic violence. There's no mystery why the HDP hitched its wagon to her organization before the national election, when it was scrambling for the women's vote. And even now that the HDP is in power, it has a vested interest in looking progressive and keeping women on board. If someone high up in the HDP suspects that Himco—a Behera Group company—was behind Mr. Narayan's death, well, they wouldn't want that fact advertised, would they?"

"I see."

"I also believe the Hindu party has something else up its dirty sleeve when it comes to women," Kulkarni continued. "Something that could alienate large swaths of women voters, as well as progressives, and, well, just about everyone else with a sense of decency. I'm not ready to say what that is. But, if I'm right, the HDP is going to need Ms. Kaul's center more than ever after it shows its full hand. Anything that might sully the good reputation of Behera House—or should I now say the Lalita Devi Center—could obstruct the party's bigger game plan."

"Like a murder."

"Exactly. Now think back to what I said earlier: the only person I can think of with a motive to kill Narayan is Arun Gupta, the Himco advisor. As I said, just imagine if it got out that a *Behera* company executive had eliminated the husband of the director of *Behera* House. Not so good for HDP's business, wouldn't you say? Moreover, Mr. Behera was a major contributor to the party, and the HDP will surely be wooing his widow to keep the money spigot open. It would be a bit awkward for those bastards to approach the grande dame if a senior advisor to a Behera company were indicted for murdering the husband of the executive director of her husband's pet project, wouldn't you say?"

"Okay, I get it," Simon replied, "but I'm really not sure Gupta did have a motive, if by that you mean Himco's air-conditioning business was threatened by Kesh's proposal. As I said, it is unlikely that multinational companies would buy Himco systems with or without the changes he's been pushing for LEED."

"You may be right—after all, you're the expert—but do you think the HDP has the faintest idea how LEED really works? It would be easy for someone high up in the party to conclude Narayan's proposal would hurt Himco's sales. Look how quickly I jumped to that conclusion."

"Wait. What are you saying? That the Himco advisor, what's his name, may not have committed the murder, but that someone in the HDP might think he did?"

"I don't really know who committed the murder. But I assume that someone high up in the HDP called my boss and told him this crime shouldn't be investigated. Why? Because that someone *suspects* Himco is involved."

Simon thought about the HDP operative's threat to Meena: if she cut her ties to the party, it would make sure Gita was indicted. That would be convenient for the HDP, since it would let Gupta and Himco off the hook. Of course, if Meena were to break her ties with the HDP, the party would still care about the reputation of her institute, which it funded. And, it *would* care about Mrs. Behera's continued support, which would be jeopardized if Gupta were indicted.

Kulkarni's intercom buzzed and a secretary announced his next appointment had arrived. He glanced at his watch. "You've been very generous with your time, Mr. Bliss. Thank you so much for coming in. Now, if you'll excuse me . . ."

The men stood and shook hands. As Simon walked to the door, he heard the officer's footsteps behind him. A moment later a heavy hand landed on his shoulder.

"Mr. Bliss, I've been ordered not to investigate Narayan's death. But there's nothing preventing *you* from finding out what you can. I'm still betting on Arun Gupta, even after hearing your doubts. You might want to pay him a visit. I'd also have a little chinwag with that two-faced priest." The DCP handed Simon a piece of paper with Gupta's contact information in Mumbai. "Just an idea."

Without thinking, Simon wagged his head. He walked onto the street and shrugged off a beggar. The idea of poking his nose into the circumstances of Kesh's murder—if it even was murder—seemed outrageous. If Gupta did kill Kesh to stop him from meddling with LEED, wouldn't Simon want to let sleeping dogs lie? Uncovering a link between Himco and Kesh's death would be just as bad for Meena as for the HDP. Simon stuffed the paper into his pocket and started walking in no particular direction. A few schoolchildren shouted, "What is your name?" and giggled as he passed.

The sky darkened; it soon burst open and drenched him. There was no taxi or rickshaw in sight. Across the street an old, toothless woman sat on the step of a shrine stringing marigolds into garlands. An Indian businessman approached and offered Simon his umbrella. The man said he was used to late monsoon showers. Simon thanked him for his offer and insisted he was fine, but the stranger would not take no for an answer. He pressed the open umbrella into Simon's hand and walked on.

Simon closed it and stood still, like a madman, as the rain poured onto him. It brought back the memory of his monsoon treatment—the twelve-hour shower that was supposed to flush the chemicals out of his teenage body after his accident. Then his mother's voice. *You've been through a monsoon without even making a trip to India.* He smiled as a taxi pulled up and asked where he was going. Simon shook his head. After a few minutes, he began to walk through the rain, the folded umbrella dangling from his wrist. He thought of Raj, his old neighbor, and had a sudden urge to find him. Yes, he thought, he would go to Mumbai to interview Gupta and, afterward, head to Colgate India. Why not?

CHAPTER 27

Meena puttered around the kitchen waiting for Gita. She nervously rearranged appliances on the counters and took items in and out of drawers: napkins, rubber bands, an egg timer, whatever. If only her eyes had windshield wipers, she thought as the tears started to irrigate her cheeks once more. Kesh stone dead, and now Madhav. They say three-fourths of human body weight is water—now she believed it. It seemed like her tears could raise the level of the oceans. She chuckled at the thought that her grieving could undo years of Kesh's effort fighting climate change.

Gita showed up around ten with a bag of croissants from La Madeleine, the new French bakery. They sat in the open courtyard, shaded by a blossoming jacaranda tree. Two white-throated kingfishers played cat and mouse as the women savored the buttery treats with spice tea. After breakfast, Gita offered to rub Meena's shoulders. Why not, Meena mused. She felt like someone who had been mugged in an alleyway and left for dead.

As Gita pressed her thumbs into her tight muscles, Meena was distracted by thoughts of the inauguration. Would the HDP hijack the ceremony with their dreadful speakers? And was it serious about carting in half-naked priests, who would drone on forever as they poured clarified butter into a sacrificial fire? Why not add some bears riding bicycles and a trapeze artist? She cringed at the thought of an HDP flag on the dais. What would the residents think seeing a Vedic altar with a ritual fire, especially those who had suffered burns? An image of Kesh flashed through her mind. *I warn you, Ms. Kaul, your deceased husband is not a pretty sight.* And now, the holier-than-thou prime minister was confirmed. Would he mount the podium and start singing the praises of auto-urine therapy? And why did the HDP insist she use the full name of the institute every time she mentions it? *The Lalita Devi Center for the Advancement of Women.* How utterly pretentious, as if we were some Washington think tank!

"Ouch, that's too much," Meena squeaked. "Softer, please."

Meena felt so alone as Gita's fingertips pressed into her skin. To whom could she turn? Madhav was gone, and Gita's advice had proved useless. Her deputy still hoped to convince Sanjeev to break the story before the big event. Bloody fat chance! The fate of the new campus was not his priority. As he so eloquently put it, he's got bigger fish to fry.

"I hope you won't forget how difficult Kesh could be," Gita said as her hands migrated to the middle of Meena's back. "I'm sure you're grieving, but maybe there's a silver lining to his passing."

"Did you say silver lining?"

"I don't know," Gita drawled, moving her fingers toward Meena's lower back, "it's just that he could be so . . ."

"Difficult?"

"Well, yes."

"Why don't we go inside where you can lie down on the couch?"

Gita asked. "And how about some oil? You can pretend you're at some fancy spa in Paris or London."

Fearing oil could drip onto the couch, Meena suggested they move to the bedroom. She removed her shirt, undid her bra, and lay on her stomach. Gita straddled her just below the buttocks and began to rub lavender oil into Meena's back, drawing her whole forearm up and down in slow, broad strokes.

"Do you remember when Kesh was in the hospital after his motorcycle accident?" Gita said.

"Yes. It was a year ago, almost to the day. I was in Mumbai and asked if you would visit him and bring flowers." How could she forget? It was the day she lured Simon to her hotel after he presented his preliminary design.

"Well, Kesh and I had a long conversation—if one could call it that—and he told me he was planning to leave you and run away with the first devadasi."

"My dear Gita, you mustn't believe half the things that man said. You know how Kesh likes—liked to talk rubbish just to get a reaction."

"And do you know what I said? 'Good! Then Meena and I can be together.'"

"What on earth are you talking about?"

"I was just pulling his leg, since he thought I'm some kind of flaming lesbian feminist." Gita paused before speaking again. "Do you mind if I ask you a personal question?"

"Of course not."

"Have you ever wondered what it would be like to be with a woman?"

"No, not really."

Gita bent down and slid her hands under Meena's torso and began to caress her breasts. "Does that feel good?"

"Yes, Gita, but, no, I'm not comfortable with that."

"Why not? Because I'm gay?"

"Well, yes, I suppose, if I'm being honest."

Gita withdrew her hands and worked on Meena's lower back again. She applied a few drops of oil to Meena's arms and gently twisted the skin in opposite directions. Next, she massaged Meena's fingers, twisting and tugging each one. When she was done, she drew a small pipe and lump of hash from her pocket.

"Do you mind if I smoke?"

Meena twisted her upper body to look at Gita. She hesitated but gave her consent. Gita rolled off the bed, lit up, and inhaled deeply.

"I have a confession to make," Gita said as she smoked the pipe.

"A confession?"

"It's not easy to tell you this, but I owe it to you as a friend." Gita returned to the bed and gently ran her fingers up and down Meena's leg. "I sent some incriminating photos of H. C. Tewari to Arun Gupta, who is this hotshot advisor to the president of Himco. Sanjeev's photos, which I finagled out of him. I suggested he, Gupta, could use them to blackmail the dishonorable minister of home affairs. The photos showed Tewari fucking Amrita."

"I'm totally not getting this," Meena replied, turning onto her side and facing Gita. "You sent photos of Tewari, the home minister, screwing the devadasi? And you sent them to whom?"

"To Arun Gupta, this Himco chap. I suggested he forward the photos to Tewari with a little note."

"I'm still confused. How did you get photos from Sanjeev? And why would you send photos to Gupta? I thought we were out to get Tewari so we could break with the HDP. What does this Gupta person have to do with anything?"

"I wanted to kill two birds with one stone, as it were. You see, I talked with a staff person at the India Green Building Association. She told me that most of the air-conditioning companies, including Himco, were livid that Kesh had won the election. Apparently, Arun Gupta was organizing fellow industry members to call for a new election based on some trumped-up charge."

"You're kidding?"

"No. Gupta pulled together a coalition of companies that opposed Kesh. All those companies that make stuff that isn't very green."

"Gita, where are you going with all this?"

"Sorry, all I'm saying is that I came to realize there was no love lost for Kesh when it came to that Gupta chap. He wanted your husband to back off from his crusade to change LEED. To get his nose out of Himco's business. So, I thought I would help Gupta out by sending him some of Sanjeev's photos of Tewari dipping his pin-sized wick into dear Amrita, the devadasi."

"What?" exclaimed Meena, sitting straight up. "You what?"

"The man is no idiot. But like most businessmen, he lacks imagination. So, I included a note, suggesting he tell Tewari to find a way to stop Kesh's campaign to tighten the LEED requirements if he didn't want those photos to show up on the front page of the *Times of India*."

Meena shot up, practically throwing Gita off the bed. She covered her breasts with her shirt. "What on earth are you talking about?"

Gita repeated what she had just said.

"Let me see if I got this right. You somehow got hold of Sanjeev's photos and used them to get this Gupta person to blackmail Tewari so that he'd stop Kesh from changing IGBA's green building rating system?"

"Yes, that's it. I was hoping Tewari would just threaten Kesh. I wanted to give your husband a little scare, to clip his wings, that's all."

"Clip his wings? Is that what you just said?"

"Yes, give him a little manicure."

"A little manicure?"

"Let me finish."

Meena stepped back and felt dizzy. She gripped the top of a chair; her shirt slipped from the arm to the floor.

"Now, Gupta called me and said he liked the plan." Gita riffled through her pocketbook for more hash and lit the pipe again. "And please trust me when I say I was very explicit. I told the Himco chappie, 'Kesh is my boss's husband, so make sure Tewari doesn't do anything drastic. Just tell the minister of affairs, or should I say minister of secret affairs, to get Kesh to back off this LEED thing. I knew how much that would upset Kesh. That's all I wanted—to rile him up a tad. Really, I thought Tewari would just blackmail him. I had no idea the honorable minister would let his thugs loose on Kesh. That's so déclassé. These politicians really do lack imagination."

"What on earth are you saying? Tewari had Kesh murdered?"

"Well, I'm afraid—"

"Oh my God," Meena blurted. She picked up her shirt, pulled it over her head, and sank into the chair. She sat stunned for a full minute. She finally asked, "So what happened? He hired some thug to hide behind the scaffolding and push it down on top of Kesh?"

"I suppose."

"And Amrita? Was she paid to turn a blind eye or even help, since she appears to have come out unscathed? Is that what happened? TELL ME, GODDAMN IT!"

"I guess. I really don't know the details."

Meena's face turned into a giant scowl. "What the hell were you thinking?" She got up and paced the room, both fists tightly clenched.

"I suppose Tewari couldn't think of a way to blackmail Kesh, so he just, well, you know, had him bumped off. I really didn't think my plan would end this way. I'm terribly sorry."

"You're terribly sorry! IS THAT ALL YOU CAN SAY?"

Gita started to move toward Meena.

"Stop right where you are, and don't you dare come any closer!" Meena burst into tears and stomped her foot. "But why? Why did you want to help Gupta? What do *you* care about Himco or LEED?"

"I don't give a flying fuck about Himco or LEED. I just thought it would be easier to approach Gupta with my plan than going directly to Tewari. I felt nervous about blackmailing a minister. To clip Kesh's wings, that is."

"So, you had Gupta do your bidding?"

"Well, yes. I figured he would, since his day job is dreaming up ruthless schemes to promote Himco's business."

"Gita, you've gone mad!" Meena cried, holding her head with both hands. "But why? What did Kesh ever do to you?"

"Well, he tried to rape me, for one. That day in the hospital last year, after his motorcycle accident." Gita disclosed the incident in detail. But Meena brushed it aside, blaming his behavior on the morphine.

"And I thought we were friends," Meena groused before she burst into tears. "I can't believe you'd do this to me!"

"We *are* friends. You must believe me—I had absolutely no idea Tewari would have Kesh you know what. I'm so sorry, really, I am. And when I found out he hired thugs and had him, well, eliminated, I felt terrible . . . although, I have to admit, I did wonder whether you'd be relieved, I mean, at some deep level. And that you and I could—"

"Relieved?" shouted Meena, bolting from the chair. "Did you just say relieved? Gita, please leave this house immediately. I can't believe what you're telling me! You're not the Gita I know. Get out, this minute!"

"Well, if you're going to be like that," Gita huffed, climbing off the bed, "I'll go. But there's something else you might want to know. Something larger—and I'm not referring to your husband's *maha*-lingam."

"His maha-lingam?"

"Yes, his big dick!"

"Gita, that's enough. Now GO!"

"Don't you want to hear what Kesh said in the hospital when I asked him why he resorted to prostitutes and devadasis?"

"No, I've heard enough."

Gita grabbed her purse. "Well, I'll tell you. He said, 'Because I'm the boss. I do whatever I want, like give the naked hussies a good spanking and fuck them in the ass. They can't complain that they're too tired or have a headache or have too much bloody work. They do what they're told, like slaves!'"

"He did not!" Meena cried, chasing Gita out of the bedroom.

Gita scurried to the front door, then turned around abruptly. Her face softened, and her voice took on a pathetic, pleading tone. "Meena, do you really think Kesh was better than the brutes who beat their poor wives to pulp? Just think about the women who land up at Behera House. Try to imagine, for just a moment, what India would be like if we didn't have to take shit from men day after day."

"Gita," Meena said, her fists so tightly clenched her nails were digging into her palms, "my husband was not like the men who beat their wives. He was a big talker, but he wouldn't hurt a fly. Now get out of here. I've had more than I can take!" Her eyes narrowed. "You know, Gita, you're no better than those goddamn HDP fanatics who want to boot Muslims out of the country. Except you'd substitute men."

Gita's voice softened into a supplicating tone. "Don't you understand?

What I did wasn't just some act of women's liberation. I did it for us. Meena, I love you, and, well, to tell you the truth, I thought you were warming up to me, even sending me signals that you—"

"You WHAT?" Meena shouted. "YOU LOVE ME? YOU LOVE ME? And this is how you show your love—by hatching a plot to kill my husband? Gita, you're a coward! I thought we were friends. But I guess I was dead wrong. I'm done with you! Now get out of this house before I call the police!"

"Call if you like," Gita responded, running her hand through her short curly hair. "The police won't touch me."

"What? Do you think you can get away with murder?"

"Well, yes. First off, I didn't kill Kesh or even have him killed. Tewari did. And even if I had, do you think the HDP can afford to have the deputy director of the new Lalita Devi Center charged with murder? The very institute they've yoked their wagon to? There will be no murder charges against me or anyone else, Meena. I'm untouchable! Oh, I do like that. A true Dalit. It sounds so politically correct, so twenty-first-century!"

"You evil bitch!" Meena cried, suddenly remembering the threat from the HDP operative. Cut ties with the HDP and they'd pin Kesh's murder on Gita. *That's just what I should do!* She could cut all ties with the HDP and have the party arrest Gita for the crime. But she quickly realized her institute would be dragged right into the mud along with Gita.

"If you don't believe me," Gita continued, "I'll call the police and turn myself in right now."

"Gita, get out of my house this minute. It's people like you who are ruining India, not the likes of Kesh!"

Gita threw her bag over her shoulder and stomped out the front door. Meena collapsed onto the couch, only to spill another ocean of tears.

CHAPTER 28

The same day

Simon was heading to his hotel in an auto-rickshaw, still thinking about his meeting with DCP Kulkarni, when his cell phone rang. It was Meena. She sounded hysterical and insisted he come to her house straightaway. The rain and wind had picked up, pushing buckets of water into the open vehicle.

Meena answered the door in a sage-colored silk robe. "You're drenched! Let me get you some dry clothes." She disappeared and was soon back with Kesh's bathrobe. "Try this, I doubt anything else of Kesh's would fit you."

Simon changed into the robe covered with happy-looking panda bears. But before he could even sit, Meena's mouth was moving a hundred miles an hour, as if her jaw were hooked to an electric motor. It took her only a few minutes to recount Gita's confession in painstaking detail. When she finished, Simon produced a faint smile.

"Did I say something funny?"

"No, but there's a silver lining in the dark cloud of Gita's story."

"Are you out of your mind?"

"If she is telling the truth," Simon continued, gazing at his bare knees, "Kesh's murder went right up the chain of command to the home minister."

"So?"

"So, what if we could come up with some evidence that Gita sent Arun Gupta compromising photos to blackmail Tewari? The note Gita sent him, for example. Or even better, proof that Tewari ordered the murder?" He fiddled with the end of the belt, noticing that the last panda had no head. He remembered that one of the items found at the crime scene was the cigarette wrapper with Gupta's cell number scribbled on it. "Just one piece of evidence, and you could tell that Tewari bastard where to go. You'd be free of the whole Hindu cabal before the event this Sunday."

Suddenly, a crashing sound. Meena walked over to the window and saw a huge branch had come down.

Simon went to the window and looked out. "I just got an idea, an excuse you can use to postpone the inauguration. Something to give us time—more time to find the smoking gun we need to shove in Tewari's pockmarked face. Maybe even time enough for Sanjeev to break his story."

Simon suggested Meena call the HDP operative, who had left his number, and say the engineers who installed the solar panels on the community center discovered a flaw in the way they were attached. There was a risk one or both panels could come crashing down, hurting or even killing guests, even the PM. The manufacturer agreed to replace the mountings, but the changeover would take a month. Surely the inauguration could wait.

Meena liked the idea and made the call, but the operative wasn't buying the goods. Since the event was already in the prime minister's calendar, a change of date was out of the question. The prospect of a photo opportunity at Sunday's prestigious opening clearly outweighed the risk of a massive solar array nose-diving onto the heads of dignitaries. The HDP's priorities could not have been clearer.

Simon collapsed onto the couch. He remembered Kulkarni's final words to him. *Mr. Bliss, I've been ordered not to investigate Narayan's murder. But there's nothing preventing you from finding out what you can.* He told Meena what the DCP said and suggested he fly to Mumbai to interview Arun Gupta. Why not? Who knew what might turn up?

Meena pleaded with Simon not to get involved. Indian politics was a dangerous game, and she didn't want to lose him as well. But Simon was on autopilot. It was as if Kesh's restless spirit had wormed its way into his soul. He demanded his clothes and hurriedly changed back into them, even though they were still damp. He kissed Meena on the cheek, darted out of the house, and found a taxi to take him to the airport.

As the cab pulled onto the departure ramp, the driver claimed he had forgotten to turn on the meter. The man wagged his head and muttered, "*Aap ki marzi*, pay whatever you like." Simon handed him a one-hundred-rupee bill and jogged toward the entrance. The driver chased after him, demanding one thousand as Simon disappeared into the crowd.

The next flight to Mumbai departed in forty-five minutes. He bought a ticket and raced through security, stepping onto the jet bridge just moments before the gate closed behind him. Once in the air, he gazed at the white puffy clouds and fancied himself as Meena's knight in shining armor. Her Lancelot. Napoleon valiantly poised on a white stallion overlooking the battlefield at Austerlitz. But he soon came to his senses. *What the hell am I thinking?*

His thoughts turned to Kulkarni. Why was the DCP so keen on investigating Kesh's death? Police follow orders—that's what they do. But Kulkarni clearly wasn't willing to toe the line. He seemed personally invested in the case. Was he hiding something?

◆

The plane landed at 2:50 p.m. Simon hailed a taxi and ordered the driver to take him to Behera Towers. He took the elevator to the top floor and strutted through the glass doors. Simon told the receptionist he needed to see Mr. Gupta, and no, he didn't have an appointment. The receptionist buzzed the Himco advisor, who agreed to meet Simon.

Gupta was seated behind a nineteenth-century French writing table made of burr elm and supported by molded splay legs. He welcomed Simon and pointed to one of two period chairs facing the desk.

The Himco advisor, a thin man dressed in a well-tailored business suit, seemed surprised by the visit, but was cordial nevertheless. When asked how his mobile number got onto the cigarette wrapper at the crime scene, Gupta said he had no idea. But he flatly denied any motive for the murder and was adamant Himco's business was just fine with or without the "Prince of Gond," as he sarcastically called Kesh. Sure, requiring LEED projects to be more energy efficient would force companies to buy high-performance cooling systems. But Himco was prepared. Its upcoming model, GreenChill, could compete with the most energy-efficient chillers on the global market. "It's dark green, almost bloody black," Gupta bragged.

"But, Mr. Gupta," Simon queried like a prosecutor, "I've heard that Himco has run into problems during the beta testing. That performance is sub-optimal at high loads." Simon was fishing; he knew nothing about GreenChill.

"There are some bugs we need to get out of the system," Gupta admitted, "but I fully expect the product to be ready for the market by the second quarter of next year."

"By that time, many IT companies constructing factories in the Technocities will already have specified their cooling systems—isn't that the case?"

"Some, possibly. I wouldn't say many."

"But, with Kesh gone, isn't it likely the next chairman of the India Green Building Association will have different priorities, and the IGBA might take its sweet time to implement Kesh's changes? Maybe soften the proposal or drop it altogether? And wouldn't such a delay give you just the time you need to get the bugs out of your GreenChill system?"

"Mr. Bliss," Gupta snapped, "if you are implying that I or anyone in my client's company had sufficient motive to kill Mr. Narayan or have him killed, well, then, this meeting is over. I suggest you turn your investigation elsewhere." Gupta picked up a pack of cigarettes, drew one out, and started tapping it on his desk. "Forgive me for being blunt, but why are you asking all these questions? You're not the police. You're not even a citizen of this bloody country."

"True, but I was a friend of the deceased."

"Yes, and I hear an even closer friend of his stunning wife."

Simon did a double take.

Gupta stood up, walked over to a coat rack near the door, and drew a lighter from his jacket. "More to the point," he continued, "I assume you're doing Mr. Kulkarni's bidding, since he's been ordered not to investigate the prince's death."

How the hell does he know that?

Gupta moved close to Simon. He was tall for an Indian man, almost as tall as Simon. "Mr. Bliss," he said, rolling his thumb over the wheel of the lighter. For a moment, Simon thought the Himco advisor was going to set his hair on fire. "Let me give you some advice, since I assume everything I say will get back to our good police officer in Sompur. It would be professional suicide for the DCP to pursue a case against anyone connected with Himco, even if he had evidence as hard as the diamonds on that family girdle the prince sold to Mr. Behera, which he does not."

And how does Gupta know about the girdle?

"As you well know," Gupta continued, "the Center—that's our federal government—plans to make a national media event of the inauguration of the Lalita Devi Center." Gupta sat down again. "The event is just five days away, and I assume the lovely Ms. Kaul has clued you in on their game plan."

"What's that?"

"Look, everyone knows the HDP funded that new campus. And those few who've been living in Himalayan caves for the last year will find out on Sunday. So, how do you think it would look if the senior advisor to the president of Himco, the flagship company of the Behera Group, were suddenly charged with murdering the executive director's husband?"

"What are you saying, Mr. Gupta?"

"I'm saying if Kulkarni makes one move to indict me or anyone from Himco, his boss, Sompur's commissioner of police, will boot him right out of his job. Next thing you know, your buddy will be hawking DVDs in front of Sompur's railway station."

This is ridiculous, Simon thought. Gita used the same line. That the police wouldn't touch her since it was in the government's interest to uphold the spotless reputation of Meena's institute. Now Gupta is claiming the same immunity. "Are you so sure?"

"That the police would never come after me? Yes, as a matter of fact, I am. For one, I have an understanding with people at the highest level of government."

"An understanding?"

"Yes, a goddamn understanding. In any case, tell that *Cool*-karni he's barking up the wrong tree."

"Excuse me?"

"He's barking up the wrong tree. Barking, woof, woof. He should investigate that dhoti-wearing charlatan who calls himself a priest. Uppity, isn't that what people call him?"

"And what might *his* motive be?"

"Look, this isn't rocket science. Our prince, poor old Kesh, was screwing the queen bee of Upadhyaya's temple, that girl named Amrita. And the home minister was dipping his wick into the same pot."

"How do you know that?"

"Let's just say I have my sources. So, the Honorable Tewari finds out that he's sharing the deva-damsel with the prince of Gond and gets paranoid. He thinks the girl might spill the beans. That Narayan could blackmail him. After all, our prince has an agenda, which is to force the government to require LEED for all government construction. Now, our good friend Tewari knows he doesn't have any influence over the Ministry of Urban Development—that's the ministry that would have to approve Kesh's plan. In fact, Tewari and the urban minister have no love lost for each other. So, if Kesh knew about Tewari's trysts with Amrita and tried to blackmail him to promote LEED among government projects, he'd get nowhere fast. Tewari couldn't pull any strings for Kesh if his life depended on it. So, Tewari orders the priest to kill Kesh and nip any potential blackmail threat in the bud. That's quite good, isn't it, the priest and the prince. It could be the title of a bestselling thriller."

"And why would Upadhyaya do Tewari's bidding?"

"You really don't know the first thing about India, do you? Because the bloody temple program falls under the Ministry of Home Affairs, and that charlatan makes a lot of money for the party and for himself by running his National Temple Program, or should I say National Prostitution Ring. Don't think Upadhyaya isn't getting rich himself. He's taking his cut. This is India 101. No charge for the lesson."

Gupta leaned back in his chair and sucked in the smoke from his cigarette in a deliberate, almost teasing fashion. Then he blew a perfect smoke ring. "Look here, Bliss, what I'm saying is quite simple: the HDP has the priest by the *b-a-l-l-s*. Yes, priests have balls too, especially that Upi or Uppity or whatever the hell he's called."

Simon felt stupid. He really was in way over his head. Indian politics was not only a dangerous game, as Meena said, but a damn complicated one.

"So, you believe Upadhyaya killed Narayan on Tewari's orders?"

Gupta gave a subtle wag of his head.

If Gupta was right, thought Simon, Tewari was behind the murder. It didn't matter whether or not Gita sent incriminating photos to Gupta, as she claimed. In fact, it didn't matter if Gupta was involved at all, so long as the trail led to Tewari. But Simon was eager to hear Gupta's reaction to Gita's confession.

"With your permission," Simon said—his heart pounding as if a professional boxer were trapped inside, trying to get out—"I'd like to share an alternative theory with you."

Gupta raised his eyebrows and snuffed out the cigarette.

"Someone sends you photos of the home minister screwing the devadasi. The sender suggests you forward them on to Tewari with a little note. *Eliminate Narayan within three days or the photos show up in the Times of India.*"

Gupta drew a ballpoint pen from his shirt pocket and started clicking the end with his thumb.

"From what I can tell," Simon continued, "you have a strong motive to have Kesh knocked off. You get your hands on these photos and think, *Holy Krishna,* or whomever the heck you worship, *how very convenient. I can have the home minister do my bidding without putting my toes in the fire.*"

"Listen, Bliss," Gupta said, tossing his pen on the desk, "I didn't kill Narayan or blackmail Tewari. As I said, Himco is just fine with or without the prince and his machinations. This meeting is over. You can see yourself out." Gupta picked up the phone and turned away. Simon stood up and walked to the door.

Then a voice from behind.

"Bliss, you seem like a decent chap, so I'm going to give you some friendly advice. And there's no fee, which is good for you, since I normally charge foreign clients $300 an hour."

Simon thought of telling Gupta he was cheap, since his Washington lawyers had gouged him with an hourly rate of $500. But this wasn't a time for humor.

"What's that?"

"Tell Kulkarni to pin the murder on one of the big foreign air-conditioning companies, like Trane or York. Or even Haier, the Chinese company. Take your pick, any one will do. I can assure you, these multinationals are just like Himco—they make much bigger profits selling cheap, inefficient systems. The prince was just as much a thorn in their side as he was in Himco's."

"You think so?"

"Or your buddy can pin the murder on all the foreign air-conditioning manufacturers. He can call it an industrial conspiracy and get the whole lot of them kicked out of the country."

"You'd like that, wouldn't you, Mr. Gupta? No more foreign competition!"

"Fair enough. But Kulkarni wins too. He'll have solved the murder without getting his precious fingers burnt. He might even be promoted to additional police commissioner or even joint commissioner. In fact, I'll guarantee it."

"And how's that?"

"Easy. I'd have the Behera Group pull a few strings. They still have the HDP by the balls, even without Mr. Behera. In fact—" Gupta coughed. "Pardon me. In fact, I'll even sweeten the deal for the good policeman. How about $250,000 deposited in a Swiss bank account with his name on it? Welcome to India, Mr. Bliss."

Simon felt like slugging the dirty wheeler-dealer, but he kept his cool and didn't respond. He thanked Gupta for his time, took his leave, and caught the next flight back to Sompur. It was only after he had boarded the plane that he realized he'd forgotten to locate Raj, his old neighbor. Just as well, he thought, yawning.

It was 8:30 p.m. when the plane landed. The line for taxis went on forever, so Simon climbed into an auto-rickshaw and ordered the driver to take him to the Sompur temple. With its two-cylinder engine, it was like riding a lawnmower on wheels to Mars. Simon cursed each taxi that whizzed by. His butt was sore from the constant bouncing, and gusts of wind periodically treated him to a generous dose of fumes belching from passing trucks.

As the three-wheeler crawled toward the temple, Simon looked out for the farmhouse where he'd seen the woman hanging out the saris that billowed in the wind—his inspiration for the photovoltaic "sails" on the new community center. But dark thunderclouds distracted him. The wind picked up and the auto-rickshaw struggled to keep a straight line. Then the sky burst open. Simon sat inside, helpless, as sheets of rain pushed into the open vehicle. He was thoroughly soaked by the time he reached the temple an hour later.

A sexy young woman answered the door to Upadhyaya's residence. Was she one of those devadasis? Upadhyaya entered the room and seemed startled to see the American standing in the entranceway, dripping wet. He ordered his servant to bring dry clothes. She disappeared and returned a few moments later with a white kurta pajama outfit. Then she showed Simon to a room where he could change. It was so ridiculously small that she and the priest couldn't hide their laughter. The arms of the kurta barely reached the middle of Simon's forearms, and the pajama pants exposed half his shins. Simon excused himself for dropping in so late without notice.

"Ms. Meena, coming she is with you?"

"No, she needs time alone right now."

A scraggly boy limped in with chai, spilling tea onto the saucers. Simon and the priest talked about the strange week that took the lives of both Kesh and Behera. Upadhyaya looked particularly distraught as he slurped the drink from the saucer. His face was covered with two dark splotches that looked like snake eyes. After a few minutes, Simon got to the point.

"Was there any sign of a struggle at the workshop?"

The priest shook his head.

"What could have caused such a massive scaffolding to collapse?"

"No, sir, I am not thinking."

"You mean you can't think of anything?"

"Yes, sir."

"If Narayan and the young woman were lying on a bed, could one of them have accidentally kicked the scaffolding and knocked it over?"

"*Ho saktaa hai*, sir," replied Upadhyaya.

"Excuse me?"

"It is possible, but with very hard kicking only. And if this is so, she would have been squish-squashed too."

"Is there anyone who wanted to kill Kesh? Someone who could have been hiding in the background and pushed the scaffolding down?"

"Only Himco, sir, the air condition. Mr. Kesh told me he was being the bull's-eye. Air-condition company is not liking him, since he was doing his level best to make tighter the LEEDS."

"Anyone else?"

"No, sir, I am not thinking. Mr. Kesh was a very honorable man."

The priest made it clear he had another appointment. It was already past the time for him to bathe and dress the temple deities. Simon realized it was his last chance to test Gupta's theory, to move in for the kill.

"Guruji, I think you should know the DCP is preparing to arrest you for Kesh's murder. The police officer has evidence that Mr. Tewari ordered you to eliminate Kesh. Everyone knows Tewari was making regular visits to the devadasi."

"I am not following," Upadhyaya squeaked. His double cowlick seemed to stiffen, like two sentinels ready to defend their general.

Simon carefully laid out Gupta's story: that both Kesh and the home minister were patronizing the devadasi. The minister feared Amrita could have told Kesh of the minister's weekly trysts or known that Sanjeev's people were taking photos that could be used against him. To avoid being blackmailed, Tewari wanted Kesh out of the way, and so he ordered the priest to do his bidding.

Upadhyaya, biting his nails, admitted the home minister was having weekly dalliances with Amrita. But he denied that either Tewari or he had anything to do with Kesh's murder. "The good minister never ordered myself to do killing of poor Keshji. I am swearing on *Bhagavad Gita* only." The priest threw himself at Simon's feet and began to weep. "Please, sir, no arresting of me."

He held onto one of Simon's legs and tugged at the bottom of his pajama pants, inadvertently yanking them down all the way to his ankles. Simon, standing in a pair of skimpy black briefs, quickly bent down to pull up his pants; but at that very moment the priest started to stand and their heads collided. Simon immediately straightened up, but Upadhyaya's head, which was hit hard, plunged right into Simon's crotch. Simon noticed the young woman and pushed the old man's head away. He managed to get his pants up, but the damage was done. The servant covered her mouth to hide her laughter as she handed over his pressed and neatly folded clothes.

Simon left the priest's residence feeling like the biggest idiot to ever set foot on Indian soil. He was no closer to solving Kesh's murder. He approached a taxi stand and climbed into the nearest car. Simon ordered the taxi to drive to his hotel. The taxi sped away before Simon realized he had forgotten the auto-rickshaw was waiting to take him back to the city. The three-wheeler bolted after the taxi, but soon gave up the chase. Simon felt terrible about cheating the *rickshaw-walla* out of his return fare, but there was nothing he could do.

As the taxi cruised through the countryside, he kept shaking his head, embarrassed by the day's events gone wrong. He tried to focus on the conversation with Upadhyaya. The priest seemed to be telling the truth. But if he were innocent, then Gupta must be the culprit. After all, his phone number was found on the foil of the cigarette pack at the crime scene. But something didn't add up. Sanjeev would not let Meena see the compromising photos he claimed to have in his possession. So why would he have shown them—much less given them—to Gita? If Gita didn't have any incriminating photos, she would have nothing on Tewari. Why would she confess to engineering a crime she didn't orchestrate? If, on the other hand, Gupta had simply contracted a hired gun to kill Kesh—independent of Gita—Simon had nothing to implicate Tewari.

He was falling off his feet as he entered the lobby of the Grand Savoy Hotel. He stood in line to get his key and overheard the person in front of him. He glanced at his watch. Who would be checking into a hotel at 1 a.m.?

"Enjoy your stay, Mr. Mainkar," the hotel receptionist said.

It was none other than Sanjeev Mainkar. He was wearing a tight yellow mesh shirt. His torso was bursting with muscles, as if barbells of various sizes were stuffed under his chest and arms. The man could surely get his goddamn article to press before Sunday, thought Simon, if only he'd spend less time at the gym.

As the journalist started for the elevator, Simon approached him and introduced himself. He asked if they could have a short talk. Sanjeev said he was tired and declined. Simon insisted and Sanjeev agreed to a quick nightcap in the lounge.

When asked what brought him to Sompur, the journalist said he had come for a meeting with Gita. Sanjeev was surprisingly responsive as Simon posed various questions. Yes, he had dozens of incriminating photos of Tewari, as well as other cabinet ministers and industrialists. But he maintained the photos were kept in a locked safe in his office. He had shown a few to Gita, but she had no access to them. And he didn't know Arun Gupta from a hole in the wall. There was no way Gita could have sent Gupta any photos to blackmail the home minister or anyone else. At least not *his* photos.

Gita's confession went up in smoke, and with it, Simon's spirits. He slouched in his chair. He asked Sanjeev why it was so difficult to break his story by Sunday, October 1, since he already had sufficient evidence of misdeeds at the temples.

"I had hoped to be finished by now," Sanjeev admitted. "But a wrench was thrown in my wheel. Well, it was more like manna fell from heaven."

The journalist explained how he was offered a trove of tapes that revealed HDP crimes far greater than the priest's temple shenanigans. "It was like seeing God in the burning bush," he said. "Or, rather, the devil." The young man insisted he needed two to three more weeks to transcribe the tapes and write the more damning story—one that would sure as hell bring down the HDP and catapult him to everlasting fame. He talked as if he had unearthed a new gospel, a scandal far bigger than TempleGate.

Simon pleaded with Sanjeev to expedite the transcription of tapes. He offered money to hire more worker bees. But Sanjeev wouldn't budge. He already had a bevy of college students working day and night. The more people involved, the greater chance of a leak.

By the time Simon left the lounge, it was past 2 a.m. So much for finding his inner James Bond and saving Meena from the jaws of the HDP. He might look like Pierce Brosnan, but the comparison ended there. Why, he wondered, would Gita weave such an elaborate story—one that implicated herself—if she had no access to Sanjeev's photos? He came up dry. Before long, he was flooded with self-doubt. What an idiot he must have looked like to Gupta! And then that awful scene when Upadhyaya's head landed in his crotch!

Simon was beating up on himself when he got to his room. He walked over to the window and started to pull down the blind. He noticed a large, brightly lit billboard outside his window. It was an advertisement for a Bollywood movie. A mustached man leaned over a woman with his arm raised, about to strike her. The woman's eyes were wide open with fear. The man looked like a dark version of his father, who wore the same trim mustache when Simon was a young child. In the corner of the room, a toddler lay on a bed wailing. Next to the bed, a heart monitor. It was a hospital room. Simon's insides tied into a knot and his knees locked.

CHAPTER 29

Kulkarni was all ears when Simon showed up at his office the next day to report his findings. The DCP thanked him for making the trip to Mumbai and listened attentively, rolling a sharpened pencil between his fingers. When Simon got to the point where Arun Gupta offered to deposit half a million dollars in a Swiss bank account, the pencil snapped in two.

Simon eventually shared his own analysis. Since Gita didn't have access to Sanjeev's photos, she couldn't have been part of a plan involving Gupta and Tewari. The home minister might be India's sleazebag-in-chief, but it didn't look like he had anything to do with Kesh's murder. And the priest might be India's chief overwhelming officer, but he didn't appear to have overwhelmed Kesh. Gupta must have acted alone. Of course, such a big man would not do the deed himself. He used a hired gun, which explained his cell number on the cigarette wrapper. But Simon didn't think Gupta was just out to get Kesh. His real motive was to rid the country of foreign competition by bribing Kulkarni to pin the murder on a cabal of multinational corporations. Why Gita would confess to having hatched a scheme that led to Kesh's murder, he did not know.

"So," Kulkarni responded, "just another case of corporate monkey business?"

"I think so," Simon said, staring at the DCP's thumbs, which seemed disproportionately large.

Kulkarni was impressed and joked that Simon could have a job as assistant deputy commissioner of police. But Simon wasn't in the mood for jokes. He slouched in the chair and sucked his lips halfway into his mouth. Without evidence implicating Tewari, there was no hope of prying HDP's albatross off Meena's neck. Of ending her torment. *Of winning her love.*

"I feel bad for Ms. Meena," Kulkarni said after a long silence. "It's a question of timing, isn't it? As long as Ganesh Shukla's car is parked in 7 Racecourse Road, the Lalita Devi Center inauguration will proceed and the place will be forever linked to the HDP, for better or worse."

"7 Racecourse Road?"

"Sorry, the prime minister's residence. If, only weeks after the big day, Sanjeev's story breaks and a major scandal erupts, her precious center could go down with the Hindu party. Or, at least take a big hit."

"Mr. Kulkarni," Simon sighed, "it's Wednesday. Four days until D-Day, and we've got nothing."

"By the way," Kulkarni said, "forensics confirmed my suspicion. That white, chalky powder in the jar found at ground zero was scorpion feces. My guess is that our murderer came into the workshop and let a scorpion loose on Narayan's foot. Those buggers sting like the dickens. Poor man must have shot up and knocked the scaffolding down himself. So, we're one step closer. The hatchet man, or woman, has a taste for French jam.

Wild blueberry, to be exact."

"A woman?"

"Why not?" A long silence ensued before the DCP continued. "I don't know many professional hit men who eat French jam. Just a thought."

"Mr. Kulkarni, if you don't mind me asking, why do you care so much about this case? You were ordered not to investigate Kesh's death. Isn't that what policemen do, take orders? I mean, why risk your job by disobeying?"

Kulkarni bit his lower lip and closed his eyes. He seemed to be fighting back tears as he joined his hands together. His fingers pointed up to form a steeple, while his two thumbs looked like heavy doors to an ancient fortress. His face was that of a man guarding a heart-rending secret.

"I have two daughters. One of them, Shobana, is twenty-five and lost her husband nine months ago."

"I'm so sorry."

"She's a brilliant scientist," Kulkarni boasted, reaching for a family photo on his desk and turning it toward Simon.

"Shobana took a combined M.D.-Ph.D. from Harvard and was immediately offered a lab position at Harvard Medical School. It was a project funded by your National Institutes of Health on DNA sequencing and cardiovascular disease. But she decided to return to India, married Nikhil, her high school sweetheart, who happened to be a top-notch engineer, and accepted a job at AIIMS, that's the All Indian Institute of Medical Sciences. Last January, the poor chap was diagnosed with pancreatic cancer. By the end of May, he was gone."

"I'm so sorry," Simon repeated. "But what does all this have to do with the HDP?"

"I'm getting to that." The lines on Kulkarni's face seemed to deepen. "The very day after Nikhil died, when preparations were being made for his cremation, I get a call from Tewari, who had just been appointed home minister. Tewari wants to see me, not my boss. What's more, he insists on coming to my home. Something didn't compute, but I agreed, and he came that evening."

Simon was having trouble hearing and moved to the edge of his chair.

"Tewari says he heard about my son-in-law's passing and offers his condolences. We talk about my daughter and her many accomplishments. Then he looks me straight in the eye and asks whether she loved her husband. I'm thinking, *what a strange question—of course she loved him. And what does that have to do with the price of tea in China?* He goes on about how Shobana must be so devastated by Nikhil's death. The conversation is getting stranger by the minute. He says, 'A. J.'—mind you, I don't know the man and he's calling me A. J.—'it's highly educated professional young women like yours who are role models for the new India. They are the future of our great Hindu society. So, I was wondering if she's thought of showing her devotion to her deceased husband and to the nation.' I'm thinking, what on earth is he talking about? Then he comes right out and asks if she's thought of following him into the afterlife, just like in the olden days. 'She would become a national hero,' he says. 'This I can assure you.'" Kulkarni removed a handkerchief from his pocket and dabbed his eyes. "Simon, have you ever heard of sati?"

Simon nodded.

"This sister-fucker, excuse my language, wanted to know if Shobana, my Harvard-educated daughter, would commit suicide for her husband, like some peasant in bloody Rajasthan!"

Simon was now leaning so far forward he felt the back legs of the chair rise up. He quickly caught himself and leaned back.

"Can you believe it? I wanted to throw the snake out by his ears. But I was too stunned. I didn't know what to say. So, I'm sitting there, dumb as a doorknob. Now Tewari takes my silence as a sign that I'm interested. He says that such an act would be publicly lauded by the prime minister and would give the new government just the case it needs to repeal the law against the practice. After all, Tewari says, what could be wrong with a custom practiced by our elite? The Brits outlawed sati a hundred years ago, as they should have, although it's still going on in certain backward areas. Tewari promises that a national holiday would be created in Shobana's name!"

Simon felt like reaching out and grabbing the DCP's hand.

"Then the lizard says the Mumbai police commissioner is retiring, and offers to personally arrange for my promotion. Not only does the Mumbai police commissioner make four times my salary, but Tewari promises to throw in fifteen million rupees as a bonus. That's what, about a quarter of a million US dollars!"

Simon shook his head in disbelief.

"So, I lead the bastard to the door of my house. My fists are clenched and I'm doing everything in my power not to grab that ridiculous combover and yank those hairs out of his stinking head. But I restrain myself and say, 'Mr. Tewari, don't you ever, I repeat, ever step in this house again. You are not welcome here.' He has the nerve to thank me! He hands me his business card and asks that I call his direct line should I change my mind. I slammed the door so hard I practically broke the goddamn hinge."

Simon thought back to what he had overheard Gita say to Meena on his very first day in Sompur. *There's simply no way we can take money from a party that says it's a woman's right to roast herself on a barbecue pit!* He would never forget those words.

"You should know," Kulkarni continued, "the HDP's agenda isn't simply to bring back sati. Tewari wants to wrap the flag around it and make it the symbol of his twisted idea of modern India. He was looking for just the right case to pull the trigger, if you'll excuse the mixed metaphor. Not some illiterate woman from the deserts of Rajasthan throwing herself on her husband's pyre. That's old school. No, he wanted a doctor like Shobana or a high-tech executive from Bengaluru. The bastard has no shame, Simon. From the day that snake walked out of my house, I vowed to do whatever it takes to bring him down, and, God willing, the whole lot of them."

Simon asked if it were possible to get a cup of coffee. Kulkarni pushed a buzzer and a peon entered. He gave an order in the local language and the man scurried out. Then Kulkarni smiled and said there was some good news.

About six weeks ago, someone from the national government approached him, saying he was fed up with all the corruption under his nose. The man, the seniormost staff member of a cabinet minister, handed Kulkarni the private mobile numbers of the entire HDP cabinet and said he was free to use them in any way he pleased. In short, this person—who asked to remain anonymous—gave the DCP license to tap the cell phones of the entire HDP leadership. And tap he did. The result was over fifty hours of conversations revealing various illegal schemes at the highest levels of government. Kulkarni handed the tapes over to a journalist, who was already investigating the temple program.

"The HDP is finished," Kulkarni said as the peon returned with coffee and biscuits. "That's the good news. The bad news, at least for Ms. Kaul, is that the journalist won't break the story for a few more weeks."

"I know about the tapes," Simon said. "I just didn't know you were the one who had given them to Sanjeev."

"Ah, so you know about Sanjeev."

"Yes, he's a friend of Gita Sen, Meena's deputy." The puzzle was almost complete, but Simon was no closer to helping Meena defuse the ticking time bomb. Then he had a thought. "What if Meena were to call the home minister and say she knows about that sordid visit to your house? What if she were to say she's through with him and will leak the story unless the HDP quietly walks away from the inauguration?"

"It's a nice idea, Simon, but Tewari doesn't have the power to cut the HDP's ties to Meena's institute. The government's relationship to Behera House is too deep. It goes all the way up to the prime minister."

Simon slouched, his foot furiously tapping the floor.

"Listen," continued the DCP. "Let's get Sanjeev in here. I've already told him about Shobana, but I'll say he can't use the incident unless he busts ass and gets his article to press before Sunday. He'll be devastated. Sanjeev is smart. He knows a personal story—the one I just told you— will pull at the heartstrings of Indians all over the country. It will give his piece a human face. He needs it."

"You can try," Simon grunted, rolling his shoulders up and back to relieve the tension. "But I'm not going to hold my breath. Sanjeev is too smart. He'll assume you're bluffing. If he knows your story, then he knows you hate the HDP as much as anybody and would want to see it reach daylight. He'll call your bluff and take his sweet time."

"You're right. So, I'll just get him in here and say he has to expedite the story, period. He owes me. Look, I was the one who gave him the bloody tapes! And he probably doesn't want to mess with a high-ranking police officer."

"Good luck," Simon said, "but I'm not optimistic. Sanjeev looks out for nobody but Sanjeev." Simon thanked the DCP and dragged himself out of the office.

As he sauntered down the busy street, a teenage girl approached with a baby slung on her hip. She put out her hand and made that pitiful *help-*

me-feed-my-hungry-baby face. Simon ignored her, then reproached himself. She probably *is* hungry. He turned back, pulled a few rupees from his wallet, and handed them over. She bent down and picked up a folded paper that had fallen out of his wallet with the bills and gave it to him. It was the famous *sah* poem, which Kesh had written out for him after their visit to the Sompur temple over a year ago. Simon must have stuffed it in his wallet and forgotten about it. He watched the girl walk off to her next customer, then read the poem.

> *On the porch, she, and in all directions,*
> *Behind she, she in front.*
> *In bed she, and on every path of me sick from separation.*
> *Alas, oh heart, here is no other entity—*
> *She she she she in the whole wide world. Why talk of non-duality?*

But there *was* a duality, he thought, pounding his fist into the palm of his other hand. He felt a spiritual longing to be one with Meena. And it wasn't just hormones speaking. He wanted to merge with her. Like the half-man, half-woman form of Shiva. Not forever, but just long enough for their souls to touch. Once. To have a piece of her inner self rub off on him. A kind of spiritual transfusion.

But this wasn't going to happen. She would have little emotional capital left for him in the coming days. And even less after Sanjeev's story hit the press. Every moment of her day would be spent trying to distance the new Lalita Devi Center from those monsters. He had failed Meena in her moment of need.

CHAPTER 30

Mumbai

Behera's three-story house on Malabar Hill sat high above the hustle and bustle of Mumbai. A twelve-foot wrought-iron security fence sealed off the premises. The top of each vertical bar looked like a spear ready to impale unwanted visitors and toss them into the Arabian Sea, far below.

Two Sikh guards in black Nehru jackets and crisp white turbans gawked at Meena and Simon as they passed through the gate. Their dark eyes looked like small cannonballs. Inside the compound, tall cedars lined both sides of the pathway to the residence. Various topiaries dotted the manicured lawn: a deer here, a peacock there. Ganesh, the pot-bellied, elephant-headed god, looked particularly pleased with himself.

Meena and Simon joined a long line of guests waiting to offer Mrs. Behera condolences. The grande dame was shrouded in a white sari, as if she were ready to join her husband. Her stiff bouffant reminded Meena of the towering headdress worn by Shiva in the Panchavati caves. On her right hand, a diamond the size of a golf ball. Next to her, on an easel, a portrait of her husband in a dark business suit. A garland of yellow marigolds hung around the top, emitting the bitter smell of death. A bevy of condolence cards and telegrams covered an Elizabethan side table. One from the prime minister was prominently displayed on a silver platter.

The house was crawling with politicians, marked by their long, black Nehru jackets. Corporate tycoons, generally taller and with fewer pots in their bellies, milled around in well-tailored European suits. It was like an insect colony where two species coexisted, but with little interaction. Except for Sompur's mayor. He worked room after room, poking his pockmarked face into everyone's business.

Meena and Mrs. Behera exchanged polite kisses on both cheeks. As Meena turned away from the old lady, someone bumped into her.

"Pardon me," the man said.

"Mr. Tewari!" Meena blushed, eyeing his extraordinary comb-over. A few black hairs wound endlessly around the home minister's bald spot, as if doing extra duty. She introduced Simon, who smiled wryly. Tewari's jaw jutted in and out like a fish in search of a meal. Or was he in search of his next devadasi? *Slime bag!*

"Dreadful thing," Tewari coughed, "this fire business in the workshop. Oh, by the way, I must tell you I was infuriated by Deepek Ranga's op-ed in this morning's *Times of India*. You know, where he accused Behera House of selling out to the HDP. I don't know how in the world Ranga found out about the grant . . . Oh, I suppose it doesn't matter, since the cat will be out of the bag on Sunday. Still, it's not right. We support an institute for battered women and next thing you know the media is accusing Behera House of being HDP's marionette—isn't that the word she used? No good deed goes unpunished, isn't it?"

Meena felt ill. How could she have missed the op-ed? Then a short man in an oversized green suit approached Tewari.

"H. C., how very nice to see you."

"*Namaste,* Jagdish!" Tewari answered. "I'd like you to meet the famous American architect who designed the new Lalita Devi Center for the Advancement of Women."

"Only the community center," Simon said.

"Mr. Raghavan owns Best Quality Marble Supply Company, Ltd. It's the largest marble mining company in India. He's got ninety-nine-year leases on fifty quarries in Rajasthan. And, I might add, he's a big supporter. He's donated the marble for many of the temple renovations and additions."

Meena wondered if that included the statue that landed on Kesh's head. Raghavan wagged his head stiffly, as if it was also cut from marble.

"Too tragic about Mr. Behera," Raghavan said. "I mean, having a massive heart attack and not even seventy. Ghastly business, isn't it?"

"Ms. Kaul is also recently widowed," Tewari gushed, as if he were nominating her for a Pulitzer.

"Oh, I'm so sorry," Raghavan said. "Was it a health issue? I was reading how we should all be cutting out the red meat."

Meena walked away. She felt like grabbing a nearby vase and smashing it on the man's head when Raj Majumdar approached her. He wore round tortoiseshell glasses and sported a flowing mane of shiny white hair. A few yellowish strands rolled over his scalp like ocean waves in the moonlight. He could have passed for a Harvard professor of classical literature were it not for the immaculate business suit and bright yellow tie with blue medallions. In his hand, a large manila envelope. He kissed Meena on both cheeks. She pointed to Simon, who had gone to the bar to get her a fresh-lime soda. Simon was walking back to Meena when Raj approached him.

"Simon Bliss," Raj said, extending his hand. "You probably don't recognize me."

"No, I'm sorry."

"No surprise. It's been more than thirty years."

Simon gave Raj a dismissive look and scanned the room for Meena.

"Raj. Raj Majumdar," Raj said, still extending his hand.

"No!"

"Yes, indeed."

"Jesus Christ!" Simon exclaimed. "What on earth are *you* doing here?"

"It's a long story. But first, let me look at you." He was studying Simon when Meena approached and stood slightly behind the two men. "My, what a handsome chap you've become! Come, let's sit."

Meena hung onto Simon's arm as they walked into the garden and spotted an empty seating area.

"Oh, I'm sorry," Simon said, turning to Meena. "I forgot to introduce you. Meena, I'd like you to meet . . ."

Raj and Meena swapped glances.

"Wait, you know each other?"

"Yes," Meena said. "Raj is an old friend of Madhav and his wife."

Simon looked puzzled.

Raj turned to Meena. "By the way, I am so very sorry about Kesh and regret I couldn't make the funeral; but I was in China last week. We're building a toothbrush factory outside Shanghai. It will be the world's largest—the size of two football fields! Oh, dear, I'm sorry. This is not the time to be carrying on about my business."

"This smells like a conspiracy," Simon said. "What the hell is going on here?"

A waiter approached with an assortment of drinks. Raj took a whiskey.

"Sorry to spring this on you so suddenly, son. I'd hoped we'd be meeting under happier circumstances."

"I don't understand. How did you know Mr. Behera and . . . and Meena?"

Raj took a sip and smiled. "Madhav was a dear friend of mine. We met shortly after I returned to India in '74. A few months before your sixteenth birthday." Raj went on to explain that he'd bought a house two doors from Madhav's. The two businessmen became close friends, playing golf or tennis almost every weekend. Behera introduced Raj to Meena and Kesh in 2000, shortly after Meena was recruited for Behera House.

"So that's how I won the competition to design the new center, huh?"

"No, Simon," Raj said. "You won on your own merit, although I did tell Madhav how very pleased I'd be if you were selected."

Simon looked at Meena. "Did you know all this time that Raj and I . . ."

"Yes. Let Raj tell his story."

Simon turned back to Raj. "How did you even know I was practicing architecture?"

"Simon, you were like a son to me. When your mother died, I felt so sorry for you, but I'd already shifted back to India and knew it wouldn't be appropriate for me to show up at your mother's funeral. Also, I'd just started the new job at Colgate India and it would have been difficult to extricate myself. Years later, I was able to track you down with the help of the Internet."

Simon turned to Meena again. "Why didn't you tell me?"

"Raj made me promise not to say anything until the project was fully designed and constructed. He didn't want you to think you'd been given the commission on his account."

Meena could almost see the wheels turning in Simon's head and excused herself. They needed some serious private time.

"Son," Raj said, "I have something important to tell you. It's about your mother and me."

"I already know." Simon gulped. "Dad told me about the affair after I'd found a photo of you and Mom in India. I suppose he knew all along, didn't he?"

"Well, no, actually. He learned about us shortly before I got my job offer in Mumbai. Your mother and I had already been seeing each other for almost a year."

Simon squeezed his eyes shut to hold back tears.

"You must know that I loved your mother. Her relationship with your father was, shall we say, difficult. But he wasn't a cruel man, although he could lose his temper. Sometimes badly. I would not have come in between them if it had been a happy marriage—you must believe me. I begged your mother to divorce your father and marry me. I wanted all of you to come live with me in India. We would have made a very happy family. But she thought the transition would be too difficult. Our affair ended after I'd given her a two-week tour of India."

"Yeah," Simon scoffed, "she told me she was going to stay with her dying sister." Simon thought of the photo of Raj and his mother kissing in front of the Taj. The kiss of death. How depressed she was after Raj left. How she resorted to alcohol. Then drugs. In the end, the combination killed her.

Raj leaned forward and placed his hand on Simon's shoulder. "I'm sorry, Simon. Truly I am."

Simon looked away. His eyes fell on a fishpond, where brightly colored koi fish were swimming in circles. After a few minutes, he looked up at Raj. "My father once said there was a particular incident that happened when I was young. Something that turned my mother against my father. For good. It was early on in their marriage, but he never wanted to talk about it."

"Marriages rarely fall apart because of a single incident, but there was one she mentioned that stuck with me." Raj pulled a thin box out of the manila envelope he was holding. "This should answer many of your questions."

"What is it?"

"It's your mother's diary. It's not easy reading, but I think she would have wanted you to have it."

"How on earth did you get her diary?"

Raj told Simon he had found it in their hotel room in New Delhi after he'd brought her to the airport on their final day together. She had forgotten it, or maybe she left it behind on purpose. Raj wasn't sure. When he called her in America and offered to send it back, she asked him to hold on to it. She said reading about all the good times they had in India would depress her. A month later, Raj received the telegram from Simon's father inviting him to her funeral.

"I didn't go, of course. It would have been too painful and awkward for everyone." Raj extended the box with both hands. "You do know it wasn't suicide, don't you? Your mother adored you. She would never have abandoned you willfully."

Simon sucked in his lips and cautiously received the box, as if it contained his mother's ashes.

"Simon, here's my business card with my mobile. Unfortunately, I have to head out. Call me anytime if you want to meet again. I'd love to take you to dinner and continue this conversation. But if you don't want to meet up, I'll understand."

The men embraced, forming a tight knot. Then Raj turned and walked away. Just as he had done thirty-two years ago.

CHAPTER 31

Sompur

Meena dragged herself into the kitchen and made a soft-boiled egg. She whacked the top off, piercing the yolk, which spread over the eggcup. Suddenly a crash in the laundry room. She looked in, only to find the room covered with white chalky powder; the dryer was vibrating so hard on spin cycle it had thrown an open box of detergent on the floor. But she didn't have the energy to clean it up. She went back to the kitchen and turned on the small TV.

Deputy Police Commissioner of Sompur A. J. Kulkarni said today that new evidence has emerged linking the murder of Mr. Keshav Narayan to a conspiracy of foreign air-conditioning companies. Mr. Narayan, an award-winning architect who was serving as chairman of the India Green Building Association or IGBA, was found dead . . .

Meena fumbled with the remote to turn up the volume, but pressed the wrong button and got Kermit the Frog singing, "It's not easy being green." It took every bit of concentration to find her way back to the news.

Speaking at the India Press Club in New Delhi, DCP Kulkarni said Mr. Narayan had tabled a proposal to raise the energy efficiency standard for LEED certification—a move opposed by certain members of the IGBA, including foreign air-conditioning manufacturers. Narayan's proposal required LEED projects to be at least twenty-five percent more energy-efficient than the industry standard set by the Indian Society of Heating, Refrigeration, and Air Conditioning Engineers, known as ISHRAE. According to Mr. C. P. Batra, president of ISHRAE, the proposed change would significantly reduce air-conditioning demand in private- and government-funded projects seeking LEED certification. In other news, a twelve-story residential building in Kanpur collapsed. Thirty-five people are confirmed dead, but the number is expected to rise as more—

Meena's hand was still shaking after she managed to click the off button. She called Simon and asked him to meet her at police headquarters straightaway. She honked her way through the snarled morning traffic as if she owned the road and parked in a spot reserved for police cars. Then she stormed into the lobby.

"Meena Kaul here. I'd like to see Mr. Kulkarni."

"Do you have an appointment?" the receptionist asked.

"No, but this is urgent."

"Everything's urgent around here, madam. You'll have to wait until the DCP has finished his meeting. Then I'll ask him if he can see you. He's got back-to-back meetings this—"

"This is nonsense! Tell him it's Meena Kaul and that I won't wait more than fifteen minutes."

"I got your name, madam. Please have a seat."

Meena scowled at the woman and sat. Two lime-green geckos chased each other, ricocheting from one wall to another. A light fixture cast a shadow on the wall; it resembled a woman's lips, half-opened as if yearning to say something. Meena's head began to ache. She was searching her handbag for aspirin when Simon entered. She told him what she'd heard on the morning news. The overhead fan was grinding away like a jet engine and wobbled furiously. She imagined it breaking from its mount and slicing both of their heads off when a policewoman approached and ushered them into the DCP's office.

Kulkarni sat motionless, immobilized by a neck brace. He excused his appearance, saying he'd woken up yesterday with a very stiff neck and even the slightest turn of his head hurt like the dickens.

"Mr. Kulkarni," Meena thundered without a word of sympathy, "what's this business I heard on the news about foreign air-conditioning companies being responsible for the murder of my husband?"

The DCP took a long breath and admitted the story had been ginned up to cover the HDP's "fat ass." He apologized, but said his hands were tied. He suggested they take the conversation outside. He told his secretary to have his deputy take his place for the rest of the morning.

They walked a few blocks to Motilal Nehru Park and took a bench shaded by a banyan tree. Meena sat straight as a ramrod, her legs tightly crossed. Her right foot was so firmly tucked behind the left calf that it began to hurt. In front of them, a vendor was setting up a large three-sided display on a folding table.

Meena proceeded to give Kulkarni a blow-by-blow retelling of Gita's confession, beginning with how Gita had sent Sanjeev's photos to Arun

Gupta so that he could blackmail the home minister—a move that was intended to "clip Kesh's wings."

"Are you done?"

She gave a quick nod, as if the police officer didn't deserve a verbal response.

"Was that a yes?" Kulkarni asked, straining to see her with his peripheral vision.

"One more thing," Meena said. "I've learned from Simon that Gita did not have access to Sanjeev's photos. But she must have gotten hold of at least one, since there is no reason on earth she would implicate herself in a crime she had nothing to do with."

"Listen," Kulkarni said, facing the vendor across the walkway, "I've been in the police force thirty-six years and I can tell you, without any doubt whatsoever, that Gita's story is, well, a pile of cow dung." Simon and Meena turned toward Kulkarni in perfect unison like synchronized skaters. "Your deputy spun a hell of a yarn."

"But why?" Simon asked. "Why would she concoct such a story?"

"I think it was to test your reaction, Meena." Kulkarni was still looking straight ahead. "Hold that thought and allow me to explain what actually happened. The real story is much simpler, as it always is. When I'm finished, you'll know what I mean."

"You know who did it?" Simon asked.

"Yes." Without moving his head, Kulkarni turned his whole body toward Meena. "The coroner discovered a scorpion bite on your husband's foot. Simon may have told you we found a jar at the crime scene. In it was a white chalky substance, which turned out to be scorpion feces. Our murderer came into the workshop with a scorpion in a jar and let it loose on your husband." The DCP turned his torso back to align with his legs, his eyes fixed on the vendor straight ahead.

"The jar!" Simon blurted, turning to Meena. "Did I forgot to tell you about the—?"

"Wait!" Meena shrieked. "Kesh was killed by a scorpion?"

"Well, yes and no," Kulkarni said. "Now, scorpions deliver a real punch when they sting. It's possible that Kesh jumped up like the devil and smashed into the scaffolding so hard the damn thing toppled over. But I'm guessing the same person who deposited the scorpion on his leg also gave the scaffolding a little help. In either case, one or more statues hit your husband on the head and either killed him or knocked him out." Kulkarni moved his mouth up and down stiffly, like a ventriloquist's dummy.

"So, he didn't suffer the fire?" Meena asked.

"That's my guess."

"So, it *was* Gupta?" Simon blurted.

"Patience, I'm getting to that." Kulkarni again turned toward Meena as if every vertebra in his neck and back were fused together. "Now, if I'm correct, you went to that new bakery in the cantonment, La Madeleine, and bought a gift basket for Gita."

"Well, yes, it was her birthday last week. How did you know?"

"The jar found at the crime scene was for wild blueberry jam made by Bonne Maman, a French company. La Madeleine is the only shop in Sompur that sells it. My men checked."

Meena was momentarily distracted by the vendor posting photos of cows, sticks of butter, and curds. "Yes," she finally said, "but how did you know I bought the gift basket?"

"I met with the proprietor. She remembered selling one to a very beautiful, light-skinned woman in her early to mid-thirties. She said it was the only gift basket she'd sold since the store opened its doors several months ago. Oh, yes, the lady mentioned the customer spoke impeccable French. A simple background check revealed you studied French in college."

"But," Simon butted in, "how did you know Meena gave the gift basket to Gita and not to someone else?"

"Come now, you must give a police officer with three decades of experience some credit. Gita is Meena's deputy, so she was the likely recipient. It wasn't hard to find out she just had a birthday. The proprietor told me that every gift basket contains a jar of Bonne Maman jam. So, I broke into Gita's flat and searched it."

"You broke in?" Simon asked.

"I had to, since I'm not supposed to be investigating this case. And there it was, right in front of my eyes, the gift basket. But no jam jar. I'm thinking, it's highly unlikely that a person living alone would consume a full jar of jam in a week. A baguette, maybe. Even a wheel of French Brie—I'd certainly be tempted—but not jam. So, I'm thinking, what happened to the jar?"

"So, it was Gita, after all?" Meena said.

"Yes, but not as she told the story."

Meena started sobbing. She was distracted by Simon's hand rubbing her back and asked him to stop.

"But how could Gita have committed the crime with Amrita there?" Simon asked.

"They were in it together. Gita came to know Amrita when she was looking into that crooked priest's temple program. She learned that Amrita's sister was brutally killed by her husband. The old petrol and match trick. We found the file on her sister's death. The husband went missing before charges could be brought against him. It wasn't hard for Gita to figure out the devadasi shared her dislike of men. Well, that's an understatement. A man had killed her sister and a male priest was forcing her to spread her legs for dirty old men two and three times her age. Oh, sorry, Meena. I didn't mean to imply—"

"It's okay," Meena said. "Please continue."

"Amrita wanted revenge—any man would do—and found the perfect outlet when Gita revealed her plan to kill your husband. In return for Amrita's cooperation, Gita offered to arrange for the sale of the girdle, which, you remember, went missing the evening of your husband's death."

"But how did you come to suspect Gita in the first place?" Simon asked.

"Honestly, it was just a hunch. If the murderer were just any old thug doing his daily rounds, he would have shot or stabbed his target. Your run-of-the-mill hit man doesn't go to the trouble of finding a scorpion and planting it on a target's leg. And you certainly wouldn't expect him to carry his weapon in a jar of French jam! So, I'm thinking, who *would* concoct such a plan? There was something naïve about the scheme, and, if you'll excuse my saying, the plot seemed to me to be the work of a woman. After I had gone to the bakery and figured out it was you, Meena, who bought a gift basket, and that the basket contained a jar of wild blueberry jam, I checked up and found out that Gita had a birthday recently. It wasn't hard to put two and two together."

Meena buried her head in her hands.

"But why?" Simon asked. "What was her motive? I don't get it."

"Ah, yes, the motive," Kulkarni said, cringing as he tried to loosen the collar. "A little research revealed that Gita was arrested in college at a rally for gay rights. The protest turned violent, and she was charged with throwing a firebomb at a police car. So, I start to wonder if we're not talking about the oldest motive in the world. *Love.* Well, I guess money is right up there, too. Am I right?"

"She tried to seduce me the other day," Meena sniveled, lowering her head.

"Wait," Simon blurted, "you're saying Gita killed Kesh in the hopes of having Meena for herself?"

"It sure looks that way. As for the crime, Gita and Amrita were in it together," Kulkarni said.

"So, Gupta's innocent?" Simon asked.

Kulkarni's head wagged ever so slightly, like a grace note. "Ouch!" He closed his eyes and grasped the back of his neck. "I really did a number on my goddamn neck." Without moving his head, his eyes migrated toward Simon. "Sorry, what did you ask?"

"Gupta, he's innocent?"

"As far as Kesh's murder. But the man is one clever son-of-a-bitch. He didn't waste a minute in contacting my boss and offering the perfect cover-up—that the murder was hatched by the multinational air-conditioning suppliers. He wanted to use the murder to serve his client, Himco. Casting the blame on foreign air-conditioning companies was a scheme to get rid of Himco's competition."

"Oh, dear God," Meena wailed.

"But why did you go along with it?" Simon asked. "I mean, why were you trying to protect Gita?"

"I wasn't."

"You were protecting me and the institute, weren't you?" Meena asked. "It was just as Gita said after she tried to seduce me. She joked she was untouchable, since convicting her could spell ruin for the new Lalita Devi Center."

"Bingo," said the DCP, revolving toward Simon. "Isn't that what you Americans say?"

Meena's face whitened; she covered her mouth and stumbled away from the bench. Simon sprinted to her and held her arm as she bent over to vomit. But nothing came out and they returned to Kulkarni.

"As for the HDP," the DCP continued, "their days are numbered. In fact, they've got two days left." Kulkarni fumbled in his pocket for a pack of cigarettes. "Sanjeev called this morning. He's already submitted his story. Apparently, the *Times of India* has already contacted the prime minister's office and shared a draft, inviting it to respond within twenty-four hours. It's protocol. The article will hit the streets Sunday morning. The HDP is finished. You're a free woman, Meena."

"Free?" she repeated, her head reeling.

"Yes, madam. The HDP had nothing to do with your husband's unfortunate fate, but that seems like the only goddamn mess they didn't engineer. They're toast! Or should I say toast with wild blueberry jam?" He chuckled. "You can postpone the inauguration, cancel it, or just go ahead without the HDP. Whatever. It's your call."

Simon smiled at her, but Meena just stared into space, more puzzled and anguished than ever.

"And you?" Simon said, turning to Kulkarni. "You must be a happy camper!"

"A happy camper?"

"Yes, it means—"

"I can guess," Kulkarni interrupted, smiling. "Yes, I'm a very happy camper, except for this bloody stiff neck."

Kulkarni went on to describe the bigger HDP scandal, brought to light by the tapes. The country's industrial houses were paying mega-bribes to cabinet ministers in return for no-bid contracts valued in the billions of rupees. The money was used to fund the HDP foundation, as well as to pay for the usual indulgences, like large fleets of luxury SUVs for the political elite. He also explained how the devadasis were made to sweeten the deals for industrialists. But no money actually exchanged hands. That was how the HDP protected itself from potential accusations that the priest's scheme was nothing more than a national prostitution ring. Kulkarni started to describe a third HDP crime, but Meena interrupted.

"Stop. No more, please."

"I think that's enough for today," Simon said, taking her hand. "Let's go."

As they started toward the park entrance, Meena thought about Gita's confession. *Did she really expect me to fall into her arms and declare my undying love after admitting she had hatched a scheme that killed my husband?*

Kulkarni excused himself for a minute. He backtracked and walked over to the vendor, who wore a T-shirt with a picture of a soda bottle and the words: *Protect the Cow, Drink CowPa Cola.*

"Officer," the vendor said, "I have a permit. You like to see?"

"I'm not here to check your permit. I just want to know what you're selling."

"CowPa Cola. Please, sir, have a flyer." Kulkarni shook his head in disbelief as he read that the drink contained 0.35 percent cow urine.

"Why drink Campa Cola when you can be drinking CowPa Cola?" the vendor asked, smiling and wagging his head furiously. The flyer described the salutary effect of cow-urine therapy. At the bottom, in small print, it stated that CowPa Cola was a small business enterprise supported by a generous grant from the HDP Foundation.

"What was that about?" Simon asked when the DCP caught up with them.

"You don't want to know," Kulkarni said, shaking his head. "You *really* do not want to know."

CHAPTER 32

Sanjeev's story hit the streets on Sunday, October 1, the same day the inauguration was to take place. It was also Dussehra, the Hindu holiday celebrating Durga's defeat of Mahishasura, the buffalo demon. Dussehra also honored the day Lord Rama killed the ten-headed demon Ravana and returned with his wife from a twelve-year exile to take back the throne, marking the revival of Ram Raj or good governance.

That the inauguration was scheduled to fall on Dussehra was no coincidence. The message to the nation was clear as day: the HDP's partnership with the new Lalita Devi Center for the Advancement of Women was an example of good triumphing over evil. The HDP was the new Ram Raj. To say the party's plan backfired would be a gross understatement. First, there was no inauguration—Meena postponed the event indefinitely. Second, there was no HDP, at least none to speak of. The government was in an advanced state of free fall.

The irony of an HDP scandal exploding on Dussehra hardly went unnoticed. The HDP was not Durga, blasted the media, but the evil buffalo demon she had slain. Nor was the HDP the new Lord Rama; if anything, the party stood for the ten-headed Ravana who had kidnapped the god's wife. Yes, Sunday was a celebration of good over evil, but hardly the way the Hindu party had envisioned.

News of HDP's crimes broke in rapid succession. The first measured 8.9 on the political Richter scale—a massive corporate bribery scheme involving eight of the ten top industrial houses, including the Behera Group. As Kulkarni had mentioned, huge sums, often worth billions of rupees, were paid for no-bid contracts. The second scandal was the blatant misuse of the devadasis under the National Temple Revitalization Program. A third offense involved spreading fake news about political opponents.

The scandal sent shockwaves around the world. Through agreements with the *Times of India*, Sanjeev's article made front-page news from Washington to Beijing. Just as the journalist had hoped, the political bomb was likened to Watergate, as well as to the Bofors scandal, which consumed India in the 1980s and '90s. It seemed like the whole world was celebrating Dussehra, and Sanjeev Mainkar became a household name overnight.

Simon sat in Meena's living room glued to the English news channel. India's president called for the immediate resignation of the prime minister and appointed a caretaker government. Prime Minister Shukla expressed his deep regret and took full responsibility, although there was no evidence linking him to any criminal activity.

Meena gloated as she watched news clips of the home minister being carted off to police headquarters, covering his face as he ducked into the police car. TV reports also showed the minister of urban development being hauled off. Upadhyaya was taken in for questioning. Talking heads chattered endlessly about the priest's contemptible program, but most concluded he was just a pawn in the HDP's game. Meena's pleasure was bittersweet. She felt like a war hero with post-traumatic stress disorder.

The successive scandals were like aftershocks following a major earthquake. But it was Kulkarni's story about Tewari's visit to his home—which Sanjeev had included as a full-page sidebar, complete with photo of Shobana—that tugged at the collective heartstrings of Indians from the peaks of Kashmir to the country's rocky southern tip of Kanyakumari. TV channels ran interviews with Kulkarni, and newspapers around the world carried photos of his highly educated daughter. Ironically, Shobana did become a national hero and a symbol of the new India. Not by throwing herself on her husband's funeral pyre, as Tewari had urged, but by surviving and speaking out against the abhorrent practice of sati. The whole country heaved a collective sigh that such a talented and beautiful young woman was alive and well. The story symbolized India's brush with an old devil. It was as if the country itself had survived a national funeral pyre.

Tewari's plan sparked a national debate about whether the life of a high-caste, highly educated woman like Shobana was really more valuable than that of an uneducated peasant from rural Rajasthan. The national conversation forced many liberals to reevaluate their long-held assumption that the lives of the rich were more valuable than those of the poor, and it led to a renewed pledge by the opposition party to step up efforts to end the heinous practice of sati.

By mid-afternoon, Simon and Meena had had enough and decided to go out. Meena went into her bedroom to change. She stared into her closet trying to recall what she had worn the day she lured Simon to the Panchavati caves over a year ago. She put on her tight jeans and the same white shirt, then stood in front of her full-length mirror adjusting her collar and sleeves. She walked downstairs, wondering if Simon would recognize the outfit. He didn't say anything, but offered up a knowing smile.

They wandered through the city streets, dropping into an occasional café to rest. Sitting in Kamala Nehru Park, they watched children play as the evening sky turned to a brilliant canvas of reds, blues, and pinks. They ate dinner at the restaurant on the hill where they had gone with Asha on Simon's first week in India. Customers were celebrating the fall of the HDP all around them. The proprietor went from table to table serving sweets and dishing out scoops of pistachio ice cream on the house.

After dinner, Meena led Simon farther up the hill to Sompur's highest point. They sat on a boulder in a quiet grove overlooking the city. The large rock, shaped like a heart, was a favorite spot for young lovers. As soon as the sun sank below the horizon, fireworks lit the sky and blotted out the full moon. It wasn't long before she initiated a three-course kiss.

Far below, people dashed about setting fire to oversized effigies of Mahishasura, the evil buffalo demon. Meena leaned on Simon's shoulder as men in colorful costumes replayed the coronation of Lord Rama following his twelve-year exile in the forest. After some time, Meena suggested they drive to the new campus. From the rooftop of the community center, they would be able to see people from the fishing village celebrating the festivities. Except for a night guard, the place would be empty, since the campus was not yet opened to residents.

They stopped at a small stand where a potbellied man sat cross-legged on a wooden crate stirring a giant vat of bubbling milk. Flies hovered, sometimes landing on an island of grey milk solids. He was making *bhang lassi*, a yogurt drink made with spices, nuts, rose water, and cannabis. She ordered two. Simon tried to refuse; but Meena insisted, saying it was an age-old tradition on Dussehra and thus non-negotiable. When they reached the new campus, Simon could not stop chuckling..

———◆———

When they arrived at the center, Simon was so stoned he could have sworn he was seeing a real ship. They climbed stairs to the roof garden and leaned over the side rail, gazing into the distance. Throngs of devotees were squatting to place painted clay statues of Durga in the ocean. The colors seemed to jump off and stay behind, long after the statues sank into the water.

Simon was having a hard time keeping the two events being celebrated apart: Durga's slaying of the buffalo demon and Lord Rama's coronation after being exiled in the forest. He kept mixing up the characters. At one point he thought Durga had returned from the forest and Rama had slain the buffalo.

"So," Simon asked, "today Durga gets back from the forest with her husband?"

"No, silly, Sita is Rama's wife. And yes, they do reunite. But, don't forget, this is India. Sita has to prove her chastity before Rama will take her back."

"Her chastity—for God's sake, didn't you tell me the woman was hijacked, I mean kidnapped in the forest? Surely it wouldn't be her fault if she were raped by the demon Rocks Anna."

"Ravana. Good try, though. And you're wrong. In India, it's always the woman's fault."

Simon thought of his wife. In his family, everything was always *his* fault.

"Sita will have to walk through the fair," Meena said. "I mean fire, to prove her innocence."

Simon was reassured—he wasn't the only one whose mind had been scrambled.

"If the fire burns her," she continued, "Sita is guilty, but if she comes out unscathed, she's innocent."

"Sounds like pretty bad odds to me," Simon replied, wrapping his arm around Meena's waist as they watched a procession bearing a giant image of Durga. The goddess wore a purple skirt and fluorescent green top; her ten arms flapped in the wind. Simon started laughing uncontrollably.

"What?"

"Oh, nothing. It's just that she looks like a giant centipede!"

"Careful what you say," Meena quipped, "or the centipede goddess will crawl into your bed tonight! Speaking of beds, I have an idea. Let's go lie down on the waterbed!"

Behera's idea of sinking a waterbed into the roof deck of the community center appalled Simon from day one. But the industrialist insisted, claiming that it would help the residents heal, and maybe even provide some badly needed fun.

"Are you crazy?"

"No. Let's be silly. It's Dussehra, after all—a time to let go. Come on."

"No," he repeated. "No way!"

"Then tell me something about your mother, what you learned from her diary."

Simon thought about her medicine chest, its shelves lined with dozens of yellow-tinted bottles. As a kid, he was in awe of those bottles. They were like trophies. He used to think all those pills were like a badge of honor, a sign of adulthood, but they ended up killing her. He pictured Alisha's dozens of miniature homeopathic pill containers. Why weren't *they* trophies?

"You two were very close, weren't you?" Meena said, gently stroking his arm.

Simon shrugged. He told her about some of the good times they had together. Summering in Maine, where they went sailing and took in the Agricultural Fair. They would take the scariest rides, laughing their heads off as they whirled around the sky. Her death was like the last day of the fair, when all the rides were dismantled and packed into trucks to go to the next town. From the day she died, he felt like a lead apron had been hung from his neck. He hardly ate and looked like a walking X-ray of himself. The family would eat dinner like Trappist monks. Sentences were like necklace strings without jewels. *Pass the salt. Potatoes are cold. Gotta do homework.*

"For years," Simon said, "I was so depressed that I stepped down from the student council, quit junior varsity tennis, and even sold Rich Kidd, my dummy."

"Your dummy?"

"Yeah. Raj bought me a dummy for my fourteenth birthday. I taught myself how to throw my voice and performed at children's parties."

"That's hilarious! I can't imagine you—"

Simon caught Meena looking at his hair. "What are you looking at?"

"Your head." Meena stroked his thick black locks with their signature streak of grey. "In the moonlight, your hair looks like black coal with a seam of silver."

"What are you saying—there's a block of fossil fuel on my head?"

"Sorry, I didn't—"

"Actually, that silver streak is the crescent moon. Didn't I tell you? I'm really Shiva, having assumed my latest incarnation in the form of an American architect. No, a *star*chitect! Look closely and you'll see stars around that moon up there. It just *looks* like dandruff."

"I'm certainly glad you don't have his mop of matted hair!"

Both laughed. Meena's perfumed face drew Simon closer. He wanted to have her right then and there, but the cannabis made his body limp and sluggish. Better not even try. He tilted his head back to take in the sky.

"You've got fabulous eyebrows," she said, stroking one.

"They're my sunshades. Keeps the glare out. I get two LEED points for them."

"And those long lashes! Do they give you LEED points too?"

"Yep. I'm actually certified LEED Platinum. Well, maybe just LEED Gold, considering I have a truckload of fossil fuel on my head!"

"You're funny. Now come on." She grabbed his hand and pulled him to the waterbed. "Stay right here." She disappeared and returned a few minutes later.

Was the weed playing games with his mind or had she really turned into an Indian tree nymph, a semi-divine deity wrapped in a diaphanous sari with no undergarments whatsoever? Simon rubbed his eyes. The sight of her dark nipples pressing against the thin cotton sari was electrifying. This wasn't an invitation to make love, it was an order. She pranced over to Simon, grabbed his arm, and dragged him to the edge of the waterbed. She slid onto the vinyl, a mermaid slipping into the sea.

"Come on, Simon." Meena reassured him they were the only ones in the building. She confessed to having bribed the night guard to make sure nobody entered.

Simon protested again, but finally pulled off his shoes and climbed on, rocking the bed and falling onto his knees.

Meena giggled like a little girl. She rolled on top of him, showered his face with kisses, and, after unbuttoning his shirt, licked his chest. Then she stretched her arms out like the wings of an airplane. "Look, I'm flying," she sang, rocking from side to side and tilting this way and that.

He closed his eyes and found himself on a raft in the ocean. Her moist tongue touched his forehead like a drop of seawater. He felt dizzy. The banging of drums below sounded like the snapping of a sail.

A bamboo flute, a foghorn.

Wind whistled in the rigging.

He opened his eyes. Her face, above, glowed like a clear autumn moon. He ran his fingers through her hair and massaged her scalp. His lips migrated to her forehead; then to her cheeks and the nape of her neck, like twin pilgrims resting at various sacred stations to pay homage. He planted kisses on her bare midriff as if he were cultivating a garden and caressed her breasts. She seemed to savor his every move, trying to reciprocate, but often too overwhelmed, enraptured.

She moaned. Crowds cheered below.

"What's going on?" he asked.

"They're dunking more Durgas into the ocean."

"I'm Durga," he joked, snuggling his head into the warm waters of her body. *And am about to dunk myself into you.* He kissed her hips, then her inner thighs. Fragrant and salty. She groaned and dug her nails into his back.

Suddenly, a vision of Upadhyaya pushing a young Indian woman into a funeral pyre. Others joined in to help, as if it were a game. Every time she tried to escape, the priest pushed her back into the flames. "Damn it, Meena, I'm fucking hallucinating." He began to freak out as images of ice and fire flashed before his mind's eye.

Lin Yang lying on the snowy ground.

Gita chewing ice.

A scorpion crawling out of a jar.

The workshop in flames.

An ice statue crashing onto Kesh's head.

Then the priest's voice: *The Hindu temple is so busy it transcends busyness. It becomes emptiness . . .* The temple morphing into Noah's boxy ark. Kangaroos and elephants jockeying to get in the door . . . sails fluttering, foghorns . . . his professor's telltale words, *don't be afraid to sail close to the wind.*

Simon's whole body jerked, but Meena comforted him with a prolonged kiss.

Her tender lips pressed against his belly. Their bodies, a tight ball of arms and legs. Her armpit smelled of seaweed. He shook his head violently, as if to rid it of any demons that might have lingered. He closed his eyes.

"Are you okay?" asked Meena, slowly opening his belt.

"I think so," he muttered, beginning to feel better. He was stark naked. How did that happen? He rolled on top of her. As they made love, Simon recalled a poem Kesh had recited about Shiva's wedding night.

> *With the day and the night the same to him,*
> *Shiva spent his time making love*
> *and he passed twenty-five years*
> *as if it were a single night*
> *and his thirst for the pleasures of loving*
> *never became any less in him*
> *as the fire that burns below the ocean*
> *is never satisfied by the rolling waters.*

CHAPTER 33

The tangle of their bodies finally loosened. Meena lay on her back gazing at the stars and fireworks. Her body felt like it had been massaged from the inside out. "Sometimes, I wonder if Kesh, the great crusader against climate change, was really afraid of being swallowed up not so much by the rising oceans but by me. Isn't that silly?"

Simon propped himself up. "Maybe you were his ocean."

Meena didn't want to be anybody's ocean.

"When I was a toddler," Simon said, "my father was carrying a pot of boiling water. He had just cooked spaghetti and was headed to the sink to drain the pot. I was crawling under him. Then the phone rang. Reaching to put the pot down, he tripped over me. The pot fell, splashing boiling water and spaghetti all over my back. I was rushed to the hospital with second-degree burns."

"Oh, dear!"

"Then, when I was fifteen, I almost burned half my face off playing with dangerous chemicals in my basement. Like the first time, I was rushed to the hospital, where they put me in a shower for twelve hours to wash all the chemicals out of my body. It just occurred to me how strange it is, me spending the last year and a half designing a community center for women who've been abused, some badly burned."

"But your father didn't *intend* to hurt you. And you burned yourself in the basement. These were both accidents." Meena turned away from Simon. She didn't want to think about burn victims.

"It gets worse," Simon said, his voice breaking. "According to my mother's diary, she arrived at the hospital—the first time, when I was a toddler—and lashed out at my father. She had come from an art class. She yelled and screamed, accusing him of disfiguring me. They had a terrible argument. Finally, he lost it and beat her. I mean, really bad. A nurse called the police and he was charged with domestic violence. So, my own mother suffered from . . ."

Meena was momentarily distracted by cheering crowds. Ravana was dead. She looked at Simon and felt his pain but recoiled from the idea that he needed her. This was not the time to rescue or even comfort another survivor. She squeezed his hand, hoping the gesture would serve as a period, an end of the conversation.

"'I'll never sleep with that man again.' That's what she wrote in her diary. 'Never again.' I don't think she ever forgave him."

Meena thought about the last young woman who came to Behera House, cigarette burns all over her arms. She had used the exact same words—*I'll never sleep with that man again.*

"I wonder if that incident somehow lodged in my unconscious," Simon continued. "Maybe that's why I've always blamed myself for my mother's death. And for my parents' fucked-up marriage. And for her affair with Raj, which ultimately did her in. After all, it all started with

Dad spilling boiling water on *me*."

"You sound like our residents, who blame themselves for the abuse they suffer."

"I do, don't I? Oh, shit, I didn't mean to hit you with all this shit."

"It's okay." She nibbled his ear to distract him.

"Stop, that tickles!" Simon said.

She drew back.

"So here we are," he continued, "relaxing on the roof deck of the community center, which I designed as a ship! An ark of sorts, to bring your people to greener pastures."

"It's your ark, too."

"Wow, that's heavy. But I guess you're right. You know, I feel happy right now. It's like my mother had been sitting in a corner of my head for the past thirty years, like a guard in a museum. Now, all of a sudden, she's gone."

Meena got it. He needed his mother for protection, like the special goddesses she asks her new residents to choose when they arrive at Behera House. But what did *she* need? Simon, yes. But the man, not the survivor.

Simon laughed.

"What?"

"I was just thinking about Kesh, one of his jokes. He could be so damn funny!"

Meena offered up a half smile.

"Unlike me, 'Serious Bliss.'"

"You don't have to be as funny or as witty as Kesh."

"Really?" He stretched out on his back again. "My mother used to say I'd do fine in India because I'd already been through a monsoon. She was referring to the time they shoved me into that shower for twelve hours after my accident with chemicals. Water pounded my teenage body like an Indian monsoon. Those were her words. She started calling it my 'monsoon treatment,' and liked to say I didn't need to go to India since I'd already been through a monsoon! Who would have thought I'd come to India and fall in love with you, fish eyes?"

Meena's limbs stiffened. *Love?* She wanted a lover, not love. She thought of Kesh—the man she knew *before* they'd moved to Sompur. *Before the wretched girdle!*

"From the very moment I met you," Simon said, "and gazed into those sea-green eyes. Those monsoon eyes!"

Simon's words brought back memories of her first years with Kesh, how he would shower her with lines from Sanskrit love poetry.

"Meena, you said the center is my ark too. But I think my ark is more than the building itself. It's all the people I've met. Kesh, Asha, Raj, and most of all, you."

"So now I'm an ark?" Meena chuckled. She suddenly felt an urge to flee. She didn't want to be Simon's ark any more than she wanted to be her husband's ocean. "Wait here, I'll be right back." She rolled off the waterbed and looked around.

"My sari, it's gone!"

Simon giggled as she bent down, fully naked, and poked her head under a chair. She crossed one arm over her breasts, the other over her private parts. "You stole it, didn't you?"

"Look over there." Simon pointed to the far side of the waterbed. "No, sorry, I think it's over there," he said, pointing to another corner. She finally found her garment folded neatly behind a chair.

"Rascal!" She wrapped the sheer cloth around her waist and flung the remaining yards over her chest.

"Call me Krishna!" Simon said. "Didn't you once say he stole the clothes of the cowherd girls when they were bathing naked in the stream?"

Without responding, Meena hurried to the bathroom and stared into the mirror. *What does he want from me—a lover, a wife, a mother?* She noticed the first signs of crow's feet around the corners of her eyes. She looked so tired. After redoing her eye makeup and getting dressed, she returned to Simon, who was fully clothed and seated on a wicker chair.

"Come on, cowgirl," he said, rising, "let's stretch our legs." They started down the outside stairwell. When they reached the atrium, Simon stopped short at the Pink Ice, the prayer tree. He looked over the strings carefully, picked one, and tied it to a small branch. "There! It's the inaugural prayer string!" He turned to her. "Do you want to know what I prayed for?"

Meena shook her head. "The wish must remain a secret if it's to come true."

"Damn, all right. It's never just about the building, is it? Every project should be an ark. Someone's ark. Hey, I'm now an *ark*itect! Get it?"

Meena struggled to produce even half a smile. They continued walking, past the round metal plaque awarded by the India Green Building Association.

"You know," he said, "I've always had this *thing* about LEED. That it forced architects to design by checklists. Design should be organic! My wife, always the therapist, insisted it was because my father used to write down family chores on a blackboard in the kitchen. He never talked to me about the chores; he'd just list them. Every day, another list. Rake the leaves, wash the car, fold the laundry. Dad would check them off on the blackboard, just like architects obsessed with LEED certification: highly reflective roofs, check; radiant floor heating, check; waterless urinals, check. I wonder if my anger was more about how LEED ignores the people the building is supposed to serve than about that checklist of green strategies."

"It's the same thing, isn't it? Your father was making lists and ignoring you. You mustn't blame LEED. It's just a rating system, a guide, nothing more." Meena's words felt almost scripted. How good she had become at comforting those in need. She pulled the cotton sari tightly around her.

"You're one beautiful mermaid. Now, if I were a mermaid, or a merman—is that a word?—I'd live with you in the ocean. After all, what if the waters become turbulent and one of your residents falls off my ark? I could catch her."

"Nobody's going to fall off."

Meena suggested they go back to the roof deck and gaze at the stars. Maybe they could catch the end of the festivities, the last display of fireworks. There wasn't much time left before they would have to head to the airport, where he would catch his flight to Washington. Simon agreed, but asked if she would wait a few minutes while he ducked into the Bird's Nest. He descended a flight of stairs. Meena waited, becoming more and more restless when he didn't come right back. He finally emerged, quiet and peaceful.

"We'd better make a move," Meena said. "Your plane departs at midnight and they want you at the airport two hours—"

"No need."

"What?"

"I cancelled my trip."

"You what?"

"I cancelled my trip. I'm in no rush to go back. Look what happened to my mother when she decided to leave India. Anyway, I've got another ark to build. Didn't you say the Ford Foundation requested a proposal to fund a new center in Mumbai?"

"Yes, but . . ." Meena gulped hard. "What about Alisha? Your kids? Your practice? Surely you—"

Simon placed two fingers over her mouth and led her back upstairs to the edge of the roof deck, the ship's bow.

Meena looked out over the water. In the distance, a lone schooner was lit up by the full moon. A bird swooped down, hovered over the vessel, and finally landed on the mast.

The festivities had ended. The buffalo demon was dead and Ram, the righteous ruler, was back on his throne. A soothing silence filled the air. She stared at the bird and recalled the story of Noah. How he sent a mourning dove from his ark to determine if the floodwaters had finally receded. Had Kesh come back as a mourning dove? She thought of her nutty, prescient, peppery husband, the man who, on their wedding day, recited romantic Sanskrit love poetry.

Suddenly, an arm around her waist. It felt comforting, then constraining. She didn't react, but kept her eyes fixed on the bird. She turned away, freeing herself from Simon's grasp. In a flash, the bird darted upward, soaring on unseen currents of air, and disappeared.

The End

ACKNOWLEDGEMENTS

This book would not have been possible without the tireless support of my wife, Jennifer, and my publisher and dear friend, Merrill Leffler. I am grateful to both for their many thoughtful suggestions over countless drafts.

The following works are gratefully acknowledged. Asha's story in Chapter 13 is based on various narratives that appear in Sudhir Kakar's *The Inner World* (Oxford University Press, 1978) and *Intimate Relations* (Viking, 1989). The Sanskrit poem at the end of Chapter 31 is from *The Origin of the Young God, Kalidasa's Kumarasambhava*, translated by Hank Heifetz (University of California Press, 1985, page 131).

My source for the esoteric dance rituals performed by the devadasis in the Jagannath temple (Chapter 22) is Frederique Apffel-Marglin's *Rhythms of Life: Enacting the World with the Goddesses of Orissa* (Oxford University Press, 2008, pp.63-63, 76 ff.). The author regrets any errors he may have made in describing these rites and in no way intended to disparage the devadasis or brahmin priests, or to denigrate their role in these Hindu rituals.

The translation of the "sah" poem in Chapter 9 and 28 is the author's. The spelling "sah" has been used for the Sanskrit "sa" throughout the novel to better convey the long "a", i.e., that the word rhymes with English exclamation "ah."

ABOUT THE AUTHOR

Ken's love of India began in 1971, when he spent an academic year in Varanasi. He earned his Ph.D. in Sanskrit and Indian Studies from Harvard University and lived in India for more than five years as a college student, postdoctoral fellow, and business consultant to US clean energy companies. He has served as Special Assistant to the Dean of Harvard University and Vice President of Brandeis University. In 2000, he founded Environmental Market Solutions, Inc. (EMSI), an international green building consulting company. EMSI pioneered the commercial green building industry in China and was recognized by the US Green Building Council as the first company to complete 100 LEED projects outside the US. His writing has appeared in various literary and academic journals, including the *Harvard Review, The Satirist, The Woven Tale,* the *Vineyard Gazette,* the *Taj Mahal Review,* and the *Journal of the American Oriental Society.* Ken's short stories and blogs can be found on his website, kenlanger.net.

And yes, the Harvard graduate student whose theory of "sah" was plagiarized by the Sompur priest in Chapter 8 is indeed the author!